Stoker & Bash: The

Sing a song of sixpence
A stage full of fright
One two-faced blackbird
Won't last the night

When a phantom presence lures Hieronymus Bash into a deadly game, threatening to kill one of the players at his beloved Gaiety Theater each day until famed actor Horace Beastly returns to the stage, London's premier consulting detective is on the case. The trouble? Horace Beastly is Hiero's alter ego and the true object of this murderous obsession. When the current star of the show is struck down, Hiero has to risk everything by stealing back the spotlight.

After a golden summer together, DI Tim Stoker would do everything in his power to protect the man he loves. But a specter from his own past proves an unexpected, and perhaps fatal, distraction.

Scheming prima donnas, grudge-fuelled critics, and an axe-wielding theater ghost are all out for blood. Will Hiero and Tim unmask this menace before the final curtain call, or are they past the point of no return?

Praise for Stoker & Bash

"*Stoker & Bash: The Fangs of Scavo* is a witty, thrilling romp through Victorian London I couldn't help but fall in love with. If you enjoy paranormal historical, go ahead and clear a space on your keeper shelf for this book."

— Jordan L. Hawk, Author,
Whyborne & Griffin series

"I adore the outrageously sexy Hieronymus Bash! If you love sexy Victorians solving mind-boggling mysteries, you'll love *Stoker & Bash.*"

— Joanna Chambers, Author,
Enlightenment series

"*Stoker & Bash* reads like Sherlock Holmes meets The Mentalist, with a flashy con man hero and his staid and steady partner... Kray turns necessary prevarication into a source of tension and passion. Plus, the mysteries are damn good."

— Sarah Marrs, Film and Pop Culture Critic,
LaineyGossip.com/Cinesnark.com

Stoker & Bash: The Death Under the Dark Arches
Copyright © 2020 by Selina Kray
Cover Art: Tiferet Design (www.TiferetDesign.com)
Editor: Nancy-Anne Davies
ISBN: 978-0-9959925-6-6
eBook ISBN: 978-0-9959925-7-3

First Edition
October 2020

STOKER & BASH

The Death Under the Dark Arches

SELINA KRAY

To my Starbuck,
my crazy bean, my tiny dancer, my fuzz bunny,
the heartbeat at my feet

Past the point of no return
No backward glances
The games we've played till now are at an end
Past all thought of if or when
No use resisting
Abandon thought and let the dream descend
What raging fire shall flood the soul?
What rich desire unlocks its door?
What sweet seduction lies before us?
Past the point of no return
The final threshold
What warm, unspoken secrets will we learn
Beyond the point of no return?

— *"Point of No Return,"*
The Phantom of the Opera (1986),
Charles Hart & Richard Stilgoe

Dramatis Personae

THE DETECTIVES

Detective Inspector Timothy "Kip" Kipling Stoker, Scotland Yard

Hieronymus Bash/Horace Beastly, actor turned consulting detective of growing renown

Calliope "Callie" Pankhurst, Bash's ward, pistol aficionado

Han Tak Hai, fixer, confidant, master of whispers, sculptor

SPECIAL GUEST STARS

Maxine Marks, gossip columnist

Gerry Tumnus, manager and moralist, Gaiety Theater

Damiane and Seraphine Vauquelin, much-celebrated Parisian ingénues

Marius Lamarque, epicene costumier

Silas Flint, long-suffering stage manager

Randolph Terriss, the Brad Pitt of the 1874 theater scene

Genevre de Casterac, prima donna, first lady of the stage

Monsieur Charles-Rainier, le Vicomte de Croÿ-Roeulx, devoted patron and investor

Polly Nichols, ballerina

SCOTLAND YARD

Colonel Sir Hugh Winterbourne, Commissioner of the Police of the Metropolis

Superintendent Julian Quayle, Tim's direct superior

DS John Littlejohn, Tim's nemesis

BERKELEY SQUARE HOUSEHOLD

Lillian Pankhurst, Callie's mother, rejuvenated

Shahida Kala, her companion

Aldridge, the butler

Minnie, the cook

Angus Fotheringham, the chauffeur
Yu-Jie Fotheringham, the ladies' maid
Ting, their daughter
Feng-Huang, their adopted son
also Admiral The Viscount Apollonius "Apollo" Pankhurst, Callie's
uncle and Bash's former lover, deceased.
and Tobias Warren, one of Han's little rabbits

Prologue

Tim looked up in time to see the chandelier crash.

He fought his way up the center aisle through the stampeding crowd toward The Gaiety's stage, arms raised as a shield. The mangled remnants of the grand chandelier popped and sparked like a felled dragon. Stagehands led trembling actors across a razor field of glass shards and steel daggers. The bituminous stench did little to choke off the audience's screams as they ran from the scene. And on a set balcony above it all stood a hooded villain, cackling their delight at the chaos they'd created with the swing of a scythe.

Hiero, stage left of the crash site, ran up to prevent the murderous interloper from escaping or, worse, doing further damage. Tim glimpsed his progress between dips and dodges around people while racing to his aid. No fighter, Hiero used the props available to him, smashing fake lanterns and swinging pulley weights at his opponent. Tim almost slowed when the fiend toppled over the rail. But a blink later, they vaulted back and had Hiero cornered.

The hooded villain lashed one of Hiero's own weapons around his throat, struggled to knot a noose as Hiero wrangled with the rope. A burly man knocked Tim to the ground. He missed the dénouement as he clawed his way back to his feet. The next pocket of space saw Hiero tripping his opponent. A heartbeat later, Hiero hugged the rail, his legs dangling over the side.

Tim swallowed a cry as he rammed toward the stage, cursing his lack of height, his postinjury weakness, the idiotic plan that had left Hiero exposed. By the time he broke through to the orchestra pit, it was all over. Hiero tumbled over the rail.

Even in flight, Hiero curved in a graceful arc. The arms that held Tim through the worst of his recovery, the chest that berthed him most nights, the head that nestled over his heart, all poise, all elegance as they shot toward the metal spikes of the chandelier.

The howl and crack of Hiero's impaling broke the world.

In a blink, Tim was at his side. He crushed Hiero's limp hand in his, searched his vacant eyes for a final glimmer. Ignored the gory metal pike that protruded from his chest. Embraced the icy rush of agony that froze the blood in his veins. Tim pried his gaze away from his beautiful, battered Hiero and looked up at the balcony from which he'd fallen.

There he met the black eyes of a red skull mask and swore a merciless vengeance.

Chapter 1

ONE WILL FALL EVERY DAY
HORACE BEASTLY STAYS AWAY

The note burned a hole in DI Timothy Kipling Stoker's pocket as he surveyed the scene before him. A gang of constables shouted a noisy crowd back behind the wooden barrier erected at the end of the alley that led to The Adelphi Theater's stage door. Pub patrons with windowside stools had front-row seats to the drama unfolding in Bull Inn Court. A detective sergeant Tim didn't recognize argued with a red-faced man he did: Mr. Gerry Tumnus, newly appointed manager of The Gaiety Theater and the man responsible for his lover Hieronymus Bash's early retirement from the stage. As for the sheet-covered body lying in the center of the court, Tim couldn't identify him by the make of his shoes, but he dreaded the knowledge all the same.

Tim shared a wary look with his colleague Han Tak Hai as they wormed their way through the crowd. A flash of his warrant card got them through the barricade, but Tim waited on the perimeter as a professional courtesy. Bad form to intrude upon another officer's crime scene. As he followed a trail of blood from the body to the entrance of a building, Tim prayed the murder and the note were unrelated.

3

Two familiar figures wrenched the front door open and stepped gingerly around the blood spatter as they exited. Comically mismatched in height and build but sporting twin sourpuss expressions, Superintendant Julian Quayle—knuckle-dragging barbarian—and DS John Littlejohn—bulldog with a schnauzer's yap—deepened their scowls when they spotted him.

"Stoker," Littlejohn sneered. "Nosing about where you're not wanted as usual, eh? Well, you can piss off back to your sickbed. This here's real detective work."

"I rather think this case begs for someone with more than half a brain," Tim shot back. "You'd best see to the crowd. Your constables are struggling."

"My constables, nothing. Ain't you heard? I'm an inspector now."

All too aware of their superintendent's beady, assessing eyes on them, Tim grunt out, "Then congratulations are in order." He turned to Quayle. "Best of luck to you, sir."

"We'll need more than luck for this mess," Quayle sighed. "What's your game, Stoker? That cat's anus Tumnus call you in?"

"Happened by, saw the commotion. Who's the victim?"

"Randolph Terriss." Tim didn't school his features quick enough to avoid Quayle's notice. "Know him?"

"Only by reputation." One of the most beloved music hall stars of the day, Randolph Terriss's celebrity was eclipsed only by the royal family. Tim marveled that the crowd wasn't treble the size. When word got out, there would be weeks of public mourning.

A mule like Littlejohn couldn't handle a case of this magnitude, and Quayle had to know it. Tim stifled a chuckle.

Perhaps sensing the change in the wind, Littlejohn quipped, "Surprised your fancy man let you off the leash. I hear tell you've moved out of your flat."

"During my convalescence, yes." Their last case had concluded in spectacular fashion, with Tim barely escaping a chemical explosion.

Even now, a slight rasp underscored his breaths, though his doctors expected a full recovery in time. "Easier to be more selective with our cases when I'm not consulting from across town."

"If that's what you want to call it."

Tim stared at him, wrestling his instinct down.

"An' a rose by any other name will get you clobbered up the ear," Quayle growled at Littlejohn. "Go see to the bloody crowd."

"But, sir! It's my—"

"Do I need to repeat myself?"

"He's not even on duty!"

"Crowds, Detective *Sergeant*." He glared away Littlejohn's next objection. "Another word and I'll kick you to constable."

"Sir." Littlejohn glowered at Tim. "Arse-licker."

If only he knew, Tim thought as Littlejohn stormed over to the barricade. Then shuddered because Littlejohn's insinuations had skirted the truth. He made a mental note to stop by the Yard, see if any serious rumors swirled. During the events of their last case, he'd earned a powerful ally in Commissioner Winterbourne by finding his missing son, but even such a high-placed guardian couldn't protect him if his relationship with Hiero was discovered.

Just as his concern threatened to boil over into anxiety, Quayle asked, "Have the docs cleared you, then?"

"They have, sir, though I'm to avoid any arduous physical activity, like chasing." Tim pointed to Han. "Fortunately, Mr. Bash's man has the speed and skill to second me."

Quayle grimaced. "That'll do. Why you really here? An' don't sing me that 'happened by' rubbish."

"Shall I whistle a different tune, then? Something along the lines of 'I should take this case'?"

"For once, Stoker, we're in harmony." A hard laugh. "Tell me why."

Tim considered how to compose this particular refrain. Hit the wrong notes, and he risked exposing Hiero's former identity as actor

Horace Beastly. But if he didn't make the connection between Terriss and Beastly, someone else would. And if that someone were a jealous Littlejohn...

"I provided security for The Gaiety before I became a constable. You might know they've recently had a change in management. One of their actors, Horace Beastly, received this yesterday." Tim showed him the note.

"This the same Beastly whom Terriss replaced?"

"The very one."

"He hire you?"

"Not anymore."

"Good. Because I'd say he's suspect number one."

Tim swallowed his protest along with his worry. So long as Quayle gave him the case, he wouldn't have to know where, or with whom, his loyalties lay.

"Our heads are on the block with this one, Stoker, soon as word hits the streets. You think the upper-ups are merciless? Try the masses. And fallen angels make great press. Find our man, and quick. Give 'em someone else to hang for this."

Tim nodded, rubbing his neck, well aware of the weight he'd just placed on his own shoulders.

Han stood still as a statue on the far side of Bull Inn Court, watching, waiting to catch a glimpse of the clue others would miss. As the constables shooed off the last of the crowd, other officers formed a human shield around the body as Tim made his examination. Han declined to join him. He preferred to remember Randy Terriss as he'd been in life: jolly, witty, dedicated, more than a little vain, with appetites befitting his name. Han's fingers twitched with need of a hammer and chisel, a slab of rock from which to etch out

Randy's cherubic face, which had earned him steady work on the Strand and won him such a fanatical following. He'd evoke the man behind the scenes, a merry prankster who could nevertheless recite the entirety of Byron's *Don Juan*—and frequently did to the ladies he wooed. But first, Han would concentrate on avenging him.

One by one, he considered the windows of the buildings that surrounded Bull Inn Court. Most drew their curtains once the police arrived. Unlike the looky-loos of the Nell Gwynne pub, residents in this part of the Strand didn't care for any officer of the law intruding on their affairs, business or otherwise. Han focused on the edifice from which Quayle and his minion had emerged, a slender, three-story building of Cotswold yellow brick sandwiched between the backs of The Adelphi and the row of shops on nearby Maiden Lane. Known as Mistress Manor, more than a few popular actors kept their most devout admirers in style there, tucked away from their wives but conveniently located mere steps from their theaters down a discreet, low-traffic alley.

Just as Han considered paying a visit to flat number three— where one of his little rabbits had told him Terriss was known to entertain—a woman's face peered out between the curtains. Soon followed by a shoulder, an arm, a hand armed with a pencil, and... a notebook. Eagle eyes flicked down, spotted him. Widened. Flew.

Han crashed through the front door, running past the main staircase to the end of the hall. No servants meant no servants' exit, or none he could see. He paused, listening for the clack-clop of heels. A jump from a second-story window would give the police another body; she wouldn't dare the roof. Han inched back toward the stairs. Keeping to the shadow side, he climbed. On the level above, he had the choice of two directions. Toward the front, the obvious choice, would probably result in him finding an empty flat. Toward the back gave her the chance to escape if she gambled right. As he approached the landing, Han glanced up into the next set of stairs...

...and found her perched high on the rail, candlestick raised to strike.

Their gazes locked. She arched a brow. He quirked a lip. And they laughed.

He wanted to paint her. There, just as she was, the deep plum of her day dress highlighting the mellow gold of her loose hair; her regal profile against the spare decor; her flint-gray eyes, sharp with mischief and curiosity; her weapon at the ready. Tissot couldn't have done her justice. Han would have relished the chance to try under more ideal circumstances. Less murderous, certainly. She lowered the candlestick and tucked it under her arm as she slinked down the stairs.

"You're Hieronymus Bash's man, aren't you?" A Mona Lisa smile. "How invigorating."

Han wondered if they had met before. Randy Terriss tended to treat his companions as disposable, though it had been some years since Randy and Hiero costarred together. Still, not a man who prized intelligence in his paramours. On first impression, the lady before him appeared rather unforgettable.

"Do you reside here, madam?" Han asked.

"Does anyone?"

"I imagine so."

"Well, then you're lacking in it."

"If you're insinuating—"

"Ah, playing the innocent. Has that ever worked for you?"

Han stammered, caught short. He inhaled a clarifying breath. "No. You?"

"On occasion. With very old, very drunk, or very blinkered men." Despite himself, Han smiled. "Will Mr. Bash be taking on Mr. Terriss's case? I hardly think a stabbing in the street worthy of his talents."

Han opened his mouth to reply, then realized. "Is that theater or street gossip?"

"Will I get an answer to my question?"

"No."

"Because you do not know the answer, or you don't care to comment?"

Han squared his shoulders, met her piercing eyes with shields fully raised.

"Oh, I *like* you," she said.

They observed each other for a time, the spark of challenge never dimming between them. A thousand questions popped and fizzled in Han's mind, but he held firm.

She could, of course, end the standoff at any moment, with a scream. Unlike Hiero, Han could never forget how precarious his position was in the world, how the wrong word, a brusque gesture, or the very look of him could spin a normal encounter into a spider's web—and he the fly.

The hum of busy voices reverberated up from the alley below. A dozen officers raring to respond to a shriek or a cry, and the glamour of his associations would not spare him. He'd learned to make himself invisible, to avoid provocation, the only means of survival for a Chinese man in the Western world.

She stepped down to his level and stretched out a hand. "Maxine Marks, *The Pall Mall Gazette*."

"Han Tak Hai, investigator."

"Enchanté."

They shook.

"Now," she announced. "As to our little impasse... What might convince you to answer a few questions?"

"Rather the same as for you to respond to my inquiries."

Miss Marks sighed. "So it seems. A pity, I say. I wager you'd make a fine drinking companion if ever you unwound enough to have some fun."

"As quick to judge as to presume, I see. Not a terribly fine quality in a reporter." Out of options, Han took a step back, enough for her to sneak by him.

She stopped at the top of the stairs to the ground floor, her gaze lingering behind. She must have known he could give chase, catch her with ease, just as she gambled he would not, for all the reasons left unsaid.

"It truly is a shame we didn't meet under different circumstances, Mr. Han. You are the rare gentleman in a city of scoundrels."

"Most gentlemen included?"

"Quite." The playful, cunning look she'd worn this whole time sobered. "Tell Mr. Bash to look to The Gaiety. A ghost haunts its stage, one that may have just claimed its first victim."

Lost in thought as he worked through this revelation, Han missed her departure. But he finally noticed the trail of blood on the floor, one that led straight into flat number three. From which, if his instincts served him at all, Miss Marks had emerged.

Han carefully walked around the spatter into the flat. The most glaring evidence he discovered was that of a police search, employing their usual "running of the bulls" method, though it was impossible to say how unkempt the flat had been prior to the murder. Framed playbills and photographs of Terriss in character decorated the walls. An open wardrobe of suits told him Randy kipped there at least some nights of the week. Significantly, Han found no women's clothes or pictures of anyone Terriss might have kept there. Nothing business related either. Just a small, well-appointed bedchamber, a cozy sitting area around a hearth, a nook for brewing coffee or tea, a drinks tray, and a pool of his life's blood seeping into the carpet.

Stabbed in the comfort of his flat in the middle of the day, likely not by the scandal-rooting reporter who stole in after the police. Randy had chased his assailant out into the street, where he collapsed. A simple everyday crime—rudimentary, even.

So why did Han scent smoke on the wind?

"Here you are," Tim said as he entered. Han stood back that his colleague might examine the room, his expression reflecting Han's disappointment. "I see the Yard has done their damndest to destroy any potential evidence."

"Do you expect there's much to be found?"

Tim sighed. "Impossible to say. But needs must."

They silently set to the task, each taking a side of the room by unspoken agreement. The police had not-so-helpfully dumped the contents of most drawers on the floor, which had them tiptoeing around, trying not to stomp on any evidence. This awkward ballet might be comical to anyone observing, but Han's steps slowed as he moved deeper into Randy's secret hideaway. He came upon a patch of letters beside the bed, their pages skimmed and flipped like a pile of used handkerchiefs. Han felt a scoundrel of the highest order for tying them back together with their discarded ribbon. None of their previous cases had ever become so personal, intruding on the life of a friend.

Or threatening those closest to him.

"The body," Han asked as they neared completion of their circuit of the room. "Anything there?"

"I'd say so, yes."

Tim handed him what at first glance he took to be the note sent to Hiero. Same stationery, same form of address on the envelope: *To Mr. Hieronymus Bash, 23 Berkeley Square*. Except when Han pulled out the card, the riddle had been replaced with a big, bloody one. Dried blood. Randy's blood.

"One has fallen," Tim confirmed. "And so it begins."

Han stared at the note until he saw only red.

Chapter 2

*H*ieronymus Bash swept by the window for the tenth time that quarter hour, his animosity toward the empty street growing by the minute. He continued to stroll around the room under the pretence of considering this new character of Callie's from every angle, but everyone present recognized the charade. Including Hiero himself, who clacked the heel of his shoe on the floor as he did an about-face and stationed himself at the corner between windows, which gave him views of the front steps and the side-street entrance to the mews. If and when his Kip returned, he would know it.

Ever since they received that dreadful, thrilling note the previous morn, Hiero had been plagued by an unfamiliar emotion: worry. At first he was flattered an admirer so clamored for his alter ego Horace Beastly's return to the stage. To be so missed after being dismissed from The Gaiety by that dung beetle Tumnus, to be adored, to be acclaimed... Well, these were the very reasons he tread the boards. By the time the team assembled in the study, Hiero had composed a soliloquy on why he must be allowed to return entitled "Fie, Tumnus! Fie!" and prepared to deliver it to the man himself later that afternoon, only to be outvoted.

Method. Madness to him, imperative to the team of investigators of which he was the least essential but most glamorous part: Kip, his detective inspector lover; Callie, his genial ward; and Han, his partner-in-everything save romance. Instead of following his quite reasonable suggestion, the team would scout, examine, plan. Han would send his little rabbits hopping to the Strand. Callie would chase down the provenance of the note. And Kip would scrutinize every speck of the paper, the ink, the envelope, the word choice, the handwriting. By evening, they'd formed a plan of attack. That morning, they launched it. And somewhere between, in the wee hours, whilst swishing the dregs of his whiskey around his glass and watching Kip slumber atop the desk, Hiero was struck by a realization.

Someone would be harmed in his name.

He hadn't known a moment's peace since, especially when Kip insisted Hiero remain at Berkeley Square while he and Han paid a visit to The Gaiety to see how things stood. Hiero could not, after all, appear as Hieronymus Bash that morning and Horace Beastly backstage that night. As skilled at disguise as he was, the key to maintaining two personas had been existing in separate worlds, with different audiences. If someone from his aristocrat-adjacent life happened to see him perform, well, there was costume, setting, the stage. Bribery, if all else failed. But to attempt to fool his fellow players by presenting two different faces in one day...

Hiero couldn't fault Kip's logic in this—mostly since he possessed none of his own—but found himself fretting nonetheless. If The Gaiety required the help of both Horace Beastly and Hieronymus Bash, how would he ever choose between them?

"There." Shahida sat back on her heels, fought to catch her breath. Kneeling down by Callie's side to pin her trousers, she rubbed her belly as she took in the entirety of this new character's costume. With barely a month left of her pregnancy, the babe within her looked to be already half its mother's diminutive size, which made every movement a chore. But carrying the equivalent of a sack of coal round her middle had not slowed Shahida, who had devoted the better part of her day to refining the character's look with her friend. "A stroke of luck, it was, that Mr. Stoker's your size. Suit only needs a few nips and tucks."

Hiero tried to refocus on the task at hand. "Disturbing, more like. But needs must."

"Find me a bit too fetching, do ya?" Callie queried in her worst Cockney.

Clicking his tongue, Hiero gestured toward the ceiling. "Up, up, up. A class, at least. Better two, if you can manage it. Remember who this... What's his name?"

"Calvin."

"Mmm, young Mr. Calvin. Or should it be Cameron? Would Scottish be too distracting? Yes. Yes, Calvin hits the right note. And so should your accent. So who are you?"

Callie brushed a hand through her recently shorn locks, rubbed the now-bare nape of her neck. The shoulder-length inches of hair she'd grown out over the summer ringed the floor around a nearby chair. Archie the pageboy, the guise she occasionally adopted for cases, wouldn't suit this kind of investigation. But neither could a lady go traipsing around the demimonde of the Strand and its theaters without attracting the wrong kind of notice, and so Mr. Calvin was born.

"A man of twenty, eager for experience. Apprenticed as a clerk but longed for something more adventurous. Met DI Stoker on one of his cases and pressed him for advice. He took me on as..." Callie broke character. "Should I be a constable, do you think?"

"Ain't earned the title, have you?" Shahida reached for her hand to help her up. "Best not give them a reason to question you."

"Mmm, yes, quite." Callie tested out a new Calvin voice. "I do the parts of the job the DI finds too tedious, and in exchange, I study with a master. Hope one day to join the Yard myself."

"Ah, yes, always steal from the best." Hiero nodded, approving this reappropriation of Kip's biography. "Nearly there." Then he spotted an approaching carriage out of the corner of his eye, and panic cinched his throat.

Until Hiero spied the coat of arms on the side door. He slid over to the edge of the window frame, peering down so he might observe without being observed. The sleek, gold-accented carriage glided to a stop. With headdresses sprouting white and yellow feathers and ornamented harnesses, the team of horses acquitted themselves with more style than some ladies of his acquaintance. Only the royals were ferried about in such luxury, and they on grand occasions. Someone who couldn't make a call without announcing their presence to all of London in dramatic fashion was someone Hiero cared to meet.

"Who d'you think it is?" Shahida asked from so near Hiero almost spooked. She and Callie shamelessly craned their heads over the sill, faces just short of glued to the pane. "A dastardly duke? A vice-riddled earl? A poxy prince?"

"Perhaps if we were living in a penny dreadful," Callie snipped.

"We saved your mum from a bunch of madwomen who were torturing her in the cellar beneath their creepy house with dead babies in the garden. What would you call it?"

"Thursday." Callie sighed. "I take your point. And I don't rec- ognize the family, but from the fleur de lys, I would wager our visitor is French."

"Intriguing." Hiero found his smile. Normally he would defer to Callie or Kip before meeting a new client, but he needed the distraction. "It seems our reputation is spreading."

Shahida snickered. "That or Madame Dansereau finally clued in to the fact you didn't actually exorcize her poodle."

Hiero shot her his most mysterious stare. "Never underestimate my powers of persuasion." With a final appraising look at Callie, Hiero said, "You might care to revisit the jacket. Mr. Calvin's still a touch too hourglass," and snuck down to his study to await his guest.

Fortunately, Kip had not tidied the desk before departing that morn. After assuring himself nothing significant or incriminating lay out in the open, Hiero repositioned a few books, scrawled a few nonsensical notes on a fresh pad, and posed himself in an air of deep contemplation. Which he held for several long minutes, and then several more. Just when his neck began to creak in protest, he heard the bell.

After a knock whose tattoo indicated a new client, Aldridge ushered in a man with a perpetual pout and spectacles too wide for his face. Hiero rose to greet him, but a pair of upraised white gloves halted his progress around the desk.

"Pardon the intrusion," he asked in French, "but are you the famous Monsieur Bash?"

Hiero, a fluent speaker of French, replied, "I am indeed, Monsieur...?"

"Jean-Georges Bocuse." The man performed a little bow. His relief at the change of language seemed palpable. "Secretary to the venerable Vicomte de Croÿ-Roeulx, who has charged me with inquiring if you might agree to a short interview."

"I can't think of a more diverting way to spend an hour than in the Vicomte's company," Hiero assured him. "Is he with you now?"

"He is."

The man was so intense that Hiero couldn't help but have a little fun at his expense. "But surely you did not make him wait in the carriage?"

"I... That is..." Monsieur Bocuse stammered for what felt like a full minute before managing a coherent reply. "He requested that I do so."

"Ah." Hiero struggled to control his grin. "Then, please, invite him in."

After another resplendent bow, Monsieur Bocuse hurried out to fetch his master. Hiero indulged a brief laughing fit as he waited, thinking he should get it all out now so as not to insult his guest. Such men were always a source of great amusement to him, their self-importance overwhelming their sense of duty. But then, the charge of self-aggrandizement had also been laid at his door, mostly by his Kip, who...

A frisson of anxiety iced the last of his laughter. Hiero silenced all thoughts of The Gaiety as the door swung open. The impish Monsieur Bocuse marched back in, then turned with puffed chest to announce, "Monsieur Charles-Rainier, le Vicomte de Croÿ-Roeulx."

The man who entered might not have been a king, but no noble in Hiero's acquaintance possessed half his presence or suavity. Hiero immediately recognized a creature of like habits: his manners meticulous, his grooming soigné, his dress haute couture, his bearing leonine. His silver mane had been sculpted into a pompadour that would have turned Napoleon green. The force of his magnetism bulked up his withy frame and gained him a foot in height. Hiero nearly swooned over the blade-sharp edges of his sideburns and the curlicued tips of his moustache. Before him stood a one-man shrine to the Byronic ideal.

Hiero despised him on principle. He vowed that this man, this titan of fashion and class, would be kept far, far away from his Kip. Then he performed a curt bow of his own.

"Monsieur le Vicomte."

"Monsieur Bash," he greeted, and continued in French. "Please forgive my sudden arrival. Events have conspired such that I had no choice but to seek out your counsel and, I hope, your services."

"It is my honor to receive you, monsieur." Hiero gestured toward a pair of wingback chairs before the hearth. "Please."

"With pleasure."

"Coffee?"

"Ah, oui." The Vicomte chuckled. "You see, Jean-Georges, not all Englishmen are heathens." Once they'd settled, he appeared to take Hiero in for the first time. Approval shone in his eyes. "Although by the quality of your accent, perhaps I've been too quick to assume…"

"Born in London, yes, but well-travelled. Once you've sampled the continent's bounty, it is rather a challenge to go back to tea and treacle."

"I could not agree more. I feel as if I've been starving for months on this... cuisine."

"You are being charitable with that word, monsieur."

The Vicomte shrugged. "When in Londres."

They shared a chuckle as Aldridge brought in the coffee and a plate of sugary biscuits. The relentlessly dour Jean-Georges stationed himself on a nearby divan, the Vicomte's diary unfurled and fountain pen poised to strike. A warning flag if ever there was. Never one to be particularly circumspect in his pronouncements, Hiero wished Han were there to guard his tongue. He could not shake the memory of the note's warning. In its wake, everything felt like a trap.

Once they'd exchanged the requisite politesse and were armed with cups of strong Turkish coffee, Hiero opened negotiations.

"And how may I be of assistance to you, monsieur?"

The Vicomte inhaled a deep breath. "First, I must say that it gives me no pleasure to come to a man of your caliber with such a tale. My great friend the Marquis de Cherbourg fell victim to the miser Blackwood and sings your praises every time we dine together."

"How generous of him. I'm sure there's some question of embellishment. If I recall, he's quite the raconteur."

"As, I'm told, are you. I hope that we might share a meal before this affair is done. This latest triumph of yours, finding the murderer of a child kidnapped by a group of zealots, sounds most harrowing."

"It had its moments." A pregnant silence burgeoned between them, which Hiero allowed to grow until Croÿ-Roeulx betrayed his first nervous twitch. He leaned forward and, in an intimate whisper, asked, "Monsieur le Vicomte, why have you come?"

A sharp look hardened his stare. "Because I am being made a fool of, and it will not stand."

Hiero nodded as if he had been waiting for this answer all along. "Please explain."

"Are you an amateur de théâtre, Monsieur Bash?"

"I enjoy the occasional sortie, yes. The same as any man of culture."

"For me it has always been a grand passion. It began when I, like most young men, played escort to my mother. From there a fire took hold, and I have burned ever since. As soon as I inherited, I began to invest. This led me to purchase the original Théâtre de la Gaîté—"

"Ah! On the Boulevard du Crime." Hiero smiled. "I've always relished the name. What a pity they demolished it."

"A tragedy of the highest order. And one from which we are still recovering."

"I believe you were among the few to move house?"

"Oui, to rue Papin. But we struggled to recapture the magic. And so, two years ago, the cochons I invested with voted to turn managerial duties over to Monsieur Offenbach."

Hiero fought not to let his feathers ruffle on the Vicomte's behalf. He knew only too well what it was like to be rousted from a place you loved. As he should probably mention. "A similar case to the management shift at our own Gaiety, where the exceptional Mr. Beastly was tossed out in favor of that no-account Henry Irving."

Croÿ-Roeulx laughed. "And with this you have divined the very event that brought me across the Channel. Monsieur Irving received a better offer from The Lyric and decamped last June, taking the entire company and most of the backstage artisans with him. The current owner of The Gaiety, Monsieur Gerry Tumnus, hastily assembled a skeleton troupe, but, given the blow his reputation suffered from Irving's coup, he had to double their wages. Through an acquaintance I discovered that he had a theater without a company, and since I had a company without a theater, a deal was struck. The grand opening of our first double bill, a *Don Juan* burlesque and the melodrama *Abelard and Heloise,* was to occur this very evening."

"How delightful," Hiero said through gritted teeth, rendered near speechless by the stunning reversal of fortunes at The Gaiety. "But I'm not clear on what role you mean for me to play?"

"Of course." A hint of scarlet tinted the Vicomte's cheeks,

though Hiero couldn't fathom why he flirted with embarrassment. "For a month we have been settling into our new home. The troubles began almost at once. A mislaid prop. A ruined backdrop. A costume three sizes too small. One of our crew tripped on a suddenly wet floor and cracked his head. Several rehearsals delayed because furniture was glued to the storage room walls. Nuisances, at first. A period of adjustment to a new stage, I thought. Or perhaps the petty revenge of the few from the original company who had stayed on."

"Or someone who does not care for foreigners."

"Précisément." Croÿ-Roeulx sighed. "Childish, but not unforeseeable. But then the rumors started among my own actors. A shadow, they claimed, pursuing them through the backstage. Strange gifts. The sensation of being watched, even when they were alone in their dressing rooms." A slithery sense of dread coiled around Hiero's spine. "I thought it nonsense, but the incidents kept piling up. Everyone in the company was buzzing, distracted, missing cues, dropping lines. And then today..."

Hiero felt his stomach drop. "Today?"

"A murder. Our leading man."

It took everything Hiero had to keep control of his face. In his former life, he'd lied to the worst of the worst, men so dangerous, so devious, it was a wonder he still drew breath. Over and again, with his silver tongue and his sly talents, he'd avoided the consequences of his bad decisions. But now the truth had come for him, inescapable.

He opened his mouth to speak, but no sound emerged. His conscience strangled every clever line or follow-up question he could think of in the crib. Beneath his calm exterior, he roiled with upset. Though the team had only begun to explore the details of this case, they were already too late. Some fiend had upped the stakes beyond bearing while Hiero stared out a bloody window.

Hiero reclined and steepled his hands, hoping he appeared to be giving the matter due thought. He ignored Jean-Georges's hand poised in the air, ink dripping from the nib of his overzealous pen.

He tried to blot out the Vicomte's tormented look, knowing it would only deepen his own agony. Instead he returned to one of the fundamental rules of deception his old mentor Erskine had taught him: if you cannot fake indifference, use your emotion to your advantage.

"That is"—Hiero let some of his anger and astonishment overtake his features—"shocking, monsieur. A truly shocking turn of events."

"I feel the same. But it will come as no surprise for you to learn that the members of my company—which includes the most celebrated actress of our time, Madame Genèvre de Casterac—are terrified. They have urged me to act where Mr. Tumnus has not, and so here I am, in your salon." He sucked back a fortifying breath. "Will you, Monsieur Bash, come to our aid and hunt down this monster? Will you find the ghost that haunts The Gaiety?"

Though he lowered his head in false consideration—a stalling tactic, and not a good one—Hiero was not unaware of the intensity of the stares aimed at him. The trouble was, he wanted to give the Vicomte an immediate yes. Never one to resist his instincts for long, even someone as impulsive as Hiero understood there were too many elements at play to give his word to this very earnest, very compelling man. And yet it felt like a betrayal to defer him.

But defer him he must.

"Very intriguing, your tale. But, as you must understand, such matters require careful consideration."

"Mais bien sûr. I would not have it otherwise. There is art in your method, after all."

"Gracious of you to see it that way, monsieur," Hiero acknowledged. "I will make some preliminary inquiries. You'll have my answer by the end of the day."

Tim kept a weather eye on Hiero's expression as they waited for the coffee and biscuits to be refreshed in the study at Berkeley Square. His devastation at learning of Randolph Terriss's death had morphed into an inscrutable expression, such that Tim wondered what it portended.

Though they were committed in their relationship and had been cohabitating for a couple of months, Tim could not always read Hiero's face. They had, after all, known each other for less than a year. In that time, Hiero had lifted a veil or two, but they were still learning the steps in their courtship dance. They'd yet to navigate major changes in rhythm or tempo, discover how to switch from a waltz to a jig to a tango. Let alone how to keep their places once the music stopped. And given Hiero's tendency to lead when he was meant to follow, Tim told himself he had a right to be concerned.

While the others settled in, Tim nabbed the brandy off the drinks tray and added a touch of courage to his and Hiero's coffees. Hiero shot him a surprised look; Tim returned a warm smile. He wanted very much to draw Hiero into his arms as he might have done if they were alone. But they'd promised to remain professional when business was at hand despite the family being well accustomed to their casual affections. And better they deprive themselves when in familiar company, Tim thought, than be too bold before the wrong audience. He hoped Hiero proved a more fluent interpreter of expressions than him, that he read novels of care in Tim's fond regard.

He took up his normal position—perched on the edge of the desk, chalk in hand—as Callie entered, wearing one of his old suits and a haircut Tim saw every morning in the mirror. Were she a few inches shorter and of coppery hue, he might have had a sister.

He turned to Hiero. "What's this latest ruse in your assault against my closet? Refurbishing my clothes as costumes?"

Hiero shrugged. "If the trousers fit."

"They fit me, as well."

"Not unless your tailor has questionable eyesight." He gestured for Callie to spin around. "I'd have half a mind to have Shahida adjust all your suits were I not so committed to replacing them."

"Ah, but if you were both immaculate, one wouldn't know where to look," Callie teased. "Given the right sartorial sorcery, you might even have some competition, Hiero."

Hiero opened his mouth to rebuke her, glanced Tim's way, and shut it. They shared a knowing chuckle. Perhaps they had gained some distance in reading each other after all.

"I'm afraid I've not had the pleasure." Tim extended a hand in greeting to Callie, who shook it.

"Mr. Jack Calvin," she replied in a deeper, wavering voice. "Work in progress."

"Steady on."

As she took her place on the divan beside Han, Tim flipped through his notebook to the page bookmarked by the blood-crusted number left on the body. He and Han had discussed not mentioning it until they had solid evidence that proved Hiero's admirer and the killer were one and the same. Tim may not be privy to all of Hiero's thoughts, but it hardly required a detective's skills to discern that he would, first, assume the link and, second, volunteer himself as sacrifice: a situation Tim must do everything in his power to prevent.

"So to the matter at hand," he announced. "Three unusual events coincide: the reception of the note urging Horace Beastly to return to the stage, the murder of Randolph Terriss, and the possible intruder at The Gaiety theater. Our primary mission is to prevent any further harm to the company of actors and the backstage crew. We have before us two, possibly three distinct cases, all surrounding The Gaiety Theater. Our task this afternoon is to determine how best to go about investigating them. First—"

"Three, you say?" Hiero queried.

"As many as, yes. We must discover if and where they overlap."

"I'd say it's been made quite plain."

"It's been made to appear so. Possibly. But we cannot hang our hat on assumptions."

"No, but you can bet your britches on them."

"We... what?"

"It's an elemental principle of investigation, sir," Callie added, her tenor steadier. "Consider every possible option unless there is hard evidence to prove one theory over another. And then test that evidence against alternate theories to discredit them."

Hiero huffed in frustration. "Might I remind you all there's a ticking clock. 'One will fall every day.' While you're shifting the angles and sifting the evidence, another member of The Gaiety's company might..." He fussed with the ends of his moustache, a tell Tim recognized all too well. "We must put an end to this tonight. If I—"

"No."

Heads turned. The same protest hung on Tim's lips, held back by his shock that it had come from Han.

Hiero arched a brow but did not back down. "A simple solution to a simple problem. They clamor for Beastly; they will have him. Lives hang in the balance."

"Your own above all." Callie added her regular voice to the choir. "I know not whether the person who wrote that note killed Randolph Terriss, but I promise you they're playing a game. They do not intend for their first move to be their last."

"They don't want your compliance," Han agreed. "They want you to play witness to their grand scheme. If you give them what they want, they will change the rules." He sighed. "You know the game better than I. You excel at it. So keep your wits about you and play along."

"Randy's life," Hiero hissed. "Another tomorrow. And the day after, ad infinitum."

"But *not* yours." Tim caught his eye and held it. "If you perform as Beastly tonight, you spread yourself on the altar before this villain, lamb to the slaughter. If we're dealing with a mind so twisted as to kill to provoke, there is always another sacrifice needed. They are a trickster god, an agent of chaos. No amount of blood will ever be enough." On impulse he plucked the bloody note from between the pages of his book and tossed it over to Hiero, who recoiled. Callie snatched it from the floor. "Horace Beastly is but a number. Hieronymus Bash, however..."

"Is preceded by a far more winning reputation. Yes, I see." A sudden suspicion-stirring twinkle lit Hiero's dark eyes. "There is, however, still one minuscule obstacle to my participation in this case."

"Which is?" Callie dubiously queried.

In reply Hiero whirled a hand around his face.

Tim inhaled sharply, the realization choking his breath. "The company knows you as Beastly. Damn." He began to pace around the desk, always thinking more clearly when in motion.

"But only one or two of the most loyal crew members remain at The Gaiety," Han said.

Tim pounced on this. "What do you mean?"

"Those who didn't leave with Henry Irving have been run off by Tumnus's management style," Han explained. "We've so few friends left there, I hadn't even heard about this ghost business until now. And if it's as bad as the Vicomte says, those who remain will be riled enough to keep mum if they recognize Hiero."

Tim paused his pacing to ask, "And what of Tumnus himself?"

An entire argument transpired in the look that passed between Hiero and Han. Hiero replied, "Never met him."

"You mean in all your negotiations—"

Hiero scoffed. "I was informed of The Gaiety's sale and new direction by Webster, the former owner. I threatened to leave. He asked that I finish the run of *Let 'em Eat Ham* and bid me godspeed. Exeunt Beastly, pursued by a Tumnus."

"Good. For our purposes, I mean." Tim shined him a contrite

smile. "And a relief to know we may proceed as planned. Let's take an account of the facts at hand. What do we know for certain?"

"Randolph Terriss was stabbed in his apartment in Mistress Manor behind The Adelphi Theater sometime in the wee hours of the morning," Han said. "He chased his assailant out into Bull Inn Court, where he collapsed and died of his injuries."

Out of the corner of his eye, Tim saw Hiero shudder.

"The murder did not occur at The Gaiety?" Callie asked. "Our note writer might have happened upon the body and planted the note."

"A crime of opportunity?" Tim considered. "Quite possible."

"Absurd." This from Hiero.

Tim ignored him.

"Quite an escalation as well," Han observed. "To go from dis-comfiting actors and writing threatening notes to murder, I mean. A shrewd player waits for an opponent's next move, especially if the plan is to draw them out."

"Perhaps they grew tired of Beastly not responding to the rumors at The Gaiety," Callie said, abandoning her Calvin persona entirely. "A brash action like murder might be their way of luring him to the gaming table."

"By eliminating the competition." At their quizzical looks, Tim elaborated. "Terriss was the company's leading man. With him gone…" He looked to Hiero, who stared very intently at his fingernails. Tim slipped into the seat beside him, canting forward to comfort with his presence. "Did you know him well?"

Hiero shook his head as if to revive himself. "Not intimately, in either sense. We'd share many bottles and trade many tales when contracted to the same theater, but otherwise wished each other well on opening nights. Excellent scene partner, Randy. Top comedian. He played second lead on my first job—how we met. Found ourselves on the same stage many times over the years. But he had a thirst for the fairer sex, and, as you well know, my own preferred tipple..."

Their gazes locked, as they were wont to do. Tim made Hiero a silent promise then, not only to find Randolph Terriss's killer, but to protect his reputation while doing so.

"Then it is you, or rather Beastly, who is the locus of their obsession."

"Wouldn't they have offed Irving, if that were the case?" Callie asked, a mischievous glint in her eye.

"Ah!" Hiero cried. "If only!"

Laughter lifted their collective spirits.

"But let's not tarry too long in speculation," Tim noted. "Han and I made quick business of Terriss's apartment. A visit to his wife I don't believe will bear much fruit, though we will need to interview her if this drags on. Mr. Calvin?"

"Happy to oblige, sir."

"Han, might you turn your talents to that most delicate of questions—"

"Who Randy was presently entertaining after hours?"

"The very one." Tim swallowed back a surge of excitement. His inner bloodhound strained the lead, as always. "I owe Mr. Tumnus a visit, posthaste. With his permission, we'll begin interviewing The Gaiety's company and staff." A raised hand from Hiero interrupted him. "My dear?"

"The small matter of my reply to the Vicomte."

"Ah."

A second thoughtful silence enveloped them.

Callie broke it first. "We've been employed by suspects in the past."

"Persons of our close acquaintance, like Lady Odile," Han countered. "His background is easily researched, but not his character."

"First impression of Croÿ-Roeulx?" Tim asked.

"Elegance. Style. Savoire faire." Hiero sighed. "I loathed him."

Han chuckled. "Ladies and gentlemen, our new client."

At Hiero's glare, Tim nodded. "I'm afraid so. Best to secure someone's cooperation. Tumnus will likely be hostile."

"Let him but make the attempt," Hiero declared, reinvigorated by his resentment. "He may have tricked Beastly, but he'll learn soon enough what is it to reject Hieronymus Bash."

Chapter 3

$\mathcal{A}$s the others sped off to prepare for their imminent departure, a soft-skinned but meaty hand captured Hiero's own. He glanced up to find his favorite pair of moss-green eyes limned with worry, the ends of Kip's very thin, very kissable lips drooping downward. He vibrated slightly, or perhaps that was a fancy of Hiero's. By now he recognized Kip's vigor at the start of a new case, his eagerness to leap into action no matter how grisly the details. If aught, the more malicious the crime, the more forceful his need to bring the latest fiend to justice.

But instead of running off to The Gaiety, Kip brought Hiero's hand to his lips and planted a long kiss in its palm. With a shy but beseeching look Hiero's way, he twined their fingers, rubbing a soothing thumb over Hiero's knuckles.

"How are you?"

Hiero exhaled a long breath. "Horrid." A gentle tug, and Kip slid onto his lap. He knit his slender frame so tight around Hiero that it felt as if they'd been cut from whole cloth. Hiero had, of late, found particular sanctuary in the crook of Kip's neck. He found that favored nook again, breathing deep of his fresh, woodsy scent. The smell of home.

"I feel as if I haven't touched you in months." Kip burrowed his face in the crown of Hiero's hair, breathing just as deeply of him. "Was it only yesterday we lounged in bed till noon? Blast that note and its writer."

"I cannot object."

"Couldn't they have been a bit more considerate in their schedule?" Kip quipped. "'One will fall every week Horace Beastly...'"

"'Looks très chic'?"

A chuckle from above. "Yes, very good. Of course, that would be every week. Unless you'd lower your standards to buy us more time?"

"Not if the Queen herself were on the chopping block."

A traitorous snicker escaped Kip. He tipped Hiero's chin up to meet his kiss, pouring new life into his sad and somewhat defeated state of mind. Hiero opened to this, their indelible connection, which for a moment transported him back to their sultry summer, with its lazy afternoons of togetherness and nights of endless conversation. This golden time lost none of its luster for having come to an end. Though by the heat in Kip's consoling embrace, perhaps it had merely paused while other matters preoccupied. Hiero certainly had to repress the urge to chase after Kip when he pulled away.

"Better?"

Hiero considered saying no just to have his kiss again. "Restored."

"You see the logic of it, don't you? Keeping Beastly in reserve."

"Never my forte, but I bow to keener minds." *For now*, he failed to add. "But in return for my compliance, in this and other things, I demand terms."

"Name it. Note my use of the singular."

"I do." Hiero, much to his relief, found it in him to laugh. "I demand your particular attentions, in whatever form you might choose, once per day, for the duration of this case."

From below, Hiero watched Kip's jaw stretch to accommodate the size of his smile.

"You have my solemn vow that I will rouse, wreck, and thoroughly divert you once, perhaps even twice per day until justice is done."

"Then I am, for the moment, satisfied." Hiero reclined his head that he might meet those shining green eyes anew. "Shall we shake on it?"

"That's no way to seal an intimate compact," Kip murmured, then claimed his mouth.

Hiero's lips still buzzed from Kip's soft attentions when their carriage halted before The Gaiety's performer's entrance, a sliver cut into an otherwise seamless brick wall that overtook an entire block of Wellington Street.

Unlike most theaters, The Gaiety stood on a small island offshoot of the Strand, the main thoroughfare of London's entertainment district. Catherine Street to the east and Exeter Street to the north, where the royal entrance was located, completed the square. Though every one of the many, many societies for the public good and charitable trusts warned against its vices—anything and everything of which could be found on the Strand and its offshoots—pleasure-seekers clogged the streets every hour of the day. The beating heart of the demimonde, Hiero had felt far more at home here, amongst the struggling artists, prolific pornographers, crafty card sharps, and rogues and prostitutes of every flavor, than at Berkeley Square until Kip moved in.

Possibly because he had led the lives of a struggling actor and crafty card sharp, among others, before his former lover and benefactor, Admiral The Viscount Apollonius Pankhurst, bought Hiero his respectability. For Apollo he'd taken on the persona of Hieronymus Bash. For Callie, the ward Hiero inherited along with his fortune upon Apollo's death, he'd transformed into a consulting detective of growing renown. In Kip he'd found something of his own, someone with whom he could be his true self. Not Horace Beastly, ruler of the stage; or the son of immigrants he'd been born; or even Hieronymus Bash, his greatest creation.

With Kip he'd been made new, into someone Hiero himself was still becoming acquainted with. But in his heart of hearts, he welcomed the change. He sensed it would be the role of a lifetime.

But that gentleman only emerged in the privacy of their rooms at Berkeley Square. The present drama demanded someone with the command and panache of the most sought-after detective in London (and his faithful partner, of a mind so clever he'd been wasted at Scotland Yard). Someone who'd make such an impression that any lingering trace of Horace Beastly would be snuffed from their memories.

Hiero rapped on the roof of the carriage. "To the front, Angus!"

Slumped into the seat opposite, Kip grinned. "Putting on a show, are we?"

"All the world's a stage, my dear."

"And might I request a private viewing later?"

"If the requisite homage is paid."

"I am, as you know, deeply devout to your particular brand of showmanship."

"As I am eager to entertain a patron of your... generosity."

The carriage lurched to a second stop at the curb end of The Gaiety's covered walkway. A cylindrical glass canopy jutted out from the arched doors of the main entrance, supported by thin poles embedded in the sidewalk. Twin posters flanked the doors, announcing the double bill of *The Tragedy of Abelard and Heloise* and *The Be-Deviled Tale of Don Juan, the Libertine*—and that the show would go on. Seeing the small circle of flowers and notes in tribute to Randolph Terriss on the sidewalk sobered Hiero for the task at hand. He remembered that the pomp and power of his arrival was in service of a greater good.

Hiero stole a moment to center himself. He could feel Kip's anxious eyes upon him, waiting to offer comfort and care, but, when it came to his performances, Hiero prepared alone. Like a racer at the starting line, he awaited the pistol's crack.

The door opened. Hiero leapt into the street and strode for the main doors, Kip but a half step behind. He crashed through the entrance. A ticket agent, quick on his feet, ran up to stop him, but Hiero flicked him off with a wave of his hand. He marched over to the foot of the grand staircase—by which time the entire front of house staff had collected around him—jumped onto the third stair, and whooshed around to face them with a twirl of his cape.

"The manager of this establishment." Hiero's announcement silenced the din. "Inform him Hieronymus Bash has come."

With the grace of spooked dodos, they fell over each other to obey. Kip strolled through the scrambling mass, a smile playing on his lips.

"Are you certain this strikes the right chord?"

"My dear, I defer to you in matters of investigation, ergo…"

"Apologies, maestro."

Within minutes, an usher appeared to escort them to the office. Not that Hiero required an escort, having performed at The Gaiety for the better part of a decade under his Beastly guise. He wondered why Kip had not yet shown his warrant card, which might have gained them even swifter access, but knew better than to voice the question. Kip's policing ways were as mysterious to Hiero as Hiero's were to Kip, perhaps why they succeeded as a team and a romantic pair. They couldn't help but surprise each other.

At the top of the grand staircase, a wide corridor diverged, leading to the restaurant on the right and the theater on the left. If Hiero had been the one to lose his leading man to nefarious forces, he would have staged a three-day wake at the table the maître d' always reserved for him. But they veered left into a hallway narrowed by the manager's office on one side and the ladies' parlor on the other.

A cacophony of voices thrummed the door to Tumnus's office. A pair of low baritones fought against the shrieking soprano of an agitated woman. The usher held his knock while the voices shredded through octaves of argument. Hiero cleared his throat. The usher reached again, heard an anguished wail, halted. Just as Kip shoved him aside, the door slammed open, and a figure in operatic fury stormed out.

The prima donna herself, Madame Genevre de Casterac, fixed them with a furious, then curious, eye before disappearing into the theater. A shouted threat, and the Vicomte de Croÿ-Roeulx followed, his anger tempering when he spied Hiero and Kip.

"Monsieur Bash, enfin." He bowed in greeting. "Perhaps one of your skill can make him see sense. *Moi, je m'en lave les mains!*"

Hiero reclined his head ever so slightly forward, peering into the office without appearing to do so. The glare off a perfectly round, perfectly bald pate almost blinded him. Bent over his ledgers, Tumnus gripped his pen like a man poised to sign his death warrant.

"I presume you mean this evening's performance?" Hiero asked, gambling that Tumnus could not understand French.

"The idea that the show must go on after such an event is the height of absurdity!" The Vicomte shouted the last of this over his shoulder. He inhaled deeply, fighting for composure. "Is there no way you can force his hand?"

"Given that we've not been introduced," Hiero remarked, "and his obstinate nature, I cannot say. But I will try."

"And I will succeed," Kip seconded.

"Ah, oui!" Hiero chuckled. "Forgive my manque de politesse. Monsieur le Vicomte, may I present my associate, DI Timothy Kipling Stoker."

"A detective of Scotland Yard?" Croÿ-Roeulx shook Kip's hand a bit too warmly for Hiero's liking. "I should not have doubted that a gentleman of Mr. Bash's prestige would surround himself with the most savvy allies. Si je ne m'abuse, you are the same Inspector Stoker who resolved l'affaire Leblanc?"

"The evidence resolved it," Kip replied, demure as an ingénue. "I merely thought to look."

A fulsome laugh restored the Vicomte's spirits. "Eh bien, I look forward to hearing the full tale."

Before Kip could answer, a voice like an ice saw cut through their mirth.

"Croak, croak, croak!" Tumnus griped. "If I wanted to hear a bunch of frogs, I'd go to a pond. Shut the door and take your business elsewhere."

After a shared look of sympathy with the aggrieved Vicomte, Hiero sauntered into the office with Kip and Croÿ-Roeulx acting as retinue. He walked up to the very edge of the desk, letting his height, wingspan, and magisterial splendor tower over the little turtle at his task. Tumnus finished the sentence he was writing, stabbed a period on the end, then lifted his head. He hadn't been smiling, but Hiero recognized all too well the hardening of the mouth and the winnowing of the stare that signaled a specific brand of disapproval. Hiero made a mental note to wear his most luxurious suits and taunt Tumnus with his wealth at every opportunity, a helpful reminder of what Hiero had achieved despite those who would punish him for the color of his skin.

"And who might you be?" Tumnus demanded.

"That you do not know does not work in your favor." Hiero waggled a finger to quiet further protest. "By way of introduction, let me tell you three truths and one lie. You may guess which one is the falsehood. Agreed?"

"Get your poncy ass out."

"Wonderful." With a swish of his cape, Hiero set off on a parade around the room. "Point the first: You are not merely the manager, but the owner of this theater, and you stand to lose everything if the current season is not a success. Point the second: Though hired for his popular appeal, you'd been shorting Randolph Terriss on the terms of his contract with the promise to make it up out of box office receipts if he drew in the crowds. But you've begun to lose confidence in the play, realizing he'd been miscast as the profligate Don Juan, and you must find a way to cut your losses."

That got Tumnus to his feet. "Now listen here—"

"Point the third." Hiero spun on his heel to begin another revolution.

Kip caught his eye, mouthing, *How do you know all this?*

"Han," Hiero whispered as he passed him. "The only ghost that haunts your stage is the specter of your very own machinations. You yourself started the rumor and caused the disruptions to draw suspicion away when something happened to Terriss. You required extra funds, you see, to keep this enterprise afloat, so you had to be rid of both his inferior performance and the mighty sum he earns."

"That is a lie!" Tumnus bellowed. "How dare you waltz in here and accuse me of such... such a monstrous sin! You have no cause, no proof!"

Hiero swooped back to the desk, meeting and matching his hawkish stare.

"Ah, then you agree that evidence should be collected before leaping to conclusions about what happened to poor dear Mr. Terriss?"

"Of course it should."

"And you concur that the goings-on at this theater point toward a gathering menace toward the members of your company and crew that cannot be ignored?"

Tumnus sighed. "I wouldn't have said so before this morning—not even sure I believe it now—but... Yes, it does bear looking into."

"Excellent." Hiero straightened and spread his arms wide, flaring the ends of his cape for an extra bit of spectacle. "Then you will give my associates and I unrestricted access to The Gaiety and everyone in it, so that we may resolve this matter to everyone's satisfaction, and you can go back to the business of, well, the show." He let Tumnus stammer awhile before adding, "And of course you must cancel tonight's performance. There's simply no question of continuing on until the theater has been inspected for safety and everyone has been interviewed."

The sheer volume of words and ideas left Tumnus adrift. "Given that Terriss's understudy just gave notice... I suppose I have no choice but to delay a night. But just one night."

"Considerate of you," Hiero concluded.

"And just who are you to conduct such an investigation? Scotland Yard is on the case."

"DI Timothy Stoker," Kip piped up, warrant card unfurled. "This is my associate, Hieronymus Bash. We're here on Superintendent Quayle's order."

"You might have started with that," Tumnus snapped. He fixed his beady eyes on the Vicomte. "Your doing, this fancy man? Don't trust our English detectives to see justice done?"

"Au contraire," Croÿ-Roeulx replied, his words covered with a layer of frost. "I thought Messieurs Bash and Stoker to be the perfect marriage of our two cultures."

"Oil and water, if you ask me." Tumnus slumped back into his seat, deflated. "You have a day's grace while I find a new lead, and no more."

"An extravagance of time," Hiero said. "Now go back to cooking the books, and we'll see if we can't stir up some savory bits of information ourselves. We'll speak again before night's end." He shooed them all out before Tumnus could rally his energies, then shut the door behind him.

"A command performance if ever I've seen one," the Vicomte exclaimed as soon as they were out of earshot. "Have you ever considered the stage?"

Hiero struggled to keep the mischief—and the triumph—from his smile. "The only public I serve is the greater good, monsieur."

"Ah, well, I for one am grateful for your service."

Tim half listened to the rest of Hiero and Croÿ-Roeulx's conversation as they walked toward the auditory. He ruminated on the idea of a pious malcontent like Tumnus owning a theater. A manager set the tone. If he kept too close an eye on the bottom line when making creative decisions, that might frustrate those being paid to let their imaginations run wild. No one bought a theater hoping to win their fortune—or if they did, they were fortune's fool, as the Bard said. And Shakespeare would know, having run the Globe Theater for much of his life. Tim wondered what had led Tumnus into this particular line and what he sought to gain from it. He didn't seem the type to chase fame. Those called to the stage tended to make the world their audience.

Tim stole an admiring glance in Hiero's direction. He had forgotten, over their summer's leisure, just how commanding his performances could be. And Tim did so enjoy being commanded by him. He stifled a shiver as they passed into the corridor that arced around the backs of the private boxes. Croÿ-Roeulx meant to lead them down to the stage, but Tim diverted down the passage to the balcony stalls, wanting to observe the working theater without being observed. On his cue, Hiero made their excuses to the Vicomte and joined him.

They stood silent in the back row for a moment, reflecting. The Gaiety never failed to take Tim's breath away. The newest auditory on the Strand, constructed only six years previous, The Gaiety might not be the most popular or the most innovative theater, but it was certainly the most beautiful. Four tiers rose up from the ground stalls—the balcony, the lower and upper boxes, and the gallery—buttressed by stone arches supporting an elaborate cornice and covered ceiling. Side boxes flanked the immense stone proscenium that framed the stage, topped with a painted frieze depicting a medieval royal court watching a masque. Friezes adorned the two side lunettes above the stacks of private boxes, pastoral scenes representing epic and lyric poetry. The act drop—currently raised for the rehearsing performers—had at its center a vignette of a lush

Italian villa. This, along with its engraved columns and deluxe fabrics, imbued the auditory with a Romanesque flair. One truly felt, seated there, in a high temple of the arts.

Well-versed in the vulgarities that regularly crossed its stage, it didn't surprise Tim to find the actors portraying the two unrequited lovers, Abelard and Heloise, pretending to gamahuche the priest who would marry them while waiting for a set adjustment. Various crew members buzzed in and out the sides and circled around the queen bee, Genevre de Casterac, who appeared to be the director.

"Shall we take the stage?" Hiero asked, sotto voce. He'd reclined over to speak directly into Tim's ear, his purr reverberating through his entire body.

Tim's gaze drifted over to Box 5, the site of one of their first intimate encounters. His traitorous mind flickered through images of all the men he'd known and been known by at The Gaiety in his youth, prior to joining the Metropolitan Police. All the firsts he'd experienced here and in other theaters, the endless hours of pleasures dramatic and carnal. He'd come of age in the Strand's private boxes and dressing rooms and back alleys. And in his favorite leading man, he'd found something more: love.

Tim ached to tell him so but hadn't found the moment, the words. Too much between them remained unspoken, no matter how close they'd become. So instead he grazed his knuckles across Hiero's hand—the quietest gesture they could dare while in public—as he turned back down the passageway.

"First, an errand." He waited until they had a small measure of privacy before asking, "Do you know of any still here who might recognize you as Beastly?"

"Only the stage manager, Silas Flint."

"Ah, yes. Then we must seek him out and, well..."

"Silence him?"

"In a less ominous fashion than Mr. Terriss, yes."

Hiero chuckled. "Silas is faithful to one, and only one, mistress,

Lady Gaiety herself. So long as we act in her best interest, he'll claim the Pope's a protestant."

"Then let's hope he's renounced that false idol Tumnus and his penny-pinching ways." Tim gestured for Hiero to guide him to Flint's office. "Take me to church."

Easier said than done. The Gaiety was something of a labyrinth, especially if one wanted to travel from the auditory to the backstage. The ground and balcony stalls had their own entrances and exits to limit the hoi polloi's access to areas where more fine-feathered patrons flocked, such as the lounges, boxes, and the restaurant. With double the amount of staircases as an older theater, even the staff often found themselves in the gallery when they meant to go to the dress circle. Tim would go to his grave before admitting he'd regularly depended on the ushers to guide him to Hiero's dressing room on nights Beastly trod the boards. Little wonder the ghost—or whoever haunted The Gaiety—had eluded identification. The only person Tim knew with a perfect mental map of the place was his current escort. Which begged the question…

"Our stalking specter," he said as they descended a staircase. "How do you think he gets about?"

"Apart from the obvious, you mean? Floating through walls and the like." Hiero chuckled.

"Expedient as that would be, I was thinking in more practical terms."

"Such as?"

"Navigation."

"I don't follow."

"How do they know where to hide?"

Hiero stopped. "Someone who knows their way around."

"Precisely. Or who possesses an exceptional sense of direction. The crew is new. The company is new. And this Mr. Flint—"

"—is the only member of the old guard still standing. Yes, I see." Hiero crossed his arms and pressed a crooked finger to his lips, all of his earlier pomp and artifice cowed under the weight of his concerns. "I may be walking into a trap."

Tim moved closer to him, wishing they could embrace. "You did the minute you strode through the front doors. Bravely, I might add." This caught Hiero's eye, and his smile.

"Yes, well. I could hardly leave you to it. The fiend would be stalking the orchestra pit while you'd be lost in the flies." Tim feigned an injured look, which brought out Hiero's twinkle. "Puts our note writer in something of a different light."

"How so?"

"Causing chaos so Tumnus will sell, I grant, is a possibility with Silas. But Randy was beloved by all—Silas would no more murder him than chew off his own leg. If he is our ghost, and he sent the letter, perhaps it was more a cry for help than a threat?"

"A dramatic way of calling Beastly back, you mean? And once he's back and sees the state of the place..."

"Sets the wheels of change in motion." Hiero sighed. "Wretched plan, of course, but he's a stage manager, not the Count of Monte Cristo. Whom I played to thunderous acclaim some years ago in J.S. Houseman's melodrama—"

"—*Served Cold, or A Revenger's Tragedie*. I well recall."

"You were in attendance?"

"On five occasions, no less."

This earned him a tender look. "I do adore you."

They hovered in each other's space, unable to touch but unwilling to part. Tim knew he should rein in his softer impulses, concentrate on the case, but the setting and their isolation and his smoldering partner proved a worthy distraction. Hiero, incorrigible as ever, only stoked his fire by backing him up to the nearest wall and... leaning. He craned his head over Tim's and inhaled deeply; Tim felt the air between them crackle. His fingers itched to make quick work of Hiero's tie, to flick open the button beneath, press his nose to the cleft at the bottom of his throat and smell him in return.

Instead he pinched the inside of his thigh until his prick thought better of perking up.

"A promise is a promise," Tim reminded him.

He dared a look upward, caught the last embers of Hiero's heated stare.

"So it is." He fluttered a hand in the direction they should take. "To the underworld."

After creeping through a series of doors Tim would have been hard-pressed to retrace his way through, they broke into the bowels of the theater. The artisans' workshops were housed beneath the stage: costume warehouse, prop storage, set-building, backdrop painting, and offices for the heads of each crew department. Tim couldn't keep himself from peering through the few open doors. Though he'd visited many times, he never missed a chance to catch a glimpse of the magic of stagecraft.

Even the rehearsal schedules on the wall outside Mr. Flint's door intrigued, though in a more professional capacity. They'd knocked twice to no response when the man himself barreled past them, chased by two bickering stagehands. Flint ignored them all as he rifled through the drawers of his desk to retrieve a heavily annotated script. He threw this at the man closest to him.

"Give this to her nibs," he ordered, grabbing a paper out of the second man's hands. Flint scanned the document closely as he fumbled for a pen. Three ticks and a sloppy signature later, he shoved it back. "Tell her it's initials, or to get someone to help her. No x's."

Grumbling, the men slunk out of the office. Hiero tapped out five silent beats on his wrist, then knocked on the frame.

"A word?"

Flint, head down, barked, "No time, no solicitations," as he rearranged the piles on his desk into... different piles.

"Not even for an old friend?"

Flint glanced up, snorted. "I was wondering when you lot'd turn up."

He waved them in, motioning for Tim to shut the door behind him. There were no chairs to speak of, only a dusty stool tucked in a far corner, on which sat the room's least attractive feature: the most garish lamp Tim had ever laid eyes on. Considering he resided in the house Goya burped up during a bout of artistic indigestion, he could only sympathize with Flint's aesthetic limitations. Perhaps the reason he managed the stage instead of acting upon it.

"I'd offer you a place to sit, but..." He came around the side of the desk to clasp Hiero's hands. "I like to keep 'em on their toes."

"As I well recall."

They shared a poignant look, and then Flint reached out to Tim.

"Glad you've come." Flint moved over to a small cabinet, which he opened to reveal a choice selection of whiskey. He pulled out three tumblers and a bottle of 1855 Glenturret. "The lads are bothered over Randy, but it's not the same as us that knew him."

They waited in somber silence as he poured them each a glass, then joined him in a toast. The scorch of the whiskey down his throat burned off the last of Tim's earlier fever, sobering him to his task. One of unforeseen revelation since most of the old Gaiety staff knew him as Horace Beastly's lover Kip, not as himself.

"How had Mr. Terriss been coping with the change of guard here at The Gaiety?" Tim asked.

Flint raised an eyebrow. "It's like that, is it?"

"Worse, I'm afraid." Hiero offered a sheepish grin. "May I present my partner, DI Timothy Stoker."

"The Yard?" Flint whistled. Tim watched as he did the math in his mind, adding Kip to the Tim that stood before him and solving for Beastly's alter ego Hieronymus Bash. "You do like dangerous living."

Hiero chuckled. "Is there any other way?"

"Suppose not, with the world at your feet." Flint took in a long draught of whiskey, then replied, "Randy was an affable sort. Went where the work was. No complaints. Half the reason he became so popular was managers were happy to book him for extended runs. Company loved him, crew loved him; he had the right kind of talent. The mob always turns out for comedy and romance."

"And yet..." Hiero tinkled his nails on the side of his tumbler. "An odd choice for Don Juan."

Flint laughed. "Jealous?"

"Never."

"Would have been yours if you'd stayed." His sadness returned. "Best that you didn't."

Tim shook his head against the very thought of someone threatening Hiero's life, then played it off as agreement.

"Better that this ghost rumor had been taken more seriously." At Flint's grunt, Tim asked, "What are your thoughts?"

"Seen him myself, haven't I?" He shuddered. "Chased him 'cross the walkways and down the back stairs, all the way out into the street. Almost had him, too, but he ran into the Arches."

"The Adelphi Arches, you mean?"

"Would've got the drop on me if I'd followed him in. And didn't fancy anyone else giving me the chop for trying."

The Adelphi Arches, nicknamed the Dark Arches for the illegal goings-on in its shadowy alcoves and subterranean passageways, were a series of brick archways that bordered the Thames and supported a series of luxury apartments. Wedged in at the bottom of a downward slope from the Strand, and thus well away from the constables patrolling the main thoroughfare, they were a haven for thieves, gangs, and criminals of all stripes. Poor individuals of good character and families in genuine need of a refuge stayed away—Tim didn't know if the tales he'd heard were more fact or legend, but the fiends who lurked there took advantage of even the most desperate, weak, or penniless. Few of the officers he knew would follow a suspect into the seething dark of the Arches, where a thousand knives waited to slit your throat.

In other words, the perfect nest for the viper they sought.

"You did right," Tim assured him. "This is a matter for the police. As you're a witness, this goes beyond rumor and nervy imaginings. Why didn't Mr. Tumnus call in the Yard?"

Hiero and Flint shared a compassionate look, then stared baldly at Tim.

"Forgive him." Hiero sighed. "He's new to our world."

"I was raised in a maître costumier's fitting room at the Opéra de Paris, among other grand houses, I'll thank you to recall," Tim huffed, a bit annoyed that Hiero so casually ignored his mother's vocation.

"You ain't wrong, neither," Flint said to Tim. "Randy might be around if Tumnus paid more mind to anything but the bottom line. Can't says I believed in the ghost myself at first—thought he was a punter who fancied a peek at the girls in rehearsal—but with his costume and the accidents... More than enough proof, you ask me."

"Costume? What did he wear?"

"Nothing out of our vault, I promise you. Everything we have on site is from after the renovation. A cape—short, so he could run—and soldier's uniform. Belts and buckles and shiny buttons, but from no army I've ever seen. And a mask. A red skull."

"The mask of the red death," Hiero murmured with a shudder.

"Aye." Flint scoffed. "Bit obvious, but we can't say we weren't warned."

"And has he targeted anyone in particular?" Tim asked. "Were all his appearances related to Terriss?"

"I wouldn't say so." Flint downed the last of his whiskey. "A few people caught him in the corridors, but always on rehearsal nights. Course it's hard to tell if he was here later, as not many people were about. The Frenchies don't linger once herself calls it a night. If anyone stays late, it's me or Tumnus."

"Have you ever felt in danger of your life?"

"Never," he chuckled. "Why'd he want to do away with a nobody like me? Nah, he went straight for the top on the first chop."

Tim laughed with them to conceal his dread. He signaled to Hiero that their interview was at an end.

"Still, be wary," Hiero warned. "He's on the hunt."

"And you're on the chase, the pair of you?" Flint asked.

"And our associates Mr. Han and Mr. Calvin, yes. You'll see them skulking about our business, so don't mistake them for the phantom."

"Tell 'em no masks, and we're golden."

"Wonderful." Hiero added a final dram to both their glasses, winked as they clinked. "And a request..."

Flint put a finger to his nose. "So long as you catch this snide, your secret is safe with me."

They exchanged some final pleasantries. Tim extracted a copy of the rehearsal schedules for the past few months and a promise from Flint to keep them informed of any gossipy developments before bidding him farewell.

When Tim swung open the door, the screaming started.

Chapter 4

*H*an cursed under his breath as he stood on the corner of Catherine Street and the Strand, the wide expanse of The Gaiety encompassing the entire span of his vision.

"Three public entrances, two semiprivate, with bad angles and little to no cover," he sighed, "to say nothing of the sheer number of people crowding the view at any given hour... How will you manage it?"

Han turned to the towheaded boy at his right, all knees and elbows now that he'd begun to grow in earnest. But the awkwardness of his newfound height hadn't dimmed the spark in his eyes or the glee in his grin. Tobias Warren was still Han's nimblest and savviest rabbit, as well as the leader of the motley gang that scanned the street for an easy mark, onto the next trick before their present business had concluded.

"Like we always do, guv." Toby shrugged. "'Round the clock, hiding in plain sight." He turned the fingers he'd been using to list off his points into a gun, playfully aimed at Han. "For the right price."

"A place of your own and two square not enough these days, is it?" Han teased. He knew better than most the constant anxiety that could set in when someone used to living rough shifted to creature comforts. Not a fear of going soft, but of going dull, of losing your instincts and your ability to react to danger at a moment's notice. Of forgetting that it could all be taken away, no matter how hard-won.

Not that he'd ever be allowed to forget, as evidenced by the pointed and menacing looks he got from passersby for the crime of standing on the sidewalk. As much as he doted on his small army of helpers, Han would never fail to resent needing their help in the first place. How most ignored these poor, grubby, mischief-minded boys, permitting them a level of invisibility he could never achieve due to the color of his skin.

But *he* could do his part to relieve that anxiety, to give them a sense of worth and security. Once he'd assembled a regular, trustworthy group, he'd bought his bunnies a small house and paid for their housekeeper in the hopes of keeping them hale, whole, and loyal. He'd lost a few rabbits over the years to the usual vices, right around the age Toby was now, so he knew he'd better sweeten the pot.

"A rugby Sunday. I'll stand your first bet, and Minnie will pack us pies and cider."

Toby's smile almost split his face. A bit of attention and a shoulder to cry on, Han had found, proved of far more value to the boys than another penny in their pocket.

"Step to, lads!" Toby shouted. "This 'un's for the rugger."

With a whoop and a holler, the boys slapped hands. Then, one by one, they disappeared into the crowd to take up their prearranged lookout positions. Toby, as usual, had been five steps ahead of Han, scouting the location and planning their approach before they even met up with him. Han waved them off with a proud nod and a tap to the corner of his eye: be vigilant.

Not that any of them knew who or what they were looking for. There might be a ghost haunting the theater, but Han doubted it wore a white robes and chains. *If* the ghost ever left The Gaiety— another possibility Han didn't care to contemplate, though contemplate it he must, along with the roof, the small building tacked to The Gaiety's far left corner like a belligerent younger sibling, and any underground passages yet to be discovered.

To think he was once pleased to find the theater had multiple escape routes. He'd been the one to encourage Hiero to take up a residency there, against Apollo's wishes, due to the fact that Han could spirit him away at a moment's notice should the wrong sort of acquaintance be in the audience. And had done on numerous occasions. Han would never admit to his bosom friend that he preferred Hieronymus Bash to Horace Beastly, that he was relieved when Hiero retired from the stage earlier that year. The risk of someone from their past making the right connection between Beastly and Bash was a necessary evil when they first broke out on their own. But now that they dabbled in detective work...

And yet Han couldn't shake the sense that he had not been vigilant enough. That he had missed a face well known to them in all those crowds. Or one in disguise. Not even the most deranged fan would start with murder as a gambit to attract Horace Beastly's attention. But there certainly was no shortage of people who wished them ill, whom they'd tiptoed away from in the gray period of their lives before Apollo's patronage.

Han stowed those thoughts away as a gamine figure skipped out of the chop house beside The Gaiety's main entrance. He'd tasked Callie—still practicing her Mr. Calvin guise—with persuading the proprietor to allow them access to the roof. Not that Han required it. He'd mapped the route from The Gaiety side during Hiero's first year at the theater. But he'd never attempted to convince the current tenant to grant a stranger off the street said access. By the spring in Callie's step, she had succeeded in doing so, which did not bode well.

However, the devil spark in her eyes when she landed beside him did much to revive his mood. He fought the urge to tuck a stray forelock of her raven hair back under her hat.

"Gait."

Her soft mouth made a perfect moue, which he enjoyed almost as much as throwing her off-kilter. "I have news."

"I expect so. How will I take it?"

The twitch of her left cheek told him she fought not to roll her eyes. Mr. Calvin, of course, would never be so bold.

"I could not presume to say, sir."

"Hmm. First, your gait. You skipped."

"I did not—"

"You did. Off the step. I thought you might break into song." He flattened a smirk of his own when she scrunched her face in displeasure. "Now what have you to report?"

"My complete and total failure." She struggled not to smile. "To secure access to the roof, I mean. Mr. Parbat, the maître d' of the chop house, and Mrs. Sikorska, who oversees the seamstress circle on the top floor, both say they have been warned by Mr. Tumnus not to allow anyone access to The Gaiety from their building, on penalty of doubling their rent. And they had a similar agreement with Mr. Webster before him."

"Sensible. I wonder if there was—"

"An incident?" The corners of her lips perked up, but she forced them down again. "One that occurred a little over a month ago, perhaps?"

Han had to credit her instincts. "Do tell."

"A woman claiming to be a dancer banged on the door to the roof, begging to be let in. Said she'd jumped over on a dare and was too scared to climb back. Mrs. Sikorska let her through, with a caution that next time she'd be brought to Mr. Tumnus for a reprimand. The woman began to sob, confessing that something had chased her up there. Crossed her heart it would never happen again. That was the first Mrs. Sikorska heard of the ghost."

"Or an incident she attributes to the ghost without proof. The dancer, if that is her true occupation, was quick to change her tune. Did Mrs. Sikorska recall her name?"

Callie assayed her best enigmatic look. Han thought she'd make a poor card sharp.

"It seems she disappeared without giving one."

"Astonishing. Description?"

"Blonde. Tall. Doesn't recall her eye color. Curvy, she thought, for a dancer."

Han snapped to attention. As Callie listed further insignificant details, an idea formed in his mind. At once eager and reluctant to pursue it, he shelved it for later contemplation.

"So any girl from any theater on the Strand."

"Twenty from The Gaiety alone—I credit that. But..." Her energy, when about to share a theory, buzzed at a higher frequency. Her teeth glinted, the ends of her hair frizzed, her aquiline features grew sharper, bolder, brighter. She lived for these moments, and Han lived to witness them. "What if this woman *is* the ghost?"

"Testing her boundaries, you mean?" Han nodded. "It's possible. Terriss was one for the ladies, and stabbing someone in the chest doesn't require an enormous amount of strength, especially if one is impassioned."

Callie grinned. "Precisely."

"However. Perhaps it's an unconscious bias of mine, but the note to Hiero..."

"If you're about to utter the words, 'It doesn't read female'..."

"In your presence? I've a far better sense of self-preservation."

"That remains to be seen."

They shared a complicit look, effortlessly in step as always. Their rapport had been in evidence from the day they first met, her but a girl, him the newest addition to Apollo's carousel of a household. She'd grabbed his hand and given him the grand tour, the second person he'd met in England to do so without prejudice— Hiero being the first. They swapped tales, anecdotes, observations, as if they'd known each other all their lives. He was astounded she'd been permitted such a free-range education. Insatiably curious about all things, she wanted to know everything about his early life in Macau and his experiences at sea, no matter how harrowing. With her, Han felt at home in a way he hadn't since living with his mother on their boat.

Until Apollo's death. That dark day had transformed her and Hiero both. One closed and the other opened. The real Hiero retreated behind the Bash persona until Tim came along and saw to the heart of him, whereas Callie became a Persephone emergent from Hades on that first spring day. She'd learned to bloom in the dark.

He'd been captivated ever since. And suddenly all too aware of the societal obstacles to any togetherness they might seek: the difference in their ages, her inexperience of certain harsh realities of the world, the privileges she unconsciously relied on... But most of all, the thought that he might lose her forever if they tried and failed. Han had learned long ago to cherish what he had rather than long for what might never be. In their friendship, and their Berkeley Square family, he'd found his joy.

Han paused a minute to consider how best to voice his concerns. "Put plainly, I cannot envision a woman being a fanatical admirer of Horace's. Perhaps his own predilections skew my judgment. But also experience. In his time on the stage, he received a mountain of gifts, invitations, love notes, and some very boisterous suitors, many of which I was charged with dismissing, and the most difficult, by far, were the men. They also outnumbered the women by a significant margin. When a woman sought to seduce him, she was direct. Others, by necessity, were more discreet and conniving." He chanced a glance in her direction. "Am I marked for death?"

"Spared the noose, but only just." Callie sighed. "Trouble is, I rather agree."

"Oh, dear."

"Quite. Hair shirt for me this evening." She bit the inside of her lip as she worked through the problem. "If the ghost, the murderer, and the note-writer are one and the same, then I must agree. It's the show of the thing. If a woman plotted to dispatch Mr. Terriss and cause chaos at The Gaiety, all to lure Horace Beastly back to the stage and usurp Tumnus, her revenge would be more artfully done. She'd leave no trace. This killer wants to be seen, to have the craft of his deceptions be uncovered and acknowledged."

"An elegant observation," Han complimented, admiring despite himself how it lit up her face. "One to bear in mind. But this is a theatrical affair. Everyone involved loves to put on a show."

"And none more so than the lead detective."

They shared a laugh. Han fought not to take a step closer. He'd found it easier to remember the obstacles to intimacy between them when Callie enacted the part of dizzy ingénue, costumed in her wigs and finery. Her bare face and natural hair made invisible the all-too-real barriers between them. Without extra caution, Han would brain himself on the glass.

"Are your rabbits in their warrens?" she asked, breaking through his fugue.

"With pocketfuls of carrots, yes. Now we need only…"

A ticket seller exited The Gaiety, cancellation signs tucked under his arm—the signal they awaited. As he proceeded to hang them on the posters and sidewalk board, Han nudged her toward the performers' entrance on Wellington Street. Hiero and Tim had successfully talked their way in through the front door; now he and Callie would test the rear. With owlish precision, Han rotated his head left and right, finding Catherine Street quite empty. He slowed his pace until he fell a few steps behind her.

"Less sway."

She half turned. "What's that?"

"Your center. Too high. Lead with your hips and kick out in brisk strides. Not like Archie, low and hunched. Mr. Calvin should be straight and strong."

She harrumphed but made the correction. "You're enjoying this far too much."

A hundred replies launched off his tongue and crashed into his clamped teeth. He embraced the silence.

Callie fell back into step beside him. "Add a bit of swagger, should I?"

Han didn't have to look to know she imitated his walk. Knew he shouldn't, but chanced a glance anyway. Regretted it.

"You're an observant mimic, but mimicry is not a full performance."

"Neither is parroting Hiero true critique."

He chuckled. "I dare say, between Hiero and myself, he would claim the more colorful plumage, and I the falconer's glove." He stole a final glance as they rounded the corner...

...to find the stage door open and unguarded, and Miss Maxine Marks peering into the black.

Hiero white-knuckled his instinct to flee when the screaming started. Why must their every case involve racing through tight underground passages after a shriek or a cry or a deranged zealot obsessed with setting fires? He had never before noted the similarities between the below-stage corridors of The Gaiety and the tunnels under Castleside, the compound once owned by the sadistic Daughters of Eden and where he and Kip were almost blown to kingdom come not five months earlier. He demanded their next case be on a mountaintop or in an open field. On a boat, perhaps, a flat Viking boat—

A rough tug from Kip, and not the kind he preferred, saw Hiero striding purposefully toward... where? The screaming transformed into quiet sobs and murmurs, not as easy to track. Flint pushed past them, broke out in a run. Kip, the newly fit traitor, set off after him. Hiero managed a jog, wishing he'd chosen a less-constricting tie, a shorter cape, a decade's less indulgence, and a regular exercise regimen. Also, a profession that required him to be outdoors.

But not really.

After a few wrong turns, Hiero nearly crashed into the small circle of onlookers surrounding one of the dancers. He stopped just short of leapfrogging one of the stagehands into the poor woman, waving his outstretched hands over this human barrier's back before Hiero paused to collect himself. He peered between two heads, then jolted back from the shocking scene.

The dancer—Polly, they were calling her—lay slumped in the arms of two of her sisters, her leg bent at an impossible angle. An iceberg shard of bone jabbed out just beneath her knee, gushing blood. The small platform that should have been beneath the trap door to catch her had been overturned, its legs sharpened into spikes, with a few lethal extras added for maximum carnage. How Polly had avoided impaling herself, Hiero could not say.

Other performers craned their heads through the open square above her, and a crowd of gawking backstage workers surrounded her but made no move to help. Only when he dared another look did Hiero discover why.

There, painted on the floor beneath her, was an enormous two. Fiend or ghost or singular madman, they'd struck again.

"Back off, all of you," Flint bellowed, clapping his hands to wake them from their stupor. "Give them space."

As the crowd retreated a few steps, Hiero steeled his posture and pushed through them, announcing his presence. Gratifying whispers followed him along the edge of the room as he walked the long way around Polly to Kip, who examined the scene and their surroundings with eagle eyes.

"You there." Hiero summoned one of the stagehands, flicking out a card with a snap of his fingers. "Fetch my physician posthaste."

The young man took the card and looked to Flint, who barked, "Now, you spineless git!" He stomped a heavy boot, sending shivers through the crowd. "God's teeth, this isn't a matinee. You up there, away with you! And you, Useless, fetch blankets. Drooling Donny in the corner there, get a bucket and a mop. The pair of you take your friend Twiggy and find the rolling sleigh we used in the panto last Christmas. The rest of you, grab everyone you can and wait in the auditory until we're done here. No one hides, no one leaves, no exceptions!"

In the scrabble that ensued, Hiero sought a private word with Kip, or as much of one as they could manage amidst Polly's wails and Flint's busybodying.

"A penny for your thoughts?"

"I doubt they're worth that much," he sighed.

"Are we certain it's..."

Kip gestured at the monstrous two. "They've made it rather impossible to ignore. And kindly let us know Terriss was killed before midnight."

"So The Gaiety Ghost is our letter-writer and the killer?"

"Signs point to yes, but our ghost, like most specters, remains elusive. But the other two are now one and the same."

Hiero permitted his dread to dampen the fury that ignited within him. He forced himself to confront Polly's anguished face. She suffered through the pain of her injury and the knowledge her career had ended with a thundering crack. Two more of her company had snuck down to succor her as one of the dressers wrapped her leg. If only the guilt that bit at his insides could be so easily contained.

"How was it done?"

"Long before we arrived, at a guess." Kip pointed to the latches where the platform had been locked in. "Those took time; the hatch as well. Give me a boost?"

Hiero recoiled. "Under no circumstances."

"All the stagehands have gone."

"You mean to press the bottom of your boots into these"—he thrust out his palms with excessive flourish—"marvels?"

"Unless you care to carry over a stool."

Hiero shuddered. "Oh, very well."

He squatted into the most ungainly position his limbs had ever taken on, forming a basket with his arms. He ignored the flash of amusement that brightened Kip's expression.

"Think you can take me?" Kip whispered as he holstered his foot.

"Oh, you're more than enough for me," Hiero said into his navel as he hoisted Kip up. By the time Kip planted a shin on his shoulder to leverage more height, Hiero found himself nose to groin, which silenced any further complaints but did little for his concentration.

"Tampered with, as I suspected." Kip performed an athletic dismount Hiero would insist be repeated at a more private hour. "It appears as if they loosened the latch so that it would wear over time. We'll have to test it, but there's only one possible conclusion."

Hiero blinked, waiting. After several beats, he asked, "Which is?"

"Oh." Kip chuckled. "Forgive me. There was no specific victim intended. Our fiend might have stayed and waited for a certain performer to pass overhead but instead left it to chance. Which leads me to a far more unfortunate conclusion."

Hiero fought against the constriction around his throat. "Do tell?"

"Everyone is at risk." They both watched, concerned but helpless, as they shifted Polly onto the prop sleigh in order to slide her to a more comfortable location. "Terriss wasn't a statement of purpose but a grand opening. I thought at first only the principal players would be targeted, but no. Our killer is demonstrating their versatility. They might maim at random; they might strike true. Ingenious, after a fashion. Also impossible to plan for."

Hiero digested this like a vat of putrid eels. "Except."

"Except?"

Hiero sought reassurance in the pale canvas of his face, where the pattern of his freckles could oft be read like tea leaves. He found none. "Isn't there always an exception, even in the grimmest of circumstances? A hint or a clue or an unexpected turn? A measure of hope?"

Kip only shrugged, then moved to catch Polly before they carted her off.

"Miss Nichols, a word?" Polly whined through another painful shift of her leg but nodded. "In as much detail as you can manage, can you describe your fall?"

"I was doing the pas de chat with Mary-Anne and Charlotte, there. I heard the trap rattle but didn't think nothing of it. The panel don't fit right, so it always seems loose."

"But this time it was?"

She sniffled through another spill of tears. "I was lucky. Felt it give before the snap, so I caught the edge of the stage when I dropped. It was so black I couldn't see anything below. But I knew someone'd stole the platform, 'cause you crouch when you fall in. Just standing, the punters can see you. So I swung out, but my shoe caught. Spike still got my leg."

"But not your life." Kip helped wrap a blanket around her shoulders. "And for that we are grateful."

Polly whimpered a reply, succumbing to her pain.

After a great deal of grunting and scuffling, he and Kip found themselves alone. Hiero stared down at the giant blood-smeared two and clung to that measure of hope with both hands.

The clack of a closing pocket watch woke him from his worrying.

"Eight hours' reprieve," Kip said. "Sixteen if you wager our fiend won't strike in the wee hours, when the theater is empty."

"Then we'd best hasten to make our introductions to the full company. After you reveal what you've been keeping from me, my dear."

His Kip, at least, had the grace not to deny it. "You're fraught enough over this. I wanted to be certain before—"

"—you leapt to the obvious conclusion? The one we'd all anticipated, that the note and the murder are connected?"

"Before I added wood to the fire you've been roasting over. Note the metaphor. You didn't choose to be on the spit, Hiero. You were bound there by this menace, same as the others." Kip's arms jerked, but he restrained himself from reaching out. Hiero could have flung moral convention into the flames as well. "They've come for you. There's no use denying it. They want you to suffer over every accident, every death. Remember that their sweetest pleasure is your torment. But, dearest, I will not let you burn."

Hiero nodded, overcome. He locked on to those eloquent green eyes, wishing they were at home. He moved closer, canted into Kip's side, as if they conferred.

"Imagine I'm embracing you," he said sotto voce.

"Imagine I'm very, very appreciative."

Hiero sighed. "How long till we need no longer imagine?"

"I cannot say." A tender touch pressed into the small of his back, retreating all too soon. "For now, your audience awaits."

Chapter 5

$\mathcal{J}$im never tired of seeing his Hiero take the stage. He appeared to grow a foot in height as he crossed to stand on an imaginary mark before the audience of assembled company and crew members. They shouted down Tumnus, who stood in the center, losing his religion as he attempted to reassure them. A hush fell over them when Hiero found his light, hovering beside Tumnus like the angel on his shoulder.

Tim skirted around the curtains, waiting for his own cue. He looked out over the crowd of irate faces, apathetic faces, curious faces, and wondered which harbored the secrets he sought. He picked out the Vicomte de Croÿ-Roeulx in the front row, growing testy as Tumnus pontificated on safety measures, as if mere caution could stop the attacks. Genevre de Casterac, presiding over two seats beside him, fought against her drooping eyelids.

Tim swallowed a yip of excitement at spotting the famous Vauquelin sisters, Damiane and Seraphine, in the middle of the second row. The actress siblings had earned international renown for their portrayals of tragic lovers like Romeo and Juliet, Tristan and Isolde, and now Abelard and Heloise.

Movement in the back row drew his attention. Vision limited by the glare of the lights, Tim inched closer to the front of the stage. To his relief, it was nothing more than a few late arrivals. He recognized the stagehands who had helped with the injured dancer and...

someone new. Old and new, if Tim's eyes weren't deceiving him. He set a hand to his brow to cut down the glare. An instant later, Tim found himself hoping it masked his surprise. More than one specter haunted The Gaiety, if the ghost from Tim's past sitting in the audience was anything to go by.

Not a genuine ghost, of course, but a very real, very grown-up Marius Lamarque.

Tim staggered back into the wings, reeling, and almost stumbled into Callie. Or, rather, Mr. Calvin. He forgot his own preoccupations when he saw her frown. "What's happened? Another incident?"

"I'd ask you the same. One of the dancers, I heard?"

"A rigged fall, yes. Broke her leg."

"No accident, I take it?"

"Not unless it's their custom to draw an enormous bloody two under each trap."

"Blast," Callie said under her breath. "Not even a day's grace to get our bearings."

"They do seem rather desperate for our attention."

"Ours, or his?" Callie nodded in Hiero's direction.

Tim watched Hiero's usual theatrics—the flaring of his cape, the underscoring of his impatience with his busy conductor's hands, the silent commentary of his sharp eyebrows, his warmth and charm and grandiosity—with a mixture of admiration and apprehension. No matter how he maneuvered Hiero away from the spotlight, some trick of light always found him.

"They've got us all, regardless." Tim sighed, sought a diversion from his worry. "Did Han not accompany you?"

She shook her head. "We had an incident of our own."

"Oh? Someone attempted to flee?"

"The opposite. Sneak in." She cast a concerned glance behind her. "Han is interviewing her now. I heard the commotion and left him to it."

"Do you think her a creditable suspect?"

She huffed out a breath. "I'd count her in, but only because no one can be discounted yet. She's a professional eavesdropper for *The Pall Mall Gazette*. Given the very public nature of Mr. Terriss's death... tongues will wag."

"If only there were a way to muzzle them until the killer is caught."

Callie snorted. "I dare say our ghost will be more easily stopped than the rumormongers. Gossip is of higher social currency than murder itself." A thought appeared to strike her. "We must connive a way to use it to our advantage."

"In this, I defer to your superior skills."

This, at last, earned him a half smile. "As expected."

A great, echoing "ahem" blasted through Tumnus's babble, startling them all. Without waiting for an introduction, Hiero all but shoved him off to the far side of the stage, taking his pride of place in the center. The crowd, which had resumed its caterwauling, broke into laughter. But all fell silent at Hiero's deferential bow.

"Good afternoon. I am Hieronymus Bash, consulting detective, and I have come to your aid. My associates and I have a wealth of expertise in solving esoteric cases such as this. You have perhaps read of our triumphs over the Demon Cats of Scavo or the fanatical Daughters of Eden. Where things go bump in the night, we're called in to make things right." Tim felt a surge of relief when a chorus of chuckles rang out. "But I must be forthright. The situation will likely sicken further before its color improves. And the only way to apprehend this villain is if all of you proceed as normal. Tonight, The Gaiety is dark. But tomorrow the show must go on."

The shouting began anew, with several people jumping to their feet. Hiero raised pacifying hands, to no avail. With nary a crack in his confidence, he waved Tim on.

After his own introduction, Tim shuffled onto the stage, angling his body so he could not see the back row. He tried to force thoughts of Marius from his mind as he confronted the crowd, but he couldn't help but wonder if he'd been recognized in turn. He shoved back the thousand questions that pushed into his head the second he thought of his long-lost friend, and what it might mean to encounter him under such difficult circumstances—made no less so by the man standing next to him, expectant.

"We will find them," Tim reassured his audience. "Those responsible. That is our promise to you. But in order for us to do so, you must make us a promise in turn: honesty. Mr. Bash and I are not here for your secrets or your petty crimes. We mean to stop a murderer. We hope we have your full cooperation in that endeavor."

The crowd buzzed, anxious and unsure. Before Tim could continue, a figure rose at the end of the second row. Genevre de Casterac knew how to create a moment and took full advantage of her innate melisma now. A diminutive woman decorated in enough silks and sparkles to draw the envy of a queen, her fashion amplified her already commanding personality.

"A noble ambition, to be sure, gentlemen," she addressed Hiero and Tim. "But one with an intolerable risk. How can you ask these good people to continue on as before, when at any moment they might fall victim to this murderous ghost? Their careers ruined, their lives lost! And all for what? Nothing but that man's greed!" The accusing finger she pointed at Tumnus might as well have been a stake to the heart.

Cheers erupted. People shouted in support. Tim marveled that they didn't throw flowers. Madame de Casterac knew how to play to her audience.

"No matter your grievances with Mr. Tumnus," Tim yelled over them, "the attacks may not stop if the theater remains dark. At the moment, the incidents have been contained to the Strand. But if you disperse, they may follow you home. The only way to see how and why this is being done is to remain here, continue your daily routines, and catch them in the act."

"Intolérable!" Genevre whipped her arms back and forth, encouraging the crowd to chant, "In-to-lé-rable! In-to-lé-rable!"

Tim looked helplessly to Hiero, who observed the riled crowd with a Cheshire Cat smile.

Vive la révolution, he mouthed to Tim before raising both hands to silence them. Madame de Casterac countered this by standing on her chair and clapping in time with their chant.

Dueling conductors, Tim thought, watching Hiero and Madame de Casterac fight for control.

"Enough!" Tumnus took over the stage anew, meeting Madame de Casterac's defiant stare head-on. "Let me be clear: you either help Mr. Bash, or you're done here. Choice is yours."

A cold silence froze over the company, their faces caught in angry expressions. But none dared take Tumnus on, not even the pouting Madame de Casterac. When one lived hand-to-mouth like so many in the theatrical trade, no one could afford to lose a job or stain their reputation.

"Come, come." The Vicomte de Croÿ-Roeulx intervened. "Let us not quarrel so. We all want the same result, non? I myself invited Mr. Bash and his associates here to The Gaiety. As they say, it is useless to fret over this *fantôme*. La solidarité, that is our way. 'We are such stuff as dreams are made on.' N'est-ce pas, mes amis?"

Begrudging mutters of "yes" and "oui" could be heard amidst the chastened crowd. Tim took advantage of their momentary distraction.

"Merci, Monsieur le Vicomte." Tim bowed his head at their patron. "We will do everything in our power to keep you safe and to resolve this matter as swiftly as possible. To that end, when you leave the theater tonight, please make sure you do so in pairs or groups. Make arrangements to spend the night with someone trustworthy while this is going on." He felt a surge of gratitude at the whistles and catcalls this produced since it meant they finally listened. "How many amongst you have had firsthand encounters with this ghost?" A half-dozen hands, a few hesitant, sprang up. "We'll interview you this evening. The rest of you may depart once you've had a quick word with one of our associates, Mr. Calvin." Callie raised an eyebrow in his direction but nodded.

"No one is to remain in the theater overnight," Hiero added. "No one."

"Stay together, be vigilant," Tim concluded, "and thank you for your time."

A livid Tumnus set upon Hiero as soon as the hum of chatter resumed. Tim, with a smirk in Hiero's direction, sidestepped that conversation, disappearing into the wings to sneak into the auditory. After a few wrong turns—the architects had made even such a simple transition into an Orphean journey—Tim emerged in the orchestra pit. He vaulted the short wall separating it from the audience and landed in front of the line of ghost witnesses. Some frowned, some fidgeted, but all appeared eager to share their tale.

Including Marius, waiting at the tail end with bright eyes and a shy smile aimed squarely at Tim.

He remembered.

Though he'd backed Miss Maxine Marks into the corner of the performers' entrance doorway, Han felt boxed in. If he interviewed her in the alley behind The Gaiety, they might be overheard. If he brought her inside, he gave her what she sought: access. He could not so much as reach a hand toward her in public—and by the superior, defiant cant of her jaw, she knew it. She could have cried murder, could have called in a posse of gallants from the nearby Strand, but she did not.

Which meant he was of use to her.

"Not much for conversation, are you?" A smile played on her lips. She fixed her quicksilver eyes on him, a challenge in their depths. But what game was she truly playing?

"I'm waiting," Han said.

"For?"

"An explanation."

She scoffed. "I'm a reporter. You're an investigator. An actor at this theater was murdered. Use your imagination."

"None required. Especially after my interview with one of the clerks at *The Pall Mall Gazette*. Where no one seems to have heard of you."

Miss Marks smirked, undaunted. "I contribute to the society pages as Mr. Devon Standish, scold and social assassin. Was the clerk a man? No mystery there."

Still not a quaver or flinch of remorse. Han thought her remarkable.

"What position do you hold in the demimonde, I wonder, that avails you of Strand gossip?" he asked.

"A great many I'm certain you've never attempted. Though if you care to, disabuse me of the notion."

Han would have liked to rebuke her, but every second wasted put someone else at risk. He reminded himself her lies had consequences to those he loved.

"Did you witness the crime?" he asked, thinking better of accusing her.

"From across the city? Hardly."

Han scoffed. "Do *me* the favor of not insulting my abilities, and I will not discredit yours."

This earned him a smile. "Touché."

"Did Terriss keep you, or were you simply there for the night?"

Miss Marks glared at him. "My services are not paid by the hour."

"Were you in the room when it happened?"

Finally, a crack in her armor. She sagged into the corner, her delicate fingers working a loose piece of mortar between two bricks.

"No. I'd run out of matches. I was a floor above, fetching another box from a friend, when I heard dear Randy's roar. By the time I ran down, he was chasing after whoever stuck him. I glimpsed him from above on the lower stairs. But I couldn't see..." She plucked out the piece of mortar, dashed it on the cobblestones. "I wasn't dressed to go out, so I went back to the flat, to the window. Didn't notice the blood till I saw him in the courtyard."

"You saw him collapse?"

"Yes."

"And didn't go to him?"

She lifted her stare to meet his, hard but heartfelt. "No."

"Too many eyes?"

She nodded. "The pub was full, spilling out into the street. We only ever met in the flat."

"It might have spared you being a suspect."

Miss Marks shrugged. "If I cannot respect a man's wishes in his final moments..." She straightened, and the stubborn jut of her jaw and the enigmatic glint in her eyes returned. "Make your judgments. I know what I am. And I *do* work for *The Pall Mall Gazette*."

Han considered her for a long moment, then took a step back, and another. A calculated risk, but one he felt confident in making. If she fled, he would only find her again, nosing her way into The Gaiety through other means. The theater contained something she could not do without, be it a story, an item, or something of indiscernible value. Regardless, Han was coming around to the opinion that it might be best to keep her close, as one did with dangerous enemies.

"I prefer observations to judgments," Han remarked, "as I'm in no position to rule over anyone."

To his astonishment, she crossed the short space between them, hopping down the two steps of the performer's entrance. For the first time in their brief acquaintance, they stood on an equal level—or, rather, Han looked down upon her, the crown of her head hovering just below the line of his shoulders. Yet when she gazed up at him with indomitable eyes, she grew ten feet.

"I wouldn't say that, precisely."

Han ignored the insinuation in her tone. "Did you and Terriss ever meet at The Gaiety?"

"Has Mr. Bash formally taken on the case?"

"I can make no comment."

"Then likewise."

"Is that what you're after? Terriss's continued support, postmortem?"

"Is that an observation or a judgment?"

The corner of his lips twitched; he firmed his mouth. "You could have fled the flat once Terriss collapsed, but you chose to remain. Or was it return? And now here I find you again. You must see how it looks."

She raked her eyes down the length of his frame, making no secret of her opinion of what she saw. Miss Marks wouldn't be the first suspect, or the last, to try to seduce her way out of an interview. Han might have been flattered, if he thought her attentions motivated by something other than desperation. He, too, could call out the dogs.

"One drink, five questions each," she declared. "Those are my terms."

"Inside The Gaiety, I presume?"

"No. I'll grant you that concession."

"Your generosity overflows."

Miss Marks threw back her head and barked a laugh. "Oh, I do like a dry wit. Preferably with some aged cheese." She strolled a short distance down Wellington Street, then turned back to beckon him. "Shall we?"

Han bristled, unconvinced. "Why should I share information with someone I've twice caught sneaking into crime scenes?"

"Why should I divulge anything to someone investigating me as a suspect?"

"Your intentions *are* suspect."

"Then allow me to uncomplicate them for you."

She offered him her arm. Though her smile held a tinge of mockery, Han could not refuse such a prime opportunity. He took a cautious step forward, keeping a respectable distance.

"How do I know you're not luring me away to do me some mischief?" he asked.

"You don't. Spoils the fun."

Chapter 6

$\mathcal{I}$f Hiero had had hackles, they would have raised at the sight of the kitten pawing at *his* Kip. Beside him, Tumnus snapped, Madame de Casterac emoted, and the Vicomte blustered while Callie scrambled to herd them all into a more private space. But Hiero could not take his eyes off the pretty creature who batted playfully at Kip's shoulder as they conversed. Who presumed to have permission to touch Hiero's beloved. He abandoned those speaking at him without a word of warning and marched to the far side of the stage, where he leapt down into the auditory—a practiced trick from his time playing Mercutio in *A Piss-Up in Verona: Two Star-Crossed Lovers Lose Their Livers.*

Hiero took some relief in noting he bore only a passing resemblance to this semiadorable miniature, as if someone had plucked all of Hiero's iridescent plumage and left only a skinny, scrawny, featherless peacock. They shared the same dark hair and eyes, but his was cropped in the severest style of the day, and he lacked Hiero's signature twinkle. Dressed in maudlin tones more befitting a graveyard attendant, the only thing Hiero could credit was the cut of his suit. The fit suggested the man knew an excellent tailor. A pity he appeared to be colorblind.

Hiero emphasized every aspect of his magnificence as he approached.

"DI Stoker," he interrupted. "A word?"

"Ah, Hiero." Kip beamed such a smile at him that Hiero struggled to recall if he'd ever seen him so elated. Alas, he had not. "Please, let me introduce Monsieur Marius Lamarque, the costumier of the French company and a very old, very dear friend. Our mothers were seamstresses with the Opéra de Paris. Only Marius had the talent to follow in their footsteps."

"I dare say you've done well enough for yourself, Monsieur l'Inspecteur," Marius remarked. "Though hardly a surprise. Timée used to insist we finish all our schoolwork before we could play." Hiero felt the shock of the pet name like a slap to the face. "He's always done things à la lettre."

Kip snickered like the schoolboy he'd been. "I seem to recall doing our schoolwork in costume most days."

Marius shrugged. "It was the only way I could learn, dressed as a pirate. And you as a... What was it? Ah, oui, a gendarme. Plus ça change..."

They fell into paroxysms of laughter. Hiero fought a pout.

"What an incredible coincidence," he hissed. Hiero marveled that Kip did not feel the same at the sudden appearance of this figure from his past. But then Hiero had learned the hard way not to believe in coincidences. He attempted to convey as much in the grin he plastered on his face, but Kip was too aswoon over this impromptu reunion. And Hiero was unable to put so much as a finger on him to remind Kip of—and alert Lamarque to—their connection. But he could remind him of their purpose here. "And have you, Monsieur Lamarque, been visited by the phantom?"

"In a manner of speaking," he replied. "If you would be so good as to come down to my studio, I can show you."

Before they could agree, the shrill cry of a prima donna belted out from center stage. They all turned to see Madame de Casterac dressing down Tumnus and the Vicomte.

"The entire evening, spent in this death trap? Ça, non!" She stamped her foot. "Only an imbecile would keep all these people here, on a night we are supposed to be dark, to submit to interviews that would tell us what? We have a ghost? A murderer? C'est évident!" To Hiero's horror, she threw out her arms beseechingly toward him. "Monsieur Bash, je vous en prie. Bring some order to this madness."

All eyes shot to him, expectant. The way it should be.

Performing a bow, he flattered, "Madame, in this and in all things, I am your servant. If you repair to your dressing room, Mr. Stoker and I will attend you presently. My associates will conduct the rest of the interviews to speed the process along."

Madame de Casterac huffed. "That is but half a solution, and a poor one at that. Separating and isolating us in the place we're most likely to come to harm."

"No one has been killed in this theater!" Tumnus protested.

"Polly ain't dancing no more," one of the witnesses interjected. "Close enough, innit?"

"The ghost could be here now," another said.

"Watching us quarrel, waiting to strike!" a third warned.

Hiero silenced their clamor by clearing his throat.

"Ladies and gentlemen, I remind you that it is vital we learn as much as we can from you if we're to have any hope of finding this fiend. You have my solemn vow that no one who remains to be interviewed will be in danger. By the ghost's own timetable, we have until the stroke—"

"'Timetable'?" Tumnus demanded. "What do you mean?"

Kip hastened to intervene. "Mr. Bash is merely parroting a theory I suggested, that there has been one incident a day, and thus they may continue in that pattern. But it's far too early to know for sure, and you are right to insist on certain precautions."

"If I may," Croÿ-Roeulx said, "I propose the interviews be conducted in the restaurant, which I'm told prepared a full service before the decision to close. Messieurs Bash et Stoker can use the private room, and the rest will wait together. Since all of you have been so kind as to give your time, it is my pleasure to invite you to dinner."

"A generous solution, Monsieur le Vicomte." Recovered, Hiero nodded in Croÿ-Roeulx's direction. "Madame, does this quiet your concerns?"

Stone-faced, she replied, "For the moment."

"Then allow us to confer, and we will rendezvous with you there."

Madame de Casterac led a procession of witnesses off the stage and up the center aisle, a queen in all but name. Hiero might have found her antics more amusing had he not understood the need for them. Tumnus and even the Vicomte acted to protect their reputations, their company, and its name actors, in that order. If this also hung an umbrella over the stagehands and craftspeople, all the better, but they would just as soon leave them out in the rain. Hiero could not help but admire how Madame de Casterac used what little power she had to shelter all.

He turned back to find the obsequious Lamarque in close conference with his Kip. Being of equal height, their heads bent together in kiss-close proximity. Hiero fought the urge to charge between them, had enough presence of mind to know playing the bull never won you anything but a spear in the gut. But that did not keep him from moving closer, nor letting his height intimidate. After a glance in Hiero's direction, Lamarque gasped and slipped away, but not without a goodbye clench of Kip's arm. Hiero caught Kip's flinch, fighting the instinct to return the gesture.

Privately he fumed.

"We should split up," Kip suggested.

Hiero did a double take. "Under no circumstances."

This earned him a raised eyebrow. "We've a good deal of ground to cover before midnight, and Madame de Casterac is not wrong. With what might yet come, the company deserves a night's respite. We cannot proceed if they refuse to return tomorrow."

"Very well." Hiero bristled. "You keep the appointment with

our prima donna, and I will venture down to Mr. Lamarque's lair."

Kip didn't feign his look of surprise. "You'd begrudge me a few private moments with an old friend?"

"Perhaps I'd be more fair-minded if they weren't so private."

Kip laughed. "You're jealous!"

"With cause." Hiero jutted his chin in Lamarque's direction. "He's measuring your inseam with his eyes."

"He's waiting for me."

"With his tongue out. It's most unbecoming."

Kip's shy smile did nothing to assuage his fears. "You're terrible." The affection in his tone, however, did mollify Hiero some. "I believe I made you a promise earlier. Am I not a man of my word?"

Hiero exhaled a blustery breath. "I confess you are."

"Then think on that." Kip began to retreat. "While you interview Madame de Casterac."

He'd rejoined the odious Mr. Lamarque before Hiero could object. He sighed loud enough for Kip to hear, and ignore, and spun around to find Callie snickering into her hand.

Thus, Hiero found himself tapping on the door to one of the restaurant's private rooms, begging permission where once he'd held the keys. Located on the second floor above the Strand-side entrance, what was once The Bard and Bullwhip bar, where his Apollo and their bosom friend Odile had flirted and feted their way through every nubile aspiring actor and well-rode mary-ann on the strip, was now a temple of haute cuisine to rival the restaurant at The Savoy. One of Tumnus's ill-conceived innovations, an attempt to draw a higher class of theatergoer. Unlike the crowds at the Lyric or the Theater Royal, the lords and ladies who snuck into The Gaiety did so incognito or escorted by their paramours. They searched for escape from the strictures of social morality, a hit of bawd, a tingle of excitement, a soupçon of wildness. Here they looked for a bit of grit under their nails.

But the extraordinary smells emanating from the kitchen did hint at other forms of seduction...

Hiero shushed his gurgling stomach before the door swung open. A young woman in a uniform a nun would think too severe curtsied and waved him in. Madame de Casterac held court at the head of a long, empty table, sipping from a bowl of consommé in which floated three fat croutons. *The actresses' diet,* Hiero thought to himself, relieved he wouldn't be tempted to steal her dinner. Her maid must have been in the process of unpinning her hair, because one side rippled down her back and over her shoulders in thick, dark-red coils—a blood rain. She didn't glance up at his entrance but continued to scrawl notes in the margins of a heavily annotated script.

Hiero cleared his throat. No acknowledgement. The maid snuck back behind her and resumed her work.

"Good evening, madame," Hiero said in French to put her at ease.

"Ask your questions," she ordered with supreme disinterest.

Had all of her earlier ire been playing to the crowd? Or was this some sort of test? Hiero felt the weight of his inexperience and wished Kip had accompanied him. Then he considered how he would have cared to be addressed, once upon a time when he commanded the stage.

"Forgive me," he sighed. "But I cannot miss the chance to mention how glorious you were as Célimène in Moliere's *The Misanthrope*. The way you flirted and taunted your four suitors, your comic touch light but your dramatic fire burning deep beneath. Ah, it was sublime!"

Madame de Casterac set down her pen but did not raise her head. "You've attended one of my performances?"

"Not just one," Hiero insisted. "Seven or eight the year I was in Paris. Your Bérénice in Racine's masterpiece broke my heart. And your Cornelia in *The Death of Pompey...*" Hiero pressed a hand to his chest, not unlike Madame de Casterac's aggressively mediocre performance, which he had in fact seen. "Better than Bernhardt."

He did not miss how her maid gasped at that compliment, or the little twist to her mistress's lips. She approved.

"I did not know I was in the presence of such a connoisseur."

"It is my honor to be in *your* presence, madame." Hiero took the seat she offered at her side. "And to quiet any concerns you might have about our ability to solve this case."

She let out a soft harrumph. "Elodie, please fetch Monsieur Bash a menu." Then, to him, "I trust even detectives take time to eat?"

"Only when in such rare company." Hiero waited for the maid to scurry off, sneaking envious glances at Madame de Casterac's bottle of wine.

Which drew her notice, as intended. "From the Vicomte's cellar. The food in this restaurant is tolerable, but they lack even the most commonplace vintages. Fortunately, Rainier brought several casks along with him."

"Does he keep them on site?"

"No, at our apartments," she replied, answering all the questions he couldn't ask on the subject. "He knows me well."

"And lives to please, I imagine."

"Quite so." She chuckled. "A temporary investment while we are abroad, but such is the nature of our work. We are nomads, you see."

"Searching for a new home? I understand Monsieur Offenbach is responsible for your exile."

Madame de Casterac huffed. "Too much has been made of the rivalry between Rainer and that upstart. Theater is the business of the new. Change is in its blood."

"And yet you've cast your lot with Monsieur le Vicomte."

She pulled one of her cascading coils straight, then curled it around a finger. "Ah, but with his offer came the potential for change. For fifteen years, I have been told what to play and how to play it. Monsieur Offenbach wanted more of the same: another Gertrude, another Fantine. But the chance to be the director, to play

Don Juan... There's a reason to endure this godforsaken country."

Hiero noted a flaw in her pattern. "But I thought Terriss had been set for Don Juan."

Madame de Casterac scoffed. "Oui, hélas. That was the compromise forced by Mr. Tumnus. And still, with Monsieur Terriss gone, he will not bend. But at least I still have Abelard and Heloise all to myself."

"It amazes me that such a strict man chose to run a theater."

"One of the great mysteries of life." She grunted. "Perhaps one of your skills can shed some light."

"It would require far more than mere skill to explain Mr. Tumnus."

They shared a laugh, a look. Hiero held her gaze longer than intended, thinking not of earning her trust, but of the company his Kip kept. Two could play at that game.

She aimed a challenging glint, sharp as a saber, straight at him. Not one to duel with anyone other than her normal partner, then. Which shred any theory that she and Terriss might have been parrying in private. Though Hiero did wonder if the Vicomte was as fiercely protective of his virtue.

"Bon à part ça, as pleasant as it has been to gossip with you, I fear I must do my duty and ask about our phantom."

"The bête, you mean, who has come for our throats?" Madame de Casterac scoffed. "Bring him to me when you catch him, so I may wring his neck."

"Have you come to some harm at his hands?"

"Moi, non. But he attempts to ruin Rainier and our company's ambitions, and for that I will not stand idle. We have already lost one home; we will not lose another, however temporary. And there is, if I may be frank, the whiff of antiforeign sentiment to his actions."

"How so? So far both victims have been English."

"Of late, oui, but before Monsieur Terriss, the fiend terrorized our troupe. Dear Jean-Michel, who paints our backdrops, hit in the head by one of the framing beams and trapped beneath it all night. We discovered him unconscious the next morning. He will recover, but he had to return to France. The ghost preyed upon my very own Elodie while she brewed my morning café au lait, chasing her all the way down to the waterfront. If she hadn't encountered one of your gendarmes patrolling the Thames, she might have been the first victim. And then there is the campaign he has waged against Mademoiselle Vauquelin, pretending to be her secret admirer, only for his gifts and billets doux to turn ugly, dangerous."

That pricked up Hiero's ears. "Dangerous? How do you mean? And which of the Vauquelin sisters was targeted?"

"Seraphine, bien sûr," she chuckled. "Damiane has a greater command of her instrument, but there is no doubt Seraphine is the beauty between them."

"Of course." Hiero played along. "How foolish of me."

"An easy mistake when one is, si je ne m'abuse, of your persuasion, Monsieur Bash."

Hiero feigned outrage at being found out; Madame de Casterac pretended contrition and signaled her thoughts on his earlier attempt at flirtation. Their conversation continued, both safe in the knowledge that nothing particularly noteworthy had been revealed about the other. Such were the ways of theater folk.

"But surely Seraphine has had her share of zealous admirers. Are you certain this is the work of the ghost?"

Madame de Casterac shrugged. "You'll have the full story from her, of course, but as I understand it, he serenaded her one night, from Box 5, beside the stage."

Hiero's tongue went numb, strangling his ability to speak. Apollo's box. Also favored by his Kip. He no longer believed in coincidence.

"An exceptional tenor, or so she said. Perhaps you should test the men in the company. From what I understand, she was rather flattered. This was before she found cockroaches in her chocolates and wolfsbane in her bouquet."

Struggling to form a coherent thought, Hiero rasped, "And you? When did you see him?"

That challenging, imperious expression returned.

"I haven't," Madame de Casterac almost laughed. "Mes excuses, Monsieur Bash, but it is my duty to take the measure of any wolf with his eye on the lambs in my company. But I see you are a hunter of a different breed. Let us pray that you, too, possess l'instinct de mort."

Tim all but floated down to the costume vault, buoyed by this chance reunion with Marius and, if he were honest, the jealousy it sparked in Hiero. In his darker moments, Tim had occasion to wonder why someone as devastatingly handsome as Hiero had set his cap on him. Tim felt confident in his strengths, his intelligence among them. That intelligence made him well aware that he was not as swoon worthy as, say, Randolph Terriss, or even Apollonius Pankhurst. It whispered in his ear, on those lonely nights of Hiero's dinner party absences, that the reason he had not yet said a certain four-letter word in reference to their relationship was because of Tim's aesthetic limitations. Hiero, like Keats, was a devotee of beauty before truth.

So the fact that Marius appeared to be an object of temptation for Tim, at least to Hiero's mind, was… well, delicious. As was the prospect of proving to Hiero just how wrong he was. Repeatedly. Rigorously. Indeed, Tim hoped he and Marius could renew their acquaintance so that every so often he could play the sword that stirred the waters. And, of course, to know him again as a friend.

He was thirteen years old when he last clapped eyes on Marius. Thirteen more years had passed since Tim's family moved back to

London from their three-year residence in Paris. Less than a year later, Tim's parents would be gone and his life forever changed. His time in the City of Light had been golden, a glut of art and excitement and adventure, with Marius as his constant companion.

Having worked his way to his employer's right hand, Tim's father had been able to afford to hire him a tutor. Tim spent his mornings learning the classics and exploring the city with his teacher, Monsieur Renard. Afternoons, he and Marius made mischief around the opera house while their mothers mended and sewed the elaborate costumes. In the evenings, the family would come together to enjoy the bustle and fizzle of Paris by night. Though the memory of their togetherness and contentment pinched his heart—what he wouldn't give for a single clench of his parents' warmth—Tim welcomed the feeling.

He once thought he'd never know such happiness again. But now, with his Hiero, he'd found something better than even that gilded age. All of which proved a winning distraction to a mind that should be tracking down a murderer.

"A wonderful coincidence, isn't it, that we should be reunited in this way," Marius commented in French as they crossed into the corridors under the stage. "In a theater, I mean."

"I cannot think where else we might have been reunited," Tim said. "But yes."

"It almost..." Marius shook his head. "I won't say I expected it, but when Monsieur le Vicomte invited me to be part of his company, I did think of you. I always wondered if you'd taken to the stage. You had such a passion for it."

"From a distance, in the auditory. I'm afraid I've little talent for dissimulation."

"Hence the profession that did call you home." Marius winked. "Also not a surprise." They shared a knowing laugh. "Ah, here we are."

As Marius worked on the heavy, intricate lock to the costume vault—another of Tumnus's innovations, and a smart one at that, given the workmanship that went into each piece—Tim stole a moment to note the changes in his friend. Like Tim, he had not gained much in terms of height or breadth, although his early teenage paunch had slimmed into a withy frame. His hands, delicate but callused, bore the pinpricks and scars of his trade. His thickly lashed eyes and full mouth took on a bedchamber quality experience had taught him to wield to his advantage.

Marius had been a boy of attitudes and high emotion. Life seemed to have tempered his intensity but not his expressiveness, as evidenced by the flourish with which he slid open the lock and pointed Tim inside.

"Shall we to business, or is there time for a chat?" Marius asked after flicking on the lights.

"Duty calls, alas." Tim tore himself away from the ever-fascinating sight of rows upon rows of costumes. "But I'll stand you a supper once this mad affair is done."

Marius smiled as if he'd swallowed the world. "I'll hold you to it."

Surely Tim didn't imagine Marius held his gaze a touch too long? They'd been too young, too awkward, too unknowing for anything to blossom between them before. Rather, Tim's thoughts hadn't veered in that direction for anyone his own age at the time. He'd harbored secret crushes on actors, at the opera and in other companies on the Boulevard du Crime, but nothing that might require him to act on his feelings until years later. Even as he acknowledged that Marius must do well for himself, Tim—perhaps uncharitably—considered how to rebuff any advances he might make. Because he had his Hiero, and no one else compared.

"Is this where you encountered our intruder?" Tim asked, refocusing on the investigation.

"After a fashion."

"So you said earlier."

"And then, as now, I was correct."

Marius gestured Tim over to a wide rectangular table, across which fanned fabric swatches in different color palettes, various costume sketches, and history books opened to illustrations. One glance gave Tim the feel and texture of the play—he couldn't wait to see these images and creations brought to life by the actors. Marius retrieved a more sober-looking tome from the bottom of a pile. Carefully setting it down where it would do the least damage, his workspace a marvel of organized clutter, he pulled on the bookmark ribbon and flipped to the relevant page.

A ledger. At last, something within Tim's realm of expertise. He scanned the contents.

"The costume inventory?"

"Précisément. As a former flâneur on the Boulevard du Crime and someone who has trafficked in the demimonde, you'll understand when I say this is not the first time the gendarmes have come searching for evidence in my studio."

Tim chuckled. "As a current gendarme, I can attest we like nothing better than solid proof."

"Eh bien, feast your eyes." He tapped a much-abused finger on a listing he had marked with an asterisk. "I have learned from hard experience to take inventory when I start at a new theater. Managers..." Marius sighed. "Some are quite severe and quick to accuse. And the person who gets accused is the person in charge when a theft or whathaveyou gets discovered, even if they have only been at that theater one or two months."

"Ridiculous," Tim agreed. "There must be twenty years' worth of costumes here."

Marius clicked his tongue. "Twelve, to be exact, from the remodel in 1862. Vous, les policiers, vous aimez les chiffres, non? I have some numbers for you. We arrived eight weeks ago. So it has been seven since I completed the inventory. And five since this red skull mask, this velvet cloak, and this black soldier's uniform disappeared from the vault. Three days later, the first incident."

Tim noted the name and date of the production the costume was used in: the last staging of *Don Juan* in 1868. One Tim remembered well, as it starred Horace Beastly in the role of the famed doomed soul. In the grand finale, a phalanx of red-skulled solider demons dragged him down to hell at Satan's behest. Tim felt sick at the idea of history repeating itself, fiction made real by their fiend's dark design.

Tim struggled to clear his constricting throat. "Someone has seen the ghost in this costume?"

"Those who have caught more than a glimpse, oui."

"And you're certain it was stolen from the vault and not recreated?"

"Absolument." Marius motioned toward the fitting area, where costumes lined the walls. "Monsieur Tumnus requested a certain continuity with an older production, so I pulled out everything in good condition from 1868 to see what could be used now, even just as inspiration. When I left that night, the skull costume was there, on the dressing doll for alterations. The next morning, it was gone."

"Hence the new lock?"

"Oui. The one before it... Well, let me say it would not have held us back when we were young and mischievous."

Tim nodded, annoyed at the simplicity of the crime, at how penny-pinching had opened the door to murder, at how the theft endangered Marius's position in the company. He'd no doubt the Vicomte, also the one to hire Hiero, had purchased that new lock. But was their participation in this case a matter of right place, right time, or had it been engineered as deftly as the theft of the skull costume? A well-placed newspaper headline, a murmured comment at the opportune moment... Someone at The Gaiety could easily have convinced the Vicomte to engage the renowned detective Hieronymus Bash without uttering a word in his favor.

Tim cursed under his breath. Their busy little spider had been spinning its web for months, and he had no way of knowing how close Hiero was to being snared.

Marius shifted into view, evaporating Tim's fog of anxiety.

"Lost to your deductions already?" he chuckled. "And I haven't even had the chance to enquire after your parents."

The old pain struck quick and deep, such that Tim couldn't keep himself from grimacing. Marius gasped, but Tim silenced him with an upraised hand. He waited for the lance of grief to scab over, for the ache in his chest to recede. "They are no longer with me."

"Oh, mais non! Ce n'est pas possible!" Marius exclaimed. "Your maman... You know how I adored her. And your papa, always with the sweets in his pockets. Un trésor."

"They loved you too. Even spoke about inviting you over for a holiday before..." Tim inhaled deeply, wishing he'd not forced Hiero away, that he was here now to embrace him. "Before they died."

"Oh, forgive me, forgive me. The memory is fresh."

"No," Tim rallied, comforted by Marius even if he was a poor substitute. Wanting to tell him everything, even if it hurt to speak the words. "It was the year after we returned. A break-in at the warehouse. We were bringing Father his supper while he waited for the last ship of the day to dock. I was exploring. Three new sarcophagi from Egypt. I'd been begging Mother to stop in, so we did that night. The wrong night."

When he looked up, Marius had turned the sallow gray of a London sky. "They were... murdered?"

With all his heart, in that moment, Tim wished he could deny it.

Chapter 7

*H*an canted the brim of his hat forward against the unfamiliar glare of the sun. That rarest of occurrences in smoggy, sooty London, a clear day, lured out the city's pallid populace in droves. They clogged the sidewalks and blocked the steps of any establishment with libations that could be enjoyed out of doors. As he followed Miss Marks down to the Victoria Embankment gardens in search of a private spot where they might converse unobserved, Han attempted to keep a proper distance between them but repeatedly lost her in the crowd. By design, he thought, until she stopped to wait for him by the entrance to the garden path.

He surveyed the gardens after rejoining her. Flooded with sun-worshippers unaffected by the stench of the Thames, there wasn't a quiet spot to be had. While most people raised their heavy-lidded faces to the sky, more than a few turned their heads in Han and Miss Marks's direction as they descended the path. Han met each of their disapproving stares with one of his own, resentment stirring within him. The reminder that he would never be entirely welcome in his adopted country, or permitted his free choice of companion in such a racialist society, cast a dark cloud over his afternoon.

He nodded toward the kiosk selling ices, but she steered him farther on to the one selling beer. The jovial vendor appeared happy to serve anyone with money to spend, which tempered Han's annoyance. He carried both their pints as they strolled since Miss

Marks was burdened with her parasol. But this proved to be a poor strategy, giving her a reason to brush hands with him every time she reached to take a sip.

Han forced himself to relax as they walked, unspeaking, along the pebbled paths. The blunt heat of the sun, the cries of the circling gulls, and the lap of the waves against the sea wall transported him back to his youth, to the collection of tanka boats in Macau's Outer Harbor that had been his entire world. To a time when he thought of the ocean, with its serene and tempestuous moods, as an older brother. How magnificent and imposing the trade ships that docked in the distance were to his child's mind.

But Han well recalled the same judgmental looks, from foreigners and city dwellers alike, whenever he accompanied his uncle to the Inner Harbor market to sell the day's catch. The People on the Water, his people, being the lowest caste in Macanese society, were forced to cater to European sailors' and Portuguese colonizers' every whim. Then, as now, Han felt divided between curiosity about the Portuguese half of his heritage and loyalty to his Chinese family, between the wanderlust that made him long for a taste of the wider world and the comforts of their tight-knit community. He felt similarly about his life in London, though moments like this tipped the scales toward homesickness.

They found a bench by the riverside rail, away from the crowd. Han set their pints between them. Miss Marks people watched, forced to face the gardens by the volume of her dress while Han looked out over the river, remembering.

"Would you care to begin, or shall I?" Miss Marks asked.

After a final scan of the Thames, Han righted himself. He could not afford to be distracted, though everything about their surroundings worked against him. Including Miss Marks herself, an orchid in a patch of daisies. "You truly mean to hold to five questions apiece?"

"Do you often cheat on deals made in good faith?"

Han snorted. "If the situation warrants."

"You realize that's an invitation for me to be... less than truthful."

"I expect neither complete truth nor outright falsehoods from anyone we investigate. Everyone has an agenda. An honest testimony is complicated by perspective; a lie is improved by seeding in small truths. Surely you've encountered this issue whilst pursuing your various trades?"

"I have, though I've never heard it so well said." A spark of inspiration lit her eyes. "Which brings me to my first question, if I may begin." Han bowed his head in agreement. "I hope I cause no offense when I ask... How did you come to these shores?"

Taken aback, Han briefly entertained the notion she could read minds. But he recovered himself swiftly. "How do you know I'm not a native? The bastard son of an adventuring nobleman permitted to work as a servant of his house?"

She barked a laugh. "Shall I play detective for a spell? Good. You enjoy a degree of freedom unheard of among the servant class. You did not inform Mr. Bash of your departure before we set off, and I expect he's not waiting on you now."

"Perhaps he gives his investigators a long leash."

"Perhaps I'm queen of the fairies."

No, Han wanted to say, *of the dragons.* But he kept up his defenses.

"I fear you will be disappointed. Mine is a common tale. I arrived on a trade ship, enslaved to its captain. Once here, I saw my chance at escape and seized it. I had no funds to speak of, let alone the price of a return, and was not eager to spend another year on a boat with such men as abducted me, so I remained. After further hardship, I apprenticed with a magician. He performed exotic tricks. I taught him the customs of my people; he taught me the Queen's."

She scrutinized him. "And which half of that is the truth?"

"Do you mean to waste all your questions on my honesty?"

Miss Marks chuckled. "Touché. Or should I say, en garde?"

"How did you... cultivate an air of refinement, as the toffs say?"

Her face fell. She inhaled deeply, turned her attention back to the lounging throngs. "A matter of survival. It's quite easy to learn a new skill when it spares you the belt. Or worse."

Surprised by her candor, Han just saved himself from reaching out to comfort her. Not that the clasp of his hand could do much to lessen the sting of such a memory. "I think, perhaps, we had the same teacher."

She arched a brow. "Similar methods, were they? It's a common tale, where people are kept."

"But you escaped."

"That particular situation, yes." Miss Marks stared at some fixed point in the distance, appeared to be fighting a frown. "But there's no real escape for us, is there? Only more luxurious cages." She turned her attention back to him. "Perhaps I presume too much in saying so."

"Not at all. If anything, it clarifies why you've been so... persistent."

A dry laugh. "Ah. And persistence is not a quality to be prized in a woman of my station."

"To some, but not to me." Han took a generous sip of his ale, liquid courage if ever there was. "My mother fought her whole life to defy society's conventions. To wear her choices, her station, even her missteps, with pride. I learned at her table."

"Then she's to be commended." The warmth of her smile appeared almost genuine. "Are you in correspondence with her? Does she know of your achievements?"

The lance of pain at the thought of his mother not knowing what became of him never dulled. Never would.

"My people are sea-dwellers, fishermen and ferriers in the port of Macau," he explained. "Any correspondence must be sent through our elder."

"Hardly the way to express private thoughts and fears."

Han nodded. "I did send word through a trusted friend once I was more established. But by then she'd..." He'd kept the letter, even if rereading meant reliving the sorrow of the day he received it. Hearing his grandfather's voice in those bleak lines proved too precious to part with. "She was gone."

Han gazed out over the river, searching for the connection he'd felt earlier. But like most mirages, it had dissipated with a change in the wind. Now he saw only the bilious water, the rickety barges, the refuse, smelled only the soot of factory chimneys on the far side. He turned back to meet Miss Marks's gray eyes, soft with understanding. And, if he was not mistaken, a shadow of her own.

"Then you are indeed far from home."

Han repressed the urge to reveal more to this woman, who seemed to be a kindred soul. Seemed to, he underlined for himself, and wondered why the editor at *The Pall Mall Gazette* kept her at arm's length when she clearly had a talent for ferreting out the intimate details of a person's life. "Not anymore."

She brightened at this, perhaps equally relieved at the change in mood.

"With your Mr. Bash, you mean? Do tell. He's rather a blank line on the local rumormongers' ledgers. A celebrated raconteur at the most entertaining parties, but little else is known about him. I admit I find him almost as fascinating as the ghost you hunt."

Han knew a trap when he saw one and tread carefully. "To know of his cases is to know the man. He enjoys the thrill of the chase and, afterward, boasting to his friends. The killers and thieves he pursues are the persons of interest."

She smirked. "A shrewd evasion. He must pay you well."

"I am not in his employ." Only after observing the reaction this provoked did he rue his haste—and his honesty. "I confess I've lost track of the score. How many questions has it been?"

"Not nearly enough, by my tally. But then you keep dropping savory morsels, and I'm famished." She wiped a bit of froth off her bottom lip with a lazy thumb. "Have been for weeks. Scraps of news from Randy about the ghost and the usual soggy crumpet actor complaints. I need some meat on the bone, something so deliciously piggy my editors won't be able to resist." Han sensed her eyes on him, searching for an in. "What do you say?"

"About?"

"Mr. Bash. He's been celebrated until now because the public learns of his triumphs after the fact. But they're already clamoring for the name of Randy's killer. You won't be able to guide their interest for long, especially if this ghost is involved and there are more incidents. Mr. Bash could use someone on his side in the press, revealing certain details to appease the mob and writing him as the hero. If you'll pardon the pun."

Han opened his mouth to scoff but thought better. She'd voiced some of his own fears about what might transpire if Hiero became too popular. That sort of renown always drew the wrong kind of attention as well as the right. And they already walked the tightrope of whether someone might connect the Bash persona to his Beastly identity. Alas, that someone might very well be Miss Marks, if he accepted her proposal. In addition to her lack of experience and his own suspicions about her intentions. . .

He sighed, wary of discouraging her. She clicked her tongue. His gaze shot to her face like a greyhound at the pistol's crack. Her shining, defiant face.

"Too much of a risk. I understand." Miss Marks grinned in defeat even as Han worked up the words to refuse her. "I willed myself into being on the backs of the men who kept me. Perhaps it is to Mr. Bash's credit that he won't be my stepping stone."

"I've no doubt you'll climb to greater heights one day."

The wind picked up. A gust, ripe with the rot stench off the Thames, blew through them. Han chugged half his pint; Miss Marks pressed a handkerchief over her nose, their leisure spoiled.

"Of course, I hardly require your permission to write about the goings on at The Gaiety."

Han tensed. He knew it might come to this, and yet he'd hoped she wouldn't be so predictable in her ambitions. Not that there was anything commonplace about her.

"And Randy isn't around anymore to care about his reputation," she continued, "not that he ever much did. What was it you said before? 'An honest testimony is complicated by perspective'? So too are honest intentions, I imagine."

"And by circumstance, yes." Han cleared his throat. "Am I permitted a final question?"

"Possibly. Probably. I've also no head for numbers. Do go ahead."

"What, in your estimation, made you what you are?"

Han didn't think he mistook the little gasp of breath she inhaled. After a brief, pregnant silence, she again turned toward the strolling couples and sunbathing workers decorating the gardens before them.

"Let me offer you a parable," Miss Marks replied.

"Unexpected."

"I certainly hope so." She traced a finger around the rim of her pint as she spoke. "There once was a girl in a box. From the first, the box was too small for the girl, and as she grew, it remained so. But she couldn't stop growing, as girls do, though the box was made of strong stuff—the strongest material in the world. It had been made to keep her enclosed no matter what. Still, she grew and grew and grew, wriggling and worming around, desperate to fill every nook and corner, every speck of space she could. Nothing could stop her, no matter the pain. The bigger she got, the harder the box became until it wrung the very breath from her lungs. Undaunted, she battered at its sides and kicked at its seams, believing that one day, if she worked hard enough, it would finally break.

"But it held fast until she gasped her last breath and gave in to despair. For she understood then that the box had not been made to contain her. It was always meant to crush her."

Han stared at her, willing himself to hold strong to his convictions. But in the rattle of the boats and the skip of the waves, he heard the echo of his mother's voice.

"I make no promises. But I will speak with Mr. Bash."

He felt her hand ghost over his, only to be drawn away.

"Thank you."

A foolish impulse, all but fleeing the restaurant once his interview with Madame de Casterac ended, but Hiero had never been one for self-control. Not when the damnable fiend who stalked his colleagues and killed his friend left his mark on the place where both of Hiero's loves had worshipped him: Box 5. So he retreated there to… He didn't even know what. Search for evidence? Would a stray hair or a weeks-old daub of spit somehow reveal to him who haunted The Gaiety? And how many others had frequented the box since, with it no longer being under permanent reservation? It still offered the closest and best view of the stage, even better than its mirror on the opposite side.

These thoughts, and darker ones, flooded his mind as he rushed down the corridor behind the private balcony boxes and into the royal foyer that led to Boxes 5 and 6. Not that any royal had set foot in The Gaiety since its redesign, but hope sprang eternal. He zipped through the foyer but stopped cold in front of the door to Box 5, giving it as close of an examination as he could in the low light.

Nothing noteworthy stood out. Hiero couldn't say what he'd expected. The knob shone with fresh polish; the painted wood betrayed not a mark. The bloody ghost—corporeal as the next man, Hiero had no doubt—had probably worn gloves. He grabbed the knob but turned it slowly, inching the door open.

A fancy of his, surely, the notion that the fiend would be waiting for him in Apollo's favorite seat. Or perhaps the one Kip preferred.

Odd that he never noticed Kip instinctively avoided his predecessor's throne, as if some spectral energy radiated from the upholstery. Hiero hoped it fried the ghost alive if they dared to sit where kings both literal and figurative once rested. But the box was empty—of murderers, at least.

The memories would forever remain, no matter who Tumnus allowed in. The corner where Kip had kissed the breath out of him. The wall before which Apollo, on a *very* memorable evening, had knelt for him. And then the tender moments, the hidden clasp of hands, the quick caresses, the nudge of an arm or a heel or a thigh. His romantic history had played out in this snug cabin before their killer soiled it.

Hiero collapsed into Apollo's chair, overwrought. The more they learned, the more inescapable the obvious conclusion became: his actions had somehow brought hell down upon this beloved place and those who had taken up residence in his wake. Kip could argue caution until the sun turned black. Hiero felt the target on his back like a second skin, every moment waiting for the bullet to pierce.

A faint melody echoed through the auditory. Hiero stretched over the rail, listening. The music box refrain played in and out of earshot, travelling from the orchestra pit, to the balcony stalls, to the upper boxes, then back down to the stage. It tinkled in one direction, then another, but never loud enough for him to catch the tune.

Hiero locked a foot between the seats and leaned out farther. Was he imagining the music?

A rustle from above caught him short. All of a sudden, he realized the precariousness of his position. A deft maneuver from an opponent, and he'd flip over the rail, crash into the seats below. He listened a final time for the music, still wavering just beyond his reach. Even these brief chirps of melody stirred something in him, equally elusive. Something at the far edge of his understanding. Something chilling. Something impossible.

He opened his eyes in time to see a glove fall out of the sky.

He recoiled. His foot twisted, unlatched. Hiero spun, grabbing for the glove. Watched it slip through his fingers, felt the lurch as he upset the precarious balance of his limbs. Scrabbled to right himself but caught nothing but air. Kicked the seat backs, squeezed the rail, curled his body in, anything, anything to keep from toppling headfirst into the stalls.

A soft tug at his neck gave him hope. His cape, snagged on the armrest, slowed his forward motion enough for him to push his weight back. As soon as he regained his footing, he threw himself down, hugging the carpet as he panted and shook. Stuffed a fist in his mouth when deep, cackling laughter rung out from every corner of the auditory at maximum volume.

Hiero crawled toward the side curtain, wanting to shroud himself in its velvet, a last defense against the fiend that stalked him. A hairsbreadth from safety, he choked—his cape was still caught. He huddled down behind the seats, cursing his size, waiting for the final blow.

The cackling stopped. Footsteps above. A door creaked open. Then... nothing.

Hiero waited, minute after endless minute, his pulse pounding in his ears, his shuddering breaths near suffocating. But no one came. No fiend snuck into his box. No strange, familiar music lured him out. Still he waited, in the eerie quietude, for a lifeline. Wondered when a place he'd once considered his home had turned against him.

The unmistakable sound of someone crossing the stage set his nerves alight. But the intruder strode at a normal businesslike pace. Hiero heard them stop at stage left, listen, then hop down into the stalls. A whistle and some scraping below set him at ease. He poked his head up, scoured his surroundings, then stood.

Below him, Han examined the glove. Red leather, with some sort of embellishment over the knuckles. A memory scratched at the back of Hiero's skull. He mirrored the gesture, hoping to dig it out. The movement caught Han's attention.

"Waking from a mid-case nap?" he called up.

Hiero scoffed. "I might ask you the same. Where did you skive off to?"

"Followed a person of interest."

"To the investigation?"

Han graced him with one of his enigmatic looks, which was promising indeed. "As your Hamlet might say, 'There's the rub.'"

Hiero snickered. "That's old Bill's. My Hamlet said, 'Where's the rub, and where can I get one?' If you'll recall."

The expression on Han's face was no longer so enigmatic. "Will you come down, or shall I go up?"

Hiero glanced at the door to the box, those mad cackles still echoing in his ears. If only there were another means of egress. He briefly considered forcing Han to catch him, then realized that would mean jumping over the rail. Regardless, they couldn't converse where their phantom foe might overhear them. "Meet me in the lounge."

Hiero waited for him to exit the stairs at the left of the stage before decamping from Box 5, so that they might walk the length of the corridor together. Before Han could speak, Hiero snatched the glove from his hand and gave it a closer examination. He almost flung it back over the balcony when he saw that the over-the-knuckles embroidery formed a series of *HB*s.

Don Juan, 1868. One of The Gaiety's rare melodramas, with him in the lead. Their costumier at the time liked to add personal flourishes that the audience couldn't see, as a tribute to the actors she pampered and adored.

"The glove has been thrown," Hiero murmured.

"And now, the duel," Han finished for him. "Of the minds?"

"One can only hope. I've raised swords in my time, but never any sharp ones."

Hiero couldn't help but take a quick peek down both ends of the corridor and into nearby boxes before waving Han into the lounge. He nudged him over to the farthest table, the one he knew from experience—far more pleasurable experience, it must be said—existed in a sound vacuum. He worried a finger of the glove between his thumb and index as he considered whether to tell Han about his recent interlude with the ghost. Or prelude, rather, if the fiend had his way.

For well over a decade, they'd been confidants, friends, something deeper than brothers. They crawled out of the pit of poverty and societal prejudice together, knew each other better than any potential mate ever would. This blood-thick knowledge spoke to Hiero of Han's newfound distraction, of the wheels of his mind spinning in a different direction than the team's. Making deductions, at the best of times, proved more difficult for Hiero than herding cats into a bag, but his feline instinct for survival, the nimble way he avoided shedding any of his nine lives, warned him now.

Something had turned Han's head.

"Manage a brief sojourn to the South of France, did you, during your time away?"

Han performed his usual curt, exasperated head shake. "I walked from the Embankment."

"Without a hat?"

"The sun's rather strong. Which you'd know, if you ever took any exercise."

"My preoccupations of late have tended toward the gymnastic, if you'll recall. If you'd prefer Kip and I enjoy them out of doors—I say! Is that sour whiff off your breath the scent of beer?"

Han sighed. "An interview. For the case."

"With a bottle of Gherlain's Eau de Cologne?"

"She wore Floris's Malmaison," he grunted. "Which you couldn't possibly know, because I did not touch her." He shot Hiero a look of studied blankness, but Hiero saw the ripples within. "Satisfied?"

"Not nearly. But then I never am, am I?"

Han ignored this. "The glove. You recognize it?"

Hiero's face fell. This game was not as fun as the one he'd been playing. "I couldn't fail to, which was the idea, I imagine."

"Anyone come to mind? An admirer or a rival from that time? A scorned lover?"

"You well know I'm a faithful sort."

Han raised placating hands. "Of course. Someone who tried to lure you away, perhaps, and was rejected?"

"They were all rejected, and there've been too many to account." Hiero let out a frustrated huff, slapped the glove on the table. "Six years since this production. Terriss, my first costar. The haunting of Box 5. This ghost has been a dedicated follower for my entire career."

"Or is close to someone close to you."

"A betrayal? I don't believe it. I *won't* believe it of anyone this close."

Han curled a large hand over his forearm. "We've weathered worse. We'll weather this."

Hiero nodded, craving Kip's reassurances. Unable to forget everything and everyone at stake. "So we have."

Han fell suddenly quiet. Not his usual attentive quiet, or his stealth, disappearing quiet. A loud quiet. A screaming quiet. "I've had a thought."

Hiero listened for more. Wanted more, words upon words, arguments and speculation, not just the one statement, so deep with meaning it became a bottomless well. He sometimes wished they didn't understand each other as they did, that he couldn't hear the terror in Han's silence. Understand everything that went unsaid.

"No."

"This scheme. It's elaborate."

"No."

"Vicious, manipulative, but with... a certain dramatic flair."

"Impossible." Hiero leapt to his feet, clasped his hands behind his back to keep them from shaking. "Don't ever speak of it again."

Han rose as well. "We must at least consider how it might be done."

"I don't want any part of it!" He covered his mouth, realizing he'd shouted. "It simply cannot be."

Han moved to block his retreat. "If anyone could manage it, it would be him."

Hiero retched, swallowed it back. Han pressed a heavy grip into his shoulders. To themselves, they both counted back from twenty. Their old trick.

"Take every precaution," Hiero whispered, "but see if it could be done."

"I've already begun."

Chapter 8

*T*im kept watch from the third step of the grand staircase as Tumnus ushered the last of the restaurant staff out The Gaiety's front entrance. The actors and stagehands had been sent off earlier in pairs, with a few paper-light reassurances and a rock-solid word of warning. Still, Tim couldn't help but feel the weight of his helplessness piling like stones on his chest. Impossible enough to protect the company in the labyrinthine amphitheater of The Gaiety. Out in the wide world, short of issuing every individual a personal police escort—and Tim shuddered at what Quayle would think of that plan—the killer could prey at whim.

A fiend's promise, in Tim's experience, was wasted breath. They would keep to their schedule of one incident a day until they chose not to, no matter the response. Only one thing was certain: the accidents would continue until they tired of the game and changed the rules, or they achieved their goal and found another reason to continue. Tim supposed he could pray for an act of God, but such supplications had never shown much result. Perhaps he should appeal to the Muses, as Hiero did.

The man himself descended the grand staircase like a war king triumphant, his magnificent black hair fanned out, his cape billowing, his hands reaching out in a gesture of munificence. Han clopped down behind him, the sober consigliere to Hiero's drunk-on-power monarch. Tim knew them both well enough by now to see the entrance for the performance it was. The clues abounded: lint on Hiero's trousers, his waistcoat slightly askew, the left curl of his moustache skirting his nostril. Something so traumatic had occurred that he'd neglected to right himself, and Hieronymus Bash never disregarded his toilette.

Tim moved to meet him, to look him dead in the eyes. What he saw reflected there added another layer of stones to the pile.

"That's the last of them, Bash," Tumnus announced as he threw the bolt to lock the front doors. "For all the good it's likely to do."

"You've spoken too soon, Mr. Tumnus," Tim called over his shoulder, motioning for Hiero and Han to remain on the stairs while he descended. "And have done yourself no favors by securing the lock."

"How do you mean?"

"You must leave us to our investigations. If all goes well, we'll have the ghost and the murderer apprehended by dawn tomorrow."

There were so many colors to Tumnus's outrage that he might have spat rainbows. "If you are under the misconception that I'll—"

Hiero waltzed in on cue. "Your office is locked, sir?"

"It is, but—"

"And your safe?"

"Empty but for petty cash. But—"

"The restaurant is closed, the props, sets, and costumes as vulnerable during the day as at night. Everything is secure."

"You hooligans—"

"'Hooligans'? Really, sir. What will your own investors think if you refer to the men they themselves hired to resolve this matter in such insulting terms?"

Tumnus recovered with aplomb. "They will know that my word is my bond. I vowed to turn a profit inside a year, and that will not happen if you and your 'team' are set loose in my theater after dark, Mr. Bash."

"Very well." Hiero performed a curt bow. "Mr. Stoker, Mr.

Han, come along. Mr. Calvin... Where is Mr. Calvin?"

"Here, sir." Callie trotted over from the vestibule, which she'd been securing.

"Excellent." Hiero nodded them toward the door. "Time for a spot of dinner, eh? I confess I'm famished." They collected around the front exit, then, as one, turned to stare expectantly at Tumnus. "If you'd do us the service of letting us out?"

Tumnus stammered, then hurried to accommodate them. Tim thought him so befuddled that he probably wouldn't realize this left him alone in the empty theater with the ghost until he'd rebolted the door and they'd hailed a pair of hansom cabs. Which they proceeded to do, not bothering to look back or bid him farewell.

Tim turned in his seat once he'd climbed aboard, chuckling as he watched Tumnus peek back out, scan the area, then make his escape.

"An ingenious bit of maneuvering, Mr. Bash," Tim complimented. Tim found Hiero's hand and squeezed. Held on as long as he dared, as Hiero still had made no move to straighten his clothes.

They arrived home at 23 Berkeley Square in a timely fashion. With a generous tip to both their drivers, Hiero and Callie entered through the main door while Tim and Han slipped around the side to the kitchen entrance. Though Tim staggered back a few steps when hit with the heat of Minnie's cooking, he had nothing but smiles for the rest of the family, gathered around the table for the evening meal. Pleased to discover Minnie had made a traditional Macanese dish Han had taught her—minchi, minced pork and beef with onion, potatoes, and lots of sauces and spices, served over rice with a fried egg on top—Tim ignored the rumble of his stomach while he dished out four portions and Han fried up their eggs.

Only as they carried their heavy trays up to the dining room, where they would sequester in order to discuss the case, did Tim's mind stray back to work matters.

"Where did your inquiries lead you this afternoon?" he asked Han. "Bear any fruit?"

Han nodded, the golden flecks in his brown eyes muted, pensive. "Still digesting."

"Your thoughts, I hope," Tim chuckled. "This is too fine a meal to waste on a full stomach."

"That it is." Han inhaled the savory aroma and sighed. Tim could only imagine what visions of home this conjured in his memory.

A round of huzzahs heralded their arrival in the dining room, where places had already been set for them and wine poured. They settled around one of the ends, with Tim granted the head in Hiero's stead. A companionable silence fell as they tucked in, each perhaps realizing, much like Tim, how famished they were. But soon enough Han took a cleansing sip of wine and elaborated on his afternoon's adventures for the group.

"I interviewed Miss Maxine Marks," he explained. "Terriss's lover, who writes the society column for *The Pall Mall Gazette* under the name Devon Standish. Twice now I've caught her snooping, at the mistress' flat and, as Mr. Calvin can attest, at the performer's entrance to The Gaiety."

"You suspect her?" Tim asked.

"I'm uncertain." A knot of concern stitched Han's brow. "She was on intimate terms with Terriss, but she seems more interested in reporting the crime than committing one. She's ambitious. Overtly so. Suggested a barter."

This surprised Tim. "For?"

"We feed her headlines during the case, she reports on the truth once it's concluded."

Callie hummed. "Smart."

"There is much to admire in her, if you care to see it," Han said.

"But can she be trusted?" Tim asked.

"A test, surely, could be arranged," Hiero contributed.

"But does such publicity help or hinder us?" Callie considered.

"She suggested we might do well to keep the public on our side,"

Han responded.

Hiero nodded. "Shrewd as well as smart. A rare bird indeed."

"You did well to pursue her," Tim commended. "But we've not even made a day's progress. And someone championing Hiero in the press might provoke our killer. Let us see what develops overnight and revisit the issue tomorrow. With any luck, this may all be over by dawn."

Aldridge poked his head in, bearing a basket of fresh buns and fig chutney, and received a hero's welcome. And a Hiero's prodding about dessert.

Once Aldridge disappeared anew, Callie pounced. "So, gents, what's the plan?"

Tim pulled out a long, scrolled document from his inner coat pocket as the others cleared a portion of the table. He carefully unfurled the blueprints he had wheedled away from Tumnus prior to their departure, four thin layers of paper superimposed to give a detailed four-story map of The Gaiety. His companions buzzed with interest.

"We must conduct a search, bottom to top, of every room in the backstage, the stage itself, the auditory, the lounges, the entrance hall, and all offices. We have until dawn tomorrow. We are hindered by two challenges. One, the sheer size of the theater, and two, the fact that we cannot be certain what we are searching for, only that we will know it when we find it."

"In other words," Han said, "any evidence of how the ghost enters, exits, travels through, or otherwise conducts his ghostly business in the theater."

"Anything of possible relevance."

"And if the fiend himself comes calling?" Hiero asked in a subdued voice Tim didn't like at all.

"Catch them, if you can. A suspect would be ideal." Tim clicked his tongue. "But take care. As we've seen, there are hidden traps everywhere that no one meant to set, part and parcel of the normal workings of a theater." In an attempt to lift Hiero's spirits, he added, "That goes treble for you."

Hiero chuckled weakly. "You have my word as a sticky-fingered rapscallion and devout flâneur that I will leave all the work to you, dear Kip."

He favored Hiero with a fond look. "We'll go in pairs, of course." He glanced at Han and Callie. "Would that I could spare you the bother, Mr. Bash, but we're severely undermanned."

"Do you think we'll manage it in one night?" Han asked.

"Frankly, no." Tim tapped the edge of the blueprint. "So we must concentrate our efforts on key areas. We'll rendezvous at midnight and compare notes. If there's reason enough to continue, we will. If not, I'm sure we could all do with some rest."

"For who knows what the morrow will bring," Hiero aptly concluded.

The moment, however, brought Aldridge with lemon and strawberry tarts. Once their plates had been cleared and they all cradled steaming cups of coffee, Tim ventured back into the subject at hand.

"Since forewarned truly is forearmed, what of note did we learn from our interviews?"

Callie extricated her notebook and flipped to a middle page. "Thirty-seven sightings, many I'm sure on the same date and at the same time. I'll need a few hours to correlate. Two in particular were witnessed by a large part of the company. The first was when the ghost projected a menacing shadow against a backdrop during an otherwise comical scene. They did not see the fiend in person, but some caught him passing through the corridors out the corner of their eye."

"I'll wager a large portion of the testimony amounts to half glimpses and strange sounds. Usually of no account," Tim commented.

"A third challenge will be separating fact from fiction," Han remarked.

"Just so." He returned his attention to Callie. "And the second?"

"One of the actresses, Seraphine Vauquelin, has been plagued by the ghost. Thought she had an admirer, but the gifts became threats."

That detail prickled Tim's ears. "She confirms this?"

"She and her sister Damiane left after the general meeting. Haven't yet been interviewed." Before Tim could protest, she insisted, "There's more. During rehearsal one day, the ghost serenaded her from one of the boxes."

"Five," Hiero pronounced in a solemn tone. "It was Box 5."

Tim turned his head mechanically toward him, everything clicking into place: Hiero's mood, his reserve, his willingness to play possum. He shifted his leg under the table to press against Hiero's. He understood Hiero's muted behavior, recognized it as that of a man hunted. And now Tim was about to lead his rare bird into the crocodile's mouth to pick at its teeth and hope it didn't snap.

"How did they know it was the ghost?" Han inquired.

"I'm told he stole a costume from the vault," Callie replied.

"Don Juan. From 1868." Tim caught Hiero's violent reaction, met his stare with one of warmth and understanding. And resolve. "A black solider's uniform, a cape, a red skull mask, and—"

"Monogrammed gloves?" Han tossed just such an item into the center of the table.

Callie gasped. "How did you..."

"We," Han emphasized, pointing to Hiero, "came across it this afternoon. In the theater. After the meeting."

Tim again reached for, and clasped, Hiero's hand. And found it trembling.

"You had an encounter with our fiendish foe?" Tim asked.

"After a fashion."

"What happened?"

Tim squeezed Hiero's hand tighter and tighter as he recounted how the ghost had taunted him. By the end of the tale, Tim held tight rein on the urge to storm over to The Gaiety, find the very real person behind these acts of terror, and horsewhip them within an inch of their lives. Not a very detectivelike response, but some things could not stand.

"Change of plans," he declared once Hiero's story died out.

"No," Hiero insisted.

"I will not lead you into peril."

"You must." The deep brown-black pools of his eyes, void of their usual luster, implored him. "Think. The theater will be empty. No one but the pair of us at risk. We must take the chance while the company is safe."

Tim shook his head. "You make too many assumptions. They might nab someone and use them as a hostage. The theater has been their playground for months. We might outnumber them at two, but they have the clear advantage."

"And yet." Han tapped the edge of his saucer with a patient finger. "They have not acted directly against Hiero in all this time. Anyone can be trapped and dispatched given the right set of circumstances. This fiend has not chosen to do that. They are toying with Hiero, with his emotions and his loyalties. A head-on challenge might surprise them. You might learn something of value in how they react."

"But why toy with Mademoiselle Vauquelin in kind?" Callie interjected. She asked Hiero, "Do you have some connection to her?"

"None that I know," Hiero responded, appearing grateful for the diversion. "I've attended one or two of the sisters' performances before, as one does, but we've never met or shared the stage."

"Another wrinkle," Tim murmured. "Perhaps the ghost took over from a genuine admirer of hers?"

"Or perhaps there is an aspect of this yet to unveil itself," Han said.

"Either way," Tim concluded, "it's clear this interview cannot wait."

"And will require a woman's touch," Hiero added. At Callie's outraged look, he chuckled. "Come now. You didn't think they were actual sisters."

The edges of Hiero's lips curled up as she flushed in realization, silencing any objection to being left out of the hunt. The sight cheered Tim.

"Then the plan is set." Even as he said it, Tim felt the first churn of worry curdle the contents of his stomach. "Mr. Calvin will molt his skin so that Callie might interview the Vauquelin sisters. Mr. Han will provide an escort. Hiero and myself will perform a more targeted search of The Gaiety—"

"And will attempt to avoid getting picked off."

The four of them sighed in unison, stared at the blood-red glove in the center of the table. Hoped against hope it wasn't a harbinger of things to come.

Han clicked the chamber of Callie's elegant MAS revolver in after giving it a final polish. He'd never been one for deadly weapons, but, much like that of its owner, the gun's beauty had grown on him over time. However, he'd be hard-pressed to say whether it was the powerful recoil of the revolver that most thrilled him or the close-quarters lessons with his merciless and accomplished teacher. He doubted he'd need it during that evening's mission, but given the Vauquelin "sisters'" reputation—as legendary in the demimonde for their conquests as for hiding their decade-long relationship—Han wouldn't leave anything to chance.

Their very open relationship, or so the rumors went.

The creak of the bottom step of the main staircase at 23 Berkeley Square called him out of the study in time to meet Callie. He'd wondered which of her personas she would choose for this particular errand. She'd selected Mrs. Patricia Stoker, née Belmont, "wife" of

DI Tim Stoker who lent occasional aid to her husband when assigned to interview a member of the fairer sex. Patricia had been deployed on a few occasions already, notably when the Marchioness of Westhaven required a chaperone whilst confronting an unfaithful suitor. A married woman opened certain doors even Hiero couldn't charm his way through, especially where some of their older and wealthier clients were concerned. And Tim's youthful appearance, if not his rapport with Callie, helped sell a longtime marriage to a girl of twenty.

"Blonde, I thought, would be best," Callie announced by way of greeting, performing a little twirl. She'd dressed in muted colors but rich fabrics and a sensible hat with only one ribbon, befitting the persona of a detective's wife. "I have a mousier color, but if they aren't true sisters... What do you think?"

"They'll serve you with cream and berries."

After a soft, approving "hmm," Callie preoccupied herself with Han's appearance, touring around him in wide circle. For his role as Mrs. Stoker's protector, he'd changed into a darker suit with a more tapered silhouette, the better to emphasize his height and broad build. Han had given his shoes a polish but washed the pomade shine out of his short black hair, releasing its natural wave. Side-parted in the manner that best framed his thick brows and sharp jaw, even he could imagine himself stomping broodily across the moors. And together they made quite the pair.

"Perfect," Callie murmured, avoiding his eyes.

They both nodded their thanks to Aldridge, who held an umbrella for them as they descended the front steps to the waiting carriage. Angus, the chauffeur, had the door.

"Good eve to you both! Which young lass am I driving tonight?" Angus chirped.

"Mrs. Patricia Stoker," Han replied, lending Callie a hand as she climbed in.

Han caught the hiss of their brushing gloves as she pulled her hand away, and he debated sitting out beside Angus in the rain for the ride. By the strictest rules of propriety, he should have, but it also wouldn't do to conduct an interview looking like he'd swum the Thames. After he settled across from her for the short journey to the Caledonian Hotel, he stared out into the soggy night, feeling years away from the sunny embankment of that afternoon. Such were the tempers and humors of life in London.

They rode in silence, Callie studying her notes that she might commit her questions to memory. Silhouetted against the diaphanous light of the streetlamps, Han fancied he caught a glimpse of her future self. Aged by her style of dress and hat and makeup, he could well imagine her as a woman of means travelling to some appointment, preparing to share her wisdom and insight for the betterment of the world. A sight that, when it came to pass, he dearly did not want to miss.

Not a saint nor a serial flirt, he'd had his share of backstage liaisons during Horace Beastly's years treading the boards, but no one who got under his skin. He envied Hiero that, finding refuge in not one, but two faithful lovers over the course of their friendship, against impossible odds. Han had found an oasis in the arms of many a good woman over the years, but the feeling of shelter and security, of belonging, always evaporated once their passion burned out.

He chanced a glance at Callie, so focused, so relentless, and wished they were a thousand miles from any class difference or social etiquette. That their togetherness wouldn't risk spoiling their family, their team, their home. His only consolation was that circumstances wouldn't change in Macau, were she the scion of a rich family and he still the son of a boat-dweller. His parents' tale was evidence enough of that.

"A word of caution," Han said. "The Vauquelin sisters are not known for their subtlety. Or their purity."

She chuckled. "You mean they might make an advance? On a

married woman?"

"On anything that lives, breathes, and..."

"Fornicates?"

He did like it when she tried to shock him. "So they say."

"I've encountered such types before."

He nodded. No doubt she had. Though Hiero rarely entertained and Callie stayed out of Horace Beastly's life, they'd both tangled with their fair share of eccentrics and disreputable sorts. But Hiero, and Apollo before him, had kept them on a short leash around an unmarried young woman.

"It doesn't trouble you? To be... regarded in that way?"

"Why should it? I've no intention of indulging myself with a suspect. If they require that I bat my eyes and pretend a blush to give up their knowledge, then so be it. It's harmless." Another silence fell, but Han could hear her wheels spinning. "Women, alas, have few weapons at their disposal. Flirtation is one of the most useful. I dare say it's the same for the Vauquelin sisters, if they aren't in fact sisters." She laughed. "Though between their lack of a familial bond and myself not actually being married, it's a wonder any truth will be uncovered."

Han joined in her mirth, and an ease was restored between them.

The Caledonian Hotel, at numbers one, two, and three Robert Street in the section between the Strand and the Victoria Embankment known as Adelphi, catered specifically to overnight or short-stay travelers, given its proximity to Charing Cross train station. Their suites of apartments, though exquisitely appointed, were not designed to be long-term accommodations—which reflected in their exorbitant cost. The Vicomte must have brokered some promotional deal, or he knew someone on staff who owed him a favor—or, Han guessed, money spilled like sand through his fingers—in order to afford to house his top actors there. Most of the French company lodged in a rooming house not far from The Gaiety, but Madame de Casterac (with, one presumed, the Vicomte) and the Vauquelin sisters had been given suites at the Caledonian for the duration of the run.

He saw these observations and more reflected in Callie's keen eyes as they climbed the stairs. She paused before the relevant door, her attention to detail so thorough that she considered what type of knock her character might use, then tapped a firm, staccato tattoo.

The door swung open, but no one waited on the other side to greet them. The dim red light of a shadowy receiving room warned them off, but not a soul sat upon its divans and armchairs. Instead they heaved with so many discarded outfits that it looked as if someone had upended the contents of their valises. A trill of laughter echoed from another room, followed by excited, drunken chatter. Someone tinkled at a piano. The pop of a champagne bottle heralded a chorus of cheers; a glass shattered; the culprit shrieked. The chatter intensified, approached. A man in a valet's livery ran into the receiving room, barreling straight for them. He didn't bother to excuse himself before diving between them and charging out of the suite. Han recognized him as the Vicomte's servant, Jean-Georges. The rouge on his lips he could not identify.

"Like lambs to the slaughter," Callie murmured under her breath as they crept further into the apartment.

Han couldn't disagree. If the Vauquelins thought the staff of the Caledonian could protect them against unwanted intruders, or the fact that they came from France kept them off the killer's list, Han would counter with the very dead Mr. Terriss and the very injured Miss Nichols. Carelessness like this wasn't just hazardous, it was outright criminal.

Of course, a guilty party tended not to take the same precautions as an innocent.

"Hello!" Han shouted.

A head poked out into the short hallway that led to the other rooms, snickered, then disappeared. It returned a moment later, attached to a body. A staggering body carrying a cigarette in one hand and the aforementioned champagne bottle in the other. Few would have mistaken Damiane Vauquelin for a man, even with her short, slicked-back hair, tailored white shirt, and gentlemen's trousers, nor did she seem particularly invested in playing the part, given the riotous red lipstick that smeared her mouth.

Provocation, not assimilation, ruled the day.

"Oh, très bien," she purred, taking them both in. Her gaze adventured longest on Han before returning to Callie. "Un verre ou deux?"

Han hesitated. He'd never been adept at French, and they'd moved in such haste that he'd overlooked the fact that the sisters might not speak English. Thankfully, Callie intervened.

"A fine state you're in. Have you not been informed there's a killer on the loose, or is that why we find you so... undone?"

Han swallowed a chuckle, reminded once again that Mrs. Stoker was modeled on Callie's stern old governess, who'd lasted all of a month in their whirligig household but left a lasting impression.

"And you have come to straighten me out?" Mademoiselle Damiane replied in a heavy accent. "Too late, madame. You are far too late."

"And you are tempting more than just fate by allowing any old fool to walk in."

"One has certainly found its way to our door." Mademoiselle Damiane swooned with laughter. "Qui êtes-vous?"

Han cleared his throat. "Permit me to introduce Mrs. Patricia Stoker, wife of the lead detective hunting Mr. Randolph Terriss's murderer, DI Timothy Kipling Stoker."

"Who sends his apologies," Callie added. "My husband thought you might be more comfortable confiding in me. And I am grateful for it."

"Comfort," Mademoiselle Damiane scoffed. "What genius ever came from being comfortable?" She waddled over to Callie, standing right under her chin and looking up. "Art is provocation."

Callie stared down her nose at her. "That very well may be. But in an investigation, we deal in facts. Do you have any to report from your transactions with the so-called Gaiety ghost?"

But she had already lost her audience.

"You," Mademoiselle Damiane slurred, taking a long swig before pointing her bottle finger at Han. "I've seen you before."

"Quite possible."

"Where?"

"I cannot say."

"Ah! Un autre mystère." She giggled into her sleeve, evidently finding herself amusing.

"Where, if I may, is your sister?"

"Seraphine!" Mademoiselle Damiane swung around, charging back down the hallway as she bellowed. "Seraphine!"

They heard water sloshing and lively chatter before three people emerged... and Han wrenched his eyes down to the carpet.

In that brief glimpse, he'd seen enough. Soaked Seraphine, in a white, gauzy nightdress that clung to her body like a second skin, wore a crown of flowers and little else. Behind her, a harried-looking man carrying a sketch pad.

"Indecent," Callie hissed, and Han suspected she agreed with her character. "You," she addressed the man. "Fetch her a robe, or I'll bring you up on charges."

"Mais non, mais non!" Mademoiselle Seraphine petulantly cried. "Auguste!"

Spooked Auguste returned in record time with a large floral-patterned blanket, adding to the Ophelian effect. He didn't even manage introductions before making his goodbyes, in halting French, to the two demoiselles.

"Do you normally entertain men of such low character unescorted?" Callie demanded as soon as he'd gone. Han detected her reluctance even as she spoke the words.

And remembered he could now raise his head. The Vauquelin

sisters, dizzy with drunkenness and who knew what else, leaned against each other like a pair of delinquent orphans.

Actors, he thought with as much charity as he could muster.

"Auguste painted my portrait," Mademoiselle Seraphine explained, still pouting. "He's going to call it *La dame aux camélias.*"

Callie gave a curt nod. "Hopefully, you will not suffer the same fate as that classic heroine."

Mademoiselle Seraphine gasped. "Ah non! What happened to her?"

"It's a book," her sister elaborated, "by Dumas. A tragedy."

"Dumas le conducteur wrote a book?"

"She means Alexandre Dumas. The son." Callie bristled. "Beside the point. Ladies, you are both in grave danger. We must speak with you at once concerning—"

"What tragedy? What happens to her in the book?" Mademoiselle Seraphine appeared on the verge of tears.

"She dies," Callie snapped. "As will you, if you do not answer my questions."

Hearing the rumble of imminent thunder in her voice, Han interjected, "What Mrs. Stoker means is anyone could be a target. And, indeed, others have reported that you, Mademoiselle Seraphine, have received threats from The Gaiety ghost?"

"Ah, zut!" Mademoiselle Seraphine marched over to a chaise longue and plopped herself down on the end. "Tell them for me, will you, Damie?" She slumped onto her side and shut her eyes.

Han resisted the urge to check for a pulse.

"Wake her, if you please," Callie insisted. "We must have it from her own account."

Mademoiselle Damiane shoved a heap of clothes off an armchair and sat. She waved her free hand at the divan, inviting them to do the same. Han and Callie cleared small spaces for themselves and perched at the cushions' edge.

"We are always together," Mademoiselle Damiane began. "Same

dressing room, same rehearsals."

"Go on," Han encouraged.

After a small belch, she said, "We receive many gifts, as you must know. Sera, because of her"—she waggled a hand in front of her face—"receives many more. The stagehands know to only bring the important ones. From a lord or a famous director. But these... They appeared in our rooms, at her mirror. With a note in red ink, signed... How do you say it?"

"A secret admirer?"

"Exactement." She sighed. "Beautiful gifts. Extraordinary. Rare flowers. Expensive wine. Shoes from the finest houses of Paris, in her size. A necklace with a ruby so big... We thought he must be a prince. It was the only explanation."

"But you hadn't yet begun the run of the show," Han observed. "How did this admirer even know of your sister's talent?"

"We believed he'd seen us perform in Paris. Perhaps he thought to begin his wooing early, with no competition. Les hommes en amour se font des idées." She shrugged. "We asked the stagehands who it was, thinking they'd promised not to say. But they did not even know what we were talking about. That is when the notes became..."

"Less amorous?" Callie suggested.

"Aïe, qu'elles était sauvages!" Mademoiselle Seraphine rolled onto her back, hand to her head in what Han recognized as one of the eight dramatic poses of misery.

"Did you keep any of them?"

Mademoiselle Damiane threw back her head with laughter. "Keep them? Do you save all the vulgar letters sent to you, Mrs. Stoker? Do you commit to memory the insults hurled your way? A strong madame like you must receive a fair share."

"What did you do with them? Is there any way one might be retrieved?"

Spotting a lighter tossed atop the mess, Mademoiselle Damiane flicked it three times before it ignited. She played her fingers through the flame to underline her point.

"Not unless you are a… What's the word? Chimiste? Alchimiste?"

"Alchemist." Han sighed. He had a certain reserve of patience for dizzy thespians, but he expended most of it dealing with Hiero. This case might very well sound the death knell of his composure. "Did it never occur to you that you were destroying evidence?"

Mademoiselle Damiane scoffed. "Evidence? Of what? Vulgarity? Bestiality? We didn't know who left the notes."

"We thought it was Germain." Mademoiselle Seraphine giggled into a sleeve. "Or Hubert. Or François. Or Pierre-Marc."

"Would your Parisian admirers travel so far just to get petty revenge?" Callie asked.

"Or Lizette…" Mademoiselle Seraphine gasped and covered her mouth, as if someone among them might still not know their secret. When no one exclaimed in disgust, she actually seemed to give the matter some thought. "To be honest, the notes and the scary gifts made me want to believe it was someone we knew doing a… une blague. A funny. Mais dans mon coeur, je le savais. I knew it in my heart who it was."

Callie perked up at this. "Who?"

"Tumnus, le monstre."

"You think Mr. Tumnus means to sabotage the opening of his own theater?"

"No, no. I think he is angry that I would not…" She mimed a gesture that required no interpretation. Han glanced at Callie—her jaw clenched, her eyes cold. Tumnus would rue the day. "Or I thought it was that, until today."

"I don't suppose you kept any of the gifts?"

Mademoiselle Seraphine resumed her giggling.

Her sister, having found a cigarette to go with her lighter, stopped blowing rings of smoke long enough to say, "Speak to

Monsieur Flint. The rotting flowers we threw away, but the others we donated to props."

"They were very, very scary," Mademoiselle Seraphine insisted.

Han heard Callie exhale quietly to herself. All was not lost. "The serenade. Can you set the scene?"

Mademoiselle Seraphine yelped, covered her face with the blanket. Mademoiselle Damiane rolled her eyes, then drank deep of the last of the champagne before replying.

"We rehearsed the death scene. I make a little groan, collapse. On the ground, I hear a strange applause. Too far away. And a bit..."

"He wore leather gloves?"

"Oui. I saw later. There is a..." She struggled for the right word. "Everyone is silent. Normally, when a scene finishes, everyone is moving. The director, the crew... I cannot stop pretending until Genevre says, 'Assez.' But she does not. Instead a voice begins to sing. A beautiful voice, but the song... The song is like the notes. It begins very nicely, but..."

"The man in the red mask." Mademoiselle Seraphine whimpered. "I thought he had come for me. I walked to the front of the stage. I begged him to stop. In English. In French. He wouldn't."

"When he was done, he waited for his applause. Everyone was frozen, staring. If not at him, then at Sera. So he threw... Oh, it was horrible!"

Mademoiselle Seraphine bolted upright. "At me. Right at me!" She heaved a sob. "Son coeur..."

Craned so far forward it was a miracle she didn't fall off the divan, Callie demanded, "What do you mean, his heart? Another gift?"

"No." Mademoiselle Damiane had gone the color of turned milk. "A real heart. A human heart."

Chapter 9

*H*iero leaned against the performers' entrance of The Gaiety, sheltering Kip with his cape while he worked his magic on the lock. A thick cloak of smog hid both the incessant drizzle of rain and their less-than-righteous actions from any passersby. But neither the damp nor the soupy murk snuffed the wisps of white smoke Hiero blew out as he waited for Kip to apply the right pressure to just the right spot. Normally a man of incomparable dexterity, Hiero did begin to wonder what was taking so long.

"Not stalling, are you, my dear?" he asked, more out of boredom than curiosity. His cigarette was almost out, and lighting another would be bothersome with one hand occupied.

"Believe it or not, I've not spent a lifetime sneaking into places I don't belong."

Hiero scoffed. "Some might accuse you of a lack of imagination."

"Would you care to take a crack?"

"Hardly. Han did the honors on the rare occasions we had to resort to—"

"Breaking and entering?"

"Improving the odds through whatever means necessary."

Kip chuckled. "Were you ever caught?"

"Only once." Hiero sucked a final puff off the butt, then flicked it into the street. "Old Horace had been invited to perform a few soliloquies at a manor house in Surrey for a particular gentleman's twenty-first birthday. Beastly's early days, you see, before Apollo's patronage. After playing to the assembled guests, the young lord in question's praise to Horace had... well, one might say a rhapsodic quality. And the way he'd cornered him by a statue of Achilles and Patroclus held a certain symbolism. So rather than retiring to the servants' quarters, Horace thought to present his admirer with a rare and precious birthday gift."

"Himself?"

"Precisely."

"A fortunate son indeed."

"Too much so, as it turned out. A recently widowed cousin had a similar notion and better access to the matron's keys. We broke in to find her spread across the bed like cream on a crumpet."

Kip snorted into his sleeve, hands shaking as he clung to the lock-picking instruments. "You must have had a time convincing her you weren't up to no good."

"Han proved to be the more persuasive. I barely saw him for the rest of our time there and had to entertain myself with the library's meager offerings. And strolls. Endless strolls."

"Physical exertion? Scandalous. However did you cope?"

"Poorly, as mentioned." Hiero snuck his now-free hand down to rub the nape of Kip's neck. He loved the bristly bits at the base of his scalp. "If only we'd known each other then."

"I daresay I wouldn't have outdone the meager charms of that library as a lad of fifteen."

Hiero took his time considering this. "Paints an image. I do wonder what you looked like?"

"Slim, wan, bookish... A giant freckle."

Hiero tugged back Kip's collar to peek at the speckled expanse of his back, the skin hugging tight dunes of muscle. It was perhaps an uncharitable thought, but he didn't regret not knowing him then. Not with such bounty to explore now, to claim with touch and lips and tongue.

"You're letting the rain in, dear," Kip protested with a shiver.

Just as Hiero thought of a way to tease and retaliate, the lock clicked. With a hum of satisfaction, Kip rose to his feet and eased open the door. They slipped into the blackness before the smog dissipated, exposing them.

Into the ghost's lair. As Kip switched on the backstage lights, Hiero reminded himself he had volunteered for this. Designed not to distract the audience, hanging lamps dappled amber puddles along tight, shadowy corridors. He'd once found their dim cast warm, the dark fathoms between a welcome place to hide. Before Apollo, the theater had been his home: he, its creature. This fiend had transformed it into a treacherous landscape where the wrong step could lose him everything he held dear.

That everything gazed at him in such a way just then that he nearly grabbed Kip by the arm and dragged him back to Berkeley Square. To the oasis of their apartments. To the bed that they should never have abandoned that morn. Kip appeared resolute, but Hiero read the subtler lines of his face: his worry, his fear, his protective instinct, his affection. He raised a hand to squeeze Hiero's shoulder, but Hiero caught it, pressed it to his cheek. Kissed the palm, though it smelled like iron and sweat.

Once upon a time, he would have run away. Found a new city, a new profession, a new identity. Life four of nine, he had plenty to spare. Not a moment wasted mourning those the killer might have targeted in his place. Now that he had some money of his own, he might be anyone, live anywhere. Take along those from the household who wanted an adventure. Even Kip he could have convinced. They'd bored deep into each other; his Kip would not abandon him. What did he owe this new troupe of actors, Tumnus, and the Vicomte, after all? Only Flint remained from Hiero's time, and he was already half-persuaded to resign his post.

To Hiero's great shock—rare as a comet streaking the night

sky—he'd become a different man. No ghost would spook him out of his theater. No fiend would terrorize in his name. No one would suffer in the sanctuary that gave so many lost souls a soft place to land.

A final kiss to Kip's palm. "Lead on, my dear."

Kip nodded but did not let go of his hand. His boyish features tightened into the pinched look he got when about to say something of which Hiero would disapprove. The fact that someone cared enough to earn his approval endeared him all the more.

"I still can't quite believe I've agreed to this."

"It is rather unlike you."

"No weapon, no escape route, only a sketch of a plan. It is rather a Hieronymus Bash way of going about things."

"And yet you agreed despite your reservations."

"A concession to your lesser angels."

"And?"

Kip mashed his lips together, fighting between a smile and a frown. "This phantom foe of ours is playing the long game. Lurking. Teasing. Seeing what we're up to. I wager they've left us a few well-chosen breadcrumbs. They want to be chased, perhaps even be found. We're to bear witness to their grand design."

"And dead witnesses can't tell tales."

"Not if their true aim is to lure out a wild Beastly."

Hiero took a few moments to map out the trail of his logic and attempt to follow him down the same path. "The workings of your mind never cease to enthrall me."

Another squeeze reminded Hiero that Kip had yet to let go of his hand. He pressed into that firm grip as he inched his way toward a question. "Then why threaten me this afternoon?" Hiero asked.

"Proof of concept." Kip chuckled at his confusion. "We shudder, ergo they are dangerous. We realize they could strike anyone at any moment—even one of us—ergo we have a personal stake in their great game. Every master villain, after all, must match wits with a cunning detective."

"And Beastly's secret is safe for now?"

Kip gave this careful consideration. "I believe so. But not enough to stake anyone's life on it, especially one so dear to me." He pressed a soft kiss to the knuckles of Hiero's hand, then, with visible reluctance, let it go. "Stay close."

They'd hardly walked ten paces when Kip stopped cold.

"What is it?" Hiero whispered. Kip cast a sheepish look over his shoulder. Hiero swallowed a snicker at how a code breaker and linguist could be foiled by a few curving corridors. "Would you care for me to lead?"

"If you please."

"I do. Where are we going?"

"The manager's office. Let's discover just how desperate Mr. Tumnus's situation is."

After an eternal hour and several infinite minutes watching Kip scan through a pile of ledgers whilst resisting the lure of Tumnus's not-so-well-hidden bottle of scotch, Hiero rather wished their ghost would stage a haunting. Stealing into a dark, vacuous theater to search for evidence should, after all, have some entertainment value, be it shocks or scares or sensual interludes. Every drop in the well of his boredom—the waterline nearly up to his neck—drained some of the terror from his close encounter with their fiend in Box 5. And Kip's earlier arguments, given he'd had half a lifetime of waiting in which to revisit them, replenished his nerve.

The snap of a shutting ledger woke him from plotting mischief. Hiero skipped over to the door as Kip scribbled a few final notes and carefully replaced his reading material.

"Your verdict?"

Kip sighed. "As expected. Somewhat. He's extended himself to the limit and will need five years of solid successes before he'll see a return on his investment."

"Ha! With his dramaturgical failings, impossible."

"Ah, but Tumnus isn't acting as The Gaiety's artistic director." He pointed to the correspondence Hiero had been meant to skim through but abandoned when he grew drowsy. Hiero could barely endure the man's speech, let alone his pious pigeon scratchings. "He has some influence—rather disturbingly, he's insisted on plays with a 'strong moral message' that 'teach the audience about the perils of sin through spectacle'—but isn't well-read enough to commission new interpretations of popular tales."

"Alluring for the Vicomte, the opportunity to program an English theater with great French works, exposing their writers to a new audience."

"Precisely. But Tumnus is, as we've seen, a cautious man. I'd assumed it was the Vicomte who was reluctant to invest fully in The Gaiety, waiting until his company had a proven success here, but according to their correspondence, it's Tumnus insisting on the delay."

"Even with so much of his own money at stake?"

"Another interesting wrinkle." Kip slid a stack of letters into a folder. "His purchase of The Gaiety appears to be the fulfillment of a lifelong dream. Tumnus is wealthy. Very wealthy. He inherited a northern coal-mining empire from his father and his uncles. As the only male heir, their three shares of the business went to him. He corresponds with the head of a firm he's hired to manage these investments, so he still has a finger in that pie. But he saw an opportunity when The Gaiety went up for sale to, as he puts it, 'act in service of the two great masters of my heart, the arts and the Lord.' So his work here is something of a pilgrimage. Also no serious personal risk, as his businesses will absolve him of any debt the theater might incur."

Hiero scowled. "So our ghost is little more than a nuisance to him?"

"Not exactly. This is his big gamble. I imagine more than a few tongues wagged in his northern friend circles when he set aside his lucrative business to play missionary in London's den of scandal and sedition. His reputation is at stake, and he can't be pleased with the disruption and the waste. He's the sort to have a dozen contingency plans, some of which our fiend has already foiled. Care to know which?"

"I wait with baited breath."

"He endures the Vicomte but cannot abide Madame de Casterac. Yet it is she who will take over as artistic director if their contract becomes permanent. So Tumnus was making moves to sign someone else before any potential partnership with the French company." Kip stared at him, expectant. Hiero hadn't the foggiest who Tumnus had approached, but did appreciate the will-o'-the-wisp glow of Kip's green eyes.

Then lightning struck.

"Terriss?"

Kip beamed, a proud parent. "The very same."

"And rather inconveniently dead."

"Ah, but not for our purposes." He paused, reconsidered his words. "I mean, his death is tragic, of course, but his potential alliance with Tumnus sheds some light on why a 'ghost' might haunt his theater and murder his leading man."

"Motives all around!"

"I daresay. And our first solid link between the murder and the happenings here. Although it does appear to absolve Tumnus of any wrongdoing."

"Of the criminal variety. His efforts to bring about The Gaiety's ruin through mismanagement and Puritanism are still very much en vogue."

"Alas." Kip moved out from behind the desk and offered Hiero his arm. "Shall we?"

"Not quite yet." He hooked his arm through Kip's, but only to tug him into a tight embrace. Bemused but no less phosphorescent eyes beguiled him, drawing him down into their depths. "All this talk of piety has roused the devil in me. Should we christen Tumnus's office?"

Hiero wanted to wrap himself in the warmth of Kip's resulting chuckle.

"You are temptation incarnate," Kip whispered before anchoring a hand on Hiero's neck and drawing him down for a kiss.

Hiero thought he'd won when they staggered back against the desk, Kip's legs parting in welcome as their bodies found each other anew. All the day's anxieties fell away as Kip's fingers dug into his shoulders and their torsos pressed hot, deepening their kiss, reviving the lust that had fed them all summer. Hiero chased after his silken lips when they pulled away, sighed when Kip rested their brows together.

"A promise was made. I have not forgotten."

"Nor will I."

"Good. Hold me to it." He brushed a final tantalizing kiss across Hiero's pouting mouth. "Once we're safely enclosed in our apartments. Wouldn't do to give the ghost an eyeful."

"And therefore more leverage." Hiero eased out of their embrace, though not before giving Kip's buttocks a thorough grope. "Where to now... my most beauteous and generous lord?"

Kip couldn't help a grin. "Devil take me."

"I'll be the one doing—"

A music box played somewhere in the distance, the same seductive tune that had taunted Hiero that afternoon, which he now recognized as Daaé's *Nocturne*. His unspoken words clogged his throat. Kip moved to the door, opening it a crack to listen.

"Is that...?"

Hiero nodded. Kip waved him over as he bent to slip his truncheon out of his trouser leg. They crept as one out the door, peering down the short corridor into the black void of the auditory. A hypnotic andante beckoned them into the dark, its lazy rhythm a mockery of the heat of their recent embrace. Certain auditory lights flickered to life, illuminating a path they were doomed to follow. Kip shot him a final bolstering look before setting off at a cautious pace. Like Orpheus before him, Hiero could do naught but pursue his beloved into the underworld—or whatever hell the ghost had prepared for them.

Despite his porcupine quill nerves, Hiero matched Kip stride for stride. He kept his ears attuned to any discordant sound: the whistle of an arrow or a poison dart, the whoosh of a falling object, the pop of a gun. After his previous encounter, he suspected the music masked the fiend's movements, an old theatrical trick. Henry Irving, the hack, had been a particular fan of juicing the orchestra when actors needed to move in and out of the crowd. He made a mental note to mention this to Kip, wondering what other hoary gags the ghost might attempt.

Too many sprang to mind, most of which could be turned murderous.

He pulled closer to Kip, who'd halted at the threshold to the backstage. The lit path unmistakably pointed in that direction, but Hiero sensed his ambivalence. One thing to stumble into a trap, another to willingly be ensnared.

The music increased in volume and intensity, bouncing off every curve of the auditory to resist being traced. Worse, they'd stopped in one of The Gaiety's acoustic sweet spots—the equivalent of a sonic maelstrom. Still, Kip considered his options with an untroubled expression.

Hiero longed to cover his ears.

"It's no good," he thought he heard Kip grumble. He bent his head almost to Kip's shoulder, wishing he didn't smell quite so delectable. "We've no reasonable options."

"How do you mean?" Hiero yelled.

"If we follow, we give in. If we retreat, we gain no knowledge. If we feint, we risk too much." A trace of a smile attempted to brighten his dour expression. "Is there a Hiero way out of this?"

Hiero could have kissed the life out of him and back in again. Moments like these, in his never-humble estimation, were why he dared to dabble in detection, a profession that otherwise ill suited him. Kip reminded Hiero how best to be himself.

Hiero turned to consider the auditory and immediately saw how gullible he'd been. Outraged by the use of Box 5, intimidated by their ghost's methods, he'd never thought to question how they created such atmosphere. Or to fight back.

Hiero charged through the backstage door, cranked on the house lights, and marched to the center of the stage. He stood there, arms folded, the challenge clear. He may have spared a glance upward to check for loose sandbags or flies—a simple matter of self-preservation. He waited for their phantom to make a move against him, tapping his foot to goad them into action.

Listening, listening all the while for the first quaver in the music, giving him a hint as to its location. Kip, taking advantage of the distraction Hiero provided, stomped along the edge of the curtain line, attempting to force whatever device played the music to skip. With the floorboards sealed tight to prevent any creaks, his efforts had minimal effect. So Hiero joined in, pounding the stage until the music hiccupped.

There.

Kip dove behind the curtain, truncheon at the ready, but the distorted music masked the patter of any retreating footsteps. Hiero found himself tiptoeing after Kip as he pulled back several curtains to better illuminate the small storage area not ten paces from where they originally stood. Small wonder the music had been deafening. Alas, nothing among the set pieces and props piled there screamed music box.

Kip focused on a prop statue near the curtain's edge. One of the Catholic saints, Hiero assumed, the cross on his chest being a dead giveaway. Its two arms jutted heavenward in supplication, one holding a lopsided urn and the other a poppy with the center carved out. An odd couple in terms of symbolism, but then, he was hardly Bible schooled.

Kip, for his own eccentric reasons, found the base of the statue fascinating. When Hiero opened his mouth to question why, a loud crack shocked him quiet. The statue tilted backward to reveal not one, but four music box cylinders configured to play in perfect harmony. Kip reached behind the base, stilled the crank, and, with a wrenching sound that nearly shattered their eardrums, blessed silence fell.

"Rather ingenious, don't you think?" Kip tinkered with the various cogs and springs of the music box. "Synchronized to play all at once, intensifying the sound. Positioned at the perfect spot for amplification and hidden in the statue... I fear we've underestimated our fiend's knowledge of stagecraft."

"Do you think they've gone?" Hiero whispered.

"Unlikely. Did you see where the path of lights led?"

"Mmm. A dressing room we are intimately acquainted with. Inherited by dear old Randy."

"Who continued our tradition, no doubt."

"Rather more return of the conquering hero." Hiero sighed, wistful, as they moved from the music box to the room in question. "Randy showed me the ropes, after all."

"And by that you mean..."

"Taught me everything I know."

Kip's brow furrowed. "You said he was one for the ladies."

"Ah! Yes. Forgive me. He led by example, not demonstration."

Kip's chuckles died in a gasp as they entered Hiero's old dressing room.

Not a trap but a message. The room had been ransacked beyond all hope of discovering anything of worth. More objects littered the floor or hung from the furniture than could be found in the open empty drawers and cabinets. The wardrobe doors had been pulled off their hinges, the chairs and dressing table overturned. Any garments belonging to Terriss had been shred to ribbons, save the costumes pinned to the walls in garish tableaux of obscene behavior.

But the pièce de résistance, if one could call it that, was the collection of newspaper clippings glued to the full-length mirror. Negative reviews from almost every production in Horace Beastly's storied career, most with a familiar byline: the critic Charles Arascain, not a fan. The nastiest bits had been underlined in thick swathes of blood-red ink, and certain words had been circled. Before Hiero could blink, Kip had deciphered them.

"Act Three, a poem

One was doomed
That I may be exalted
Another missed
For which I cannot be faulted
With a third trick
I'll have earned my acclaim
By the fourth act
Who will they blame?
Return who's lost
And you might find
Not a measure of truth
But some peace of mind
A small price
In a longer game
I ask you again
Who will they blame?"

Hiero recoiled from the mirror, the message, its meaning. Stumbled over a piece of rubble and landed, with a crunch, on a pile of chair kindling. Kip, soundlessly repeating the riddle over and over, didn't turn to check on him, even at Hiero's groans and curses. They grew louder the more annoyed he became, at his lover and at the situation.

It all came back to Beastly. This lunatic would burn the forest down to find the trunk of one felled tree. Hiero grabbed a broken chair leg and stabbed the jagged end into the stuffing of a ripped cushion. He felt not a whit better, so he threw it at the far wall, glorying as it snapped in two. Kip still didn't flinch. Hiero inhaled a deep, lung-stretching breath, wishing he could breathe fire.

He understood Kip's warnings, his seamless logic, about not giving in to a fiend's demands. That they would only move the target before Hiero could hit that bull's-eye. That reviving Beastly would be no better than a shot in the dark. But he'd never been a creature ruled by reason. He was a twitchy, impulsive thing who thrived amidst chaos. He lived in the wild seconds after a wager was struck, the breathless instant after the dice were rolled.

He knew then he had to find a way to risk it all without breaking his word.

Chapter 10

*T*im stopped at the top of the second-floor stairs at 23 Berkeley Square, leaning his hip against the rail as he waited for Hiero to ascend. He imagined the box of evidence they'd collected from Terriss's dressing room wriggling under his arm, as excited as he was for it to find its place on the house library's shelves. *His* library, behind whose vaultlike mahogany door he'd have bolted himself away to examine every letter of the killer's latest message, were it not for the man climbing—with a slight crick to his back?—up to meet him. Whose dark-sun eyes had lost their luster while they'd finished their work and returned home.

An undiscovered country, this pull to comfort Hiero before and beyond the needs of the case. The shift had come with his injury some months earlier, but Tim didn't think that was the cause. He'd had accidents before, even a short hospital stay, and continued on just as diligently with his duty. But he'd never had a person take hold of his heart with such... dominion. He'd never had a Hiero.

Tim tucked the box into the short back passage that led to the library, then turned and opened his arms. Hiero sank into them before reaching the top step, an indulgence their uneven heights rarely permitted him. Tim gathered as much of the day's weight onto himself as he could, resting his chin on Hiero's crown so he might feel completely enveloped. Only once Hiero let out a soft grunt of discomfort did Tim draw him up to the landing, loosening his grip but twining their hands as he led him toward the mighty library door. Thick enough to snuff even their loudest moans.

"Admire your work as I do, my dear Kip, I don't feel especially compelled at the moment to admire you while you work." A soft tug in the opposite direction conveyed Hiero's wish to retire. "No matter the memories the sight of you manning a desk calls up."

They had indeed been quite thorough in their testing of the desks in Hiero's study and the one in Tim's room, now transplanted to the library.

"And if we were to make new memories?" Tim pulled forward until Hiero's fine frame trapped him against the door. "I am, as mentioned, a man of my word."

To Tim's dismay, the gaze that Hiero foisted down at him was neither playful nor amorous.

"And for this night only, I release you from it." He sighed, pressed his forehead to the wood paneling. "We must put an end to this madness, and soonest."

Tim hugged Hiero in anew, hating the tension that stiffened his limbs and not more fortuitous parts. "We will. Of course we will." He burrowed his face in the notch at the base of Hiero's neck and drank deep of that inimitable musk, smoke and spice and everything nice. "But even detectives require rest, if not a bit of distraction, to sharpen their minds. Won't you, couldn't you, be persuaded to distract me awhile? In the name of expediency?"

This got Tim the chuckle he sought, and Hiero caressed the familiar curves and clenches on his very roused, very eager body. He pressed the hard column of his erection into Hiero's thigh and, to his relief, felt an answering nudge at his navel. He slammed down the door handle and backed them into the room before any second thoughts could take hold. A frantic fumble for the lights took several delightful detours up and down Tim's person, but Hiero's soft gasp when he finally saw the refurbished library was worth their untwining.

Tim hovered near, never losing sight of that beloved face as it shifted through expressions of awe, elation, and quicksilver sadness at seeing what was once Hiero and Apollo's sanctuary remade. As soon as they'd acquired the villainous Lord Blackwood's collection of occult tomes and esoterica, along with many more practical books on history, philosophy, and art, Tim set to work organizing the shelves. Row after row and column after column now gleamed with gold- and silver-lettered spines. Tim had acquired a few of Lord Blackwood's statues of ancient gods along with the collection, but only Bastet, Bacchus, and Arianrhod stood vigil.

He'd tucked his desk over at the far end, the better to note anyone who might enter—or sneak attack. He did tend to get absorbed in his work. Under the glittering skylight, he'd placed an Arthurian round table, around which a circle of plush chaises and divans gathered. Though the library had been gifted to him, Tim hoped it would become a headquarters of sorts, a place where their team could discuss cases, review evidence, or contemplate the darker shades of the criminal mind. A place of sanctuary and reflection away from the more brutal realities of their work.

And to properly bless the place, they'd first burn a little carnal sage.

Tim decided to play valet, moving to undo the buttons on Hiero's jacket and slip it off his broad shoulders as he acclimated himself to the changes. Tim folded Hiero's jacket and his own, then draped them over a nearby chair. Never let it be said he hadn't learned at the foot of the master when it came to sartorial etiquette. And more. Taking one of Hiero's hands, palm up, in both of his, Tim unlatched the cuff link and spread open the fabric to reveal the gnarled skin of Hiero's wrist. He swished a thumb across it, relished the sharp intake of breath. He repeated the motion on the other hand, lingered even, mapping the veins, the ridges, the fine lines on his palm, the tree-trunk rings on his long fingers. Tim wondered in which of Hiero's lives he had earned each one, or were they erased and redrawn with each new identity? One of Blackwood's books might teach him to chart the course of their relationship in the etchings on Hiero's palm, but Tim preferred the surprise. Reacting moment to moment had become something of a way of life, the only way to be for someone like his beloved Mr. Bash.

Tim glanced up, found Hiero's black-brown eyes upon him, glints of amber simmering in their depths. Recovered, then, from his earlier funk, and not a moment too soon. Tim shifted to his neck, skirting his hairline with greedy fingers and smoothing along the slender column before undoing his cravat. It slid to the floor along with his waistcoat, and Tim popped the buttons of his shirt. Hiero arched his torso to meet Tim's outstretched hands as he stroked up his chest, shrugging off his shirt and grabbing for Tim, who halted him.

Hiero toed off his shoes and took a step forward. Tim retreated a step, maintaining the very short distance between them. With an arched brow, Hiero watched as Tim undid his trousers, guiding them down to his long, lean calves and petting his feet as he shed them. These, too, Tim shook out and folded before returning to his tall, dark, and exquisite lover, who stood, confident and bare, in the glow of the gaslight. From the velvet waves of his hair to the taut roundness of his buttocks, to the scarred misery of his back to the sinuous grace of his form, Tim still felt humbled ever time he beheld his beautiful, bewitching Hiero. It swelled his heart and thickened his prick to know he was the only one permitted to see him thus: naked, hard, ready. He vowed, as he always did, never to forget how precious a privilege that was.

"How would you have me, my dear?" Hiero asked, impatient as always.

Tim stripped as he strolled in a circle around him, just out of arm's reach. By the upward jut of Hiero's cock, he no longer harbored any reservations about their imminent tangle. Tim paused as he dropped his own shirt, searing his gaze down the length of him until Hiero twitched.

"Have you? Will I be?"

They'd given themselves to each other in every possible position and fashion, save Hiero being taken. In general, Tim preferred to be commanded, but every so often, usually while Hiero sucked him into oblivion, he did crave a reversal. He never pushed, never even asked Hiero if he'd care to try it—not that Hiero had ever failed to voice his desires. If he wanted Tim in that way, he had only to ask, and as he had not done so... Still, no harm in clarifying.

Hiero's resulting hesitation told Tim all he needed to know.

"If you wish," he almost whispered.

Tim stopped his progress, went to him. "No. Only if you truly desire it."

"I do, at times." Hiero welcomed Tim into his embrace, shivered at the gentle press of their bodies. "And you, always. But..."

Tim gave him a moment to rally his thoughts, then kissed his collar. "I see no reason to hurry along. The point of the exercise, to my mind, is to take our leisure."

"And pleasure."

"Most especially that." Tim plucked a sensual trail to the base of Hiero's neck, tonguing the fragrant little notch he so loved. "And how may I best please you this evening?"

Tim thrilled at the low moan such a simple question produced.

"On your knees."

Hiero staggered as Tim led him over to one of the chaises, a larger reproduction of their faithful fainting couch, but in a less outrageous color: indigo. Stretched across its luxurious velour, he looked every inch a Persian emperor or a Mesopotamian god. Tim gave himself the role of consort, adding pillows in strategic places, an extra layer of comfort for Hiero's head and back and legs. And one dropped to the floor for his own still-creaky knees. Crafted to Tim's specifications, this particular chaise curved up under the hips, offering the recliner's crown jewels to any who might care to plunder them. Tim's gaze lingered on every one of Hiero's treasures, a connoisseur at a particularly impressive auction.

His prick, not nearly as discerning, pulsed in reminder of how long a day it had been and how very much he'd been wanting this. Hiero reached for him and teased Tim to full, throbbing hardness with his elegant fingers. His legs shook under the strain of remaining upright while being frigged by a master. Hiero thumbed Tim's slit till he saw stars. Fists balled at his sides, he tore at his bottom lip with his teeth. Any protest he might have voiced escaped as a moan. But who would refuse such singular attentions, the long, vigorous strokes his meaty hands could never mimic? The satin-soft hold his hips bucked and bucked into until the sweat slicking his chest met the seed trickling down his cock and dripped around his aching bollocks.

Too quick, Tim thought as the first starburst of pleasure erupted at the base of his back. A sharp squeeze to his balls almost amplified it, instead snuffed it out. Tim cried out—though whether in frustration or ecstasy, he wasn't sure.

"Down," Hiero commanded.

Tim dropped blindly to his knees, only realizing he'd clamped his eyes shut once he hit the pillow. A few blinks restored a much better view of Hiero resplendent on his throne, a glittery sheen of perspiration enhancing the rich brown tones of his skin. Hiero released the grip coiled around his cock to caress Tim's face. Tim leaned into the touch, parting his lips to welcome the thumb into his mouth, a pantomime of revels to come. He met Hiero's scorching gaze with a fire all his own. They flirted silently awhile until Tim could bear it no longer, pushing his hand away to claim a deep, delirious kiss.

Reignited, Tim blazed a trail down Hiero's chest before palming his cock. A few painstaking strokes had him pushing Tim's head down, playfully but insistently; the first decadent lick had Hiero crooning. Tim loved how Hiero twined his fingers in his hair as Tim sucked him, the low, desperate noises he made and his total abandon to Tim's ministrations almost as enjoyable as his thickness, the texture of him on Tim's tongue, his salt and smoke taste.

Tim snuck an errant finger down to stroke along Hiero's crease, the most he would ever permit, and was surprised by Hiero rocking against him. He cautiously explored the puckered ring of his entrance, giving Hiero every chance to warn him off. Instead he spread his legs and began to writhe.

"My dear?" Tim eased off to ask. The sight of Hiero with his head thrown back, limbs askew, wetting his lips in anticipation of being penetrated, was enough to bring Tim to the brink of climax.

"Please, Kip. Please."

Tim took him to the root as he delved inward, massaging his way to Hiero's core. Between the heaviness on his tongue and the tightness around his fingers, Tim quaked as if he were still standing, still throbbing deep in his groin, at the mercy of Hiero's powerful hand. He shed the last of his restraint when Hiero began to thrust.

With a keening shout, Hiero shot down his throat. Tim moaned around his cock as Hiero rode the wave of feeling, giddy at having brought him to such an end. Once his breaths evened, Tim crawled atop him, stiff and wanting, but Hiero and his miraculous hand soon found a pounding rhythm anew. Tim pressed their brows together, intoxicated by the fumes off Hiero's afterglow, by the mercurial man in whom he'd found his match. Basking in the tender look Hiero shined up at him, he babbled heartfelt nonsense until the fever flushed him from crown to toe tip in scarlet sensation… and he spent and spent and spent.

A whisper of a kiss brought him back down to Earth, though his senses still popped and fizzed, love drunk.

"I wish there were three of you." He flopped onto Hiero's chest, sated and utterly blissful. His sticky chest, but Tim could hardly complain of the mess he'd made.

"Dare I ask why?"

"One for each orifice."

This earned him a throaty chuckle and a naughty backside grope. "But then I couldn't have my every which way with you."

Tim applied the relevant sex-brain logic to this and snickered. "No, you'd have to share. With yourself, though, so not a bad deal."

"Spoken like a true glutton."

Tim lifted his head to look Hiero in the eyes, somewhat surprised by his comment. "Am I? A glutton?"

"When it comes to affairs of the flesh." Hiero, still not done with him, carded his slinky fingers through the thicket of his hair. "If I'd known, when first we met, how ardently you'd give yourself to our interludes, I'd have been far less suspicious."

"Or you'd have used me for my body and been done with me. And then where would either of us be?"

Hiero made a moue of displeasure. "Doesn't bear contemplation."

Tim beamed at him, hoping the look in his eyes conveyed something of his deep feelings toward Hiero, however complex they could sometimes be. He cared for him in ways too immense and unruly to be encompassed in a four-letter word—one Tim knew he had not yet spoken. But a small part of him, the part that had found the two people he loved the most in the world dying in a pool of their own blood, still fought against the tide of his softer emotions, afraid everything would be swept away again. He had barely survived that first shipwreck, near drowned by the loneliness, the emptiness of a life with no attachments. Hiero had revived more than his carnal appetites in giving Tim an oasis, a family. And reminded him of how much more he stood to lose if they could not weather future storms.

"No," Tim murmured both to Hiero and to himself as he lay his head back down. He blanketed Hiero as best he could with his shorter frame, only too aware of how inadequate a barrier against the ills of the world he proved to be. "Rest here while I work?"

"Only if I can enjoy your particular attentions again sometime before dawn."

"Now who's being gluttonous."

"One man's feast is another man's... preserves?" Tim felt, more than saw, Hiero shake his head. "No matter. I fear tomorrow will be even more trying than today, so best we be as relaxed as possible."

"Mmm. Yes." Tim hugged him tighter, anything to delay even the short walk across the room. "It does afford one a certain clarity, doesn't it? Fucking, I mean."

"Only when done right."

"Well," he sighed, kissing into the coarse dark curls over Hiero's heart. "We've yet to put a foot or sundry other parts wrong, in my estimation."

They laughed for far too long over such a silly—if compelling—notion, then fell into lazy contentment.

Dawn, in late-summer London, didn't announce itself by haloing the roofs of the eastern houses in a rosy glow, as Homer might have described it. Instead the gray clotted-cream cloud cover lightened by degrees, from soot to slate, from slate to iron, from iron to ash. Whatever coolness lingered in the air moistened with the rise in temperature until the humidity licked at Han's cheeks like a dog's drooly tongue. Still, he preferred to wait in Berkeley Square for one of his little rabbits to hop along, at least until chimney smoke above the house signaled Minnie had started on the morning baking.

Han reminded himself that Toby wasn't late. That he may not come at all. Twelve hours was rather a quick turnover for this type of information, especially since, were circumstances different, he should have made the relevant enquiries himself. He'd entrusted this to his shrewdest, wiliest, most appearances-may-be-deceiving bunny, and he needed to give him time to work his magic. Time they did not have, if the answer was the one he expected.

It was a fallacy, he knew, to think this way. A true investigator examined the facts and came to an objective conclusion. Trouble was, Han could see no other conclusion in the evidence they'd gathered but the one that haunted his dreams. And so he waited for word that what they'd thought impossible had indeed come to pass and threatened everything and everyone they held dear.

At the far end of the square, a horse-drawn cart came to a lurching stop. A rowdy pack of newsboys, a few of his rabbits among them, crowded around the back as an older boy distributed the packs of newspapers. Han whistled to one of the boys, an apple-cheeked lad named Samuel, and tossed a shilling in the air. As expected, Samuel was more interested in the brown-paper pack of sandwiches Han had nicked from the kitchen, which he exchanged for a newspaper, than the shilling, which he negotiated for news about Toby. Of which there was none.

Cheeky indeed, but Han expected no less.

So freshly printed the ink stained his fingers, Han ignored the rabble-rousing headline declaring Terriss's death a murder, instead flipping back to Mr. Devon Standish's column, a tribute to Terriss with praiseful quotes from such Strand luminaries as Henry Irving, Nellie Farren, and the like. Not the thrilling exposé Miss Marks had anticipated writing, but enough to earn her a spot on the third page.

Han flipped through the paper, searching for the rugby scores. A bold headline on page five stopped him cold.

TERRISS MURDER INVESTIGATION SUFFERS A BASH
Special commentary by theater critic C.D. Arascain

The blood of beloved stage actor Randolph Terriss had not yet been washed from the cobblestones of Bull Inn Court when Mr. Gerry Tumnus, manager of The Gaiety Theater, called on the notorious Hieronymus Bash to head a private investigation into his murder. This on the heels of rumors of dark goings-on at The Gaiety, where, in the day since Terriss's stabbing, dancer Polly Nichols was injured and a former headline talent mysteriously disappeared. For weeks now, theatrical circles have been abuzz with stories of The Gaiety's troubled change of management.

Upon taking the reins, Mr. Tumnus made a series of controversial decisions, from bringing in a homeless French company, led by noted scoundrel the Vicomte de Croÿ-Roeulx, to casting light comedy marvel Terriss as the roguish Don Juan. A mass exodus of The Gaiety's backstage talent followed.

What effect will hiring Mr. Bash have on the case, other than free publicity for all involved? The question begs an answer. This critic cannot help but think the solution lies not in the questionable methods of a detective more interested in headlines than headway, but in the triumphs of the past. Mr. Horace Beastly has not graced a stage with his capable presence since the turn of the year, the result, a source claims, of Mr. Tumnus's takeover. Mr. Beastly's Don Juan was the toast of the 1868 season. Surely The Gaiety's salvation—and renewed faith in Mr. Tumnus's managerial abilities—lies in luring Mr. Beastly back, and not in the scandal-chasing ways of the talentless Mr. Bash.

Han read the item through three times, each with more foreboding than the last. He folded the paper under his arm, relevant page up, to stop himself from overanalyzing. His gaze stuck on the swiftly disappearing stacks off the cart, the flock of newsboys carrying them to every street corner of the square, the borough, the city. In two hours, more people would have skimmed that item than would have recognized Randolph Terriss on sight the day before. People who'd never stepped foot in a theater could parrot a critic's opinion on the whole sordid plot and every one of its players, all because of two deft paragraphs. Han felt a new appreciation for the power of the press.

Abandoning all expectation of meeting with his best rabbit, Han retreated back to the kitchen of 23 Berkeley Square, where a cup of strong coffee and a slab of thickly buttered bread would set him to rights. Or so he hoped. Without a shred of evidence, he blamed himself for this latest development. Hiero's antics had always flirted with exposure, so some preparations had been made in case of a doomsday scenario. But Han, stupidly, had always expected Hiero would be the engineer of his own demise, not an enemy from without. He took the lesson to heart.

He charged in to find Tim fussing over a breakfast tray. By his rumpled but cheerful air, he and Hiero had managed a brief respite from the demands of the case, which relieved Han. He didn't begrudge either of them their moments of leisure, even in the eye of the storm. Han smiled at the sight of Tim snipping the thorns off a rose before laying it across Hiero's tray.

And yet Tim's detective instincts served him even in such a tender moment. Without so much as a glance in Han's direction, Tim shooed Minnie off to the library with Hiero's breakfast, grabbed a loaf from the bread basket, and cut off four generous slices. These he hung in the toasting frame to brown over the fire while he poured the coffee and fetched the butter. Han watched while he decided how to voice his suspicions, marveling anew at how Tim extended his care for Hiero to all the members of the household. His respect and appreciation for having been invited into their little family showed in his every action, from remembering how they took their tea to helping with tedious chores to bringing home little treats they favored. If Tim's closely detailed observations were at times unnerving—he really didn't miss a trick—the way he thoughtfully used this knowledge reassured.

Han certainly didn't object to being served the exact meal he had craved minutes after entering the kitchen, nor Tim's quiet company while they both indulged. A pauper's repast to some, Han remembered how decadent he thought his first taste of buttered bread so many years ago, behind an inn at the Portsmouth docks. If this rich, creamy spread and fluffy loaf were considered scraps, then he'd truly reached the land of plenty. Though life soon taught him how naive he'd been, he'd always crave the simple luxury of butter.

When Tim returned from putting four more slices over the fire, Han slapped the newspaper by his plate, saving his wary look for when Tim had finished reading. Tim tapped the edge of the table, a sign he considered his words with the same care he'd shown Han just then. "Not the most unexpected turn of events."

"Is there a code of some sort, perhaps?"

"None that I can see. And the message could not be clearer, no matter how unwelcome." Tim reached into his waistcoat pocket and unfurled a piece of paper, the message in his own hand. "The latest from our obsessive friend, conveyed as underlined words in a series of negative Beastly reviews."

Han's mouthful of toast lodged in his throat midway to being swallowed. "The same byline?"

Tim nodded. "The same Arascain. Though I'd heard he decamped for New York and the lure of Broadway some time ago, which does lead one to wonder..."

Han thought, with some regret, of Miss Marks and her ambition. Had his delaying tactic brought on this retribution? "On many fronts."

"Quite." Tim fortified himself with another half slice before asking, "Do you think her capable?"

Han didn't hesitate. "Of this? Certainly. Though I question whether the editors at *The Pall Mall Gazette* would permit such speculation from an untested source."

"On the fifth page."

"She did mention a struggle for her work to be recognized."

"A plausible theory, but unreliable evidence. Still..." Tim sighed, rubbed his face with his hands. "Too little time, too many variables in play. I'd wager on it being another manifestation of our specter."

"Get the heartbroken crowds clamoring for Beastly's return?"

"Just so. Tumnus would be a fool to ignore them, no matter his promises to the Vicomte. In these matters, the audience always wins. And if it's Beastly the audience wants..."

"But would there be a theater without the Vicomte?"

Tim related what they had discovered the previous night about the state of Tumnus's finances. "So, you see, if it's a choice between saving face and satisfying the terms of his contract, it's likely Tumnus will salvage his reputation first. You see the trouble?"

"He'll go back. No matter what move we make, if the audience demands it, our Mr. Beastly will return to the stage."

"Giving our fiend what he wants. Never ideal."

Han considered this. Tim's personal stake in the matter colored his view. But he also thought Tim, no matter how deep his affections ran, still underestimated Hiero's abilities. Han and Hiero, in their roughest years, had survived worse than an invisible foe.

"You think we should kill Beastly once and for all?"

Tim emitted a pained noise but nodded. "Perhaps not kill. But someone has asked a question, and we must provide an answer. Before Tumnus and the Vicomte take action."

Han sighed. "Agreed. Leave it with me."

"Actually..." Tim grinned. "For this subterfuge to come off, I fear we must read in the man himself."

"That I'll leave to you, Romeo, O Romeo."

"Deny my father and refuse my name? I very well might have to in order to persuade him."

Han chuckled. "And Miss Marks's proposal?"

"If we join her game when the stakes are this high, we'll never be able to bow out," Callie, or rather Mr. Calvin, declared as she descended the stairs. Tim rose to put the kettle on. She plunked herself in the chair directly opposite Han; he heard the unspoken en garde. "The odds will be against us from the start."

In riposte he slid the two documents over for her perusal. With her usual meticulousness, she reviewed them until Tim delivered her a pot of tea, a bowl of sugar, and one perfect Callie-style cup.

"We have an answer," Tim explained as he retook his seat. "My concern is it won't be enough."

"They've got the public's attention, you mean?"

"And will continue to milk that bountiful teat."

"With Miss Marks's help, we might be able to draw them out," Han said. "They aren't the only ones who can stir up sentiment."

"Provoke them into an error or a misjudgment?" Callie sighed. "I fear we'd fall victim to the same. With heavier consequences. We are already at a disadvantage, responding to their notes and items, never knowing when the next threat or incident will come. This will not give us the upper hand."

Their eyes locked across the table, not in challenge, but in something far more complicated. Han knew Callie would not argue a point without merit, would privilege the case over her personal desires. For the first time, he struggled to do the same. Perhaps it was the restrained way in which Miss Marks related her tale of woe; perhaps it was the echoes of his own struggle in her story, but Han wanted to defend her.

"You're right," Han conceded, taking some pleasure at the shock on her face. "If we behave as they would, we are no better."

Tim resumed his tapping, lost in thought. "Or perhaps we simply have not found the right use for her."

Chapter 11

The clip-clop of horses' hooves, each footfall like a stomp to the head, chipped away at Hiero's peace of mind as he slumped into the darkest corner of the carriage seat. A dull pressure forced him to squint every time he opened his eyes. The rain-fresh stench of London oozed through the door seams, polluting the long breaths he drank in to—ostensibly—clear his head. Even Callie and Shahida's quiet chatter, punctured by the occasional snort, pelted the left side of his face like buckshot. He needed a hot bath and a half bottle of Scotch. Barring that, a bucket of ice water to dunk his head in. Barring that, a Kip to massage away his biyearly migraine.

Not that his sweet Kip hadn't done his damndest to distract Hiero from his worry the previous night. Curled up in postcoital languor on that very cozy chaise, he could almost have ignored the day's events, forgotten the ghost's threatening words. While Kip dozed, Hiero had stared up through the library's skylight at the overcast sky, worrying that this time he'd met his match. When Kip rose to work, he pretended to sleep, comforted by the scritch of his pen and his long, ponderous sighs. Only when Kip crawled back into his arms in the wee hours had he found true rest.

And woke two hours later to what felt like an ax lodged in his skull.

As the carriage slowed, the usual clamor of passing voices grew louder. Hiero assumed this to be the migraine's next wave of assault, amplified by pounding echoes in his ears, but Callie and Shahida hushed, listening. Angus, their driver, knocked out the warning signal, a blast like cannon fire on Hiero's vulnerable senses. He clamped his eyes shut to corral his tears, inhaled slow, steadying breaths through his handkerchief as he braced for further onslaught. When a gentling hand covered his knee, he almost lost the last of his composure.

"Stay in here," Callie cooed in a tone he'd never heard from her. "I'll instruct Angus to wait around the back. Once we're done with Tumnus, you'll accompany Shahida home."

"We'll hide you away in the attic so you can rest," Shahida agreed. "Lil will be glad of the company."

With his debonair attitudes and refined airs, Hiero tended to give off the impression that he was as sturdy as a croquembouche. Even those who knew something of his history tended to forget he had scraped his nails raw climbing up from the gutter.

"Out of the question," he hissed, forcing himself to straighten in his seat.

"Anyone can see you're indisposed," Callie insisted. "You'll be of no use—"

"Save your lectures," Hiero snapped. He stole a moment to dab away the perspiration on his brow—and contain his darkening mood. "If we're to exorcise this phantom from my theater, then you know as well as I that the show must go on. I have top billing in this black little farce, after all."

Hiero desperately wanted to down the entirety of his hidden flask, but he knew it would not help his cause. Once he felt capable of enduring them, he met their pair of looks—Shahida compassionate, Callie fuming—with a defiant one of his own. He even managed a grin.

The carriage jostled. Angry fists hammered at its sides, angry voices chanted, "Justice for Terriss!" and, "Bring Beastly back!" along with racialist slogans aimed at the French troupe. Hiero almost lost what little breakfast he had hard swallowed at the movement. A peek through the curtains did him no favors. The crowd gathered in front of The Gaiety made up in volume what it lacked in size. Hiero frowned at them, wishing they would save their outrage for worthier causes. Fortunately, a mob of theatergoers didn't intimidate the way a group of, say, underpaid factory workers might have, so Silas Flint had no trouble pushing through them to rap on the carriage door.

At Hiero's signal, Callie unlatched it long enough to let him in, kicking away a few of the more zealous protesters before slamming the door behind him. On noticing Shahida's state of advanced pregnancy, Silas raised an eyebrow but made no comment. His eyes widened far more when he saw how poorly Hiero fared, recognizing the nature of his distress from the many times he'd suffered similar bouts backstage at The Gaiety.

"Coal miners at work again?" Flint tapped his temple as he fell onto the seat beside Hiero.

"Incessant, though they've long since depleted my store."

"I'd have Maggie brew you up some of her special tea, but." He shrugged.

Maggie Armitage, Hiero recalled, was a gifted fortune teller and an even more gifted herbalist, but she had decamped along with the rest of The Gaiety's crew. Yet another strike against Tumnus—not that Maggie's elixirs had ever brought Hiero much relief.

"How's the mood in there?" Callie, in her Mrs. Stoker guise today, asked.

"Same as out here, though I wish I could tell you different." Flint grunted. "Ghost's had his way with the dressing rooms. Walls plastered with everyone's worst reviews. From the French papers too."

Hiero cursed, himself far more than the situation. They hadn't been thorough enough in their search the night before, and the fiend had scored again.

"The theater was meant to be locked till our arrival," Callie said.

Another shrug. "Welcome to life between a rock and a hard place. Tumnus says black, Frenchies say white. Neither of 'em listened to DI Stoker. Tumnus came to work on the books. Madame de Casterac called a morning rehearsal. Ghost laid his tracks in early. Result: powder keg." Flint's hands mimicked an explosion. "Got what they deserve, if you ask me."

As he braced through another tectonic shift in his brain, Hiero pondered this. Flint understood the pressures of mounting a new season as well as he did. Was it any wonder their specter used these to their advantage? With so many volatile personalities involved, they would be a fool not to. Again, Hiero came back to the theory that the ghost could only be someone intimately involved in the theater community. Though someone in the company itself would be better able to mix the various elements into a fiery concoction.

The stage manager, for instance, the only link between the crew, the actors, and the management. Keeper of secrets large and small, fixer of situations rough and delicate. The ghost's identity seemed to be the only thing Flint didn't know about The Gaiety's present woes. Or did he?

As he regarded Flint's haggard face, the way his salt-and-pepper hair spiked out in every direction, and the ever-present stoop gained through years of backbreaking work, Hiero felt a traitor for even thinking Flint could be holding the strings they found themselves hanging from. No puppet master, him, but a man who'd made his career finding a way to service his betters while making sure those beneath him never suffered. Hiero well recognized the determined uptilt of his jaw, the unspoken question in his mud-brown eyes. In his own quiet way, Flint had come for the same answers as the clamoring crowd.

Ignoring the vise that ever tightened around his head, Hiero knocked on the ceiling, instructing Angus to take another turn around the block.

"How's Betty?" Hiero asked. Not his best dodge, but needs

must.

Mention of his wife never failed to bring a smile to Flint's hard face. "Good. Rounder than that one." He inclined his head toward Shahida.

"Your third?"

"Fourth. And the last, God willing." He chuckled. "I love 'em all, mind. But we've not a moment's peace between us."

"Is that why you stayed?" Callie asked. And Hiero cringed. They'd have to review how to cultivate a confessional mood once the case ended.

Flint, thankfully, preferred the direct approach. "No. Had me pick of jobs, if I'd have left. Tumnus knew it and offered double the going rate."

Shahida gasped. "Lucky."

"You work hard, you make your own luck." Flint's smile faded as he turned his attention to Hiero. "Kind of you to ask after Betty, but let's get down to brass tacks. Are you coming back?"

Hiero raised a hand to forestall the women's looks of alarm at the revelation that Flint knew of Hiero's dual identity. "How do you mean?"

"You know what I mean. Beastly. Don Juan. One night, and all this ends."

Squinting as the pain sliced and diced his gray matter, Hiero could not bring himself to answer. Because, of course, he understood. Worse, he agreed. But clearer minds had argued otherwise, and, in his present straits, Hiero couldn't argue with that.

But Shahida could. "So you'd what? Put Mr. Bash here in danger just to maybe lure this ghost out? How do you know he'll stop once he has him? How do you know he won't turn on the audience? The other actors? Kill him on the spot? And how's the coppers supposed to catch him?" She scoffed, rubbed her belly. "I don't see no good coming from giving 'em what they want."

Callie chimed in. "Believe me, Mr. Flint, when I say we've considered every option. It gives us no pleasure to play by the ghost's rules, but until we know more..."

"You're sending lambs from your very own flock to the slaughter." Flint stared at Hiero. "The Beastly I knew was a better shepherd than that."

"An easy choice when there's no wolf at the door," Hiero shot back, agony making him brittle.

"Came up together, you and I," Flint reminded him. "From the streets to the stage, and desperate not to slide backward. Have you forgotten what that's like? Kipping in the storage room so you can walk half the night. Stealing scraps from the headliners' half-eaten plates. Saying yes to everything and everyone, even if they scared you half to death. Anything to earn your place." He shook his head. "That's who you're feeding to the wolves."

Hiero could only shrink farther into his seat, wishing someone would knock him unconscious.

"That's not fair," Callie objected. "The fiend has been plotting this for months. We've only had a day. Grant us a bit more time to get a result."

"Your pardon, madam, but have you ever gone a day in your life without a proper meal?" Flint spoke soft as silk, but Callie still gasped. "Any wait's too long if there's an obvious solution."

"You know nothing about the circumstances of my life," she seethed. "But you've made your point."

Flint waited a beat, perhaps thinking they would concede. Hiero cursed all the other forces at play that held his tongue.

"I have, for all the breath it's wasted." Flint sighed, the weight of the world sinking back onto his shoulders.

"Not wasted," Hiero reassured.

Flint's gaze found some warmth for him. "You've given better performances. Must be the pickaxes."

"I must conserve my energies for the final act, as you well know. Can't give it all away in rehearsal."

Flint chuckled. "No. Shame I won't be there to see it."

With all the pressure on his cranium, Hiero thought he'd misheard. "How do you mean?"

"I'm done." Flint bowed his head, shamefaced, when confronted with Hiero's shocked expression. Here was not a man who quit on a whim. "You'll see when you get in there... The lot of 'em have gone mad with it. Screaming over who plays what part, do we open tonight or not, all while work is being destroyed, while people are dying. I won't make my Betty a widow over that lot."

Hiero began, "Silas—"

"They'll scapegoat you," Callie insisted. "You're giving them, and us, every reason to suspect you."

Flint offered his arms up for cuffing. "Arrest me, then. If you truly think I could plan and plot something this horrible, clamp me in irons and take me to the Yard."

Hiero fought for the mental focus to steer the conversation down a different path. Just as he found the words, the carriage stopped, and the crowd attacked anew. Clinging to both his seat and his sanity, he shouted above the din, "Under no circumstances. Of course you are free to go. I ask only that you speak to DI Stoker before you do so, that he might give you advice on how to take the proper precautions. And if you would be so kind as to show him the vandalized dressing rooms."

"I promise to see out the day. No more."

"Perfectly reasonable."

Hiero threw a hard, silencing stare in Callie's direction but recoiled when this increased the ache behind his eyes. He inhaled sharply one, twice, thrice, then exhaled in a rush, attempting to center himself before facing the madding crowd. After knocking on the ceiling to indicate his readiness, he rose to his full height, squaring his shoulders and tweaking the ends of his moustache. He'd stolen a page from Don Juan and, despite the heat, draped himself in head-to-toe crimson velour atop a diaphanous cream shirt. His slim-cut waistcoat betrayed a gold flame motif over black satin. Their fiend might enjoy playing dress-up, but Hiero would show him who The Gaiety's real sartorial superstar was.

"Besides, I've never known you to miss a show," he added, then shooed Flint out the now-open door.

"Make way, make way!" the embattled stage manager shouted as he beat a path through the chanting protesters. Han and Kip, who'd left early on some errand, had already cleared away something of a path. Hiero knew the little one-act he'd prepared would move the rest.

He clasped Shahida's hands. "Ready?"

"A mite better than you. Where's your twinkle gone?"

"Enlisted, alas, by the fireworks popping off deeper inside. But have no fear. Play your part, and it will return."

She scoffed. "My beau's exact words before he scarpered."

"And I renew my vow to wring his neck, should he ever come calling," Callie reassured her, locking onto her arms.

"Nah, I'm golden, Mr. Bash." Shahida chuckled. "And if I get into trouble, I have me very own nursemaid." She elbowed Callie's side.

"Who'll spirit you back to Berkeley Square the second you're done," Hiero insisted, relieved by Callie's very serious nod.

"Just cue me when you want the waterworks turned on."

Hiero beamed. "You're a marvel."

"No, just up the spout."

The laugh they all shared loosened the vise on Hiero's head a small amount, but still he had to steady himself when he turned to the door. Then he emerged to a clamor of cheers, jeers, and awestruck gasps and let his public's attention soothe the last of his aches.

Not really, but he never could resist a crowd.

With great flourish, Hiero ceded center stage, in this case the top of the carriage steps, to Shahida. A hush overswept the crowd as she pushed out of the cabin, looking convincingly meek and woebegone. Affecting a protective air, Hiero hurried her toward The Gaiety's main entrance; the whispering speculation started halfway through the crowd. By hour's end, every editor on Fleet Street would be desperate for her name, and Han's clutch of rabbits would be only too eager to chitter all her faked details in their ears.

Hiero permitted himself a wince once they segued into the entrance hall—empty, eerily silent—to rendezvous with Han and Kip. Kip furrowed his brow in concern; Hiero redoubled his efforts to appear normal. Well, his version of normal. Still, the press of a hand into the small of his back did not go amiss, however brief the gesture.

"I warn you, they're breaking their fast on thunder and brimstone," Kip said.

"At a guess, Madame de Casterac?"

"And the Vicomte. Tumnus, of course. The company scurrying around them."

"Center stage, I suppose?"

"Where else?"

"Indeed." Hiero smirked. "Not that I've ever minded a dramatic entrance."

Hiero and the team entered the auditory and ascended stage left. To Hiero's dismay, no one onstage turned in their direction. Madame de Casterac belted her complaints with long-practiced melisma, but her opera did little to overwhelm Tumnus's sharp, staccato refusals. The Vicomte struggled to temper them both in two languages as Madame de Casterac hissed asides to him in French.

Hiero struck an imperious pose, waited for one of them to approach him. Given the huge gulps of air Madame de Casterac sucked in without losing wind, her bluster still had considerable sail. He cleared his throat.

"Mes enfants," Hiero bellowed, which caught them all short, mouths agape. "I believe DI Stoker's instructions were clear as to when you might resume your rehearsals."

"You're late," Tumnus retorted.

"Only in the sense that I am lately returned to a place I left but scant hours ago."

"Monsieur Bash," Croÿ-Roeulx implored, having the good sense to claim the upper hand, "please tell this imbecile that to open tonight would be madness with the backstage a disaster and half the company threatening to quit."

"Yes, I've just spoken to Mr. Flint, who has agreed to stay on until this evening to aid our investigation into the latest incidents."

"The latest incidents!" Madame de Casterac cried. "Il ne veut rien que notre sang! How many more incidents must our reputation suffer before you catch this, this..." She broke off into a stream of French insults in a dialect Hiero did not recognize.

Tumnus pried his beady stare off her long enough to snap, "Results, Mr. Bash. Do you have any? Or are the papers right in that you're all show and no talent?"

Hiero struggled not to roll his eyes. Only he was allowed to make bad puns. After a final confirming glance at Kip, who gave reluctant nod, he waved Tumnus, Madame de Casterac, and the Vicomte forward. No one moved. With a sigh, Hiero performed an insistent assembling gesture. They dug in.

He snapped his fingers and pointed to the ground. "You may prefer to shout your troubles to the rafters, but I'll not air the results you demand in front of the entire group of suspects." Chastened, they gathered in a tight circle. "Through interviews and various other evidence, we've learned that the focus of the ghost's obsession is your former leading man, Horace Beastly." Croÿ-Roeulx and de Casterac glowered; Tumnus's eyes popped. "Note that I say 'focus,' not 'target.' It's possible that the ghost means to pave the way for Beastly's return. It's equally possible they seek to lure him here to trap or harm him in some way."

"You see!" Tumnus crowed. "I was right to call on him."

Hiero raised a quizzical brow just as Madame de Casterac

screeched, "You had no right! The role of Don Juan is mine! I will not be upstaged by—"

"You sent for him?" Hiero interjected. "When?"

"As soon as I finished reading *The Pall Mall Gazette*," Tumnus replied. "A rather enlightening piece, I'd say, by Mr. Arascain."

Hiero shrugged. "Everyone's a critic." Opening his side of the circle, he waved Shahida forward. "Mr. Tumnus, may I present Mrs. Horace Beastly."

They stared at her, stunned. Shahida attempted an awkward curtsy, then collapsed into sobs. Tumnus recoiled. The Vicomte's eyes glimmered with tears. Madame de Casterac crossed her arms under her breasts, smug.

"Your letter." Hiero took no little satisfaction in rejecting the man who'd ended his theater career. "Returned to sender, I'm afraid. Mr. Beastly's sailed for fairer shores."

"Sailed?" Tumnus looked adrift. "To where?"

"America." Sobbing Shahida drew the word out to fifteen syllables. "Says he'll send for me when he's got work. But what am I supposed to do now, I ask you, with this one coming any day and…" She heaved a shuddering breath. "How can I cross an ocean with a young'un? Leave me family and all. He's abandoned us, I say! He's…"

She threw herself to the ground with a frightening amount of vigor, clinging to Tumnus's leg and snotting on his shoes. Tumnus's thigh twitched as he repressed the instinct to kick. Madame de Casterac snickered into the knuckles she pressed to her lips. A proffered handkerchief from the Vicomte saw him dragged down to his knees. Shahida flung herself into his arms and proceeded to soak his shoulder. He patted her delicately on the back, avoiding Madame de Casterac's evil eye.

Only his ever-pounding head stifled Hiero's laughter.

Hiero clapped his hands. Han came forward with the "documentation" he and Kip had procured that morn.

"A bill of sale from the London ticket vendor who booked Beastly's passage west. Another from the train he took to Portsmouth." Han presented each item to Tumnus in turn, unsmiling but eyes agleam. "A written statement from the harbormaster confirming that the boat left the harbor three days hence, and that everyone on the manifest boarded. And anecdotal testimony from Mr. Neville Radcliffe, noted theater patron, who happened upon Beastly at an inn and bought him a farewell drink before waving him off at the dock."

Tumnus looked as if he wanted to rip their evidence to shreds. Instead he cleared his throat. "And why have you spent the better part of a day tracking down someone who has left the country?"

Hiero clicked his tongue. "Surely one who appreciates Mr. Arascain's sensational arguments has imagination enough to figure it out."

"Mais c'est évident," Madame de Casterac scoffed. "Monsieur Beastly was cast out of his theater and refused the chance to reprise one of his greatest roles. Of course that made him suspect number one."

"And now that he has been eliminated, and our preliminary interviews have concluded, I will turn my attention to... other promising suspects." Hiero saturated his words with so much threat they all but dripped from his mouth. "Unless you prefer I hand over the case to the Yard?"

"Il n'en est pas question!" Croÿ-Roeulx objected, easing Shahida into Callie's waiting arms and stomping to his feet. He didn't tower over Tumnus, but he had enough of a height advantage to intimidate. "Monsieur Bash is in my employ, and, per our contract, the artistic decisions also fall to our company. Tonight we are dark once again, to allow Genevre time to rehearse *her* Don Juan. And so that Monsieur Bash can continue his investigation. Tomorrow, at noon, we will meet again to see where we are. Agreed?"

All murmured except for Tumnus, who tossed the evidence in

the air, turned on his heel, and stalked off.

"I'd take that for a yes," Hiero quipped, and his audience indulged in some tension-bursting chuckles.

They hammered between his eyes till he saw stars. Though that didn't prevent him from shooing Shahida and Callie back to the house, winking at Kip and Han as they followed Flint backstage, or sneaking off with the Vicomte for a private word.

Only Horace Beastly had been sent to bed. For Hieronymus Bash, it was on with the show.

Tim paced the corridors under the stage, wishing for the solitude of the library at Berkeley Square and cursing himself for it. While he and Hiero had been at play the night before, the ghost had wreaked havoc, regurgitating critics' bile onto the walls of every dressing room, staining key pieces of set furniture and back drops with fake blood, and shredding the work schedules in Flint's office into a thin layer of paper snow. They would lose the entire day documenting every squiggle and speck, and for what? Even while Tim's instinct whispered that this would bring them no closer to catching the killer, the logical part of his brain shouted that the only way to proceed was to put everything in order. And so he paced, hoping to exhaust the weaker impulse, to clear his mind until he saw the way forward.

One thing did prove painfully clear to him now: all roads led to Hiero.

Was the killer's obsession any different from his own? Again and again, Tim had made disastrous decisions, all to protect Hiero. The suppression of the notes. The choice not to resurrect Beastly. The early end to their search the night before. Even now, in the midst of berating himself for his distraction, half of him worried over Hiero's health, whether he could focus enough to steer the suspects in the right direction. The only advantage to all this was that he and his enemy both acted with the same intent: to win Hiero's attention. But Tim was damned if he could see the value in that for their killer.

He came to the trap door where Polly Nichols, the dancer, had fallen. Contemplated for a moment the giant two painted on the floor. The ghost and Hiero inhabited the same world, one of high drama and artifice. Despite the events of the past year, Tim was accustomed to more common criminals: thieves and blackmailers, fraudsters and fortune-hunters. Unsurprising that he felt so out of his element. His only guide through this hall of mirrors was Hiero, still a mystery and a half himself; Tim struggled to find the truth behind the illusion.

But how to shift the game to force their fiend to play by Tim's rules? Perhaps Tim's biggest mistake came in thinking he could.

Too itchy with annoyance to keep still, he started down another corridor. Officially, Tim waited for Han to make sketches of the vandalism so they could reconstruct it at home. Unofficially, Tim sought to assure himself no other traps lay in wait for the unsuspecting members of the crew backstage. But given the mazelike layout of the entire Gaiety structure, Tim began to consider whether to call in a few constables from the Yard to help with the search, and whether he could do so without alerting Quayle to his problems with the case. He felt somewhat consoled by the fact that he was still the only detective in London uniquely suited to solving it. Not that Quayle would hesitate to call in the rank and file should Tim make a hash of things.

Reason enough to resolve the matter as quickly as possible.

He woke from his latest musings to find himself at the door to the costume vault, propped open by a rather intimidating dummy dressed as an executioner. Tim recognized the outfit from Hiero's final Gaiety play, *Let 'em Eat Ham*, a *Hamlet* burlesque set during the French Revolution. If memory served, one of the backstage crew had played the silent role. By the breadth and build of the costume, Tim wondered if it had been Silas Flint, and made a mental note to ask Hiero later.

Sounds of weeping echoed up from the deeper recesses of the vault. Alarmed, Tim chased them down to behind the privacy screen in the dressing area, where he found Marius sobbing as he stitched together a magnificent gown. The back of the garment had been slashed to ribbons. Marius attempted to mend it by using the leftover fabric as stripes across a new layer. A basket of similarly damaged costumes sat on his right while a few repaired pieces hung off the screen to his left. By the redness of his fingertips, he must have been working for hours, with hours more ahead, on dresses and waistcoats and jackets he'd already completed before the ghost struck.

Tim might have wept too.

"Dear me," he murmured, just loud enough to get Marius's attention. The words felt entirely inadequate, but Tim couldn't think of another way of alerting him to his presence.

"Ah, Timée." He exhaled a shaky breath, forced a smile. "*Qu'est-ce que je vais faire?*" The French words resonated with a deep desolation the English translation—What am I going to do?—simply didn't possess. All at once, Tim longed for those golden years in Paris, racing through the ruelles and nicking baguettes from the food stalls and playing pranks on the street artists, the grande drame of life in the City of Lights.

"Carry on." Tim pulled up a stool beside him, not sure how a physical gesture would be received. "What else can you do?"

"A very English attitude, that." Marius chuckled as he wiped tears from his cheeks. "But I have to ask myself all the same. First we lost the original Gaîté, then the entire Boulevard du Crime, then that connard Offenbach made us orphans anew. And then years of travelling from city to city, vagabonds with no place to call our own. And now finally here, to the damp and the fog in August, for pity's sake, and still someone wants to be rid of us…"

"It is a little de trop. I sympathize."

"I do not doubt it. I still cannot believe Madame Amaranthe…" He pressed a finger to his mouth to stifle another sob. "But you seem to have found a way to cope. Please, share some of your wisdom. I'm in great need of it, as you can see."

"Would that I had gained some wisdom through the years. All I can say is that the anger fades and the sorrow diminishes in time. But nothing ever takes it away."

"Not even your vocation?"

"Ah, well." Tim laughed, sheepish. "One does feel useful, on occasion. Especially now that I've partnered with Mr. Bash. Our team is like a little family. Not unlike the Vicomte's troupe, I imagine."

Marius scoffed. "I believe you mean the minions of that celebrated tyrant Genevre de Casterac."

"Not popular, is she? You'd never know it from her rallying cry."

"Before her public, any public, yes, of course. Liberté, égalité, fraternité. And she is trying to woo Tumnus—not into her bed, but into giving her creative control over the theater. So she has not been quite as Marie Antoinette as normal. But no one in the English company has any other language, and so they do not understand her critiques."

"I take it that's a generous term for them."

"That word should not be used in reference to her." His eyes spilled over anew. "You see this?" Marius petted the gown on his lap, hem pins and all. Tim wondered if he could feel hot or cold, given the thickness of his calluses. "Not the work of the fantôme."

Tim started. "Are you certain?"

"Absolument. I had Mr. Flint change and double the locks yesterday. Too many treasures are kept here, and the ghost had already struck once. Everything was in order when I came to work this morning. I went to help with the chaos outside, and when I came back…"

"Did you see her enter or leave the vault?"

"Non. But it is not the first time. And her critiques when she first saw the finished costumes…" He pointed to the pattern he'd been stitching. "She wanted more stripes."

Tim nodded, chewing on this new information. "What has she said about the sets, the props?"

Marius sighed deeply. "I will say only this. Nothing she approves of has been touched."

They shared a knowing look, broken by Marius's sniffle. Tim offered him his handkerchief. Marius raised a hand to refuse but stopped when he saw the patch of cloth. Seeking Tim's permission with a glance, he unfurled it, admiring. Like any gift from Hiero, it was a handsome thing: silk with a discreet fleur-de-lys pattern in minty shades of green. Tim fought a blush as Marius scrutinized it, a somehow more intimate action than if he had blown his nose.

A master of textiles, Marius must have recognized the quality of the piece and would question its provenance. And make the correct assumptions. Tim schooled his features, but to no avail.

"I see you have not been as lonely as I thought." Marius reached for Tim's lapel and slid the handkerchief back into the inner pocket of his jacket. "Much to my dismay."

Tim opened his mouth but could not find the words to gainsay him. Though they'd both been young and inexperienced, their time together in Paris had not been entirely innocent. His eyes flicked to Marius's pouting lips. A flash of their first, fumbling kiss lit up Tim's mind.

"No," Tim admitted. "Not of late."

"So it is a true partnership you enjoy with Monsieur Bash?"

Tim hesitated. He knew he tread on thin ice, confirming such private information to a suspect. He had no idea if his boyhood friend had grown into a man of substance, but neither could he lie to a friend.

"We are indeed well matched in many areas."

Marius nodded, his doll-pretty features tinged with sadness once more.

"Eh bien," Marius sighed. "If his efforts have so improved your sense of couture, I cannot complain. And certainly to see you again has made my time on this cold island all the more tolerable. I hope he will not object if we spend a bit of time together once you have rid this theater of its ghost?"

"He cannot possibly. And I would like that very much." Tim gave his arm a comforting squeeze. "This cold island may not compare to the thrills of Paris, but it does have its delights."

After fetching Marius a pair of fingerless knit gloves to protect his hands from further abuse, Tim made his excuses and went to check on Han's progress. Preoccupied with weaving what Marius had said—and not said—about Genevre de Casterac into the grand tapestry of the case, he paid little mind to retracing his earlier path until he turned a corner and—

A cloaked figure blocked the corridor before him. Black military uniform. Burgundy gloves. Red skull mask. And an ax. A bloody, dripping ax.

Only too aware of the gross inadequacy of his truncheon, and his own fighting skills, against a guillotine on a stick, Tim pulled out his warrant card.

"Scotland Yard!" Tim shouted, praying his voice carried to Han. "Surrender at once! Drop your weapon at once!"

Any hope Tim harbored that the figure was one of the background actors waiting for their cue sank when they raised the glinting blade high. Tim inched forward, repeated his command, wary of losing any limbs but unable to retreat. The lord of misrule had created this favorable coincidence, and Tim would be damned if he left anything else up to chance.

"Come for me, have you, devil?" Tim taunted. "Or should I call you 'Phantom'?" The figure slashed the blade through the air but did not strike. Tim crept ever forward, stowing his warrant card and unsheathing his truncheon. "A neat trick, that, scaring them all into submission. You'll find I'm not so easily cowed." He stared into the figure's black, bottomless eyes, searching for any sign of life. "Put down the ax. You must see you're done for."

Tim halted just shy of striking distance, truncheon clamped between his fists. The drip of some fresh victim's blood plopped on the floor. The figure could have been a statue—they didn't move, didn't appear to breathe. The red skull dominated Tim's vision, a crackling white light seeming to emanate from its eyes.

A jerk of motion. The ax flew. Tim dodged, dove. Heard the whisper as it sliced over his head. Looked up in time to see the swish of cloak around the far-right corner. Pushed up and raced off.

With no heavy cape of fabric to weigh him, Tim quickly closed the distance. But the ghost proved nimble, vaulting over obstacles and slipping around tight corners with practiced ease. Tim grumbled as he ran, wishing he knew The Gaiety well enough to track the fiend's route, set a trap. Instead a game of three-pawed cat and portly mouse played out within the underground maze, with neither able to escape or pounce.

When that telltale rasp began to thicken his breaths, Tim barked out the foulest curse he'd ever uttered. Though he kicked his legs for more speed, his still-recovering lungs betrayed him. A warning cough choked off his breath. Undaunted, he spit on the floor and kept running.

Ahead, the cloaked figure snapped open one of the backstage traps, yanked down a ladder. Tim lunged with all his strength, hoping to smash them against the rungs, but his breath cut out. He stumbled, wheezed, collapsed at the base of the ladder.

As Tim clawed at his necktie, a black streak soared over him and up to the stage, after the ghost.

Han. All was not lost.

Chapter 12

*H*an leapt over a gasping Tim, up the ladder and onto the stage above. The stunned crew, in the midst of changing scenes, pointed toward the auditory, where a phantom figure dashed up the center aisle toward the pit exit. Han veered left, slaloming around actors and stagehands before breaking into the staircase. Taking the steps three at a time, he climbed to street level, battered through the royal exit onto Catherine Street, and charged toward the pit exit doors a half block down. Avoiding the noontime crowds stole precious seconds from his advance.

The ghost blasted out the pit exit doors. Han lunged, missed them by an arm's length, somersaulted over a pair of perambulators. A polite nod to the nannies, and he raced for the Strand. The cloaked figure blazed a path of terror down the crowded thoroughfare. Han, losing ground, shifted into the traffic, preferring to dodge carriages and cabs than take his chances with pedestrians. This limited his view of the ghost, who might dart into a shop or alleyway at any moment.

A clear path opened up before him. Han redoubled his speed. The ghost didn't tire. Fear of capture fuelled them, which Han wielded to his advantage along with his height and endurance. But the fiend had ruthlessness on their side.

At the traffic-dense intersection with Southampton Street, Han dared a hard turn into the figure's path. The ghost sidestepped his attack and plowed straight into the fray, spooking all the horses. Han bounded over a toppled hansom, slid between the wheels of a stalled cart, and shot out under the legs of a rearing horse. He glanced up to see a hoof clobbering down at him before diving for the sidewalk. Angry shouts squalled behind as Han found the phantom leapfrogging over signs and hissing at punters as they ran toward the alley that led to Bull Inn Court.

A confrontation at the scene of the crime? Were they luring him in, knife concealed until the last moment? Would his body be the second bloody tableau in the place Terriss perished? If so, they would have to be deft. Han had more than a few tricks up his sleeve.

But the ghost barreled past the alleyway, indefatigable. Snarled at a newsboy who shoved a pile of papers in their way, then crossed the street.

Their first mistake.

Guessing their destination, Han powered over to the corner of Durham and the Strand, the dust and dirt giving his longer strides extra purchase. He skidded, leg out, just as the figure turned. He clamped his feet around their heel; they slammed onto the cobblestones. They attempted to kick him off, but Han reeled them back by the boot, grabbing for their mask. An elbow to the chest winded him. The fiend tried to reach for their... knife? Pistol? Han never found out. With a twist and a snap, he dislocated their arm.

They roared. Han punched a fist into their back, pinned them down. He searched for weapons as they squirmed and jabbed. Only then did Han notice the crowd of surly punters forming around them, pint-holding patrons of a nearby pub. Their fight had stopped traffic—a pair of red-faced drivers abandoned their charges and stomped toward them.

Han's instinct told him to forget the mask. Whatever face hid beneath would do little to convince these ornery onlookers that he, a "foreigner," was in the right. The Red Skull, however, might save him a night in division lockup, if not the pummeling about to beat down upon him. He missed the click of the razor unfurling until it slashed his hand.

The fiend twisted away from him, flipped onto their feet, and flew toward the tunnel to the Adelphi Arches. A heartbeat behind, Han ran after them... only to hit a wall of onlookers as they disappeared into the shadows. One of the brutes shoved him with such force Han landed hard on his back.

"That's Terriss's murderer gone free!" he shouted. "Fetch the constable!" He thrust a pointed finger in the ghost's direction, swallowed back his fury at not being able to follow. The trouble that currently obstructed him would triple if he entered the Dark Arches in the ghost's wake.

"Look at this 'un, eh?" another of the brutes drawled. "Thinks he's a copper."

"Crawl back to your den, boy," a third sneered. "Leave the streets to us Londoners."

Han grappled to his feet, stood his ground. "The constable," he insisted.

"Shove off," a fourth hissed, spitting in his face. "'Fore we send you back from where you come. In a sack."

Han snapped. He snatched the pint out of his hand and poured it over his head. The others charged, but he was ready for them. He clocked his elbows into the jaws of his side attackers and kicked out, bollocking the front assailant. Three more lunged, wilier than the first round. Han punched with his wounded hand and gouged with the other. He spun around, quick and lethal, engaging all six at once, knowing if they caught him by the arms, he'd be beaten to death.

But sometimes a small measure of vengeance fed the soul in ways capitulation never would. He'd survived being press-ganged onto a boat and a year fighting off a mercenary crew; he would survive this.

When finally his attackers lay scattered around him, bruised and groaning, Han ran over to the very edge of the tunnel. His cut hand streamed a blood path behind him. The stench alone warded him off, a mixture of bilge water and charnel house, to say nothing of the thousand knives lurking in the dark. A constable's whistle sent everyone, onlookers and assailants alike, scurrying off to lick their wounds or beg innocence.

Han grunted, fell to his knees, hands raised. Wondered if he'd be in for that beating after all once the constables got him to the station house. Cautious footsteps approached, the unmistakable snick of a truncheon being unsheathed Han's only warning. He braced himself anew.

The crack of a gun caught all of their attention. A carriage barreled down Durham Street, coming to a stop with a whinny and a squeal. Han chanced a glance over his shoulder, permitted himself a small smile when he spied Angus at the reins. Callie, or rather Mr. Calvin, launched out of the cabin as soon as they stopped, shouting at the constable who hovered a few steps behind him.

Han blocked out the details of their discussion, concentrated on catching his breath. He almost flinched when a gentle grip cradled his arm. Thankfully, Callie took no offense.

"You're hurt." After sacrificing her handkerchief to his cut hand, she helped him to his feet. He waited beside her as she instructed the constable to call for reinforcements and block all access to the tunnel, deftly name-dropping Superintendent Quayle. His body still thrumming with energy though his limbs ached, Han retreated to the carriage.

He collapsed across the seat, letting out a huff of frustration now that he was alone. Their phantom was no doubt back in their lair, savoring their success. Soured somewhat, he hoped, by the need to relocate their arm. He nested his head on the soft cushions, wishing...

He woke to Callie's scrutiny as she dressed and wrapped his wound. Though she took pains to keep her touches clinical, Han found himself longing for the curl of her finger around his, a stealth caress. A flicker from a candle he'd always have to snuff out.

Tugging at her bottom lip with her teeth in that inimitable way, Callie whispered, "I'm so very sorry."

"Whatever for?"

She opened her mouth, shut it, struggled for words. "The world, I suppose."

"Ah." He shrugged. "The price of tea and spices."

"It doesn't bother you?" She shook her head. "You might have caught them."

"More likely I would've been kneecapped as soon as I entered the tunnel. Everyone who skulks under the Dark Arches risks the same. Everyone's a mark."

"The perfect hideaway, then."

"For our fiend and so many others."

Callie sighed, and Han got the gentle attentions he sought when she clutched both hands around his own. Her scarred, ruddy fingers, which told the real tale of her character, still dainty compared to his haymakers. He read many things into that connection: worry, frustration, and vulnerability, but also care, succor, resolve. He held fast, wishing he could draw her into his arms.

But he didn't know, not really, if she would welcome it. And he didn't have the strength to let her go if they started.

"Always ten steps behind," she mused, frowning. Still holding. Squeezing, really. "And able to disappear at will into a place no one will follow. A ghost not only in name."

Han allowed himself to rub a thumb over her knuckles.

"What were your impressions?" Callie asked, her investigative spark relit. "Were there any details about them that stood out?"

Han rallied his focus back to the case. He must have lost more blood than he realized. "They were slight. On par with our Mr. Stoker, but with less muscle. They fought hard and ran fast, but there wasn't much power behind their hits. It was easy to overwhelm them—they were saved by their wiles and our audience."

A raised brow. "You pulled your punches?"

"And their arm out of its socket," Han insisted. But he thought better and exhaled roughly. "Strategy. But also..."

"Safe." She squeezed harder, inadvertently reopening his wound. The pain helped.

"Less violent. Than I might have been, if we were alone. Than I was after."

Callie let their twined hands drop onto the seat cushion. Growled low in her throat. "Damned ignorance, which might have cost someone their life."

With a final squeeze, Han slipped his hand out of hers. "The story of the world."

"How do you endure it?"

He did look at her then, baldly, intently, in a way he'd never been to her before. Perhaps the incident ripped something open in him; perhaps her first show of tenderness drew him out. Han let her see behind his mask, the death by a thousand cuts he suffered through each day and the bone-deep will that helped him survive. The rage-baiting knowledge that he was one of the lucky ones, him and Hiero both. "What choice do I have?"

She did not flinch. She did not cower. But her ice-blue eyes glistened as she beheld him, and that helped him harden his resolve.

He would never let her suffer at the hands of the world.

A clang. A crank. A burst of steam. Hiero watched as the Vicomte's manservant, the fussy little gnome Jean-Georges, performed a ritual as complex as a tea ceremony whilst brewing him a headache remedy. And, it should be said, the Vicomte's midmorning café au lait. Upon hearing Hiero was poorly, Croÿ-Roeulx, ever the gentleman, postponed their meeting and ordered he take an hour's repose on the plush settee in his office. Grateful—and aching, which served no one—Hiero had indulged in a dark, silent hour and was the better for it.

Now upright across from the elegant Vicomte, so regal in even this drab office setting he might have been sitting for a portrait, Hiero felt halfway back to himself. He'd refused a cold compress for his brow—Croÿ-Roeulx's compassion likely didn't extend to damp hairlines and melted makeup—but regretted it now as pinpricks of tension, and the occasional stab, still needled his skull. The spiked tisane Jean-Georges presented him with went some way to revivifying his senses, and the espresso chaser jolted him back to wakefulness. Just in time to intuit that the gracious Vicomte had lured him with sugar but knew how to crack the whip.

Jean-Georges bustled over to his small writing desk in the corner, back turned to them but pen at the ready. Hiero admired Croÿ-Roeulx's commitment to fair negotiations. With a written record, one could rarely be swindled. It also gave him an idea how to survive this little tête-à-tête with his dignity intact.

Hiero swigged back his espresso before commenting, "Very fastidious, your little monsieur. If I may be so bold, where did you acquire him?"

"He's part of a family of servants who have been with mine for decades. Centuries, perhaps. Loyalty, you see, attracts talent."

"So you run your house as you run your theaters?"

The Vicomte chuckled. "Pourquoi pas? You can only teach what you yourself learned, and I learned from the very best."

"Your mother?"

"Bien sûr. But also a certain Madame la Marquise of my ac-quaintance." A wistful look shrouded his handsome face. "She was a marvel. One of those rare birds who can live in society, but also above it."

"Hiding in plain sight, you mean?"

"Oui. A paragon of discretion and therefore a trove of secrets. Similar to your Lord Blackwood, but not quite so..."

"Mercenary?"

"Non, le mot grec. What is the word...?"

"Ah. Hubris."

The Vicomte nodded. "I received my second and best education at her side. And, of course..." He casually threw open his hands, letting Hiero supply the rest.

He wondered if Jean-Georges wrote that down.

"And now you have Madame de Casterac." Hiero enjoyed how Croÿ-Roeulx fought to control his expression. Still, he didn't seem terribly offended. "You have a type, I think, monsieur."

The Vicomte chuckled. "Touché." He retreated into his coffee, emerging with a cloud of foam on the bottom of his mustache. He extended the moment by patting it dry with his handkerchief, a master class in stalling. Hiero waited him out, his suspicions piqued. "Genevre, of course, is more of a partner than ma chère Irma perdue."

"Or would be, if Mr. Tumnus had a bit more imagination, I presume?"

Even one of Croÿ-Roeulx's charm permitted himself a grimace of extreme distaste at the mention of the Draconian manager. He coughed, likely to mask a curse. But instead of launching into the tirade Hiero had hoped to provoke, he asked, "And you, Monsieur Bash. Where do you stand on the question of loyalty?"

Hiero poorly concealed his surprise. "I value it in my closest associates: Stoker, Han, Calvin. But when it comes to suspects... as a matter of honor and justice, I must be loyal to no one."

"Even if that one is paying your fee?"

"Is this a confession, monsieur?"

The Vicomte laughed, a heady, alluring sound. "Of a more earthly sort than our menacing spirit. Tumnus, this morning, grumbled about the ghost breaking into his office, but... Perhaps I am a bit la tête dans les nuages, and certainly I am no detective, but I asked myself why the ghost would make such a disaster of the dressing rooms and leave the office untouched. And so I thought—"

"That you would press me for information." Hiero kept a light tone but a shuttered expression. He did not appreciate being a pawn in another game, not when their fiend had been toppling knights and rooks in hopes he would make the ultimate sacrifice. Once upon a time, Hiero might have cared who ruled The Gaiety. Now he just wanted to keep all the pieces on the board.

"You must see how he lacks the proper esprit d'artiste."

Hiero tread carefully, not wanting to air Beastly's personal griev-ances.

"I do. And as a patron, I find it scandalous." He took a steady-ing sip of the tisane. "But I am here as a detective, not a spy. I cannot share anything with you, even as my employer, until the murderer has been stopped."

Croÿ-Roeulx, being a shrewd negotiator, heard the exception, not the rule. His eyes glinted with amusement and, better, satisfac-tion. "But once our fantôme has been sent back to hell..."

"One hopes, for their crimes. But—"

Jean-Georges raised his head, gasped, raced for the door. After an endless moment, he shouted from the hall, "Monsieur, venez! Venez! C'est le fantôme!"

Dubious, Hiero rose slowly to his feet, but Croÿ-Roeulx hurried into the corridor. A bit of playacting for his benefit? The Vicomte wouldn't be the first demimondaine to turn a tragedy to his advantage by faking an incident. Hiero had made a career of it in a former life. Then the distant clamor reached his ears, and he trailed Croÿ-Roeulx down to the stage.

By the time they hit the boards, the frazzled crew had retreated into the wings, gathering in tight gossip circles to soothe each other. A stagehand broke off from his group to inform the Vicomte that Madame de Casterac had locked herself in her dressing room. Croÿ-Roeulx threw up his hands and shot an expectant look at Hiero before going to deal with that situation. At a loss as to how to proceed—not being a trained investigator, and with no evidence to speak of—Hiero searched around for one, or any, of his associates. Inconspicuously, or so he hoped.

Alas not. As he strolled to the center of the stage, his natural habitat, the whispering crew members all turned to watch him. Normally, Hiero wouldn't mind any and all eyes on him, but the mistrusting tenor to their scrutiny made things a bit awkward. He could see no body nor injured party. The disarrayed furniture signaled they had been interrupted mid-set change. But by what? Or whom? Where was the blood, the mess, the crime? And why did everyone look to him before they bothered to explain themselves?

A too-familiar wheeze echoed up from behind one of the tables. Kip crawled out of an open trap hidden there—or, rather, the obsequious Marius Lamarque carried him out. An octopus might have been more conspicuous about where on Kip's person he laid his arms when, really, a shoulder's support would have sufficed. To add insult to indisposition, Lamarque murmured soft encouragements in Kip's ear as he helped him up the ladder.

Burning, Hiero wanted to shout, *The man lurched through dirt tunnels to catch a baby killer mere hours after being poisoned. He does not need your bloody encouragement to carry on!* Then he saw the state Kip was in and rushed to his side.

"Stoker!" Never let it be said Hiero could not keep in character in times of crisis. "Here, set him on this chair."

"No, I must..." Kip gasped between tortured breaths.

"Sit!" Hiero snapped his fingers, and a stagehand appeared at his side. "Fetch DI Stoker tea with lemon and a hot compress." He caught the man's arm as he turned. "A splash of brandy wouldn't go amiss."

When Hiero returned his attention to his Kip, he saw Lamarque petting his back. He bit back the first five remarks that sprang to mind, kneeling before Kip to lay possessive—and concealed from all but Lamarque—hands on his knee.

"What's happened?" he mirthlessly asked Lamarque.

Who took a beat to respond, staring as he did at Kip's trembling hand when it covered Hiero's. Lamarque ceased his petting, but was that a glint of challenge in his eye as he answered?

"Hélas, I did not," he replied in French, needlessly sotto voce. "I heard a commotion in the hall. As Timée had just left me"—did Hiero imagine the taunt in his raised brow?—"I went to see if something was wrong. I found him this way, collapsed at the base of the ladder."

"Ghost," Kip managed before a coughing fit seized him.

"Chased you? Fought you? Struck again?" Hiero forced himself to ask, wanting nothing more than to spirit them away to a quiet corner, that he might properly tend to his Kip.

Once he'd recovered his breath, Kip made a running gesture. "Han. In pursuit."

Hiero sighed, relieved that all was not lost. "A minor victory, then. Perhaps your bravery has avoided us another incident. Let's find you somewhere private to recover, Sir Gawain." The stagehand returned just in time for Hiero to ignore Kip's silent protests. "Ah, your tea." Kip grabbed the cup, breathing in some of the remedial steam before testing a small sip. When Hiero's glare did nothing to swat away that gadfly Lamarque, he thanked the stagehand. "You're a very capable young man. Please assemble your confreres and assure them everything is in hand. With any luck, my associate will return with a suspect, and all this will be at an end."

Once certain the crew's attention had been diverted and the Vicomte still played nursemaid to Madame de Casterac, he refocused... only to discover Lamarque fiddling with Kip's cravat.

"I realize the rules of decency are somewhat relaxed in this environment, but I think even The Gaiety's loose-trousered crew might cry public indecency." When this failed to elicit a response from Lamarque, Hiero tried a blunter approach. "What in Thalia's name do you think you're doing?"

"Making space for the compress." Lamarque blinked at Kip and Hiero, innocent as a babe in the woods. "It's meant to go on his chest, is it not?"

"In private, yes." Hiero shoved his body between them to offer Kip his arm. He did not miss Kip's hiccup of laughter as he latched on to him. Or how Lamarque fell onto his arse. "Fetch another tea, if you mean to be of use."

On instinct, Hiero guided them to his former dressing room, only realizing his mistake when once again confronted by the ghost's anti-Beastly collage. Kip didn't seem to mind, leaning against the wobbly remnants of the dressing table.

"You might have been kinder," he rasped after clearing most of the congestion from his throat. "He's my oldest friend."

Hiero scoffed. "We birds of prey recognize like. Would a falcon share its nest with an eagle?"

Kip attempted to chuckle. It came out as a reedy hiss.

"Well, this falconer will only ever have one feral bird on his arm. So it might do not to let lesser breeds ruffle one's feathers." Though still working for breath, Kip tugged Hiero into closer quarters. He wriggled fully onto the high dressing table that he might have the reach to tangle his fingers in Hiero's hair, though did not attempt a kiss. Hiero tended to prefer to be the one to steal Kip's breath away. "Especially when one possesses such a magnificent plumage."

Ah, but Hiero wanted that kiss.

"How's your head?" Kip asked.

"Same as your throat." Hiero set about finishing the work Lamarque had started, pressing his lips to the delicate notch at the base of Kip's neck before applying the now-lukewarm compress. "One of Minnie's poultices would not go amiss."

"As would one of Aldridge's scalp massages." A smile quirked the corner of Kip's mouth. "Say when, and we'll bugger off home, fiend and friends forgotten."

"Will buggery be on the menu?"

"Perhaps, if Han can make water into wine."

Hiero frowned. "Not the ghost, then, that led you on such a merry chase?"

Kip let out a hyena-ish grunt, planted his brow on Hiero's shoulder. "Who can say? Anyone can steal a costume. Anyone can wear a mask. Anyone can skulk about the shadows in a lunatic's wake. Anyone can stir up chaos whilst chaos reigns." He shook his head as he righted his posture. "When illusions beget illusions, how are we to seize hold of the truth?"

"By luring our fiend into a trap of our making."

Hiero's suggestion appeared to confirm something for Kip, who met his gaze with an eager look. "Agreed. But how?"

A sharp knock at the door startled them apart. Han strode in nursing a bandaged hand, Callie on his heels. By the black expression he sported, the fiend had evaded him. They had the story off him, the conclusion of which sucked all the air out of the room. Hiero turned to Kip, a weak promise to invent some sort of ruse to trap the ghost tempting his tongue, but found him grinning. With genius or madness, Hiero couldn't say.

"What?" Callie demanded. "What possible method of the Yard's could possibly remedy this... this..."

"A bluff," Kip replied with renewed confidence. "A bluff of such rage and clamor that it might just scare our ghost away."

Chapter 13

The scorch of the late-afternoon sun spared none of those assembled in Durham Street in heavy navy coats and chinstrap helmets. As constables distributed gold armbands and lanterns, Tim gazed across the sea of Metropolitan-Police blue with a mixture of pride and dread. Astonished by the variety of division letters he read on their collars—most from as close by as A and one as far as F—he nevertheless understood, by the fire in their eyes and the set of their jaws, that some had answered his call to arms in order to catch a killer, and some just spoiled for a fight.

If Tim thought for a moment the seething black of the Adelphi Arches hid any innocents or impoverished souls struggling to survive, he would never have called on Quayle to organize a roust. He had only been down there once before his time with the Yard, lured by a soft word and an agile tongue into the worst beating of his life. The incident had prompted him to take up boxing, and later to accept the offer to become a constable. But he never forgot the wild-eyed wicked faces of those who lurked there; the grabbing hands and the bruising kicks; the packs of shark-toothed men with more scars than skin; the rutting cries and the angry smacks; the sludge of dried blood and festering mud and old bones that swamped the ground.

Since then, the Dark Arches had become a legend in their own right. Every peeler on the beat had a tale of their own about the place, a subterranean purgatory so dangerous to policemen that

Commissioner Winterbourne issued an unofficial dictum that officers could not enter in groups of less than ten. When Tim proposed his—rather desperate, if he was honest—idea to Quayle, even the notoriously rule-bending superintendent expressed misgivings about sending valuable men down to, as some called it, "the first level of hell."

Still, it came as no surprise that so many among the constable and sergeant ranks volunteered. No better way to prove one's mettle than diving headfirst off a cliff into a savage sea. To emerge unscathed would earn them any promotion they could want... though not even organizing a mass arrest of the city's most slippery and violent criminals could earn Tim the respect of DS Littlejohn, whose pale, pudgy face, slack with boredom, stood out among the red-cheeked rabidity of his fellows.

As Tim waited for the whistled signal confirming the other two exits to the Arches were blocked by smaller teams and a fleet of Black Marias, he skimmed the worst-offenders list Quayle had hastily compiled as an excuse for the raid. While Tim didn't expect the likes of gang leaders, smugglers, and thieves to be lying about, waiting to be nicked, they might get lucky. But he saved all his prayers for evidence of where their red-skulled fiend hung his hat. Having tarnished his own reputation among the rank and file long ago, Tim's only ambition was to spook their phantom into missing their mark.

"Quite the assembly," Callie, in her Calvin guise, remarked as she angled the brim of her hat against the sun. "One does wonder who are the lions and who are the lambs, to see them prowling about so. Some appear to be foaming at the mouth."

"More of a question of wolves and... meaner wolves, really." Tim frowned. "It's not unheard of for the Met to recruit among the more gentleman rogues."

Callie rolled her eyes. "Robin Hood has done us all a great disservice."

"No argument here."

"And yet you've thrown in your lot with us."

Tim shrugged, unwilling to give voice to his true answer with so many ears around. "You've brought your bosom friend?" he asked instead, meaning her revolver.

"The lady herself, and her handmaid." Callie tapped her ankle on a streetlamp.

Tim nodded. "I know this question won't be well-received, but—"

"Aim for an arm or a leg, only as a last resort." Despite the smartness of her retort, her face sobered. "I've never killed a man. I don't intend to today."

"Which is precisely why I'd have no one else by my side."

She scoffed at that, but her color rose. "You mean Han's the only one with a hope of talking Hiero out of whatever nonsense he has planned while we're gone."

They shared a knowing chuckle.

"Guilty," Tim admitted. "But you're best suited, not second best. And if the need calls for it... don't hesitate. Shoot to kill."

Three short whistle bursts echoed up from the Thames-side exit, followed by three more from the ramp on Lower Robert Street. Lanterns raised and truncheons ready, the officers fell into formation: two parallel lines between which a few detectives would walk, scanning faces in the crowd for anyone of interest. If they caught a high-level criminal, they'd be pushed to the center and whisked into one of the Marias for later questioning at the division house. Tim and Callie would bring up the rear, interviewing anyone the officers found with knowledge of the Red Skull.

Tim stood at attention at the mouth of the tunnel as the peelers marched into the black, acknowledging each and every one with an encouraging look. Already the stink of fish guts and gore clogged his nose and mouth, though the camphor sharpness of the lantern oil cut through it some. Already the shouts of the earliest officers rang up from the tunnel's depths. Tim hoped no one useful would escape before he and Callie breached the entrance.

Typically, DS Littlejohn numbered among the last in line—in his mind, to monitor Tim for any sign of weakness. But Tim recognized the flash of cowardice across his smug little face at the first screams.

A final gulp of foul air, an affirming glance at Callie, and they began their descent.

The sallow lantern light reflected off the brickwork arches above them but illuminated little else. Grimy and slick, the cobblestone road was soon swallowed by sooty sand, remnants of the beach and coal-offloading dock the Arches once were. Rustlings and rumblings behind the walls tensed the men. A few succumbed to nervous titters. In the distance—one strained to tell how far—the brawling had already begun.

Tim forced his breathing into a slow, even rhythm as they navigated several blind turns. The air thick and putrid, he cursed the rasp he already felt in the back of his throat. Callie shoved a flask in his hand. Brandy, a care package from Hiero. He took a grateful swig, exchanging it for his new truncheon.

The ground beneath them evened off as they came into the main hall, a block-long barnlike structure with stabled alcoves where various criminal types plied their trades. A second lower path ran along the seaside wall, high above which a few unreachable portholes cast in stark shafts of light. The first wave of constables had weeded out a few likely suspects, cuffed facedown in the muck. Others lived out petty revenges, taking on a gang of wily toughs in one of the alcoves, or small mercies, such as herding a trio of dollymops out the Durham Street exit, to avoid the Marias.

Callie halted the hard-faced women with a whispered word and a finger to her lips. Tim caught a couple of pickpockets by the ear for an interview under duress. They gleaned nothing of use from either group. Undaunted, they worked their way through the hall, begging brief words of those who weren't snarling or punching or cursing, and some who were. Tim narrowly avoided the slash of a concealed blade as he questioned a feral-looking thug who tried to barter, then fight his way out of an arrest. Callie neatly clocked a vicious man unconscious while three officers struggled to subdue him.

Tim had begun to wonder if the Dark Arches deserved their reputation—though what a difference infiltrating with a small army made in that regard—when Littlejohn beckoned from one of the unlit alcoves. Wary of whatever trap Littlejohn had no doubt set for him, Tim grabbed a lantern and signaled to Callie. He waited until she'd unsheathed her lady to creep into the shadows that shrouded the alcove. Callie held her weapon so low in her gloved hand that not even Tim could tell she was armed, but her solid presence at his back bolstered him, especially when the light cut down to the weak flicker of two lanterns.

What little flame there was found nothing to reflect off save Littlejohn's smug moon of a face hanging over the terror-blown rounds of the witness's eyes. Cowering into a corner where twenty years' worth of drunken sots had pissed or shat or worse, the man had been so badly beaten he didn't look fit to stand. With bulbous swells on his otherwise gaunt face and an arm at an impossible angle, the man had suffered more than Littlejohn's brute interrogation technique. Tim noticed crusted brown stains on his shirt.

Old stains, long dried.

A twisted arm.

Welts on his face that could be bruises, but also might be...

Tim permitted himself a second's rage at the idea that Littlejohn might have cracked his case.

"Found this on him." Littlejohn tossed an object to Tim, who struggled to catch it, armed as he was with a truncheon and a lantern. He did not miss his nemesis's snicker... which died out as Tim bent to retrieve the item.

For good reason. Tim nearly choked on his tongue when he

raised the red skull mask into the light. Behind him, Callie hissed under her breath, a warning to tread delicately Tim didn't heed.

"DS Littlejohn, give your report."

He snorted but complied with little fuss. "I was searching this here piss hole when I almost fell over that one... er, the suspect. He was cradling that like it was his last drop o' whiskey."

"And did he require discipline, or did he hand it over willingly?"

Littlejohn looked at the ceiling and appeared to count back from ten. Tim knew all his tells, but also that he wanted to get back into Quayle's good graces. A sterling report from Tim could make the difference.

"No discipline." Littlejohn put a mocking inflection on the second word. "No point. Can't hardly stand, can he?"

"Fetch a stretcher. You'll need to see him to the Yard, once we're through."

"But—" Littlejohn swallowed back a protest, but his angry eyes spoke all. He exhaled a long, bullish breath, then asked, "We've caught the blackguard, haven't we? Limp arm, gone a few rounds, mask..."

Tim couldn't help a bit of condescension. He wasn't made of stone. "It's possible, true, that this man, weighing little more than a plucked chicken and with a face more worse for wear than a burlap sack is the mastermind behind the murder of Randolph Terriss and the slew of crimes at The Gaiety. Or... Mr. Calvin, would you care to conclude?"

"The killer dragged him here, beat him up, broke his arm, and shoved the mask at him to make us think he did it," Callie explained to a red-faced Littlejohn.

"It ain't me!" the frightened man yelped. "I ain't done nothin'!"

"Shut it, you!" Littlejohn bellowed before rearing back toward Tim.

He cut off the DS before he could open his mouth. "As you can see, our witness is in a great deal of pain and likely scared out of his wits. Now see to your duty and alert DI Woolsey that he'll require a doctor."

"So you can take the credit?" Littlejohn growled. "This is my collar."

"And you'll conduct the secondary interview, at the Yard, once his arm's been wrapped."

That concession took Littlejohn off guard. Little did he know Tim would get all he needed from the man in minutes. But the DS dove back into the chaos behind them all the same.

Reg Dover—the name the man gave—couldn't add much more to his tale than what Tim had already guessed. Nor could he give a half-decent description of the person who'd done this to him. One step ahead at every turn, their fiend had beaten poor Reg until his blood blinded him, then shoved the mask under his slack arm. And they meant for Tim to figure this out since their ghost hadn't even bothered to match the injuries Han dealt them.

The ghost mocked him, same as Littlejohn. Terrorized the company at The Gaiety for jollies and wrong-footed anyone who got in the way of their sick game. Their unseen puppet master predicted his moves as surely as if they'd stuck a stick up Tim's arse. But how to wrench everyone free of this riddler's control?

Tim barely repressed the hot, hairy need to rip the mask in two. Instead he gave it a tight twist… and felt an object within. He gestured for Callie to raise the lantern to shine into its hole, where he discovered a note emblazoned with a bloody number three.

They exchanged a pregnant look. But just as Tim reached in to pry out the note, the world exploded.

A distant blast threw a shock of light into the alcove. The hard shove of a panicked crowd rocked Tim and Callie into the far feces-smeared wall. But the press of bodies proved short-lived as everyone sought to escape. Callie bent to shush Dover's animal whimpers while Tim peered around the alcove's edge into a scene that rivaled the Peterloo Massacre.

Two masked, howling brutes lobbed flaming bottles of alcohol at the straw beds and bundles of rags in the inhabited alcoves. Enraged, many officers abandoned formation to battle anyone they could get their hands on, suspicious or not. Some denizens of the Dark Arches fought to save their hovels, bucketing sewer water onto the fiery pyres. Others brought out wrenches and pipes to fight the police or free their cuffed compatriots.

Hellish plumes of smoke swooped out the portholes, blocking the last of the sun. A barrage of cries and curses muted the pleas of the few good-intentioned constables attempting to order the chaos. Tim watched, helpless, as the flamethrowers targeted a sergeant attempting to evacuate some of the pickpockets. The burning man jumped into a deep trough of water but did not break the surface.

Tim could not tear himself away from this disaster of his own making until Callie shouted for help. "What in blazes is going on out there?" she demanded.

"The inevitable." Tim sighed. He kneeled by Dover and Callie, hoping the darkness of their alcove would discourage anyone from hiding there with them. "We must fly."

"Littlejohn?"

"Brawling or cowering outside, by my guess. He won't be coming back in if he made it out. They're working to block the exits."

"Then how will we...?"

"Recall why you're best suited for this task." Tim didn't miss the proud sheen to her expression as she cocked her revolver.

Dover screamed. Tim clamped a hand over his mouth. Not terribly reassuring, he knew, but they could not afford any intruders before they made their move. He brought his gaze level with Dover's crazed, bloodshot eyes, willing him to feel Tim's reassurance.

"We mean you no harm. You'll not survive the hour, let alone a night, if you stay. Will you come with us?"

Though he still quaked with fear, Dover nodded.

"He can't walk," Callie helpfully remarked.

"I'll carry, you defend." Tim shifted to Dover's uninjured side, praying he only required a crutch. Already he could hear the wheeze whispering under his breaths, feel the scratch in his chest from the spreading smoke. "But first I must ask you, at the cost of our lives... is there another way out?"

Dover let out a sobbing wail when Tim began to lift, his pain convincing him in ways Tim never could.

"Left," he groaned, and so they went.

They avoided the worst of the fighting by delving deeper into the Arches. Tim dared a glance over his shoulder, only to see most of the officers retreat back up the Durham Street entrance, with the most ruthless remaining to slug it out with the throngs of bludgers. The rest flooded toward the other two exits, even if it meant most certain arrest.

Callie attempted to navigate them away from that constant, clamoring stream of people but got them stuck between two columns of crisscrossing arches. When she turned to address Tim and Dover, someone grabbed her from behind, knife to her throat. She smashed the butt of her revolver in his eye. He snarled. She twirled and stuck the barrel to his forehead. A dozen hands grabbed for her lady, so she shot him in the foot.

This cleared a circle around them. Dover rapped on Tim's arm, pointed toward a man-sized sliver in the wall behind the two columns. But when Tim veered them in that direction, the crowd surged. Callie fired two rounds at the ceiling, loosing a shower of rock that only half covered their escape. It had to be enough.

The passage widened after they squeezed through the initial gap, Dover precariously balanced between them. Ten endless, choking minutes had Tim wondering if he led them to their doom—just as he had left his fellow officers, his guilt shouted—when they came upon a ladder beneath yet another trap door.

At Dover's melodic knock, locks slithered, a slab that sounded like stone shifted, and a square in the ceiling cracked open. They

emerged, battle scarred and weary, into the cloakroom of the
Caledonian Hotel.

With a strong grip on his shoulder, Han steered Hiero away from
the restaurant, specifically the lounge area, of the Caledonian Hotel.
By the redness of his eyes and the sheen of perspiration on his brow,
Han knew his friend still suffered his headache and would take every
opportunity to drown it in liquor. A desperate man's remedy, that,
useful during their years on the streets but only to numb the pain.
He'd thought it best they escape The Gaiety (and the ghost's
attention) awhile. What better than a simple errand, or so Han
hoped, that nevertheless provided a much-needed change of scene:
tracking down the Vauquelin sisters, who had not presented
themselves for rehearsal that afternoon.

That this also brought them a stone's throw from the Adelphi
Arches, where two much-beloved team members searched for clues as
to their fiend's next move, was not lost on Hiero, who had agreed
with only a hint of the usual sturm und drang. Though given what
Han had seen of the Vauquelins and their indulgences, he'd need to
short leash Hiero during their interview to avoid chemical tempta-
tions. While Hiero had never flirted with chasing the dragon, Han
well recognized the sort of pain his friend had endured throughout
this case, and it bit deeper than a migraine's fangs.

They paused beside a luggage rack to consider their approach of
the reception desk.

"Old roué or long-lost paramour, do you think?" Hiero asked.

"I wager the Vauquelins have their share of lecherous admirers.
This will require something more delicate."

"Remind me again why we simply don't sneak up there and tap
on their door?"

"Fancy our chances with two well-regarded ladies who might raise the alarm at any moment, do you?"

"I can't imagine they have pristine reputations in this or any hotel, given the scene you encountered the other night."

"Nevertheless," Han insisted and welcomed Hiero's concessionary nod. They'd talked their way out of too many such incidents—and had the scars to prove it—for Hiero to continue to protest.

"A formal declaration, then. Let us hope he doesn't read the papers."

Hiero swanned over to the clerk in question, unfurled his card, and soon earned them an escort to the third floor courtesy of the concierge.

They followed a willow branch of a man—slim, with the balletic grace and energy essential to someone in his position—up the plush blue carpet of the grand staircase. Hiero made a show of "oohing" and "ahhing" over the decor while Han observed their surroundings attentively, scanning for anything out of sorts. Four of their suspects resided in the hotel. In his opinion, they had not given the place or the threat posed to them here due consideration. He and Hiero may have gone the officious route by announcing themselves to the staff, but anyone in the theatrical trade could find a way to slip in and out unnoticed by even the nosiest doorman or chambermaid.

As evidenced by the glimpse of a certain someone that stopped him short on the second floor. Well, two someones, since Han recognized the man exiting one of the rooms far down the corridor as Dr. Lazlo Grieg, a physician employed by most of the theaters on the Strand for the little emergencies that might hold up production. The second someone hovered in the doorway to her... room? For a blink too long to avoid Han's notice. If, indeed, she had been attempting to avoid him.

After signaling to Hiero, Han broke from their procession to stall Dr. Grieg, who had treated Horace Beastly for many a minor ailment over the years and might blow the whole thing up. Han spent their brief, tedious conversation considering whether perhaps Grieg was their culprit—too haughty, he decided—and wondering how to approach Miss Maxine Marks, who did him the favor of waiting for him just inside her door.

Once he heard Grieg's footsteps descend the stairs, Han made his way down the corridor and stopped just beyond the entrance to the room Miss Marks... occupied? Invaded? She leaned against the doorframe in open invitation, though to what, Han couldn't have said. Or perhaps didn't want to know. That way he wouldn't have to refuse.

Han almost laughed as he took her in: the crimson red of her evening gown, the garden of gold and rubies around her neck and décolletage, the silk and lace of her long black gloves, the twin daggers pinning up the honey waves of her hair in almost a parody of a jezebel. Or, in his culture, a symbol of immense good fortune.

Han couldn't afford to disregard either interpretation. "Client or interview?"

She chuckled. "Am I under caution?"

"I daresay. This is the third time I've happened upon you in as many days."

"Ah, but this time it is you who is intruding on my affairs."

"You've taken a room?"

"My former apartment is, as you might recall, the scene of a crime."

"And is your tenancy sponsored?"

She let out a throaty laugh. "Yes, in fact. By Randolph Terriss. Three years of faithful service. But you'd guessed as much."

"I tend not to put much stock in guesses."

"And I don't particularly care for conversing in hallways." She moved an inch closer to the door, leaving barely enough space for him to pass through. "Won't you come in?"

"You well know I can't."

"If you've ideas about my reputation, I assure you, I have none to protect."

Han took some time with his response. "I don't care to be counted among those who refuse to treat you as a gentleman would."

"Chivalry." She raised a brow. "Not unexpected." She had a way of looking at him as if he were the rabbity upstart and she the vulpine investigator. He wished he minded it more. "Not entirely welcome."

She lunged forward so that Han had no choice but to catch her close. Miss Marks stole a moment to stare into his eyes, her own glinting with mischief and something more, before claiming a kiss.

Soft, pliant lips pillowed his. Need surged within him, not just carnal hunger, but for connection. He seized her, carried her into the room, and crushed her against the wall so hard that the bones of her corset bit into his chest. A breathy moan parted her lips. Her mouth, unctuously sweet, beckoned him. Han deepened their kiss, drinking his fill of her, relishing the tussle of lips and teeth and tongue that was only an amuse-bouche in a ten-course banquet.

Han gave his lust rein, letting her suck his mouth and yank his collar and work her thigh against his groin. He lingered too long nipping her ear because the thought that she wanted him—for herself, from the first—lit his wick like nothing else. Miss Marks shoved him, hard, at the opposite wall, then pounced anew, her kisses twice as voracious, making quick work of his trouser buttons with her deft hands. She reached out to shut the door...

...and he blocked her, pulling off her bottom lip to stare into her eyes. She arched a pointed eyebrow again in question, in challenge. Han let his gaze flicker over her scandalously red mouth, wishing it could be otherwise, then gently nudged her back.

"Most unwelcome," Miss Marks murmured, then retreated to her side of the small corridor that led to her parlor.

Han took a moment to right himself, not just his clothes, but his mind. Miss Marks, of course, required no recovery time at all.

"Why have you come?" she demanded, not quite concealing her

hurt at being rejected.

Han expected no different and therefore wondered if it was a ruse. "On inquiries. I happened to be passing and saw Grieg depart."

"The doctor, you mean? Do you know him?"

"As all denizens of the demimonde do. A man renowned for his discretion has many friends."

"But you serve a gentleman, not a demimondaine."

"As I've said, I serve no one," Han insisted. "But in the past I've had many masters, most unkind."

Miss Marks sighed, let her mask slip. Han caught his breath at the longing in her eyes. She forced her chin up, her back straight, and met him with the cool, mocking defiance he found so alluring. "Well, now that you're here, have you and your colleagues considered my offer?"

Han smiled to himself. The team had not explicitly discussed the matter since he first brought it up. But given that morning's headlines, he thought a test might be in order.

He gave a curt nod. "I have an item for you. If it appears in Mr. Standish's column tomorrow, we may proceed further."

With a quick wave of her hand, Miss Marks called for the information. But Han saw how she vibrated. "Agreed."

"Mr. Horace Beastly, former headliner at The Gaiety Theater, was seen in Portsmouth, boarding a steamer bound for Canada. Rumor is he's been lured across the pond by the Theater Royal in Montreal." He debated including the more salacious rumor about Beastly's "pregnant wife" but preferred to keep Shahida away from any trouble that could bring about.

Miss Marks scoffed. "Convenient. Especially for a certain madame."

"Very. Although I hear Beastly left before the trouble started."

"Or so he wants everyone to think."

Though Han knew he was on dangerous ground, he held steady. Hiero might be the fabulist in their partnership, but he could finesse with the best of them. "Perhaps. But I question whether an actor's vanity would permit him to create a villain of such nefarious repute and not claim credit for it."

She laughed despite herself. "And what actor could devise such a scheme? They are fed their wit by writers, after all." He lost her to that inner space of deduction. He recognized the expression well, having observed it on Tim almost daily. "Look to Mr. Standish's notes in the dawn edition. You'll find your item."

"Then I'll have more for you tomorrow."

"More." Miss Marks stalked with purpose toward him, stopping just inches from his chest. "But not enough."

His skin tingled in anticipation of her touch, every limb itching to reach for her, to resume their torrid interlude. Han hugged the wall. He wanted to fall to his knees, hitch up her dress, devour her. But if his time as an investigator had taught him anything, it was to resist such impulses.

And so he performed a quick bow and made his retreat.

Lost to reviewing the past few minutes over and over in his head, Han started when a hand fell on his shoulder as he loitered at the edge of the stairs. Hiero, on his way down, knew better than to ask what had delayed him, and by his sly look, read too much on his face. Or perhaps he noticed the trace of lip color Han hadn't been able to rub off entirely.

"Happy hunting?" Han asked before any insinuating comment could be made.

Hiero shook his head. "Not a quail or a Vauquelin in sight, alas. Theories?"

"None good."

"Indulge me."

"Given what I observed last night, they're as likely to be in an opium den or a house of ill repute as the salon of one of London's most generous supporters of the arts."

"The concierge is of the opinion that they departed for The

Gaiety without his notice."

"Astonishing. The concierge can be bought."

It wasn't often Han made Hiero smile, and not the reverse, and he felt his own grin stretch at this small victory. But the moment was short lived as Han watched the truth of their predicament sour his friend's mirth.

"Perhaps one of your little hares could"—Hiero mimed hopping—"make the rounds of the warrens."

Han nodded. "Constable or quiet word, if they're found?"

"Constable." Hiero made a moue. "I've never been one to frown on la vie bohème, but where one's safety is concerned..."

"And they missed rehearsal," Han added, following Hiero's line of thought all too well.

"One of the deadliest sins," he agreed.

Hiero waved them over to the cloakroom as soon as they alighted in the lobby.

"As to that other matter..." He turned to confront Han face-to-face, the action belying his earlier nonchalance. "Any word?"

"None."

Hiero shut his eyes, breathed deeply. "And you still believe—"

"That caution rules the day? I do." Reminded of earlier, Han frowned. "I must."

A series of three melodic knocks from inside the cloakroom broke the tension. The attendant disappeared into the rows of coats. A few moments later, the scrape of sliding stone could be heard, and the crack of a heavy door. Han drew Hiero against the wall by the far side of the counter, ears pricked. A muddle of conversation and an odd creaking followed, accompanied by an unholy stench.

Before Han could wave Hiero away that he might stealthily investigate, the counter lifted, the half door swung open, and Tim and Callie staggered out carrying a battered man between them.

Chapter 14

An arm for an arm
A Bash for a Beast
Make the exchange
And so will reign peace
Otherwise they'll know
Naught but terror and pain
A game without end
And who will they blame?
The bearer of this missive
Is but a pawn in my plot
Do what you do best
And leave him to rot
But wait for my present
What or when, who can say?
If this gift doesn't teach you
Others will pay

*H*iero flung the note across the table to keep from tearing it to
shreds. The blood-encrusted envelope—Dover's blood, no
doubt—emblazoned with a red-brown smear of a three glared up at
him when he went to smash his head onto the glossy, seamless
hardwood. He threw it as well.

On the small divan across the parlor, a doctor attended Dover, their murmuring voices rising in pitch and volume with every shift of the patient's arm. Hiero could not glare at a man in pain, especially one suffering, as the note suggested, due to Hiero's failings, so he directed his stare at the bovine DS Littlejohn, who worked his jaw as he watched over the proceedings.

Employing every one of his feline wiles to retrieve the note and envelope without Littlejohn taking notice, Hiero moved to the window instead of returning to his seat. The scene in the street below resembled a rowdy funeral. A procession of Black Marias waited to pull up to the exit to the Adelphi Arches, each to be filled with rioters escaping the underground blaze. Clouds of smoke hung around the tunnel mouth, stifled by the humidity and blending into the descending fog. Those bruise-fisted, black-coated constables not charged with herding prisoners clogged the street. Thrumming with the aftereffects of the battle, they cackled and whooped and tossed their helmets in the air as if they'd survived Waterloo.

Hiero turned his back on that hellscape, one thankfully not of his making, searching for a decent strip across which he could pace. Between the minuscule parlor and the two-person dining area, there was none to be had. The reception clerk had generously donated the room for Mr. Dover's recovery and Kip and Callie's refreshment in exchange for everyone's discretion regarding the secret entrance to the Dark Arches in the cloakroom. Of course, the only room available was the least accommodating. How Kip and Callie were getting on in the adjoining bedchamber with water closet, Hiero hadn't enough imagination to conjure. In a different mood, he might have passed the time guessing at the depth of Kip's blush.

But the note tainted everything. After tucking it in an inner pocket, he felt it like a stone over his heart, crushing the last of his patience. The only thing that stopped him serving it up to a candle's voracious flame was the chance it contained evidence. Evidence of something other than Hiero's continued inability to put an end to the suffering of the members of his former company.

Method and reason could no longer shield him. He must embrace the madness.

With no warning, the door swung open. A snide protest died in Hiero's throat at the sight of Superintendent Julian Quayle, bushy browed and glowering as ever, lumbering toward DS Littlejohn.

"Report, Sergeant."

Littlejohn stammered, darting his head about like a puppy that had piddled in the corner, when the doctor replied, "He's stable. Malnourished, so I make no promises, but he should make it to a hospital."

"Golden. Lucky you were here, Doctor…"

"Lazlo Grieg, sir. I make myself available to all the guests of the hotel."

Quayle grunted. "A few of my officers could do with a look over, if you've time. Send your bill to my office at the Yard."

"With pleasure, Superintendent."

Without even a glance at Littlejohn, Quayle stomped over to Hiero's side of the room. Though he resembled a gorilla that had squeezed its face too long through the bars of its cell, he appeared to be… smiling? Hiero shifted into a louche but defensive pose.

"Stoker about?"

"He should be done detoxifying momentarily. Though I wouldn't care to wait. The stench was exceptional."

"That's the job. Gets your hands dirty. Might've done him some good."

"Our record speaks for itself."

"*Your* record?" Quayle scoffed. "Tell that to the punters crying for your neck."

"And have you come to escort me to the noose?"

"Don't tempt me," Quayle bristled. His beady eyes locked on Hiero, searching his face for who knew what sign of treachery or worse. But even a brute like Quayle knew such impressions were no better than reading tea leaves. He was, as much as Kip, servant to the facts. "Tell Stoker I want a report on today's maneuver and an update on your case on my desk in the morning. And..."

Surprised at his hesitation, Hiero prompted, "Hmm?"

"Job well done." Quayle sighed, sheepish. "We'll make a copper of him yet."

By the time the door slammed behind him, Hiero still hadn't picked his jaw up off the floor. But then he felt the sink of the note into his breast, past the layers of flesh, into the bones that encased his heart. He watched, numb, unseeing, as they carted poor Reg Dover off to hospital, just another fly in their eight-armed attacker's web. Hiero recognized that he too was snared. Only a matter of time before their fiend came to suck him dry.

He heard the door to the bedchamber open but did not turn. For the first time in his adult life, Hiero struggled to school his features. He heard those familiar footfalls on the carpet behind him, sensed that cocooning presence near but could not bring himself to put on a brave face and draw Kip close. Not with Dover's screams fresh in his ears. Not when someone near suffered through worse, their cries unheeded, their pleas useless, waiting for Hiero and his associates to stumble over their remains.

He dug the note out of his pocket and thrust it blindly in Kip's direction.

"Ah." Kip gently pried it out of Hiero's hand. "I did wonder where I'd mislaid that."

"Perils of..." Hiero bowed his head. He could not even retreat behind his wit. "Another victim. Undiscovered."

He heard the crackle of parchment as Kip brought himself up to speed. "This gift, you mean?"

"The very one."

Kip's momentary silence spoke volumes. "We can't proceed on assumptions."

"Call it intuition, then."

"Or Dover was the fourth, and this present is meant for you. To hit at you directly. Another item in *The Pall Mall Gazette*, or a perverse gift from your very own secret admirer."

Kip encircled his waist from behind, resting his head just beneath the nape of Hiero's neck. Body to body, heart to heart, as they often lay after being intimate. Hiero longed to give over to his embrace. To speak the words caught in his throat for weeks before their fiend forced his silence.

But how could he, with a bloody four writ on an unknown someone's bleak epitaph? How could he give his Kip everything when he already knew how this would end?

"Any and all admirers will be shown the door." Hiero rallied, as he ever did, tugging Kip around to his front. "And you're the keeper of my perversions."

"Don't I know it." Kip caught him in a long, heartfelt kiss, then stepped back that Hiero might inspect him. "Decent?"

"The smell, certainly, is much improved."

"I'll send to the house for another suit."

"On its way."

Kip chuckled. He perused Hiero's face with his moss-green eyes, crinkles of concern limning their delicate lids. Hiero wished he could spend the evening running a fingertip through the fans of his coppery lashes. But the time for such indulgences had ended.

"Discouraging, this latest note, I know," Kip remarked. "It's meant to be. But my time under the Dark Arches illuminated certain things. More than expected. We can finally start eliminating suspects."

Hiero couldn't conceal his shock. "How do you mean?"

"The witnesses to our masked bandit's flight," Callie explained, exiting the bedchamber in a jacketless version of her Calvin guise.

In perfect synchronicity, Han entered through the main door with her new jacket hanging from his arm. "Not the most concrete proof of innocence, but it's a start."

Kip cleared his throat. "Locations," he declared as he escorted

Hiero over to the divan. A snug fit even with only the two of them, Hiero thought, until he realized Kip kept deliberately close, pressing their legs together as he opened his notebook and rested a hand on Hiero's thigh thereafter. "Whom did you observe, and where?"

Hiero fought to swallow the lump in his throat before contributing, "The Vicomte. We were conversing in his office when the first cries were heard."

"His motive is weak," Han said. "If he wanted control of The Gaiety, he would buy it."

"And it doesn't stand to reason that someone from elsewhere would come here to play out such a complex game," Callie added. "That holds for most of the French company, I'm afraid. Unless..."

"They're all in it together," Han finished. "An orchestrated drama to spook Tumnus out."

Kip squeezed Hiero's knee as he said, "But the notes aren't addressed to him."

"Nor to anyone," Callie pointed out. "Not even the first. It was received by a Gaiety ticket vendor, who sent it through to our Beastly proxy, who brought it to Berkeley Square."

Hiero stared at her. "How do you know this?"

She shrugged. "I enquired."

"How did they know where to send it if the envelope was blank?"

"'One will fall every day Horace Beastly stays away.' Ergo..."

Hiero huffed with indignation. "Glad to see they've taken my safekeeping to heart."

"Be that as it may." Kip steered the conversation onward. "A strike against the Vicomte is that he resides in this very hotel, along with Madame de Casterac and the Vauquelin sisters. Now perhaps our fiend exited the Arches through Lower Robert Street or Thames side after Han's pursuit, but it seems too great a coincidence that a hidden exit lets out here, where four of our suspects reside."

"Five." Han said. All eyes focused on him. "I encountered Miss

Marks during our search for the Vauquelins. She has let a room here."

Hiero recalled the near fugue state he'd found Han in after his brief disappearance. An idea, a delectable idea, began to form in the wiliest corner of his mind. One he tucked away for later use.

"With Terriss's money?" Callie demanded.

"She implied as much."

"How convenient for her."

"Especially given her journalistic aims," Kip said. "Once again she's positioned herself at the center of the action. But is it because she is the cause of it, or merely seeks to benefit? She's worth a deeper look."

"Agreed," Han replied. "I've given her a test. An item in tomorrow's *Gazette*. We'll see the result."

Kip shook his head. "Such a woman would have a wide web of connections. Chase it down."

Callie smirked. "We will."

"Now to our prima donna. I believe she was among those on the stage when the ghost ran through?"

Hiero, pondering other matters, woke to say, "Croÿ-Roeulx was called to her side when we arrived, but I did not see her for myself. Han?"

"I had eyes only for the Red Skull."

"Quite. Still a possibility, then." Kip flipped to the list of suspects at the front of his notebook. "Tumnus?"

Hiero and Han consulted each other with a look, then said, "No."

"Flint?"

"No."

"And I was aided by Mr. Lamarque..." Kip scanned up and down the page. "Which leaves the curious case of the Vauquelin sisters."

Callie raised a finger to draw their attention. "While I do not think we can entirely discount anyone at this time, I... would challenge the notion of their guilt."

Han chuckled. "I concur."

"The pair of you." Hiero snorted. "They are actors. Dissimulators by trade."

"Takes one to know one," Kip quipped with a fond smile in his direction.

"Precisely my point," Hiero replied.

"And we return, as we must, to motive." Kip clapped his notebook shut. "Arguments could be made for each suspect in relation to their desire to seize control of The Gaiety." He clasped Hiero's hand between his. "But why target you, my dear? To what end? You were out of the game, and they have taken great pains to bring you back in. If we discover the reason, we unmask our fiend."

A depressed silence fell. Hiero met his ardent gaze with one of hesitation. He'd never been one to state the obvious, to take a direct route when a circuitous one would do. But was Kip, his genial, dogged Kip, truly deaf to the only relevant suggestion on how to proceed?

"Then let me." Hiero gripped the hands that held him. "Let me lure them out and end this."

The knock that shook the door, though measured, startled them all enough that Hiero missed Kip's reaction. With reluctance, he slipped his hand out of Kip's grasp just as Callie called in the concierge. Hiero noticed at once how his feathers were ruffled, this man who prided himself on his patience and calm.

"The Mademoiselles Vauquelin have returned," he announced. "They require your immediate assistance, Mr. Bash."

Tim dashed up the steps two at a time, ignoring the itch at the back of his throat that threatened for the third time that day. The concierge matched him leap for leap, but behind them, Hiero struggled to keep up. For once Tim didn't slow to accommodate him. Even if he gained only a few minutes' advance, he needed every second to prepare for what they would encounter in the suite above. Spurred by the haunted look on the concierge's face and the not-so-distant screaming, Tim hurdled over the top edge of the staircase and broke into a run.

He didn't need to go far. An attendant propped open the door to the Vauquelin sisters' suite, from which emanated a stench only slightly less noxious than the Dark Arches' reek. With a nod to the attendant, he glanced inside while waiting for the concierge. The parlor appeared much as Han and Callie had described it—frivolity's carnage—so Tim couldn't tell what part of the shattered wine bottles, mountain range of garments, and overturned furniture happened most recently.

Mademoiselle Seraphine Vauquelin, of admirable vocal dexterity, 2qw curled in a ball atop a table, rocking and wailing. Mademoiselle Damiane was sprawled across one of its chairs, smoking furiously and berating her sister in French. One or both of them appeared to be altered, although sudden shocks often prompted strange responses, even in the calmest of people. Here it shook the air with the force of colliding storms.

Tim stopped the concierge before he could make the introductions. "A timeline, if you please, before we proceed."

The man looked grateful. "They returned to the hotel thirty minutes ago. I spoke with Mademoiselle Damiane Vauquelin briefly in the lobby, alerting her to Mr. Bash's desire for an interview. She appeared unmoved and proceeded with her sister to their suite. I do not think they discovered the trouble right away. Once they did, I believe I was summoned at once. I ordered Mr. Carson here to secure the door and then went straight to your suite."

"Very good." Tim couldn't catch Hiero's eye as he joined them, but, by his pinched look, he too anticipated the worst. "See if Dr. Grieg can be summoned back, will you?"

The concierge performed a bow, then left them. Hiero wasted no time in tapping on the door frame and striding into the parlor.

"Mesdemoiselles," he announced and continued in French. "Please forgive the interruption, but I believe you require my assistance."

Mademoiselle Seraphine ceased her wailing and stared, like a child caught midtantrum. "You... You are the detective?"

"Consulting, and yes. Hieronymus Bash, and this is my colleague, DI Stoker."

She sniffled, hiccupped. Her bottom lip trembled. Tears welled in her eyes, then spilled over her cheeks, down the same still-damp rivulets as before. "Damie," she bleated before burying her face in the ring of her arms and sobbing. "Le pauvre monsieur, le pauvre monsieur..."

Mademoiselle Damiane stubbed out her cigarette on the arm of her chair. Her glare could have cut glass, her mistrust a dagger at their throats. Tim recognized the dead-eyed look of someone who had run afoul of the law more than once in her youth. But her jaw twitched, a tell if he ever saw one. She fought to keep her teeth from chattering, smoked to disguise the tremors in her fingers. Something had scared the drunk out of her, and she wasn't accustomed to terror or sobriety.

"How may we be of service?" Hiero smoothly asked again, as one did of the traumatized.

"We received this." Mademoiselle Damiane threw a note at Hiero, but Tim plucked it out of the air.

He forced himself not to rip off the envelope, though the contents came as no surprise. A four, written in blood. He showed it to Hiero, who didn't devote more than a flick of his eyes. Tim moved closer to him, wondering how he could spare him this. He remembered the dripping axe carried by the Red Skull, and the blood froze in his veins.

Letting the chill spread to his heart, that he might endure this, Tim refocused on their witness. "And?"

Mademoiselle Damiane took her time lighting another cigarette before pointing to the corner. One could barely see the gift box beneath all the ribbons and frills and flounce, the sort of gift any young lady might giddily receive from a friend or a beau. Save for the garish red stain streaking across the carpet, where it had been kicked.

"Please make yourself and your sister comfortable in a suite downstairs while we examine the scene. Mr. Carson will escort you," Tim instructed, hoping to spare them, and perhaps Hiero, the sight of whatever lay inside.

"We must stay here? Pourquoi?" Mademoiselle Damiane demanded.

"A doctor has been called for. And we may wish to interview you."

"What else is there to say? The phantom has done this. We arrived here, we opened the box, and voilà le resultat."

Normally, when confronted by this kind of vehemence, Hiero could be relied upon to punt. A witty aside. A wave of hands. An oblique reference to Shakespeare and, poof! The bubble of tension burst.

But he stood stone still, staring at the gift box.

"We'll need to speak later," Tim attempted to dismiss them. "Once we have all the facts in hand."

"Here is what I know in my blood," Mademoiselle Damiane hissed. "Sera is the only one being forced to wear these little chapeaux de merde. The only one being tormented by a murderer. And if I lose my sister to this menace while your d'incompétents stand around and ask nonsense questions…"

With a growl, she dragged a simpering Mademoiselle Seraphine out into the hallway. Mr. Carson, pausing to bow in Tim's direction, shut the door before chasing after them.

Tim caught Hiero by the arm. "Let me."

"I have seen a babe buried in a garden, and worse." Hiero exhaled deeply. "Much worse."

Tim pressed his hands to Hiero's chest. "Enough for a lifetime."

"That's not how the game is played."

"We must change the rules." Tim struggled to read anything on his face other than determination. They were too well matched, Hiero and their adversary, in their ability to dissimulate. But he knew Hiero suffered every strike against him, with or without evidence. Knew it in the place that belonged to him alone.

Hiero did look at him then, his dark-star eyes shining with realization. "You know."

Tim sighed. "I suspect."

"How?"

"When I encountered the Red Skull... I thought it was a prop. And then Han returned from the Arches, and everything that followed..."

Hiero nodded. Not a censure, to Tim's relief. "Together, then."

Tim wanted to pull rank, but he knew better. And perhaps a small part of him did not want to be alone. Leading Hiero by the hand, Tim cautiously plotted a path around the red streak, so as not to disturb any evidence. He let go of Hiero only to don his gloves, relieved to find the ribbons already cut. They crouched on either side of the gift box, then, at Hiero's unspoken signal, Tim lifted the lid.

To find Silas Flint's severed head lying on a gore-drenched pillow.

Hiero made a guttural, animal sound.

"'The hand that mocked them, and the heart that fled.'" Perhaps out of some tender instinct, he reached for Flint's hair, only to remember himself and recoil. "'Look on my works, ye mighty, and despair.'"

Before Tim could offer him a soft word, Hiero made a swift retreat to the other end of the room, to the cabinet where the

Vauquelins stored their liquor.

Amidst the rattle and clink of Hiero's unsteady hands pouring himself a triple whiskey, Tim examined every side of the box, even lifting the sodden pillow out of its luxurious packaging. Nothing. A hole in the bottom with wilted edges confirmed only that their fiend had been a bit sloppy with execution, both of Flint and the gift wrapping. Tim hoped the beleaguered stage manager didn't suffer, but the expression that would forever be on his face said otherwise.

Tim replaced the lid and rose to full height. His mind should have been wrestling with theories and conjectures, sifting through every remembered detail of the evidence for connections to this particular kill. But he could think only of Hiero, of the thunderstorm of grief brewing behind him. That Tim should go to him. That Tim should insist that he flee—to protect himself, to protect their family, whatever reason would convince.

Not by accident did the killer target the one person in The Gaiety's company closest to Hiero. The only one who knew Bash and Beastly were one and the same. The only obstacle to Beastly returning to the stage. They'd set a perfect trap and now sat back and waited for their prey. And Tim knew of no argument or strain of logic strong enough to hold Hiero back. Especially when the next victim might not number among The Gaiety's staff, but those closest to him.

The only way to serve Hiero, or anyone, in this, Tim decided, was to solve the case.

He brushed a pile of unmentionables off one side of a half-hidden desk, then wrote out three quick notes. He entrusted these to Mr. Carson's replacement, who hurried off to send them. Tim reentered the parlor to find Hiero staring down at the closed gift box, the whiskey bottle cradled in one arm.

"When did you see him last?" Tim asked.

"This morning." His voice had lost all of its music, the sweeping notes and dramatic pauses that cast a spell upon the listener. Hiero spoke only for himself now. "Was it only this morning? In the carriage. He wanted to quit. I convinced him to wait out the day." He bowed his head. "I killed him."

"No."

"Five children. Two wives. Lost one to fever, then he found a new life with a seamstresses." He inhaled sharply. "I must confess to her."

"No." Tim approached him cautiously. "We must stay the course."

"To what end?" Hiero shouted, flinging his whiskey glass at the far wall, where it thudded on a painting and plunked onto the carpet. His shoulders sagged under the weight of this tiny defeat. "Mine? Yours? Those we swore to keep safe? Those we treasure?"

"They want this," Tim insisted, pushing into his space but still not daring a touch. "Your reaction, your pain. Impulsive decisions. Our bond strained." A potent thought occurred to him then, but he nudged it aside for later consideration. "They mean to break you."

As if approaching a starving lion, Tim opened his arms, moving steadily closer until he'd lured Hiero into his embrace. He rested his heavy head on Tim's and let out a somber moan. Tim cinched him closer still, sharing his grief, reminding Hiero that where once he struggled alone, now they stood together. A togetherness their murderous foe lacked, given the ferocity of their obsession.

"Better have failed in the attempt." After a deep sniff, possibly of Tim's hair, Hiero pressed a soft kiss to his lips and pulled away. Still weighted by guilt but seeming more himself, he said, "I am, after all, only on my fourth life."

"Fourth and final."

"Don't fret. You are cordially invited to join in any future metamorphoses." He kept a weather eye on the gift box as he declared, "I believe it is time."

"For?"

"Your complete and total surrender..."

Tim stammered, confused. "Under different circumstances—"

"...of the field of battle." With a solemn mien, Hiero presented *his* case. "Our ghost chose an ephemeral persona with good reason, perhaps even named themselves to perpetuate the myth of their invisibility."

"And therefore their invincibility?"

"Precisely." Hiero reached over to pluck Tim's handkerchief out of his pocket, began to twist and twirl it about. "You, my dear Kip, are a gentleman of logic and method. Follow the breadcrumbs through the woods to grandmother's house. But a man of your intelligence would note the size of the oven and the feast of sweets and the witch's axe collection, and take your leave whilst skinny and agile." He continued to snake the silken cloth around his hands as he spoke, so nimbly Tim had difficulty keeping track of its progress. "Our fiend hopes you'll follow his path of destruction straight into the fire. They relish luring us from crime to crime to read their childish rhymes and fret over their next vile act and fumble our way through their great game. No more."

With a flick of Hiero's wrist, the handkerchief disappeared.

"You suggest we stop investigating?"

"No. We must stop playing on their terms. We must smoke them out."

Tim took a moment to reflect. He'd long ago accepted that he'd never be able to follow the dashes and ellipses that punctuated Hiero's thought process. He had a syntax all his own—not encoded, just eccentric. A talented writer's idiosyncratic flourish. As such, his meaning was often obscured, sometimes even to Hiero himself, but tended to reveal itself in time.

The trouble being that time was of the essence, the countdown to the next incident already begun.

"How do you mean?" Tim asked.

The enigmatic look he received did not inspire confidence.

"Just that."

"'That' what? We withdraw from The Gaiety? We return the case to the Yard? Hole up at Berkeley Square and take up crochet whilst awaiting the next damnable note?"

"After a fashion." Hiero seemed to consider him, evaluating some unfathomable aspect of his character in a way Tim didn't much care for. "Tell me a lie."

Tim scoffed. "Whatever for?"

"A simple request. Lie to me."

"Hiero, stop horsing about. The circumstances could not be more dire."

"I am aware of the seriousness of our endeavor, given that my friend's head is presently lying in a box, sine corpus." The look became a glare. "Now, the lie."

"How can I convince you of it, when you know whatever I say next will not be true?" A raised, perfectly angled brow was Hiero's answer. Tim sighed. "That's the challenge."

"Tick-tock."

Tim shut his eyes, shook his head. He ran a few stomach-churning scenarios through his mind, but, in the end, he conceded Hiero's unspoken point.

"I cannot. You know I cannot." Tim couldn't keep the fondness out of his gaze despite everything. "Not to you."

A slip of a smile quirked his lips. "Not terribly well to others either, if I may say."

Tim growled out a sigh. "Ergo I cannot be apprised of your plan."

"Not if it's to succeed, alas."

Some truths, even unknown truths, stacked on one's chest over the hours and days, piling high, crushing the life out. Tim felt the hard press of such a burden now. He wanted to object, to call Hiero's darker machinations off. He suspected what some of them might involve.

But later today he would search for a body to reunite with Silas

Flint's head. Tell his widow the worst news she'd ever hear. Listen to his children wail with grief. Reread the notes, pore over the scant evidence, piece together clues the killer had meticulously planned for him to discover. Twice in his life, Tim had deviated from the rules. The first led to the discovery of his murdered parents. The second brought him Hiero. The significance was not lost on him.

He met Hiero's dark eyes with new resolve. "Do you trust me?" he asked of the man he adored.

"With my life, as you well know. But—"

"Tell me everything."

Hiero opened his mouth to reply, then sighed. "Kip..."

Tim pushed back into his arms, seizing him as tight as he dared. When Hiero went to turn away, Tim forced him to meet his stare— his ardent, imploring stare.

"Three days. Two murders. Two broken limbs. A streak of vandalism unheard of in the theatrical world. The Gaiety's company terror stricken, its performances cancelled. To say nothing of all the unfortunate souls in the Arches arrested or worse. There will be more blood on both our hands if this goes awry." Tim reached under Hiero's lapel and pulled out the handkerchief hidden there. Spared a moment to delight at Hiero's dyspeptic expression. "Tell me."

"They'll come for you. At the least sign of doubt or weakness... I won't let them have you."

"Not when you can sacrifice yourself."

"You must finish this, if I fail."

"How can I, without you by my side?" He cupped Hiero's jaw, smoothed a thumb across his stubbled cheek. "I've learned a great many things over the past year, but this above all... We're at our best only together. Rogue and righteous, chaos and reason, Stoker and Bash. That is what they cannot touch. That is what we must unleash upon them."

Something in his black-brown eyes melted, the last glacier of Hiero's reticence sinking into a sea of feeling. The kiss that gentled

Tim's lips felt chaste compared to their more sensual moments but ran deep with passion, with devotion, an oath as unbreakable as any vow they might make.

"Together," Hiero murmured into the shell of his ear, "we will hunt this phantom spirit down if we have to chase them into the fires of hell."

Chapter 15

*H*an swiped his finger through an errant daub of butter on his plate, spread it across his tongue. The last bit of luxury he might taste in a long while, he mused. He mulled a second bowl of porridge, a poor substitute for the savory congees of his youth, remembering the thirteen long hours between meals the previous day. But the ache of his healing hand reminded him of chasing the Red Skull and carrying Silas Flint's decapitated corpse up from the bowels of The Gaiety, and he thought better of overburdening his stomach. Who knew what horrors awaited them later that day?

Corpulent, rain-swollen clouds hung low over the Bruton Street rooftops as he snuck out of the kitchen entrance, the air so thick Han feared being suspended like a fish in aspic if he paused for too long. But fiercer tempests than the one brewing over Mayfair would come about if he neglected his duties due to inclement weather. He still hadn't had word from Toby. Worrisome. Part of the trouble of unknown forces moving against them was those forces were, as mentioned, unknown. Their reach might be contained to London, or to the Strand, or to their circle of acquaintances, but Han could not trust in that. He could rely only on his instinct, which had confused him of late, a dual-pointed compass pulling him in opposite directions.

He stopped cold on the curb across from Berkeley Square. Holding her parasol like the Queen her scepter, Miss Maxine Marks awaited him in the shadow of a lime tree. Her high-necked royal-blue coat draped over the ruffled tiers of her dress like a sash, secured with silver buttons. Though half hidden under a jaunty hat, none could deny the crownlike stature of her golden locks, one long curl of which bounced on her collar, the only indication that she'd hurried.

Han hesitated to cross the street. The newspaper tucked under her arm crowed her triumph; she would not have presented herself if she'd failed. And yet seeing her there, a brittleness to her poise, however graceful, gave him cause to wonder.

Instinct. A double-edged sword.

Or was it simply his own reticence? He'd been deceived by so many, so often. Had saved himself by deceiving in return. When one understood the machinations of a thing, the hints and tells and subtle techniques, one saw them everywhere. In everyone. Even those, he sighed inwardly, with obvious intentions. Such as a woman of no means attempting to claw her way out of the gutter.

He crossed the street. "Good day."

"In what passes for daylight in this alleged summer."

"Is it the weather that disagrees with you or the earliness of the hour?"

"Both must be endured, but only one by choice." Miss Marks sighed wistfully. "When you've spent most of your life surrounded by wretched, chattering people, quiet becomes its own comfort. I work best in the wee hours, before the city wakes." Her gunmetal eyes caught him in their sights, softened. "We're kindred spirits in this."

"Only when there's a case on. Otherwise I sleep deep and well."

"Untroubled by petty cares and pangs of conscience? How like a man."

"It wasn't always thus," Han insisted, stunned at how quickly she'd pushed him on the defensive. "But with perseverance and a bit of luck, my fortunes turned."

"Ah, yes, that pirate's gold, good fortune." Her expression turned somber, which made her somehow more beautiful, a heroine in a Millais portrait. "You'll need a chest of it by day's end."

She yanked the newspaper from under her arm and thrust it at him, as if a spear and not a few crinkly pages. She'd folded it to the item in question, but it would have caught Han's eye anyway, taking up generous column inches on the third page.

GAIETY PLOT THICKENS: DID BASH TAME THE SAVAGE BEAST?

by C.D. Arascain

In a turn Shakespeare wouldn't have muddied his shoe with, Mr. Hieronymus Bash, self-celebratory detective to those willing to pay to have their troubles magicked away, put on a show at the entrance to the incident-plagued Gaiety Theater yesterday, but one that far from convinced. Confronted by a crowd of theatergoers seeking only justice for their murdered idol, beloved actor Randolph Terriss, Bash instead presented them not with a theory, but with an alibi for his prime suspect.

How The Gaiety's manager, Mr. Gerry Tumnus, received the news that Mr. Horace Beastly, late of The Gaiety stage and considered the most probable cause of its current woes, had fled to the colonies, one can only guess. Mr. Bash thought parading Mr. Beastly's abandoned wife and child-to-be before the protesting crowd a worthy use of his time *and* Mr. Tumnus's money. Though I am, as a theater critic, not well versed in the minutiae of modern policing, I doubt the brave men of Scotland Yard waste their time providing their top suspects with an alibi.

Mr. Bash, of course, is merely a consulting detective of middling skill and rank opportunism. But given this latest outrage, Mr. Tumnus might start to wonder about a possible connection between Beastly and Bash. How else could the detective have amassed conclusive evidence of Beastly's departure, let alone located the wife no one knew he had, after less than a day's

investigation? Why would Mr. Bash choose to parade this innocent woman before an angry crowd? And if Beastly has truly fled,
when did he leave, the previous week, or once alerted to the suspicions against him? Perhaps by one of Mr. Bash's bumbling
associates?

Mr. Terriss's grieving public deserve answers to these questions and more. The theatrical demimonde, known for its smoke
and mirrors, has perhaps become too accustomed to spectacle
without substance. But in the words of a far lesser bard, "Where
there is smoke, there is fire."

Han growled in the back of his throat and would have done
much worse were Miss Marks not before him. He read the article
through three more times, but somehow the words did not change.
Nor the meaning, to far more than their investigation.

"*The Pall Mall Gazette* refused the item you gave me," Miss Marks
said. "I cannot fault them."

"Nor should you. Their allegiance could not be more clear."

"With the victims? Yes." In a tight voice, she added, "As is
mine."

He caught it then, the tremor under her words. Not of fear, but
fury. He chose his next comment with care. "You are asking yourself,
I gather, if perhaps you should have tasked *me* with a proof of trust."

"Would you have passed, I wonder?"

"Likely not. But not for the reasons you think."

Miss Marks scoffed. "Such as those of which you cannot speak."

Han regarded her warily but could not help striking the blow.
"We are strangers."

She worked her jaw, not ready to abandon her anger but wary of
giving sway to her upset. "Is that all?"

Han considered this, considered her. He could end it, here and
now. He should, though he would make an enemy. Her skills,
though remarkable, were rudimentary. She did not pose enough of a
threat to keep close.

And yet.

"I cannot answer to the charges here. Nor to those you've left unspoken. All I can say is we have our reasons. We have a plan. And our only care is to prevent others from falling victim to this murderous fiend. On that you have my oath."

His little speech enflamed her, but not how he'd intended. "Your oath?!" she bellowed. "I was humiliated, presenting them with that scrap of nonsense whilst their top man waited in the wings—"

"You saw him? Arascain?"

"Not through the haze of red that clouded my vision, no."

Han exhaled a long breath, hoping she would do the same. "I understand—"

"You know nothing." Her mouth pinched as if she wanted to spit. "You see only your feathered bed and buttered toast and kind master."

"I have *no* master." But Han's intuition tingled. "You watched me eat through the window?"

She wrenched the paper away and tossed it at his chest. "You don't deserve my answer."

He scrambled to guess why she might spy on him, then remembered that, not long ago, he'd been in similar straits.

"You couldn't bear to knock. To be surrounded by a life you'll never lead."

"I was set up to fail by that fraud you bow to!"

A truth hidden in a lie, Han mused to himself, at a loss as to how to remedy the situation without revealing more than he ought. How he wanted to play the Hiero: invite her in, introduce her to their ways, help her have the life she worked so hard to achieve. But they were, in the end, strangers. And neither of them had passed the test.

"Accuse him of what you will, but know that no one cares more for The Gaiety and its players as that fraud, as you call him." Han took a cautious step toward her. "And neither of us spent the night in our feathered beds, dreaming of sugar plums."

Arms coiled so tightly around her chest that she appeared to suffocate herself, Miss Marks's only response was an unimpressed glare. Han met its full force, did not flinch.

"Arascain. To your knowledge, will he attend The Gaiety's opening tonight?"

This shocked her. "They mean to perform?"

"We hope they will be persuaded."

"All actors have their eccentricities, but these don't strike me as being suicidal."

"No effort so far has prevented the ghost from striking, wherever and whoever they please. They'll keep to their own twisted timetable, opening or not."

"A rather hazardous version of 'the show must go on,' that."

"But practical. If they are together, we stand a better chance of keeping the company safe."

"And away from Mr. Arascain's criticism? But so far he's only targeted your master."

"And will continue to do so, no matter what transpires on that stage." Han allowed himself a moment to look at her with unguarded eye. Her anger. Her resilience. Though he suspected otherwise, he might never see her again. "An olive branch. A ticket to tonight's performance, front row center, first balcony, will await you at The Gaiety. I would strongly encourage you to attend."

The corner of her mouth quirked up. "What are you planning?"

"All I may say is you'll want to see it for yourself. Alone."

She barked a laugh. "Mr. Han, are you suggesting a woman of strong moral character such as myself venture unchaperoned into your phantom's playground?"

"Two tickets, then. But leave Arascain behind if you mean to have tomorrow's headline."

A sudden tremor shook the air. The first fat drops of rain pelted down on them, so heavy they poured right through the canopy of leaves. Miss Marks unfurled her parasol, posed it on her shoulder so that its frilled edge framed her face. Gold hair against royal blue against black tree trunks, all behind a watery sheen reminiscent of Degas. Han knew he would paint her someday, whether as a model or from memory.

"Oh, I do. But beware this critic's wrath if you do not pass *my* test."

She turned on her heel and strolled off through Berkeley Square. Han stood watching her until she was no more than a distant speck and he soaked to the bone.

Hiero flicked his gaze away from the glint of the straight razor as it stroked up and down the strip of leather. Though it wasn't every day one beheld a hugely pregnant woman sharpening a lethal weapon, he didn't care to tempt another migraine. After a sleepless night of preparations for their great gamble against the ghost, he'd retreated to the attic, where he hoped watching Lillian Pankhurst's quiet puttering about might lull him into a nap.

Instead he discovered a hive of activity. Callie buzzed between the corner desk and the far wall, pinning things to her evidence collage, sorting and resorting various piles and scrawling thoughts in her notebook. Lillian presided over the small dining table and chairs, packing little boxes full of knitted hats and scarves and toys for the orphan babes at the Castleside residence. Shahida had been dozing under a web of multicolored wool in an armchair but roused as soon as Hiero entered. He now sat before the grooming mirror, face swaddled in a hot tea towel, awaiting the guillotine. Or, rather, a shave.

Better, he'd thought, to sit facing the room, that he not lose his nerve. But in these final moments before he surrendered his Samsonlike powers to Shahida's cutting skills, he wished he could see more than the two fingers of space he'd poked out for his eyes. Catch a final glimpse of the majesty for which he was renowned on both sides of the English Channel. And this was only the first sacrifice to come that day, if their plan worked.

"To what purpose, all that scritching?" he demanded of Callie to distract himself from the impending assault on his person. "Surely you've completed your tasks and could do with a cup of tea?"

"I thought"—Callie skimmed her finger down a list as she replied—"since we have sent up the red flag, it might do to have someone take a crack at solving this case by combing through the evidence."

"Revolutionary."

"One might be encouraged to think so."

"Sieved any nuggets, have you? Gold, silver, copper, I'm not bothered which."

Callie straightened, sighed. Scanned over all her efforts with a gimlet eye and a clenched mouth. "Nothing of exceptional value so far," she admitted. "Only..."

"Hmm?"

"Seraphine Vauquelin."

"Ah!" Lillian made a swoony sound. "Her Ophelia was enchanting. Elegant as a swan, brittle as... as..."

"Rosemary," Shahida chuckled, "for remembrance."

"Yes." Lillian straightened the ribbon on a stuffed bear. "Our last night out with Apollo. You remember..."

"I do." Hiero swallowed hard. "At the Lyric. Unforgettable." Too far away to take her hand, he was relieved when Shahida went to comfort her. Unwrapping his face to better attend Callie, he prompted, "What of her?"

"Not what, but why?" She gestured at the tomb of evidence that surrounded her. "The notes, the crimes, the victims... Everything targets Beastly. If the aim of the game is to restore hoary old Horace to The Gaiety's stage, how does taunting Seraphine Vauquelin achieve that?"

After a long moment of vacuous contemplation, Hiero shrugged.

"It doesn't," Callie confirmed. "By your admission, you hadn't even met the Vauquelins prior to this week. Our fiend has never toyed with their prey, present company excluded. None of the other victims were tormented. If anything, the murderer used the element of surprise."

"But didn't they start by scaring the life out of the actors and such?" Shahida asked.

"They began their reign of terror by unsettling The Gaiety's players, but these incidents were random. Tricks, noises, accidents. Except for the gifts sent to Seraphine Vauquelin—gifts that started off kindly, as those of a secret admirer, then turned sinister once the company started whispering of a ghost."

"Were the kind gifts and the nasty ones sent by the same person?"

"Impossible to know," Hiero replied. "Mademoiselle Vauquelin burned the notes."

"And all this before Terriss snuffed it?" Shahida lurched back over to her wool-strewn armchair and sat with a rush of breath. "Got the wrong end of it, don't you?"

"How do you mean?" Callie asked.

"You're wanting to suggest that this admirer started copying the ghost when he saw all his wooing was for naught. Went black, stopped caring if his attentions gave her joy or misery."

"Two obsessions," Hiero murmured, "is one too many, even for a case of this nature."

"Exactly. Backward." Shahida fiddled with two balls of yarn, attempting a demonstration, but gave up. "Your ghost came first. Thought to cause a bit of bother, get under that Tumnus's skin. Murderer, plotting his evil deeds, sees what this does to the company—"

"And copies it." Callie tapped her pen rapidly against the side of her notebook. "Well reasoned."

"But what of our lovelorn admirer?" Hiero asked.

"Gave up, didn't he?" Shahida scoffed. "Even secret suitors need a carrot now and again."

"But our ghost wouldn't give up the game, even with competition," Callie said. "Instead they take over our admirer's domain to attract the murderer's attention, perhaps even propose an alliance."

"Two heads." Shahida grinned at her friend. "Always better than one. Except for the murdery bits."

"Quite." After a flurry of scribbles and strikes, Callie straightened to address her audience. "Point the second: The Red Skull. Half glimpsed or half imagined by most of the company, except on two occasions. Once during the serenade to Mademoiselle Vauquelin from Box 5, and once by Han and Tim during their chase."

"Suggesting..." Hiero blinked, attempting to stay awake. "What does it suggest?"

"Neither incident can be directly connected to one of the murderer's crimes."

"What of the bloody ax?"

"The Red Skull dropped the ax during their flight. It was a prop. Couldn't have sliced a loaf of bread."

Even someone beset by fatigue and anxiety such as Hiero could make the obvious conclusion. "There are two."

Callie nodded. "There are two. The ghost and the murderer." She dropped her notebook on the desk with a loud thwack. "A theory that only begets more questions, alas. Are they working together or apart? Do they have a shared goal? Has one done all the killing, or have they swapped roles as needed, one playing avenger, the other distraction? Are both attempting to lure Beastly back, or are they working at cross-purposes in a savage game of one-upmanship? Are they, perhaps, at war?"

Hiero repressed the sudden instinct to wrap his head not just in the tea towel, but all of Shahida's yarn and perhaps a few of Lillian's boxes, to mummify himself in a sarcophagus of commonplace household items. His exhaustion bit deep, a paralyzing sensation that robbed him of speech and thought and action. It seemed like a lifetime ago, and not the previous evening, that he'd promised Kip their tight-plotted ruse would rule the day. In light of this new information... Damned if he knew if they should proceed.

If any solution prevented the molting of another skin.

A cannon boom of a knock at the door warned of Han's entry. Everyone save Callie jumped in their seat, receiving no more than a curt bow of the head in apology. Han strode over to Hiero and slapped that morning's edition of *The Pall Mall Gazette* into his lap, soggy and folded to the third page.

The headline alone was enough to still the blood in his veins. By the time he'd read the piece through, he didn't have voice enough to beg them to check for a pulse.

Callie grabbed the paper away, canting it so Shahida could read over her shoulder. Only Lillian, her bubble of tranquility restored after her ordeal at the hands of the Daughters of Eden, floated about her boxes, oblivious, a doting fairy godmother bestowing her wishes with grace. Hiero longed to be sprinkled with a bit of her fairy dust. Perhaps he would turn into a pumpkin.

Callie cracked the skein of silence that had spread over them. "We cannot proceed. The risk is too great."

"The risk is as it ever was." Hiero didn't know from what small, secret part of him his defiance flared up, but he couldn't snuff it. "Trust in the stagecraft."

"I've taken measures to ensure Arascain won't be in attendance tonight," Han said. "But, of course, he'll have eyes and ears in the theater."

"As do the other actors, and the stagehands, and the patrons," Callie insisted. "They will make the same connection Arascain implies here, between you and... you."

"It's perfectly understandable, given our day-to-day, that you'd forget you're in the presence of the greatest actor of his age," Hiero declared with an extra soupçon of arrogance. "So I'll remind you. On with the show."

Callie growled under her breath. "And if someone makes the connection? Recognizes Beastly as Bash or Bash as Beastly? What then?"

"Then..." Hiero smiled his desperation smile, the one he'd learned to unfurl in his darkest moments, when confidence alone might save him. "We improvise."

Scowling but unwilling to give him the benefit of her anger, Callie stomped back to her evidence. Shahida placed a supportive hand on his shoulder, then set off to refresh the hot water basin. Hiero met Han's assessing stare with another of his life-or-death grins, which earned him a bemused chuckle. Hardly the direst set of circumstances they'd confronted, after all.

"Any hippity-hoppitying in the square?" Hiero inquired sotto voce.

He didn't particularly like Han's pained expression or the tone of his "no." Experience had made them unflappable, except when it came to their shared Achilles heel: someone they cared for being hurt as a result of their machinations.

"It's early still," Han responded. "Two days for such a task..."

Hiero sighed. He wasn't wrong, but they both knew something wasn't right. "Might you not send a bunny after the first bunny?"

"And have our villain make a stew?" Han grunted. "I should have gone myself."

"You couldn't be spared."

"That's a coward's argument." He grabbed the fallen paper, crushed it in his hands. "How many till we see the forest for the trees? How many till we acknowledge that we're not blameless in this?"

"Steady," Hiero whispered. They shared a poignant look. "We do shoulder the blame, but only for our share. Not an unreasonable amount. Not everything Erskine hung on us. And we use our gains—"

"To make it right. I know." Han scrubbed his face with his hands. "I know. But at what cost?"

Han didn't have to glance back in Callie's direction for Hiero to understand all the nuances of such a simple statement. If he could grant him any wish, it would be a love as grand as the unconditional affection his Kip gave him. But that was one adventure Han had to navigate alone.

"We've paid," Hiero reminded him, "in full."

"Not if..." He shook his head, unable to complete the thought.

Not particularly keen to give his own suspicions voice, and thereby new life, Hiero addressed the room at large. "I see no other way forward than to continue on our present course. The board is set. The challenge has been made. The players gather. Let the great game begin."

Chapter 16

*T*wo by two, they marched solemnly down the center aisle of The Gaiety's stalls, the greenish-yellow light from the half-mast gas lamps casting giant creeping shadows up the sides of the auditory. Mourning became the pallid denizens of the demimonde, who'd come to celebrate their latest lost son. Bedecked in black and violet hues and the occasional splash of crimson, they painted this somber palette on extravagant canvases: hats of every size and shape, some fringed with feathers, some crowned with lilies; bejeweled veils Salome might envy; parasols and fans with dagger-sharp tines; cuffs dripping with lace; skirts with more ruffled tiers than reason; coats that draped so low they might have been trains. In pairs they paraded to their seats, each performing their own internal tragic soliloquy.

Tim stood guard at stage right, gambling that if the ghost attempted another haunting during Silas Flint's memorial, they would strike the stage and not the crowd. Though given that all the drama presently occurred in the audience, he had cause to second-guess. Genevre de Casterac, taking the widow's seat at the center front, clutched a gem-encrusted cross to her chest and whispered prayers in fake, if Tim's hearing was sound, Latin. At her side, the Vicomte de Croÿ-Roeulx awkwardly patted her back. He appeared more uncomfortable than consoling, avoiding any who might approach him for a private word.

Seraphine Vauquelin, in full waifish desolation, walked as if in a trance, her body slack and her eyes floating heavenward. Chemical, Tim concluded. Or perhaps not. Once all eyes were upon her, she rushed the stage, racing down the aisle and flinging herself at the orchestra pit barrier like a bird smashed on glass. A few quick-witted stagehands pried her off before she climbed over. They flung her at her sister, who numbly offered her a shoulder. Damiane looked to have gone five rounds with her rouge and lost, her handsomeness both garish and waxen under so much lacquer. She blotted her crying sister's face with the hem of her skirt, dragging her away from the bristling crowd. A few hisses followed them to the farthest, darkest corner.

Not quite a full house, Tim thought, but enough to do Flint proud. Despite their fears about entering The Gaiety, the community made a show of force. He recognized the managers of several major theaters along with former Gaiety headliners like Nellie Farren and Florence St. John. Tim stifled a smirk when Henry Irving, Hiero's longtime nemesis, waltzed in, tapping his gaudy walking stick. Even Tumnus rose to the occasion, his waistcoat and hat band in a shimmery tortoiseshell pattern.

Tim watched him greet the guests with the air of a proud father at his daughter's wedding. He wondered whether he should have displayed Flint's head on a podium at center stage in order to give these peacocks some perspective.

"Dreadful, aren't they?" Marius whispered, echoing Tim's thoughts.

He stepped back so he could see into the wings where Marius lurked, concealed from the crowd by the side panel. His bloodshot eyes and wan countenance spoke of another sleepless night, though whether he'd lost it to worry or at Madame de Casterac's whip, Tim couldn't know.

"Far be it from me to stop them giving themselves away," Tim quipped in French. This earned him a weak smile.

"It must be difficult for you, discerning who mourns purely for show and who is doing it to hide darker intentions."

"Everyone tries to hide. Some are just more adept at it than others. But this crowd..." Tim scanned the audience, searching, like Diogenes, for an honest man. "They are masters."

"How do you stand it? Every day surrounded by liars, thieves, worse. It must harden your heart."

Or flay it wide open. Tim hoped his reaction did not betray him. He pried his mind away from thoughts of Hiero, shushed the clamor in his chest, his actual heart full to bursting. Tried to remember a time when he felt as Marius described.

When he turned back to Marius, Tim caught a glimmer in his eyes. He did his best to ignore its implications. "Far from it. We knew our share of liars and thieves in Paris, did we not? Admired some, loved some, not for their foul deeds, but for their character. Their crimes were born of poverty, desperation. I cannot condemn a man for doing what he must to survive. But these fiends I chase now are of a different breed. Their cruelty knows no bounds. There is a python among these peacocks, and I must stop it from swallowing them whole."

The glimmer flickered to full flame. Tim wanted to retreat, to return to his duty, to overexplain why anything between them was impossible, but the shadows under Marius's eyes and the scars on his delicate fingers stopped him. He could not refuse a freezing man a bit of warmth.

His reprieve came in the form of Tumnus, of all people, who climbed up to the stage in order to start the proceedings.

"You should join the others," Tim advised Marius, who nodded but made no haste to depart. "You'll want to be seen."

"I want to be safe."

Tim met the challenge in his eyes full-on, wished he could offer more than empty assurances to his oldest friend. He vowed to do better by him once this madness ended; Tim had too few connections to his past to sever this one.

Tumnus opened the memorial with a prayer. Not many bowed their heads, but Madame de Casterac raised her voice to the uppermost balconies, overwhelming even Tumnus with the force of her devotion. Within minutes of beginning his vague, rambling remarks, Tumnus lost the crowd, who twittered and fluttered and primped and made great show of unfurling their fans or affecting the perfect pose. One woman blubbered as if she'd been Flint's childhood sweetheart. One of the managers fiddled with his cigarette case. Damiane Vauquelin raised a flask every time Tumnus mentioned Flint's name, pouring as much tribute on the carpet as down her throat.

Tim surreptitiously checked his pocket watch, wondering when the real show would begin. But then, the main event did tend toward the fashionably late.

Finally, just as Tumnus invited members of the audience to share their recollections of Silas Flint, a thunderous rattle shook the doors. Silence fell like the slice of a knife. The mourners' eyes darted about the stage, the boxes, the upper tiers of the auditory; some shivered; some crouched; some stared at the doors as if the devil himself knocked. Tim swallowed a smile, counting down the seconds until...

The doors flew open, rebounding off the walls with a momentous *thwack*. The crowd yelped. A lone figure stood in the entranceway, drinking in the attention as the ghost might, were they a creature that thrived on flattery and regard like the man currently framed there.

But Horace Beastly aimed only to incite fervor, not fear, and so he strutted into the auditory as if returning from his coronation, smiling his most beguiling yet enigmatic smile as even the snobs among them gawked. When he reached dead center, Beastly paused, inviting their scrutiny, their scowls, their censure. Commanding all the sweet, sweet minutes of attention, greedy after months away from the spotlight.

Tim stopped his jaw from scraping the stage planks, his feet from taking an astonished step forward, from running into the arms of a near stranger. Having rarely had the chance to observe Horace Beastly offstage, Tim hadn't noticed how completely Hiero transformed himself from one persona to the other. His stance, his gait, the way he held his mouth, even the quality of his gaze altered when he became Beastly. Added to the fact that he had shorn his shoulder-length waves of hair into a side-parted crop more fitting with the styles of the day and—this frazzled Tim's senses for several moments—*shaved off his moustache*, Tim would be excused for believing he beheld an entirely different person.

Relief flooded him as he realized their small deception would work. But trepidation bled into the mix when he marked how easily his Hiero could disappear himself. Tim's upper lip twitched, longing for the bristly reassurance of Hiero's kiss as Horace Beastly completed his procession through the still-gaping audience.

He stared down the manager who had wronged him as he approached the stage. Tumnus's entire countenance flushed union-jack red, including his shiny bald pate.

"I have a few words of tribute to my dear friend Silas, if I may," Beastly announced.

Tumnus grimaced, a dog held by its master's command, then grunted his assent. Tense with fury, he stood guard while Beastly climbed to the stage.

"Mais c'est qui?" Marius asked, breaking the spell.

"That"—Tim fought to temper the awe in his voice—"is Monsieur Beastly."

Unnerved by the odd energy surrounding Beastly as he approached, Tim almost didn't hear Marius's following question. "The Gaiety's first Don Juan?"

"The very same."

Tim, despite himself, couldn't pry his eyes off Beastly. The plush fullness of his lips, the rich brown of his skin, the angles and rounds and slopes of his regal cheeks exposed for all to see. The dove's-down *V* at the nape of his neck that Tim would suckle to stir him on lazy mornings, when they had all the time in the world to banter and tease, to burrow so deep into each other that they breathed the same air.

"Mon Dieu," Marius swore under his breath. "Timée, does this mean—"

"I cannot say." Tim raised a hand to hush him, forced calm over his own breath as Beastly stood at the front of the stage, as if expecting applause.

A crackle of excitement thrummed through the audience while they waited to see in what direction lightning would strike.

"Home at last." Even Beastly's accent had shifted from "eccentric aristocrat of foreign birth" to "actor concealing lower-class origins." Tim felt a pang of regret that only he would appreciate these fine details. "But for the worst of reasons. It's fitting that old Silas has brought me back to this, my first theater, since it was he who heard me singing on the Strand and invited me to audition for Mr. Charles Webster. He recognized in me the same look of desperation he no doubt wore when, eighteen years ago, a prop master at The Adelphi let him kip in the workshop on a stormy night, after he'd helped him haul in some wood. Kept Silas so long as he made himself useful— and if you knew him, you knew how useful he'd become. 'Talent will get you a chance; hard work will earn you a life,' he'd often say. And don't we all know the truth of that."

One heartwarming anecdote, Tim mused, and the crowd was in his pocket. But such were the wiles of Horace Beastly, charmer of wild renown.

"'Herding cats,' Silas would mutter from the wings on those nights when missed cues and mislaid props made a mess of things." Beastly chuckled. The audience echoed his mirth. "But they were few and far between under his stewardship. Determination may have brought him to The Adelphi's stage door, hat in hand, but it was his ability to tame the most ferocious of lions that made him the ideal ringmaster here at The Gaiety. Who could forget the sight of him stalking about, armed with a giant net, the night an owl decided to roost in Titania's garden, hooting every time an actor spoke a line." The mourners, despite themselves, laughed, unable to resist Beastly's storytelling flair. "Or how he played doctor when a babe decided it absolutely must push its way into this world between acts. Box 7: the carpet's still stained." That earned him a few prim grumbles, but most continued to chuckle.

"Or the many nights he played a corpse while the understudy who owned the role replaced an indisposed actor. Given our moral degeneracy, present company included, old Silas got rather a lot of practice." The audience reared on him, booing and hissing. Beastly smirked, unrepentant. "Oh, stuff your protests. None of you knew him as I did. None of you know the history of the theater you inhabit." He turned on Tumnus. "Not even you, the mismanager who lets a killer haunt its halls."

The audience roared. Some leapt to their feet, shouting, arms thrust in the air; some wilted in their seats, sniffling and sobbing. Seraphine Vauquelin slumped to the floor and began to wail. Her sister ignored her, downing the last of her flask. Tumnus, rage red, stared daggers at Beastly but did nothing to quiet the crowd. Baffled by their antics, Tim struggled to find some clue, some insight amidst the cacophony.

The Vicomte broke from the pack to confront Beastly. "Et qui êtes-vous pour nous condamner? Where were you when your friend lost his head? At the dockyards? On your way to Canada?" Croÿ-Roeulx scoffed. "Tu fais pitié."

Madame de Casterac, hot on his heels, shoved the Vicomte aside as only a true diva could. "Murderer!" she snarled. "Do you think us blind to your true nature? Such fools that we cannot see a killer is among us? You stab poor Randolph in the street like a common brute, and then you remove Monsieur Flint, the one who knows the truth about you." She pointed a condemning finger straight at

Beastly. "Your phantom is here!"

The audience erupted anew. Recognizing his cue, Tim cleared his throat once. Twice. Pandemonium continued. He curled two fingers to his lips and let out his sharpest whistle. The sea of mourners glared at him, too scandalized to shout.

"If I may." Though he stepped toward Beastly, he avoided looking at his face, still unable to see any Hiero in him. "Far from being the killer, Mr. Beastly has himself been the ghost's principal target. Until now, Mr. Bash and I have not been able to reveal the fact that we received notes, which we believe to be from our fiend, threatening Mr. Beastly. For his own safety, we insisted that he keep away from The Gaiety until we proved that the person causing these incidents and Mr. Terriss's killer were one and the same."

"You see?" Beastly beamed. "I walk among you again not as a mere mourner, but as a savior. And tonight, when I return triumphant to the role of Don Juan, the role that made my career, I do so with a target on my back. Mine and mine alone."

A cry split the air. Madame de Casterac lunged for him, claws out, fangs bared, screeching French obscenities. It required the force of three men to hold her back, but not before she gouged a nail into a stagehand's cheek. Beastly gazed down at her like an indulgent king, smug and satisfied.

A second whistle calmed but did not silence them. Despite the gossipy buzz that underscored his words, Tim pressed on. "The risk to everyone involved remains, Mr. Beastly and the entire company. But with your help, we have a chance to end this tonight. Superintendent Quayle has dedicated fifty officers to your protection. Mr. Bash and our team will station ourselves at key points in the theater. When they come for Mr. Beastly, we will be ready. Otherwise... I cannot say when or if their reign of terror will end. Or who might be targeted next."

The audience erupted anew. Even the Vauquelins lent their voices to the fray. Those not directly involved made a hasty retreat to spread the gossip far and wide. Madame de Casterac blasted the full force of her indignation at the Vicomte, the only one who took a moment to rationally consider the matter. He caught Tim's eye and nodded.

Tim almost choked on his relief. The first of many hurdles overcome. He glanced into the wings, hoping to reassure Marius, but found him gone. Tumnus, his movements tight with affront, stomped his foot to be heard. Only Tim gave him audience.

Finally, the audience settled, if begrudgingly. "The Gaiety theater and its company will do everything in its power to comply with Scotland Yard's instructions. For *one night only*"—Tumnus shot a look at Madame de Casterac, who jutted out her chin and huffed—"Mr. Beastly is invited to play the role of Don Juan." Beastly performed a pretty bow, which won him no converts. "But fair warning, Mr. Stoker. If another member of this company is in any way harmed before, during, or after this performance, it will be the end of *your* career."

With a horologist's precision, Han pushed the tines of the trick lock into position. Though his magnifying glass brought the tiny cavity into fine focus, he couldn't use the small lantern he normally employed on such occasions, lest he draw one of the ushers' attention. He'd already had a time explaining to the constable posted to this section of the balcony tier that no one, under any circumstances, should be allowed into Box 5. The ticket sellers had been similarly wary. Word of Beastly's return had scorched a blazing path along the Strand, kindling intrigue and razing fears. The stomp and shout of staff scrambling to add extra seats rumbled up from the auditory, disturbing Han's delicate, painstaking work.

Once he heard the click, he slowly withdrew his instruments, then tested the snap-and-seal function. Satisfied that this final step was complete, he slunk back into Box 5 to review his handiwork.

A trap within a trap within a trap. A puzzle box, one might say. Han chuckled to himself at the thought. Their nemesis knew the significance of Box 5. As cunning as they'd been thus far, Han didn't think they could resist a pilgrimage to such as sacred place, especially on the night of Beastly's return. They might even have a bit of mischief planned for whatever special guest was seated in the box. But the spider would become the fly if they ventured into Han's web. Anyone who sat in either of the seats would find their arms and legs cuffed in.

Moving toward the rail but keeping to the shadows, Han stole a few moments to watch the rehearsals onstage. Don Juan was Han's favorite of Hiero's performances, and many a critic believed it to be his finest. Even years later, even muted for the run-through, Hiero sparkled as the unabashed libertine, his natural charm irresistible. For all her protests, Madame de Casterac proved a vibrant foil as both Don Gonzalo and the Devil. Han wondered if Hiero purposefully let her shine to keep her from scheming any trouble of her own.

The ghost had given them enough grief. Though they'd gambled and grifted and improvised their way out of many life-or-death situations, they'd never stood to lose quite so much if they failed tonight. The home they'd struggled so long to find. The means of providing for their large, vulnerable family. Their freedom.

Little wonder Hiero had retreated back into his Beastly persona for this final act.

Footsteps approached. In the seconds before someone intruded, Han spun, flicked off the special lock, and swooshed the door... into a shoe wedged against the frame. Beyond, Callie bit her fist to stifle a howl of pain, glaring daggers. Han tugged her inside. After shoving a stopper into the lock, he knelt to examine her foot. The impact had rent the side of her boot almost in two and cracked the sole. Fortunately, she was in her Calvin guise, so likely no damage beyond a bad bruise. And excruciating pain, if her curses were any indication.

"Can you walk?" he asked, daring a look at her face.

"Not as well as I can kick." She huffed and puffed with a dragon's indignation, limping around in a circle. Han knew the exact moment when she perceived the change to the room, which extinguished her temper. "What have you been up to?" She refused the hand he offered her as she too knelt to scrutinize one of his contraptions. Despite her aching foot, she didn't hesitate to compliment him. "Excellent workmanship. If you're not careful, I'll invite you to tinker the hours away in my laboratory."

"I'd happily accept, once this business is ended."

She shifted into a seated position, sighed. "Our true business is never at an end. But I daresay we deserve a holiday after this latest madness."

"I second the motion."

She stomped the heel of her good foot into the carpet. "Carried." With a hiss, she slipped off her mangled boot and inspected the damage. "Will we, do you think? Emerge from this unscathed?"

"We must." Han wished he could believe it.

"All of us?"

"I'm not one for empty promises."

Her shoulders sagged. "More's the pity." Never one to dwell on her troubles, she straightened. By the glint in her eyes, with purpose. "You've been whispering. With Hiero."

"Perhaps we have."

"There's no 'perhaps' about it." She pinned him with her stare, a bug on a specimen display. "I know... No, I trust well enough not to ask. But I warn you, Tim will not have the same reserves of patience if he discovers your secrecy after the fact. And given the present state of affairs between the two of them, that could prove cataclysmic. No matter what transpires."

Han nodded. "Sage counsel."

"See that you heed it," Callie insisted. "Before the point of no return."

"I will," he assured her. "When it's a matter of fact and not suspicion."

"Has there been anything but severed heads and suspicion about this case?" she mused. "A phantom indeed, our killer. Or killers." She tucked her wounded foot into her lap and began to massage it. Han flexed his hands, fingers itching. "Miss Marks. Will she be attending this evening?"

"I believe so."

"As an emissary of *The Pall Mall Gazette*?"

Han cleared his throat. "That I cannot say."

He hesitated. She waited, eyes dropped but, if he knew her, senses alert.

"I may have... misplayed my hand there," he admitted.

"That's unlike you."

Han had no answer. A million things to say, but none that could pass his lips without spoiling everything. Perversely, he wanted her counsel. Where had he gone wrong? How could he ally with her to their advantage? One fearsome woman would surely understand another. But Han knew to speak such things aloud risked breaking a deeper bond of trust than he would ever share with Miss Maxine Marks. One he would never forsake.

"You've done your due diligence there?" Callie asked in a too-light tone.

"The editor at *The Pall Mall Gazette* wouldn't confirm or deny that Mr. Standish is a pseudonym but offered that he'd made Miss Marks's acquaintance."

Callie's fingers stilled. "And before?"

"The world's oldest profession. No references available."

Her mouth firmed into a too familiar line. "And before?"

"Like many an enterprising woman of obscure origins, her pseudonym is a pseudonym. Her birth name I've yet to uncover." He grabbed her boot, attempted to push some of the torn patches back into place, to no avail. The impact had ruined it.

"Leave it to me." Callie put out her hand. Han stared until he realized she wanted her boot. After knitting back a loose stitch, he relinquished it. "You've enough, with your whispers and this plan of ours. I'll see to her."

Han shook his head, uncertain whether it was out of reluctance or agreement. He watched as she jammed her foot back into the boot, wincing in sympathy. "Let us see how the night plays out."

Callie rose, testing out her walk in a short circle. "Strategy or stay of execution?" Satisfied, she straightened to her full height. "Does she appreciate your gallantry, I wonder?"

Han sighed. "You misunderstand—"

"Do I?"

"Yes." He chose his next words with care. "I haven't looked further because I haven't needed to. She's been entirely forthcoming about her life, about her circumstances…"

"I see." Callie barked a laugh. "She was kind to you, ergo she must *be* kind."

"She isn't, particularly. But I believe she was honest."

"Lies are best swallowed when sweetened by truths. You taught me that."

"So I did."

"An unverified fact is no better than a fiction." Her face, so pink and soft despite its sharp angles, paled and tightened. "Instinct is a last resort. A thief flatters, but a killer feigns indifference. A shrewd blackmailer has no secrets. How many lessons over how many years, and yet…" She crossed her arms over her chest, scowled. "Break from her."

"There is no 'we' to be broken."

"Then *do your diligence*," she insisted, "and be done." Callie turned awkwardly on her heel and departed.

Han fought not to call her back, not to spout some disingenuous explanation. But now was not the time or place to promote the virtues Miss Marks possessed. Though Han promised himself that, once this business concluded, he would find a way to help her rewrite her story.

After making a final inspection of the mechanisms of his trap, he flicked on the trick lock and sealed Box 5. By midnight, he hoped, a suspect would be snared. And he would be spared a closer investigation of Miss Maxine Marks, whomever she may be.

Chapter 17

*H*iero poured himself a generous dose of brandy, drank. Let the smooth liquid caress his vocal chords and soothe his queasy stomach. After hours upon hours of rehearsal, a vengeful Madame de Casterac making him pay for his unexpected return in sweat and intricate stage blocking, his raw throat protested even the brandy's sweet attentions. With reluctance, he stirred in a bit of tea and honey, took a second draught. Better.

With a cunning little tool, he dug at the spirit gum under his false moustache. Not quite as magnificent as his natural one, but needs must. His wig he'd already plopped on one of the bedposts, which now bore him a passing resemblance. Hiero chuckled at the thought, resisting the urge to repeat the joke to very jolly, very dead Randy Terriss, whose apartment they'd "borrowed" for his costume switches between Beastly and Bash. It wouldn't do for London's finest consulting detective to disappear midcase, so he had made two appearances at The Gaiety that day, one in the early afternoon and one as the actors returned from their evening meals. He even picked an argument with Tumnus just to prove to Callie that people's powers of observation, especially the pale complexioned among them, were not as perceptive as they thought. She granted the point, and yet Hiero somehow felt he'd lost rather than won.

Two more transformations—one to Beastly, the other to Don Juan—and he could... Well, not rest, precisely. He had an audience to seduce, a costar to enchant, a villain to foil, an incident to provoke... and another quick change into Bash that he'd forgotten. Drat.

Living a double life was not for the faint of heart.

Footsteps echoed in from the corridor. A soft knock heralded the clank of the lock. "Monsieur le caméléon?" a familiar, and very dear, voice inquired.

Hiero rose as Tim inched into the apartment, cautious until he shut the door. Self-conscious in his state of mid-metamorphosis— shorn hair slicked back, upper lip burning from the spirit gum, himself wrapped in one of Randy's coarse robes—Hiero resisted the impulse to slink behind the wardrobe. And was glad he did when Kip's eyes found him, wide with wonder and glowing with admiration. Hiero would have pulled a Samson long ago if he'd known this would be the result.

"Hello." A wisp of a smile played on Kip's lips as he approached him. "I don't believe I've had the pleasure of your acquaintance. Mr. Beastly, is it?"

"How do you know me to be a pleasure if we've never met?"

"By reputation, of course. Though if I go by name alone..."

"There's more fun to be had, I dare say."

Kip feigned innocence. "Are you very beastly indeed?"

"Come here, little lamb, and I'll show you."

Hiero lunged. Kip swept to the side, spun around him, smacked him on the buttock, then skipped away. Hiero whipped the length of his robe dramatically as he made to give chase... only to discover Kip draped across the bed in a pose that gave no illusions as to his intent. The Grand Pyramid at the front of his trousers beckoned further exploration. Hiero was no Egyptologist, but he knew a treasure when he saw one.

And yet. "Far be it from me to protest this little rendezvous, but isn't there another suitor pounding at the door? One who won't be put off by our keens and moans?"

"They'll plight their troth soon enough." Kip shifted onto his knees, waving Hiero forward so he could lay his hands on his chest and look him in the eye. An earnest, adoring look that took his breath away. "But I couldn't let you flirt with our fiend without reminding you who awaits at home. Our sanctuary. Our family. *Our* life." Kip reached up to trace delicate fingertips across his top lip, his expression caught between melancholy and wonder. "You will return to me after this folly is ended, my Hiero."

A kiss in lieu of a lie. But after such a declaration, Hiero couldn't keep himself from claiming Kip's mouth with a long, sensuous press of lips, affirming his devotion. Then more languorously, permitting Kip to explore the fresh-shaven curves with nips and nuzzles, a courtship of caresses. But the fever that had consumed them for the better part of the year—and the fear of what might transpire that night—soon had them prone and panting.

As he made his way along the Strand toward The Gaiety some-time later, Beastly once more, he revisited every second of their interlude. The scent of Kip's most intimate places, his delectably male musk. The wildness of his expression as Hiero took him. The sag of his singing body in Hiero's arms. How Kip pulled Hiero atop him on Terriss's bed, touching from brows to toes, and held him, close and true.

He walked in the shadow of the friend whose murder he sought to avenge, from Terriss's secret hideaway to the Strand, where he'd honed his craft and earned his success, through the stage door that had welcomed him every night, into the dressing room that had been his final refuge. Hiero thought of everything that remained unsaid between him and Kip and wished he'd been braver in their last moments together.

"Remember, if anything goes awry, shout 'Stoker' and drop to the floor," Kip had instructed as he ran a comb through Hiero's hair, a tender ritual. "Grab de Casterac and exit stage left to the auditory. Hide in the crowd, follow them into the street. I'll find you there."

"And here I thought the purpose of this endeavor was to draw out our fiend," Hiero murmured, so as not to distract from Kip's ministrations.

"To out them, yes. To disappear you, no."

"Better myself than—"

"Some inferior captive?" With a final flick, Kip set down the comb and gripped his hands into Hiero's shoulders. Possibly resisting the urge to shake sense into him. "We're entering an undiscovered country. We know how they behave when they are denied. We cannot know what they will do when presented with the object of their obsession." Kip dropped a kiss onto the crown. "I'll not see another hair on your head harmed, by the ghost or any other. Not while I still draw breath."

Their gazes met in the mirror, eloquent with feeling. Hiero had never seen such ache in Kip's eyes as upon his leave-taking a few minutes after. He'd rushed to the window to watch Kip cross the courtyard where Terriss's body had lain mere days ago, until he disappeared down the Bulls Inn Court alleyway. It had taken everything in Hiero not to call him back, to cancel everything, to declare himself, to beg him to abandon this foggy island and decamp with their family to parts unknown.

Instead he screwed his courage to the sticking place.

After shutting the door on the backstage chaos, Hiero sat himself before another of Terriss's mirrors to paint his face in the colors of another tormented character. And, with a bit of luck, to conjure up the performance that had won him accolades. But where some sorcerers worked their magic with elixirs and potions, Hiero cast his spell with costume and makeup. He whispered a charm as he picked up his brush, and...

Recoiled. Stifled a scream. Fought to even his panicked breaths as he reached for the note hidden there, emblazoned with a garish red-ink five.

Sing a song worth tuppence
A poppy full of cock
Two naughty blackbirds
Rook everywhere they knock
Tired of the flash life
The birds began to sing—
What trick can we use
To trap the wicked king?

The king was in his hideaway
Plotting out his wrath
The knave was in the spotlight
Breathing his last breath
The inspector paced to and fro
But no fiend did he find
Until a phantom stalked the aisles
And snatched him from behind

Sing a song of sixpence
A stage full of fright
One two-faced blackbird
Won't last the night

On impulse, Hiero shredded the note in half, then into pieces, then into tinier pieces, which he then fed to the flame of a candle, evidence be damned. As the taunting words disintegrated into flecks of cinder and plumes of smoke, he spared not a moment contemplating their meaning. Instead he continued with his maquillage. And if his hand shook as he wielded the brush, or if his fingers trembled as they daubed rouge on his cheeks, he paid them no mind.

His audience, and fate, awaited.

Spectacle, Tim mused as he watched the seats of the auditory fill to capacity, *will forever trump safety.* Though Hiero would no doubt take all the credit for The Gaiety's full house, they both had experience enough of the public's lurid curiosity to know that their killer, and not Horace Beastly's timely return, brought out the ghouls. He wondered if, should the worst occur, the audience would cheer or jeer the ghost's latest performance piece, no better than the Colosseum's bloodthirsty spectators in ancient Rome.

They certainly appeared primed for sport, not art, if their breathless whispers and darting eyes were any indication. Tim made a final tour of the gallery level, assuring himself each constable patrolled his section. The tension in the air crackled such that the hairs on the back of his neck stood straight. Standing in the stalls, where Tumnus had packed in so many there was barely room to twitch, must be akin to being in the center of a hive, with patrons buzzing and whooping and chattering until your head spun and your ears rung.

After checking he had time enough for a final sweep of the front entrance, Tim dodged around latecomers as he moved into the main corridor. Sneaking behind an ornate vase, Tim checked that DS Littlejohn stood guard outside the manager's office. He'd assigned detective sergeants as escorts to each of the principal suspects under the guise of their safekeeping—Tumnus and Littlejohn seemed a natural pairing—but in truth, it was a precaution. This gambit of Hiero's wouldn't work twice. By night's end, Tim would see their fiend in shackles, or they would be the ones fleeing to the continent.

To Tim's annoyance, Littlejohn and his usual gang of minions gathered in a circle outside Tumnus's office, smoking cigars and snickering over some crude joke. Superintendent Quayle had insisted no others could be spared that night, and Tim hadn't doubted him. Worthier officers received prime assignments; this lot were lucky to act as glorified nannies to Tim's suspects. By the looks of things, they couldn't even manage that much. Corralling his patience, for it wouldn't do to let easy prey distract him from the hunt for big game, he stalked toward them, only to halt before he could be spotted.

Through the open door to the manager's office, Tim spied Tumnus, Croÿ-Roeulx, and several other men toasting to a successful opening night. Among them was one Colonel Sir Hugh Winterbourne, Commissioner of the Police of the Metropolis and Tim's high superior. Only Commissioner Winterbourne chanced to look up as Tim observed them. Catching Tim's eye, he gave an approving nod. Tim saluted him in return, then skulked off to the grand staircase before Littlejohn or some other could ruin the moment.

Not that Tim felt any relief knowing his actions that night would be observed by a man who could ruin his career. Commissioner Winterbourne owed Tim a significant debt for locating his long-lost son earlier that year, but he wouldn't be the first powerful man to punish, instead of reward, such service, especially given the secrets Tim kept. As he scanned over the last arrivals—morbid curiosity had lit a fire under the audience, so the theater was uncharacteristically full before the performance began—Tim felt the weight of his responsibility sit heavy on his shoulders.

Only his reputation, relationship, and career depended on outsmarting a maniacal fiend.

In the auditory beyond, the orchestra gave their instruments a final tuning. Tim took up watch at the back of the stalls. Waves of thunderous applause crashed through the audience, though the curtain had yet to rise. Tim couldn't help but suffer a frisson of excitement himself. Whatever dramatics, real or fictional, transpired on stage that night, Tim would never lose his love of the theater, or watching the aforementioned "greatest actor of his generation" entertain a crowd.

And indeed the first play, a three-act melodrama about tragic lovers Abelard and Heloise starring the Vauquelin sisters, absorbed him such that he almost neglected his duty. In this version, the story's edges dulled for English audiences, the lovers were ripped apart by Heloise's cruel uncle when she became pregnant out of wedlock. Both were forced to take religious orders despite having married in secret, their legendary correspondence their only connection for the rest of their days.

By the time the Vauquelins took their bows, Tim discreetly daubed his handkerchief at the corners of his eyes. Primed not to miss a second of the action in case some villainy occurred, few in the audience left their seats during the first interval. The horde of people in the stalls became rowdy, catcalling and criticizing the ballerinas who took to the stage dressed as angels and demons to rouse anticipation for the five-act burlesque: *The Be-Deviled Tale of Don Juan, the Libertine.*

Tim traded his handkerchief for his truncheon when the curtain dropped on the dancers and the orchestra roared back to life. A ferocious percussive overture pounded out from the pit, silencing the mischief-makers. Everyone in the auditory craned forward in their seats, peering into the low light as the curtain rose to reveal a dark stage. Footsteps echoed like the ticking of a clock, but no figure appeared. Then, a burst of light, a flood of smoke… and Horace Beastly as Don Juan, addressing the audience with piratical flair.

Rogue. Seducer. Libertine. Man of a thousand faces. Don Juan truly was the part Hiero was born to play. Tim, of course, knew the reality, the compassionate and weary soul who took on the mantle of Hieronymus Bash to survive a world so often against him. Whereas Hiero hid in plain sight to be accorded the respect some men were granted simply by virtue of birth, Don Juan used his powers of persuasion to charm, deceive, and live a life of debauchery. Still, Don Juan's story served as something of a cautionary tale for Hiero, and the similarities between their experiences brought out his best. Whether luring Dona Ana into his arms for the sinful night that set off the plot; or slaying her father, the righteous Don Gonzalo; or daring God to strike him down when confronted with his crimes, Hiero commanded the stage.

The audience, rapt, almost forgot to clap between acts. Seraphine Vauquelin often stammered through her lines, so mesmerized was she by Hiero's stare. Even Madame de Casterac, a virtuoso herself in the dual role of Don Gonzalo and the Devil, struggled at first to match Hiero's intensity and nuance. The murder scene became so engrossing Tim almost forgot to breathe.

He tore his eyes away from the stage, forcing himself to scan the auditory before the final act: the infamous last supper scene, where Don Juan invited a statue of Don Gonzalo to dinner. Dona Ana, having discovered that her lover murdered her father, begged him to repent of his sins. The Devil emerged from the stone of the statue, beckoning Don Juan to join him in Hell, promising an afterlife of never-ending debauchery. Don Juan could not resist such an offer, and burned in hellfire for all eternity. The Devil, after all, would have his due.

If their fiend, with their own twisted flair for the dramatic, meant to strike, they would wait until the last supper.

The audience gasped when the lights lifted on the scene change. Tumnus had spared no expense: a dining hall drenched in jeweled reds and dark golds, a magnificent chandelier suspended over a long black table, and, stage left, a balcony with a trompe l'oeil background, implying a second floor. Tim crouched down, attempting to see up into the flies to spot any looming danger. As the actors came to life, Tim did his best to ignore them. He looked to his allies positioned around the auditory, everyone waiting for the ax to fall.

It hit, as these things did, like an earthquake.

Just as Madame de Casterac, wily and minx eyed as the Devil, commenced her victory monologue, a familiar hooded figure stepped onto the balcony, ax replaced by a giant scythe. The audience, thinking this part of the performance, whooped and cheered. A creak, a snap, and the chandelier wobbled, dropping a few feet before springing to a stop. The actors stilled; the crowd yelped. Tim seized his truncheon with both hands.

"Timée!" Marius pushed through the constables that had assembled beside Tim, transfixed by the trouble on stage. "Timée, come quickly! Backstage, there is a..." Tim turned to him at the same time as Marius caught sight of the stage. "Mon Dieu! It's the phantom!"

Tim took him by the arms. "What's happened backstage?"

Marius shook his head as if to clear it. He bent toward Tim to whisper, "A body. Who it is, I cannot say. It is too... You must come now."

A glance back at the stage caught the hooded figure raising their scythe. With a pat on his shoulders, Tim pulled away, but Marius held firm.

"Please, Timée, you must come!" Marius wailed. "She is suffering!"

"She?! Who is she?"

"Come with me, and I—"

The audience shrieked. Marius blanched. Tim whipped around in time to see the chandelier crash into the table, engulfing the stage in a blast of splinters and shattered glass.

Abandoning Marius, Tim dove into the melee, swimming steadily upstream but unable to part the tide of the crowd to permit swift passage. Stagehands carried Madame de Casterac and Mademoiselle Vauquelin away from the chandelier's wreckage, tiptoeing around the corona of shards and splinters that encircled the crash site. And on the balcony above the hissing, spitting chandelier, the phantom cackled their delight.

To Tim's dismay, Hiero raced up to the balcony, blocking the fiend's exit with the full breadth of his frame. Even from his distance, Tim recognized the dark challenge in Hiero's eyes—one the hooded figure met with vigor. Desperate, Tim shoved people aside as he pushed to the stage. No fighter, Hiero used the props available to him, smashing fake lanterns and swinging pulley weights at his opponent. The fiend delivered a pair of cracking blows but missed Hiero's obvious dodge and toppled over the rail. In a stunning show of agility, they swung back up and slammed Hiero into a corner.

Tim swallowed a cry as he tore through the crowd. Above, Hiero bared his claws, gouging into his opponent's hood and grabbing for their mask. Rather than put them at a disadvantage, however, it gave the fiend the momentum they needed to lock onto Hiero's arm, yank him off his feet, and toss him over the rail...

...ripping a seam so wide in the fabric of Tim's existence it would never be mended.

Tim lost time. One moment he looked up to check on Hiero, and the next he knelt at his corpse's side. He cradled Hiero's limp hand in his, searched his vacant eyes for a final glimmer. Ignored the metal pike that punched through his chest like an angry fist. Stifled the wounded animal yowl that threatened to tear from his throat. Pressed a hand to his own chest, to his heart, and was startled to discover it still intact, still beating. It only felt like their fiend had ripped it out and crushed it under their boot.

His light, his Hiero, the brief candle of their love stuffed out.

The phantom. Tim pried his gaze away from his beautiful, broken Hiero, looked up at the balcony from which he'd fallen and into the vacant eyes of the Red Skull. Tim clamped his jaw on a growl, his desire for vengeance dripping like fresh blood from his mouth.

Above, the mask shifted away to reveal the half moon of an all-too-familiar face.

A face that, far from reassuring, had the gall to wink at him.

Caught between fury and amazement, Tim stared down at the "corpse" of his beloved, seeing with new eyes. The slightly too boneless slump of the frame. The putty smoothness of his cheek. The fingernails that gleamed with lacquer. Most significantly, the pristine swath of exposed chest around the pike—no hair, no scars.

Time slowed as Tim sat there, immobile, clutching a straw-filled hand.

As if in mockery of the grief that still swelled Tim's throat, Hieronymus Bash strode out of the wings, frowned gravely at the body of his doppelganger, and playacted checking for signs of life.

Tim's hands quaked, though whether out of the desire to seize Hiero in a fierce embrace or throttle him till he collapsed beside this… whatever it was, he didn't know. Reminded that despite the near-empty auditory and abandoned wings, someone monitored every move they made, Tim retreated into the only sanctuary that could save him now: doing his duty.

"DC Whitehall!" he barked, rising to his feet. "Report!"

"All actors and stagehands have been gathered in the safe room, with two guards at the door."

"Make it three."

"Yes, sir."

"DC Foxglove!" Tim shouted. A silhouetted figure appeared at the back of one of the gallery boxes. "Make the rounds. Check every exit, speak to every officer. Full reports in the front hall in twenty minutes."

"Sir!"

"Mr. Calvin!" Callie trotted out onto the stage, chin high, out of character and unrepentant as to her obvious involvement in Hiero's ruse. "See to Mr. Beastly's remains."

Her cool blue eyes flared with annoyance. "But the fiend—"

"At once."

The march step of determined footsteps echoed through the auditory as Tumnus, Croÿ-Roeulx, and Winterbourne, with Littlejohn in tow, descended from the gallery to the backstage.

Tim watched them disappear into the rear stairs and cursed to himself. "Han!"

"Checking the trap for mice," Hiero remarked.

Tim let out a long sigh. "Then all is not lost."

"On the contrary." Hiero stood, moved in close to Tim, who backed away. "Our part in this great game has only begun."

"Your part, perhaps." Tim hissed. "I am, as ever, the last to know."

It felt absurd, objecting to Hiero's methods when he'd all but given him permission to do his worst, but Tim had been sincere in his belief in their power as a team. In the strength of their togetherness. And still Hiero had deceived him, bringing Tim's nightmares to life before his very eyes. Without a word of warning. Anger only skimmed the surface of the feelings this small betrayal bubbled up.

Hiero had the grace to look dismayed. He slipped a hand under Tim's collar, gripped the join of neck to shoulder. Tim again pushed him off. Muttering every invective in every language his enraged mind could think of, he turned away to help Callie arrange the "body" in a more authentic death tableau. He retched into his mouth at now being complicit in their scheme. But nothing and no one could spare him this. He could not preach togetherness and then throw them to the wolves, though he hated himself something fierce for longing, despite it all, for Hiero's embrace.

Tim turned to confront the tribunal of severe, stern-eyed faces— with the exception of Littlejohn, who sneered in near delight— awaiting their guilty plea, their mea culpa.

"Gentlemen," Hiero greeted with an open sweep of his arms. "If you'll be so good as to follow DC Whitehall into the waiting safe room, we'll soon have a head for your noose."

Chapter 18

*A*fter a quick change out of the Don Juan costume that had permitted him to double Hiero during their fight—and Hiero to switch from Don Juan to Red Skull to Bash in record time—Han bundled all the clothes they'd dropped into a sack and escaped to the roof. Not just a ruse to hide away the tricks of their former trade, he checked the cross point between The Gaiety and its adjoining building for evidence someone had snuck over. Finding none, he walked the edge until he reached the perfect vantage over the front entrance of the theater.

Chaos reigned below. A flood of frightened patrons rushed into the Strand with no thought as to direction or destination, swamping passing carriages and mooring the few hansoms hailed by the first wave out. They poured into nearby restaurants and pubs, seeking the sanctuary of commonplace surroundings, of lively chatter—not that those that lingered in the street forgot to gossip and gasp and relive the most shocking moments again and again.

Han traced the tale of Horace Beastly's grisly death at the hands of The Gaiety ghost as it traveled, with its audience, down the length of the Strand. Already pools of teary-eyed mourners threatened to drown the flower hawkers, such was the demand for blooms to lay by The Gaiety's doors. A small group of reporters, lured away from their drinks by the pull of a bigger fish, shouted down one of the ushers for not letting them in to view the body.

Which put Han in mind of *The Pall Mall Gazette's* best source on the Strand and whether she was in the auditory when Horace Beastly jousted with the chandelier. He'd been on the lookout for Miss Marks before and during the performance, but hadn't spotted her, and the ticket he'd offered her had gone unclaimed. Han also hadn't caught sight of anyone fitting the description he'd been given of Arascain. Either Miss Marks had kept her promise, or the critic had come in disguise.

But what aspiring reporter would keep away from such a scene? Not one of her ambition. Still, he couldn't quite convince himself to chase her down after the disastrous way they'd left things. Han should have felt relief, but the thought that he'd been the one to disappoint her didn't sit well with him. He understood all too well how impossible it was to break through certain societal barriers and wanted to be of more help to her.

Yet his obligations demanded his attention. Han waited until it looked as if everyone in the auditory had left to head back in, avoiding any constables who might still be patrolling, who might see him as the sort of trouble they needed to report, thus distracting from actual trouble. As he scaled down the roof ladder, sneaking into the stairs that led to the royal entrance and Box 5, a rush of anticipation suffused him. Though he knew better than to hope their fiend had taken the bait, that they had enough intimate knowledge of Hiero/Horace's proclivities to understand the significance of Box 5, Han acknowledged it would be satisfying to unmask the phantom who stalked them.

Whether their identity simplified or complicated the team's attempt to bring them to justice remained to be seen. But whomever had stumbled into his trap, wolf in sheep's clothing, or simply wolf, Han would see to it they'd never be free again.

After a quick peek down the corridor to assure he was alone, Han shut and locked the door to the two side boxes. He patted the inner pockets of his jacket for the knives concealed there. He'd considered and discarded the idea of borrowing Callie's MAS revolver. A risk no matter how he armed himself, but a necessary one. But given how murderous this particular fiend was, Han wouldn't gamble with any life but his own.

He stared at Box 5, centered himself. Senses alert and limbs poised to strike, he measured every step until he stood before the door. The nigh-invisible hair he'd stretched across the top corner had been severed.

Someone was inside.

With a slender instrument, he worked the tines of the lock until they opened without a sound. He inhaled a deep breath, held it, eased the door open a crack. Silhouetted against the eerie glow of the gaslit auditory, a figure sat. Unless there were two of them—still a possibility—Han's trap had worked. He inched the door open farther and ensured that no one hid above or at the sides, waiting to pounce. Once confident no surprises awaited him other than the fiend's identity, Han entered with purpose.

A gentleman always announced himself, after all, with a lady present.

His heart sank when the gaslight caught the golden shimmer of her hair. Han hovered behind her for a time, wondering if this moment was inevitable from the first time they'd met, hoping he hadn't ignored vital clues because of... well, because. He'd wanted so much more for her. But then, she'd been lost to him before he ever set eyes on her.

"I've been waiting for you," Miss Maxine Marks, or the woman who'd taken that name, said without turning her head. "As soon as I took a seat and heard the clicks, I cursed myself a fool. Of course it would be you. My mistake. My undoing."

"I felt the same just now, as I entered."

"Not before?" She turned her head but still did not look at him. "I was certain I'd struck the wrong tone at our last encounter. Overplayed my hand."

"If I'd suspected then, I wouldn't have let you leave."

"No." She shook her head. "Too obvious, Arascain. Overwritten. Not my work, I assure you."

"But you were responsible."

"I played messenger. In all things." She glanced at him then, and the blue shock of her eyes still stirred something in him. Han suspected it was pity. "I still do."

"Messenger to whom?"

"Wouldn't you care to know." She stared at him, piercingly, until the chill seeped into his bones. "The boy you sent. How you waited in the square each morning for word that would never come." Her mouth hardened into a firm line. "You shouldn't have sent a boy."

Han refused to give her the satisfaction of his reaction to the dual blows she'd pummeled him with, that someone thought dead still lived, that someone who deserved a long, easy life had been struck down too soon. The former should have filled him with dread, but the latter cut deepest. Toby—not a boy by any definition, given what hardship he'd known, much like Han himself once, and Miss Marks as well, all struggling to better their place in the world, to raise themselves from nothing.

That detail, more than anything, condemned her.

"Say his name," Han insisted. "The one who pulls your strings."

"Why bother?"

"You'll forgive me harboring some doubts."

Miss Marks scoffed. "I see your doubts and raise you Horace Beastly being skewered by a chandelier. Appearances do tend to deceive."

"And the dead make easy scapegoats." He slipped a hand into his jacket, curled it around the hilt of a knife. "His name." A hint of a smile twisted her lips, as if she savored another small victory. Han fought not to shudder. "And do you bear his mark?"

The twist curled into a full, menacing smirk. "On my neck."

With due caution, Han stepped closer. "May I?"

"If you must."

With the tip of his knife, he pushed aside the curtain of her hair and plucked open the four buttons at the back of her high collar. Han peeled back one side of the cloth, revealing a fanglike tattoo of a far deadlier knife: a dagger.

Until that moment, he'd hoped Hiero's misgivings were only that, speculation based not on the facts of the case but the fears they both harbored. Well-founded fears, it turned out. If Han had learned anything from the trials of their past, it should have been to trust Hiero's instincts. Instead he'd let himself be lured into complacency by their recent good fortune, by the soft pillow of luxury.

Miss Marks, villain though she might be, saw it from the first. Their story might have had a different ending if he hadn't made himself such an easy target.

Han stole a few moments to refocus his mind while refastening her collar.

"Satisfied?" Miss Marks purred.

He dropped his hands from her neck, backed away. "Not in the least. But I will make do, as always."

"'Make do,'" she mocked. "In that big house with its warm beds and full pantry, a carriage with fat cushions, and a porcelain doll to flirt with? I wish I could go without as you have these last years." She clicked her tongue. "And all the while, the man who gave you that life survived on weevil loaves and tattered blankets beside a one-log fire."

"And thoughts of revenge?" Han wanted to spit out the sour taste in his mouth. "Any yarn teller worth her salt should know there are two sides to every story."

"I know what I've seen."

"What he showed you." Han sighed. "'The best illusions stand on the shoulders of truth' was the first of many lessons I learned under his... tutelage, I suppose one might call it. But not the most valuable."

Miss Marks raised a brow as she turned to face him, at an angle that defied her restraints. "Would that be 'where to stab the knife to inflict the most damage'?"

"No."

Han met her eyes, shining with triumph, and knew he'd been caught. The click of the gun, as she stood and took aim at him, pinged like the spring of a trap. Han reached back, grabbing for the door, but hit on something solid, human. He had only seconds to curse his luck before everything went black.

Hiero struck what he hoped was an authoritative pose as he and Kip listened to the testimony of the seven constables collected in The Gaiety's front hall. Or, rather, Kip listened and Hiero ruminated. He had never been the most attentive audience, even to those he cherished, especially when a companion could summarize for him later. This particular bout of distraction afflicted him not because of the tipsy butterfly rhythms of his mind, but out of the need to brood over the aftermath of his great gambit against the ghost.

Broody, thy name was not Hiero. Contemplation, introspection, analysis… That way madness lay. Perhaps the multiple character swaps had loosed something in his brain. Perhaps the extreme pressure of the circumstances had caused him to doubt himself. But one glance at Kip's face when Hiero emerged from the wings in full Bash regalia after Beastly's "demise" had brought forth an emotion heretofore foreign to his way of being: regret. Though he'd kept on with the performance, as any actor of worth would, he felt the force of Kip's anger and hurt like a horse hoof to the head.

Wounded and confused in his own right, he'd reached for Kip when he shouldn't have—an empty, placating gesture, he knew, but a necessary connection. A glinting hardness had sharpened Kip's stare, and Hiero almost recoiled. Even now, though an arm's length from one another, Kip might have been in another theater entirely, given the lack of attention sent Hiero's way. And so he brooded, and second-guessed, and struggled for a sense of himself, a feeling that, for all his myriad metamorphoses, he'd never experienced before. Though Hiero changed identities like waistcoats, he'd always enjoyed a deep and unconflicted sense of self.

Yet another way his relationship with Kip had bettered him.

The interviews concluded, the constables dispersed, and Kip dashed off toward the grand staircase. Hiero stumbled over his own feet as he hurried after him. He could not match Kip for speed or determination, and so fell behind. By the time he heaved himself up the last stair, Kip had jogged halfway down the corridor. Two yelps and a whistle later, Kip still did not turn.

Only a pratfall, it seemed, would do. Slightly exaggerating his heaving breaths and lack of coordination, Hiero tripped on a dense thatch of carpet, staggered twenty or so paces, and crashed into the standing vase. A fake, it failed to shatter, but the loud thud prompted Kip to spin around, truncheon at the ready. Too kindhearted to leave Hiero sprawled on the floor, he righted the vase as Hiero lurched back to his feet and assayed his most sheepish look.

Not fooled, Kip glared, though he did wait for Hiero to right himself. If only the mood between them could be improved with a few minor adjustments. A quick survey confirmed they were indeed alone. Still, in the interest of caution, Hiero gestured toward the bar area. A quick shot of whiskey, Hiero thought, would do them both a world of good. "A word?"

Kip's frown deepened. "I've heard rather enough of what you have to say for one night, Mr. Bash."

"But I fear you've misunderstood."

Kip shot him a gimlet eye. "Our suspects, and my superior, await. The night has been a shambles. We've no culprit to present to them. My lack of understanding of your latest tomfoolery hardly ranks as urgent."

"To you, perhaps."

"And there's the difference between us. Perfectly illustrated."

Hiero conceded the point with a nod. "Our methods *are* different, I grant. But you agreed—"

"To bear witness to your death?!" Kip, surprised by his own volume, pressed a knuckle to his lips. The tension in his fingers might have crushed stone. "No, I most certainly did not agree to watch as the... The only person..." Kip shut his eyes, shook his head. "Did you even consider our initial plan? Pretending the ghost nabbed Beastly? Or was this in your mind from the first moment, and I your only obstacle to carrying it out? Dispatched with a castoff lie and a pat on the head, without a care to my... To our..."

Hiero took advantage of his momentary upset to usher him into the bar, shutting the door behind them. By the time he turned around, Kip had sagged onto a stool, head in his hands.

Though Hiero ached to console him, he doubted his touch would be welcome. Instead he fetched the whiskey. Or perhaps brandy? What particular poison spoke to contrition? "The truth had to be writ bold across your face."

Kip slammed a fist on the bar. "Manipulated into a performance by the man who shares... You are nothing if not an original, Mr. Bash. Pity the audience fled before they could appreciate the breadth of your talent."

"The ruse wasn't for them."

"For the fiend, then?"

"Who else?" Hiero implored. "If you believed it, they would believe it."

"Yes, but what you fail to understand is I had to *live* it." Kip scowled at the brandy but took at greedy sip. "And you allowed it. You *wanted* me to—"

"For a minute, before I reemerged. A matter of seconds before you learned the truth."

"That no gag is too cruel if it's part of a game, even when lives are at stake?" Kip sneered. "Oh yes, I learned that all too well." He threw back the rest of his brandy, banged the tumbler down. Grabbed the bottle from Hiero and poured himself another shot. "I thought, I truly thought, that you believed in what we could be together. That all this was more to you than just another adventure."

"It is," Hiero insisted, longing more than ever to reach for him, to hold him, to prove in body the spirit of his words. "You are."

"Balderdash." Kip bowed his head, stared into the amber depths of his glass, his thirst and his ire doused by melancholy.

Hiero sighed, at sea as to how to tow Kip back to him. "One cannot mourn an illusion. The corpse was that and nothing more."

"Your hand, cold and lifeless in mine. Your eyes, waxen, vacant. The shard of metal jutting from your chest. And when we'd just begun, when we'd only..." His thin, coppery lashes fluttered rapidly but let no tear slip through. "I will never forget it."

Hiero reached out an open hand, laid it on the bar near Kip. Everything in him begged him to grasp it. "But I am here with you. You've only to—"

"Give over? Surrender myself? To what end, if I'm to be the only one steadying the boat? Either we're in this together, or..."

Hiero, tired of waiting, grasped his arm. "Or we've different notions of how to play captain." Though this didn't even win him a chuckle, he pressed on. "Your methods are... well, methodical. My own flirt with the abstract."

"And heartbreak."

"An unintended consequence, my... my dearest one." Having secured one tether, he dared two, twining both of Kip's hands in his. "I didn't think. Which was, if I am honest, my aim. To shoot wild. But I ended up wounding someone—you—who was not my target, rather than our fiend." Hiero inhaled deeply. "Forgive me?"

Kip pulled his hands out of Hiero's grip without so much as a squeeze, pushed his glass aside and stood. "Work to be done."

Hiero rushed out from behind the bar, blocked his path.

"Timothy." He caught and locked into Kip's startled gaze. "I am so very, very sorry. You are... everything. Please believe that."

"I do." Despite the telltale glistening in his eyes, Kip rallied his emotions. "You are, as ever, most persuasive, Mr. Bash. But when your actions belie your words... which am I to trust? *My* ambition is true partnership, in all things. Such a partnership requires absolute honesty. Else I cannot see a future for us."

Kip brushed past him and hurried off, the hounds of duty forever at his heels, no matter his distress.

Alone, Hiero longed to drown his sorrows in a friendly bottle. But Kip's heartache and admonishments sunk deep, and the tidal pull of their connection tugged Hiero after him, sink or swim.

Chapter 19

*T*heir footsteps echoed through the vacant auditory as they traveled through the side passages to the backstage, Tim at a quick march, Hiero lagging behind. Tim almost raised a handkerchief against the reek of terror that lingered in the air along with the scent of singed metal and scorched wood. He forced his gaze straight ahead, though it drifted again and again to the site of the crashed chandelier, where one gore-red prong jutted up from the remains.

Was it paint? Pig's blood? A perverse part of Tim's brain remained eager for answers about the mechanics of how they'd done it, though his heart could never have endured the explanation.

"Mr. Calvin." Tim suffered a small pang of guilt at the relief that suffused him at the sight of Callie waiting for them by the backstage entrance. Intelligent, cunning, capable—at least Tim could depend on one of his colleagues. Though she had participated in Hiero's daft plan, he didn't count this as a strike against her since she'd been raised in that unconventional household and their ways imprinted on her at a young age. Unlike certain bon vivants he had the misfortune to be in love with. "The body has been secured?"

"Dispatched to the coroner, sir, with Angus at the reins."

"Any word from our ghost-hunting friend?" The vague hope that Han, the second pillar on which Tim could rebuild his confidence in their team, had trapped their fiend buoyed his spirits.

"None as of yet."

Tim sighed. "How are the captives?"

"Threatening everything from our livelihoods to our firstborns if we don't release them soonish."

"Anyone unaccounted for?" Hiero swept in, glaring at the interlopers who hovered around them.

"Worse." For the first time in memory, Callie appeared uncertain. Her keen blue eyes darted from Tim to Hiero and back again, taking the temperature. Unsurprised that one of her instincts smelled the sickness that had set in, Tim nevertheless encouraged her with a nod. He could only focus on one ailing aspect of his existence at a time, and the case took precedence. "Seraphine Vauquelin has been taken."

Tim swallowed back an oath. "Taken? You're certain?"

"Yes. Mademoiselle Damiane is spitting fire. Given how inseparable the two are..."

"Not an abandonment. The work of her admirer, most like."

"Or, per my theory, our ghost."

"And we no closer to identifying them," Tim grumbled. "And Beastly's body still warm."

A cold, hollow silence descended upon them.

"Retaliation, swift and sudden," Hiero murmured dramatically. Tim shot a questioning look his way. "Not an act of desperation, but a contingency plan. If not Horace, then Seraphine. Our fiend would have his way."

"Unless *she* is our ghost," Callie pointed out. "She wouldn't be the first actress to pretend an admirer."

"With her sister as coconspirator, left behind to sell the story as an abduction?" Tim considered. "I might almost believe it, save for her face the night they discovered Flint's head."

"Need I remind you she is an actress?"

"Touché," Tim conceded. "Motive?"

Here Callie stammered before settling on: "Terriss was her first admirer, but she despised him. Afraid Tumnus meant to pack the troupe off back to France, she begins a campaign to scare the English out of The Gaiety so Monsieur le Vicomte can take ownership...?"

"And why, pray, does this involve sending complicated notes, in English, to Horace Beastly, already banished from The Gaiety's company?" Tim queried, flirting with amusement to keep despair at bay. "Not to mention she and Damiane's 'sisterhood' would come under less scrutiny in France."

Callie threw up her arms. "Then we'd best expand our list of suspects beyond The Gaiety because everyone else is accounted for. And the constables guarding the door will see *your* head in a box if you dare suggest one of them was derelict in their duty." She harrumphed. "I may know from experience."

"Hold." Tim raised a finger. "Mademoiselle Seraphine was stolen from a room full of suspects, with the door barred by constables?"

Callie gave a curt shake of her head. "She caused a fuss until one of them escorted her to her dressing room, that she might change out of her heavy costume."

"Dare I guess which one?"

"Only if you say Littlejohn."

Tim couldn't keep the smirk from his face, though both Callie and Hiero's expressions seemed to wonder if he'd finally lost his head. And certainly if Littlejohn proved to be in league with their phantom, Tim would regret his reaction. But despite the direness of the circumstances, a part of him couldn't help a silent cheer that he might finally see the end of Littlejohn.

"Same trouble, different location," Hiero commented. "Snatched from one guarded dressing room or another makes no matter. Unless she can walk through walls."

"Perhaps she is our ghost," Callie quipped, but appeared unconvinced. "Or, per my theory—"

"Now fact," Tim confirmed, abandoning his mirth as quickly as it came on. "A safe room full of suspects and a kidnapped ingénue lead to only one conclusion: there are two. Though I fear the second may be unknown to us, an understudy mentored by one of our players behind the scenes."

"Giving them knowledge about and access to The Gaiety."

"Among other advantages." Tim turned to Hiero. He fought the pang of longing that reverberated within him at the hope reflected in Hiero's eyes. "We've established that lurking undetected in a theater this size would be easy if you kept to the shadows and wore the right costume. But, in your expert opinion, could one simply... blend in with the company? Pretend to go about one's business and linger on the edge of crowds?"

"A servant, perhaps?" Callie added. "To the Vicomte or Madame de Casterac. No one pays them any mind. And we did see Jean-Georges in the Vauquelins' rooms in the Caledonian."

"Is that so?" Tim followed the logic of that line of inquiry but still couldn't see the greater pattern at work. Croÿ-Roeulx had one of the weakest motives, and Jean-Georges struck him as mundane, not menacing. Though the Vicomte did love his melodrama...

Hiero operatically cleared his throat. "In my expert opinion... Yes. Quite possible. Under the old guard, I daresay not. Webster had his faults, but he ran a tight ship. But now, with everyone new, even Silas admitted to me—under the strictest oath of privacy, of course—he couldn't keep track."

"Flint." Tim heard the familiar click, the last piece falling into place. The puzzle spread out across the plain of his mind, complete but lacking interpretation. "Terriss was killed to make way for Beastly's return, but why kill Flint?" Tim felt his pulse quickening, his breaths heaving fast and hard. "Because he would know our ghost, this shadow accomplice, was not part of the company. Because Flint made a point of learning the names and positions of everyone in the French troupe, and this second could no longer hide among their ranks."

"But who, then?" Callie threw up her arms in a very un-Calvin-like gesture. "And if this partner is doing the devil's work, how do we uncover them? Or the true mastermind, if there's no blood on their hands?"

"Patience," Hiero interrupted as Tim made to answer. Though to his annoyance, he would have counseled the same. "I'd remind you that we set our own plan in motion too recently to see a definitive result."

Tim ignored him. "For the moment, we've our betters to appease and Mademoiselle Vauquelin's disappearance to investigate. Mr. Calvin, if you'd be so good as to track down Han and see what he caught in his net. Once we know what the day's fishing has yielded, we'll be better placed to plot our next move."

With a resolute nod, she set off. Tim had nowhere to turn but toward Hiero, who wore another unreadable expression. Tim should have taken it for the warning it was but only had eyes for the case.

"Whips at the ready, then," he declared as they veered toward the safe room. "Time to venture into the lion's den."

The two officers standing guard before the door to Madame de Casterac's dressing room—the most spacious of the backstage rooms, and therefore the most accommodating—didn't bother disguising their wary expressions when Tim and Hiero approached, though they did their best to keep a stiff upper lip. They stepped to the side to let them pass without comment or acknowledgement. After dashing off a quick knock, Tim entered briskly, as if carried on the winds of imminent success. Or so he hoped Commissioner Winterbourne interpreted his speed and steadfast bearing.

His suspects and their associates lounged around the palatial room in a tableau reminiscent of the works of Augustus Egg. Madame de Casterac, propped up by a thronelike gold chaise, let herself be flattered and feted by the dancers gathered at her feet. The Vicomte, oozing with aristocratic insouciance, hovered near. His servant Jean-Georges busied himself with refilling his glass from a bottomless bottle of wine. Tumnus cornered the commissioner against the wardrobe, sounding off with religious fervor while his audience swallowed a yawn. In the far corner, Damiane Vauquelin, still in her Abelard guise, slumped over a stool, sobbing. Stagehands and other minor players clung to the walls in whispering groups, the air rife with gossipy chatter.

Tim and Hiero snuck into the only available space to address the room. Upon spotting the detectives, everyone lunged, clamoring and complaining louder than The Gaiety's audience that night. Tim raised his hands in a pacifying gesture and lifted his head to speak, only to have Hiero cut in front of him and announce...

"All is well." He whistled sharply as they piped in with their protests, and a resigned silence fell. "You'll soon be free. We've reached a crucial stage of the investigation, and so it is vital at this late hour that we have your full cooperation. Now—"

"Do you have a suspect?" Tumnus demanded.

Hiero smirked. "That would be telling."

"Et Monsieur Beastly," Croÿ-Roeulx prompted. "Is he another victim, or is it possible someone has done away with our phantom?"

"I can confirm only that, to my great regret, Mr. Beastly is very much dead." Hiero's visible sadness appeared to sober them.

"Our priority is confirming the whereabouts of Mademoiselle Seraphine Vauquelin," Tim said. "Anyone who has interacted with her in the past hour must submit to a short—"

"Typical." Madame de Casterac sniffed. "La petite connasse must always make herself part of the drama. But the true artist serves the story, she doesn't rule—"

"Assez, Genevre," the Vicomte snapped. "Let the detectives do their work!"

"A meal of it they've made so far," Tumnus grumbled. "Two lead actors dead, a stage manager beheaded, and these fools—"

"But everyone is against them!" Croÿ-Roeulx shouted him down. "As you have been from the start, Monsieur Crapaud! And why? Because you do not want the ghost found!"

Madame de Casterac threw herself into the pile-on. "From the beginning, you have wanted us out. We're good enough to line your coffers, but when it comes to art—"

"How dare you accuse me—"

"You are behind all this—"

"Stolen from me not once, but twice—"

"Ladies and gentlemen!" Tim bellowed from atop a velvet footstool. He stared them all down until quiet reigned anew, only Winterbourne's smile giving him pause. "I'll remind you that a woman's life hangs in the balance. Now who was the last to speak to Mademoiselle Vauquelin before she departed with DS Littlejohn?"

From her corner, Mademoiselle Damiane lifted her head, pointed a finger in the air. The crowd parted for them as they made their way across the room, Tim seizing the lead. He kneeled before her and offered his handkerchief, waiting as she swabbed her swollen eyes. Stage makeup smeared her lids and temples, a bandit's mask, but her sorrow restored her innocence. In her flaxen Abelard wig, she resembled nothing more than a cherub.

"Mademoiselle." Tim switched to French, hoping this would give them a pocket of privacy amidst the eavesdropping crowd. "Believe me when I say we will do everything in our power to find your beloved sister."

"I do. This monster... Like a chimera. Pretends to be a man, but at heart..."

Behind him, Hiero cleared his throat.

"Can you recount your movements from when you came offstage after the last act of *Abelard and Heloise*?" Tim asked.

She nodded sluggishly. Her sorrow had until now hidden the fact that she was well in her cups. Tim wondered, given her reputation, if she'd imbibed before or after her sister's disappearance.

"I met the Constable Winslow in the wings. Seraphine had to prepare for Don Juan, so we went out the back to smoke."

"The performer's entrance?"

"Where else?"

"And did you stay by the door the whole time?"

"Bien sûr. One cannot wander in costume."

"And when you returned?"

"Monsieur le Vicomte had invited me to watch *Don Juan* in his box. I wished Seraphine merde and went along to join him."

"Was she in high spirits? Melancholy? As normal, or disturbed?"

"Nervous, but that is normal on opening night."

Tim considered how to phrase his next question, given its delicacy. Already he could feel the room's attention sharpening when Mademoiselle Damiane spoke of the Vicomte. "And so you were escorted to a box by Constable Winslow?"

Somewhere in her stupor, she must have realized the effect this detail had on her audience. "He is a charming fellow. And Monsieur le Vicomte very graciously invited him to watch with our group."

"Who else joined you?"

"Monsieur Tortue"—by which Tim knew she meant Mr. Tumnus—"Monsieur le Commissionaire, another constable, some investors... and two wives. I don't recall their names. 'The play's the thing.' Isn't that what your Shakespeare says?"

At Hiero's deep intake of breath, Tim hurried on. "And once the incident occurred?"

"Ah, la folie furieuse!" Mademoiselle Damiane sighed. "I must confess to you, Monsieur l'Inspecteur, that I did not obey the orders of Constable Winslow. You must understand, my only concern was for Sera. After the mess with Monsieur Flint and her admirer's horrible gifts... I was afraid."

"As well you should be."

"At that moment, no. I found her in our dressing room with her guard. Constable Winslow came soon after, and they brought us here. We were alone at the start, but then the others came. I left the box as soon as the chandelier fell, so I did not see what happened to Monsieur Beastly. When the others told us... Sera became upset. She could not catch her breath. Her costume was very tight. Madame Genevre gave her a fan, we gave her wine, but nothing helped. So the sergeant... Little Man, is it?"

"Littlejohn."

"Lui. Monsieur le Commissionaire asked him to take her back to the dressing room."

"Alone?"

"I didn't care to put anyone else at risk," Winterbourne, who had been following the conversation, explained.

After patting her on the hand, Tim stood to address him. "Of course, sir. Quite reasonable." Tim took a moment to look around, not just at the avid faces hanging on their every word, but at the layout of the room. Hiero caught his eye, raised a questioning brow, but Tim moved past him. Crowded, certainly, but suffocating?

Only then did he notice two people remained unaccounted for.

"DS Littlejohn, I presume, returned to inform you of the disappearance?" he asked Winterbourne. "Where is he now?"

"Under guard in one of the lounges." Winterbourne stepped closer to whisper, "He claims innocence. That he left Mademoiselle Vauquelin in her dressing room so she might change in privacy, and waited. When it had been too long without word, he entered, and she was gone."

"And your instinct, sir. What does it tell you?"

"That the goings-on here are too mysterious to lay blame at the feet of a fellow officer."

Tim sighed. "Quite. Is that why you sent him away?"

"No." Winterbourne chuckled. "He drew too much ire from this crowd. Didn't care to stoke their fires further."

"A wise decision, sir. You have my gratitude."

Tim paused a moment to consider the situation from all angles. Being a seamstress by trade, his mother had taught him a fair bit about the costuming. Enough to quibble with Miss Damian's version of events.

"A final question, mademoiselle. Why did Mademoiselle Seraphine have to change? She could hardly appear in company without a corset. Couldn't her stays be loosened? Or the sides of her dress be let out? Especially since she suffered a fit of nerves as much as a constricting garment?"

Anger fired her watery eyes. "If you had seen her, you would have done anything to help her. She was in agony."

"Which would have been alleviated with the aid of Mr. Lamarque, surely? Is that not his job, as head costumier?"

"Putain de merde!" Mademoiselle Damiane bellowed. "What are you suggesting? That Sera did this to herself? That she was merely acting?"

Hiero, without a hint of irony, drawled, "If the melodrama fits…"

"Salaud," Mademoiselle Damiane hissed, then spit on Tim's shoe. She crossed her arms over her chest and firmed her features against him. Until tears flood her eyes, and she bent over, sobbing anew.

Despite his suspicions about her sister, Tim's heart went out to her. Until somewhere behind him a grande dame of the theater cleared her throat, summoning his attention.

"Excusez-moi, Monsieur l'Inspecteur," Madame de Casterac pronounced with the weight of a royal decree. "But who is this Monsieur Lamarque you speak of?"

Tim's mind flashed to the time before the chandelier fell. Marius's panic, his insistence, beckoning Tim away from the stage. Remembered that he'd mentioned a body backstage, another murder. How had he forgotten? Tim had had no choice but to ignore him but cursed himself nonetheless, and Hiero's deception besides. If Tim had known Beastly's tangle with the Red Skull was just more theater, he might have helped his friend.

"Marius Lamarque, the head costumier. Has no one seen him since the incident?"

A look of bafflement overtook the entire group.

"Our costumes are from our tour of France last year," the Vicomte informed him. "Or from The Gaiety's vault. We employ our neighbor seamstresses for hemming and small adjustments, but we have no costumier."

Tim stared. Idiotically, he knew, but the news paralyzed him. Heartbeat echoing in his ears, vision sparking and flaring like whiskey splashed on a fire, he could not call up the words, let alone form them with his slack, speechless mouth, to question Croÿ-Roeulx further. In crisis, Tim looked to Hiero to save him. His wolfish expression spurred Tim back to life.

"Marius Lamarque is not employed by either your troupe, Monsieur le Vicomte, or The Gaiety?" Though both Croÿ-Roeulx and Tumnus shook their heads in dismay, Tim still felt the sting of disbelief. "Very well. We will perform an examination of Mademoiselle Vauquelin's dressing room. Once arrangements have been made for a personal escort for each of you, you're free to go."

"I will happily see to those in exchange for liberty," Commissioner Winterbourne offered.

"Good of you, sir," Tim managed to reply, not missing the concern that etched his face. "I'll report back within the hour."

Tim raced into the corridor without a glance back, knowing far more vicious hounds gave chase.

Chapter 20

*H*iero stood, helpless, in the doorframe as Kip meticulously searched the Vauquelins' dressing room. Not fooled by Kip's dogged examination of each and every surface or by his use of a magnifying glass to scrutinize the tiniest speck of powder, Hiero saw what others would not: the tremors in his fingers, the flush to his cheeks, the tense stretch of his coat across his shoulders. The hundred ways in which Kip forced himself to focus, rather than screaming the house down.

He'd made a mess of it. Try as he might, Hiero could no longer color his actions as anything but... well, dark gray. He should have trusted his instincts where Marius was concerned. Trusted that Kip would listen, would intuit his discomfort was more than jealousy. (Had it been? He couldn't say. Such was the muddle.) As to the Beastly gambit, he may have misjudged there. Perhaps. At the very least, he'd best admit so to Kip. Make a concession to repair things between them.

Trouble was, Hiero had no particular talent for reparations or apologizing. Or dragging them out of the quicksand in which their relationship currently sank. His few missteps with Apollo had been easily righted; one tended to be fleet of foot in matters of survival. But with Kip... nothing connected them. Except, of course, everything of any importance.

Hiero broke out of his dire musings to find Kip with his arms propped against the far wall, head bowed, breath ragged, body shaking. Fighting the urge to run to him, to gather him into an embrace and pet him like a thunder-spooked dog, Hiero instead walked over and hovered near, cajoling Kip with his presence. Hoped some small part of him was comforted by his proximity. In the wild carousel of his mind, Hiero went round and round on what to say, how to break him out of his self-recrimination. Because Kip would blame no one more than himself for his failure to see through Marius's deception.

In the end, Hiero could be no one other than himself. He poked. "Was he your friend from childhood?"

"Yes," Kip replied, voice thick.

"You're certain?"

"I knew him at once. Before we spoke. He recollected details no other could have known."

"Hmm." Hiero let the ensuing silence do his work for him. When Kip failed to take the bait, he poked harder. "I wonder why that is?"

To his relief, Kip stopped shaking but remained in his contrite pose. A small victory. "You think him a fraud?"

"Oh, he's most definitely a fraud, in action if not in identity. I only wonder... Why continue with his ruse if he recognized you in turn? And you a detective inspector, no less. There's hubris."

"No more than returning to a theater where you once trod the boards under another persona to investigate a series of crimes."

Hiero had steeled himself against the hit, but it smarted, more than expected. But it would not be the last. He raised his shields. "A cunning observation. Connected, in part, to my own thinking. The 'why' of it, of course. Why target Beastly in those notes? Why not you directly? Someone else? Tumnus, for instance. Why force my involvement at all?"

"If you're suggesting Marius knew I would be called to investigate..." Kip inhaled deeply. "I'm well past that assumption. Into darker territory, one might say."

"Oh?"

Kip wrenched himself off the wall and made a violent turn, eyes wet and red rimmed, but hard. "A figure from my past, planted as a distraction in the very theater you occupied for over a decade, during the case that lured you back. Notes and news items all but daring you to risk exposing your dual identity. Two murders and a series of incidents, all pointing the finger in Beastly's direction should your deception be revealed." Red flooded Kip's face, but his voice shocked with its arctic chill. "Not a game. Revenge. You've known from the first who's behind this. You've known all along."

Hiero wanted to cower. To bluster his way through some far-fetched confabulation. But if he meant to keep even this tenuous hold on Kip, he must give him nothing but the truth. "Not known. Suspected."

"Hiero speak for 'known.'"

"No." Hiero met his accusing stare with one of honest intent. "Han and I believed, without a shadow of a doubt, the revenger in question to be dead. We were not permitted to witness his execution, but we assured ourselves, repeatedly, over the years, of his non-living state. And still, when signs could be read implying his involvement, doubted. Strongly. Believe this, if nothing else. If Han or I had any sense he'd survived the noose, we would not have remained in London. Nor built a refuge and filled it with those we care for, those most vulnerable. We'd have sailed for the new world, or farther, long, long ago."

To Hiero's relief, Kip's anger tempered a bit. Curiosity, ever his Achilles heel, glimmered in his eyes. "Then we never stood a chance."

Hiero sighed. "I dearly hope that's not so. Else we should gather our cherished and flee to Portsmouth this instant."

"Should you?" Kip's lips twisted, then decided on a frown.

"Should *I*?" Hiero continued to wrestle with the need to go to him, to seize him, to let him feel the force of the emotion he strangled back with all of his might. "No. Not alone. Not without you."

Kip stared at him for an endless moment, as if measuring the weight of his soul. When finally he lowered his eyes, he gave a small nod.

Not mended, but not lost. Hiero almost wept.

"So in your estimation." Kip cleared his throat, resumed their debate in a more formal tone. "Is he involved, this revenger? Is Marius his creature?"

Hiero collected himself but couldn't quite still his hands, which he wrung and wrung. "I cannot fault the logic of it. It's the likelihood that still gives me pause. Han, as you know—"

"Would not leave such a thing to chance. Agreed. Could Marius be copying your revenger's methods? Have been apprenticed to him in some fashion?"

Hiero pretended to think this through, worrying both his hands and his heart. He wanted to explain everything to Kip. Of course he did. At some later day, or hour, or year, when their future together wasn't balanced on the tip of a dagger. "Too young, I wager, to have known him before his disappearing act."

"But not after," Kip insisted. "If indeed there was an after."

That dispiriting thought queered Hiero's stomach. Revulsion filled him. He pressed a fist to his mouth, terror and disgust not as easy to swallow as sadness. Had he and Han, in their ignorance, exposed others to the lives they'd barely escaped? Had their failure endangered someone with even fewer choices than they had?

"They work in pairs," Hiero said to distract himself as much as to confess. "His minions. He plays Fagin to those in impossible circumstances, lures them in with the promise of food and shelter and knowledge. Work, after a fashion. The sort where one doesn't care to get caught. And if one does, a partner's there to pillow the fall. Part of his technique, as Callie so shrewdly observed. Someone always has an alibi."

Kip, to his credit, avoided mentioning the obvious, that Hiero and Han had been such a pair. "Seraphine Vauquelin, you think?"

"There's the rub. Why would Marius—or his partner, if not Seraphine—bother tormenting her if his master's aim is to strike at me? And if Seraphine is his partner..."

"Why not aim to distance her from Damiane?"

"Why not lure in Damiane and Seraphine, instead of Marius, to be his accomplices? He prefers pairs with an established bond."

"And yet..." Kip walked the circumference of the small space. "Isn't it more likely that Seraphine somehow bribed Littlejohn into silence than was stolen from this room, with him just steps away?"

After a quick scan of his surroundings, Hiero had to concede the point. Unless...

Hoping to prove his worth to Kip, he gave the dressing room a closer examination, checking not for points of egress but a classic Erskine trap. No cleaner than the Vauquelins' suite in the Caledonian Hotel, Hiero attempted to look beyond the discarded robes and the makeup-smeared counters and the carnage of the wardrobe.

There. Hidden behind a privacy screen, which had been folded and propped over it: a full-length mirror. Hiero shoved the screen aside, ran his fingers around the edges of the frame. At the telltale click, he watched as the glass shifted aside to reveal a hidden tunnel. He suffered a pinch of pride before turning back to Kip, who smirked in begrudging approval.

"Wait!"

Callie ran in and shoved something at Kip before doubling over, panting. Also, Hiero suspected, fighting back tears.

Kip held another note. Hiero didn't need to read the details to see the fiery red "six" emblazoned on its envelope. Or to guess the contents.

"They've taken Han." A near sob underscored Callie's every word, but she held fast against her tears. "They destroyed the trap, left only the note. There was..." She swallowed hard. "There was blood on the carpet."

One two-faced blackbird
Won't last the night

Hiero remembered the foreboding rhyme of the previous note and became so overwhelmed by despair that he ached to embrace someone. He opened his arms to Callie. To his surprise, she threw herself into his chest, burying her face against his jacket and hugging him as he gathered her in. He glanced over her hat at Kip, who studied the note with, Hiero thought, forced intensity, especially since it was brief.

"What have we done?" Callie whispered as she looked up him. "This folly of mine, playing detective, what has it wrought?"

"Now, now." Hiero cinched her in all the tighter. "If anyone is to blame, it is I, for being foolish enough to think I could continue to tread the boards when we embarked on this new way of life."

"No, it is I who asked too much of you."

"Rather, you asked *something* of me, which no one had done before, and instead of leaping at the chance to be of use, I clung to my old ways with both hands."

"But if I—"

"Enough." Kip, despite the determination that glinted in his eyes, had gone pale. "A villain is a villain. This revenger might have targeted just you, Hiero, or you and Han, but he chose to make innocents suffer. He might have shot you in the street or shoved you down a flight of stairs, but no. He preferred to embroil us all in a Machiavellian game that we lost before we even started playing. Do not spare a drop of guilt wondering if different actions might have changed the course of events. They would not. He is a villain." Kip strode over to the Vauquelins' drinks tray and poured them all a finger of brandy. "Three questions require our attention now: Who is Marius's accomplice? Where is Han being kept? And how do we retrieve him?"

"Marius?" Callie gaped at them. "You mean the costumier..."

"Is no costumier at all," Hiero confirmed. "But rather our murderer. Or the ghost. Or both. Do try to keep up."

The mild criticism did its work in relighting Callie's inner fire. She pulled away and smacked Hiero in the chest. "That slip of a man couldn't have subdued Han alone. And all the others were assigned constables. All save the reporter Han was keen on, Miss Marks. If Marius was put in place to distract Tim, and therefore distract you, she proved a ready lure for Han." Her voice only quavered a bit on his name. "Miss Marks is Marius's accomplice. How's that for keeping up?"

"The names." Hiero shook his head, annoyed with himself. "He has a penchant for alliteration, our revenger. The names prove as much."

"Maxine Marks and Marius Lamarque." Callie gasped. "Under our noses all along."

"Hieronymus Bash," Kip sighed, "and Han Tak Hai." Hiero heard a melancholy note in his voice he didn't at all care for. "From H to M. Did he cycle through I, J, K, and L in the interim, I wonder?"

Hiero gathered his courage and said, "Erskine chooses pairs with similar names as a mnemonic device. They were, and are, but letters to him."

Callie huffed. "In a grand puzzle of his own devising, no doubt."

"Precisely."

"Erskine." Kip's stare could not have been sharper if it were slicing Hiero's throat. "So he too has a name."

Ever conscious of how Kip evaluated each reply for its forthrightness, Hiero spoke the truth, and nothing but the truth. He could not lose another ally, especially one so very, very dear.

"Graves 'Dagger' Erskine is the name under which they hanged him. Also, I wager, how he's known to the Yard. But he's had many others over the years."

"The mentor you oft speak of," Callie said. "He is the revenger?"

"Perhaps," Hiero and Kip replied in unison.

"If not," Kip continued, "someone has gone to great lengths to make us believe so." He handed over the sixth and final note to Hiero, who fought to still his shaking hands as he grabbed it from him.

CHECK MATE

Your move,
E.

"Villain," Hiero seethed. What else was there to say? "Festering boil on a wart on a scab on the pustule-riddled arse of the world." He pinched the bridge of his nose until he saw stars. "What now?"

"I put the question back to you," Kip answered. "Erskine, or someone familiar with your history, has set the table. Only you can tell us where to sit."

Though Hiero knew Kip was right, he also saw the challenge for the test it was. His instincts had failed Kip once today; they would not fail him again.

"The mirror is a feint." Hiero stepped halfway through, encountered a ladder leading down beneath the stage. Light and color illuminated the bottom rungs, telling him everything he needed to know. "Leads down to the costume vault, but no farther. Gave Marius a means of terrorizing Seraphine Vauquelin but served no other function."

"Then where are they!" Callie shouted, her frustration shredding her temper.

"The only place someone as notorious as Erskine could hide while also monitoring his minions' progress. Especially as someone who used to tread the boards himself and couldn't risk being recognized on the Strand."

"The Dark Arches," Kip concluded for him, his frown deeper and his face wearier than Hiero had ever seen it before. "Surrounded by a veritable army of the most cutthroat scoundrels in the underworld."

"Don Juan triumphant," Hiero declared, twisting away from the mirror door as it shut, to be spared his own reflection.

Han woke to the scent of roses.

His skull felt brittle, gridded with fissures like the shell of an egg that hadn't yet cracked open. The yoke of his brain sloshed every time he moved his head, nauseating him. A sticky film—his own drying blood—coated the back of his neck and shirt. A small pool of it matted his hair to the floor. When he attempted to open his eyes, he felt the grit of it on his lids and lashes, fought to see through the film over his pupils. As he adjusted to the dim gaslight beyond his blindfold, pain stabbed into the inside corner of his eye sockets, lobotomizing him for a time.

Han worked his way through the whiteout ache and the screeching of his inner ear, back to semiconsciousness. The sickening floral stench, like chugging a bucket of rose oil, overwhelmed his senses, with no relief in sight. He'd been bound by someone who knew all the tricks: thick twine instead of ropes or shackles; a tight weave around arms and legs; tie hands to the sides, not together, so thumbs can't be dislocated. Knocked out, he hadn't been able to flex his wrists to gain the much-needed quarter inch of space in which to maneuver.

Still, not the first time he'd been clobbered on the head and laced up like a Sunday roast, but Han dearly hoped it would be the last.

Slowly, measuredly, he sucked in breath after breath until his mind cleared. By now he could taste the different fragrances of roses, coral and vermillion and ivory and blush, so strong, so cloying that he wondered if they'd stashed him in a florist's cold room. But the temperature felt normal, and what light he could see dashed that theory. He continued to work the problem, as experience had taught him.

Orientation: lying on his back.

Size of the space around him: large, but filled with nearby objects.

Proximity to others: to be determined.

Sounds: Hmm...

Han slowed his breathing, listened beyond the steady beat of his heart. The usual faint rustling, no chatter. But there, amidst the living silence, a whimper. Or perhaps a gasp. Someone else, a groggy someone, was lurching back to life.

"Hello?"

A groan purred to his left, the swish of sheets, the creak of a bed frame. The person—a woman, by the voice—giggled. Tipsy, perhaps, or drugged. More creaking. The clop of feet hitting the floor, followed by a lazy grunt and a few unsteady steps. Then a crash. Wild, drunken laughter. The timbre recalled someone familiar, but Han needed more to identify her. Which soon enough came in the form of wails and sobs and the rattle of metal shackles. Their attackers had gifted her more mobility, but she was just as much a prisoner as him.

Their captors' first mistake.

"Who's there?" Han asked the ether.

A definite gasp this time, and then a shriek for good measure. He must have been a sight.

"Mais... mais qui c'est?" she demanded, her words so slurred that Han barely understood the question.

Drugged, then. Han cursed himself for his lack of dedication to his French lessons all those years ago, which didn't help matters. Especially since this woman, whose identity he made an educated guess at, was his only hope.

"Mademoiselle Vauquelin?" he asked in broken French. "Are you well? Are you hurt? I am Mr. Han Tak Hai, servant to Hieronymus Bash. I accompanied Mrs. Stoker to interrogate you about the events at The Gaiety. Do you recall?"

She seemed to think this over. "That is you, Monsieur Han, under all those knots?"

"Indeed. May I ask, are you injured, mademoiselle?"

She heaved a dramatic sigh. "I am on the floor." He heard the clink-clank of a chain, which she may have been pulling. "How did I get on the floor?"

"I believe you fell."

"Ah, oui. I remember." A beat, then. "Why don't I remember?"

Han dearly hoped, for her sake as much as his own, that a similar blow to the head had caused her confusion. "Mademoiselle, would you do me the favor of removing my blindfold, if you can?"

Han heard a scraping sound as she, presumably, crawled toward him. The squeal of bed hinges and a loud thud alerted him to her failure. Then she started crying.

"Mademoiselle Vauquelin? Are you well?"

"Le fantôme," she whispered in a small voice. "We are his prisoners." And she began to sob.

The distant slam of a door alerted Han to the fact that time was of the essence. A pair of voices, Miss Marks and an unknown man, quarreled loudly. At least Han thought it volume and not proximity: the sound carrying but the words muddled. He doubted their anger would delay them long. Soon enough, one or both would walk near enough to catch any conversation or escape attempts, losing him any ground he managed to gain.

Mademoiselle Vauquelin noticed the intrusion and had enough good sense to sob into her sleeve. Their captors' presence also seemed to make her aware of the impossibility of their circumstances. She cried harder. With every sharp gasp of her breath, Han felt the force of her terror intensify, until she was close, he suspected, to fainting. Hiero might have soothed her with words or an impassioned speech, perhaps even a song, but he was no actor. He could not even offer her a shoulder to cry on. All he had, all he knew, was the need to protect those he loved.

"Mademoiselle Seraphine." Han knew he had guessed right by her tiny squeak. "You must be brave, for Damiane."

A wrack of sobs overtook her. "I will never see her again!"

"Hush, hush," Han attempted to soothe. "If you interrupt them, we've no chance. Tell me about the room we're in. Is there a door?"

She murmured a lonely "Oui."

"And a window?"

"Two."

"What else?"

"We're in a garden."

"Like a conservatory?"

"No. But roses. Bouquets and bouquets everywhere." That, at least, explained the smell.

"And you are chained to the bed?"

A wail answered him. He heard her collapse, her sobs, all progress lost. Callie, he thought, would be aghast. And halfway to making a rope out of the bedsheets. Han indulged a fleeting moment of despair at never seeing her again, at how he'd ignored her in favor of someone...

A better match. A smarter match. But he wasn't so deluded as to ignore that that had been exactly the point. That he'd been targeted as surely as Hiero.

And suddenly he knew just how to get through to her.

"I have a friend." He slowed the cadence of his voice, mimicking Hiero at his most eloquent. "More than a friend, really. A lady, who I... Well, who is very dear. As dear to me as, no doubt, Mademoiselle Damiane is to you. I long to see my lady again, to let her know I am safe. Don't you?"

"But I am not safe," Seraphine bleated.

"You could be," Han reminded her. "If you follow my instructions, I swear, you will be. But I need your help. Without you, I will never be reunited with her. And you..."

"Dami is the heroine. I am just the scenery."

The voice crescendoed, the unknown man operatic in intensity, Miss Marks underscoring him with her sardonic wit. Any minute, one or both would force an end to the argument, and they'd be upon them. Fortunately, Han had a good deal of experience with flattering someone's ego whilst in dire straits.

"I saw you tonight, on stage. You are far more than just scenery. You moved me to tears."

A sigh, somewhere between misery and contentment, escaped her lips. "What must I do?"

After a nerve-fraying amount of back-and-forth, Han discovered there was a lock on her shackles. He'd never expected to coax an intoxicated ingénue through the finer points of lock picking, but it was hardly the strangest way he'd spent an evening. All the while, he spoke of Callie—surprised by some of his own revelations—and she of Damiane. Too honestly by far, but such was a prisoner's dilemma. If he tired of her petulance by the end, Han remembered that a loose tongue should not, in a just world, condemn her to death.

And that his own stupidity in trusting Miss Marks might.

Mademoiselle Seraphine had only pushed up his blindfold by the time their captors' rage burnt out. Though they'd lowered their voices, Han could distinguish individual words. The thin walls wouldn't protect them for much longer. Han whispered his final instructions to Seraphine: open one of the windows, toss some petals over the edge, then hide in the bushels of roses, silent as the grave, until they dragged him out. Once certain of their absence, she should make her escape.

A gamble, betting on her ability to stay quiet during whatever would transpire in the room. But better that than she break a leg jumping from, if he guessed the angle correctly, a second-story window in her present state of not-quite intoxication and bone-deep fear.

The threat of imminent torture, or worse, had a way of sobering even the flightiest hearts, so by the time the door thwacked open, Mademoiselle Seraphine had resurrected her Ophelia and drowned herself in flowers.

Han, by contrast, couldn't feel his legs. The full force of his stare, however, he aimed at Miss Maxine Marks, who strutted in with a regal hauteur even Her Majesty wouldn't have dared. She arched a brow when she saw the empty bed and his missing blindfold but didn't appear displeased.

"Chivalrous and cunning." She clicked her tongue. "I will miss our duels."

She betrayed herself with a smirk before and calling her accomplice into the room. Han kept his gaze fixed on her, knowing the briefest flicker could give the game away. Still, he didn't quite know where to look when mousy Marius Lamarque marched in, such was his shock.

Shared by the man himself, who gaped at the empty bed, then ran at the window so swiftly he almost launched himself out. Marius slammed it hard enough to crack the glass. To Han's relief, Seraphine didn't peep.

Mousy, Han reflected, had perhaps been his second underestimation of the night.

Miss Marks raised a hand to forestall Marius's shouting. "Serves you right, going off book. You know the rules as well as I."

Any hope Han had of Erskine not being involved in some fashion died then.

"You have your plaything," Marius seethed. "I mean to have mine."

"Then steel yourself for Mr. Stoker," Miss Marks answered. "As intended."

"I will have them both, if I so choose, and anything else I desire. Stoker for the slaughter and Seraphine as spoils."

"Suit yourself," Miss Marks sighed, indifferent.

Marius glared, barked, "Ready him," as he stormed out. Han didn't care to know what that meant but feared he would soon find out.

Miss Marks twitched her nose, grimaced. She opened the second window, fanning her handkerchief around the room to freshen the air. After verifying the length of the drop for herself, she threw a few of the bouquets out into the street and rearranged others to distract from the missing blooms. Han concentrated on the view, though inside he begged for enough good fortune that Mademoiselle Seraphine not be discovered. Whatever gods protected boozy actresses must have shined over her, for she remained hidden.

The same could not be said for their whereabouts. A glimpse of the Adelphi Terrace down the street suggested they were trapped in the Caledonian Hotel—not a surprise, given Miss Marks rented a suite there. But perhaps a miscalculation on her part. The Caledonian and the Adelphi Arches had played too great a part in the case for Tim Stoker to fail to search there... unless they meant the location as a lure. As a trap.

And he the bait.

Under others circumstances, at the first hint that Erskine lived, Hiero would have run. They'd even agreed on a rendezvous point, if separated. The only scenario that would stop Hiero running was the one they presently found themselves in: Han in mortal danger. Though he stilled his face against any show of emotion, fury, of a force and tenor Han had not felt since his days with Erskine, ignited within him. He'd sworn then, as he swore now, that he'd never again be a pawn in the chess game Erskine made of life. If no other alternative presented itself, Han would sacrifice himself.

Once satisfied with the quality of the air, Miss Marks swaggered over to his bed and sat on the edge, her bottom snug against his hip.

She turned, as if riding sidesaddle, and leaned over him, supported by an arm wedged into his other flank. She wore the same imperious expression as ever, with an extra spark of triumph in her cool blue eyes. The hunger, as yet unsated, that once attracted him now turned his stomach. To think...

"You cannot save me." She smirked down at him with such contempt that Han wondered if she was fallen aristocracy, like Dahlia Nightingale. "I've heard your promises. I know your story. And if you think me foolish enough to believe our master was completely honest in the telling of his sordid tale, then you haven't been listening. But this is the life I choose, and I will see it through."

"Enacting the vengeance of a cruel old charlatan?" If he could move his shoulders, Han might have shrugged. "A curious way to earn your freedom."

"Better I should have bided my time until the dashing manservant with the warren of spies invited me to play housemaid in a different sort of prison?" She scoffed. "I'd have still ended up on my knees."

"Still up to his old tricks, is he?" Han frowned. "I would have thought age might have tempered him there."

"*He* never laid a finger on me. The same cannot be said for those who came before him. I learnt the price for food and shelter at an early age. And knowledge." Miss Marks leaned over his torso, almost kissing close. "I also know when something... true passes between two people. Something that could grow into a valuable partnership." Intrigued by her words, if not her advances, Han waited her out. "Does it suit you, honestly, to play second fiddle to a drunken scoundrel? To toddle around after him, cleaning up his messes whilst he wines and dines with the nobility? Seen as a servant, or not seen at all, while he's treated better than a prince?"

She let her questions sit with him awhile before adding, "I saw how they turned that afternoon, outside the Arches. How the punters cheered you until they saw your face."

Han wished this came as less of a surprise. "It was *you* I fought?"

"Who else?" She laughed, pleased with herself. "We're well matched in all things. We could be quite the pair."

Though she'd been leading him down the garden path, Han still started when they arrived at her intended destination. He'd forgotten how bold she was. "If we quit our respective masters, you mean?"

"I've been promised freedom, if I play out my part," Miss Marks coyly explained. "I mean to take it. And you, as well, if you care to second me. It's Bash he wants. So long as you lure him in, the master will overlook your past transgressions. He badly wants you back in the fold. And once he's got his revenge..."

Miss Marks moved over him, hovering her lips but inches over his. She would never prove to be less than temptation incarnate.

But no pirate's treasure compared to Hiero, to Callie, to their family.

Still, he must persuade her. Han gazed into the depths of her eyes. Scrutinized every speck of her face as he would if he had any intention of giving in. What had a decade and more of chaperoning Hiero taught him? Expressing doubt convinced more readily than any pretence.

"How am I to prove my worth?" Han asked. "I betrayed your master once before. I very well may again. What's my pound of flesh?"

"More than one, for what you've done." Miss Marks snickered. "The first: give up the girl."

Han knew then that he'd already lost. That she'd been taunting him all along. He didn't need to fake the scowl he shot up at her. "She's gone."

Miss Marks howled a laugh. "She no more jumped out that window than I flew across the Channel on wings of feathers and wax." She leapt to her feet, began tearing through the biggest of the bouquets, the one Seraphine Vauquelin had been cowering behind.

Han could only watch, heart in his throat, as the petals showered over him. But he could not focus on Mademoiselle Vauquelin, even in the last seconds of her life. He thought only of Callie, and Hiero, and Tim, and what evils Erskine's new minions would wreak upon them in the final moves of their wicked game. Worry so consumed him that he almost missed Miss Marks's growl of frustration when, after all her efforts, she revealed nothing but a bare wall.

Somehow, some way, Han had distracted her long enough to permit Seraphine Vauquelin to escape.

Chapter 21

Tim scrubbed his face with his hands before refocusing his attention on the map spread out across the table before him. Sketched out in charcoal and based on recent surveys—and, it had to be said, their imperfect memories of the place—he wished they had a more reliable rendering of the layout of the Adelphi Arches from which to plan their attack. Or that anyone or anything involved in this case proved to *be* reliable, most especially his ostensible partner, and not excluding himself.

His childhood friend, a villain of the highest order. A woman under his protection, taken. His teammate, captured. His lover, guilty by omission, an agent of chaos at the best of times, and... Tim didn't care to look too closely at the last word on his list. He needed no further distraction at this critical point. But with his trust so abused, concentration proved elusive. Especially when said partner hovered beside him, so sick at heart and transparently contrite that he barely seemed corporeal.

A part of Tim longed to comfort Hiero. Another, more strident part felt so resentful that he wanted to drop the entire affair in his lap and be done. All the while, the clock ticked down. Tim stared at the map, his mind spinning like a compass with no direction.

They'd retreated back to the library at Berkeley Square to strategize and prepare after sending a restless Callie to search the

Caledonian Hotel. In the Vauquelins's dressing room, at the height of the crisis, Tim was certain they needed to take their time and make a considered, definitive play. But now that the true weight of the odds crushed down on him... he believed there was no way out without someone getting trapped in the rubble. The one he had been fighting to protect all along.

Tim stepped back from the table to stroll around the room. He ran his fingers along the ornate spines of the books on his favorite shelf, ancient, gaudy tomes on the history of necromancy he'd probably never need to consult. A gift from Hiero, this cavernous room filled with every literary and historical delight Tim could read in a lifetime. Meant to occupy him for that lifetime of study, of investigation, of... solitude? Had Hiero suspected, even then, that Erskine would come for him?

No. Tim had known the answer before he even posed the question. This temple of arcane learning, brimming with the spoils of their first adventure, the collection they'd bought off Lord Blackwood's estate for pennies of its true worth, was a tribute to their partnership. Why else devote so much space to their shared endeavor? Why else create a cozy nook close to Tim's desk where they might—and did—take their leisure? Why else invite Tim into his home and his life and his bed?

Amidst all the drama and subterfuge of the case, Tim had forgotten what motivated the man he loved, what lay behind *his* mask: kindness and care. Such a man could not be expected to obey the rules of reason and deduction when he led, always, with his heart.

Tim returned to the table. Hiero sat on its edge, gazing up at the skylight. Suddenly overwhelmed by the enormity of what they faced and the towering stakes, Tim struggled to do what he must with the necessary delicacy. But perhaps that's where he'd erred in the past. Melodrama was Hiero's lifeblood. Perhaps Tim needed to learn from him, not lecture him, to give sway to the violent tides that moved him.

Tim gestured for them to move toward the indigo fainting couch, the scene of their intimacy only two days before. Two days. No further evidence of Erskine's upheaval in their lives was required when Tim considered that fact.

Tim stalked forward until Hiero was forced to sit on the top ledge of the fainting couch's seat. His expressive eyebrows slanted upward in shock when Tim slid between his legs, stopping just shy of full-body contact. Tim avoided Hiero's eyes by carding his fingers through his cropped hair, somehow perfect even after hours under a wig. He traced the stubbled line of Hiero's jaw with a thumb, wondering how long it would take him to regrow his mustache.

"The plan is this: You will enter the Dark Arches alone and find Erskine's chamber—or be brought there once recognized. When captured, you will put on your favorite show: teasing, goading, wit to spare. Bluster, which they will see through, but indulge. All part of the game. Their reward for having successfully brought you to your knees. They will relish it. And when their guard is down..."

"You will strike?" Hiero scoffed, but Tim didn't fail to remark that his arms had woven themselves around his waist. "They are too battle ready for that. Erskine is a master strategist. Plans inside of plans inside of plans."

"And yet you managed to outwit him once before."

"Using a method I daresay will not work to mend things between us."

"Improvisation, you mean?"

He watched as Hiero worked through every way of saying it without saying it, then abandoned all hope and ventured there. "The only way to confront someone so considered is to not consider anything at all. Pure reaction."

"Which, by fortune's favor, is a particular talent of yours."

Hiero gave a reluctant nod. "Perhaps I am mistaken, but I received the distinct impression that you don't find this particular talent of mine of any value."

Lowering his hands until they cupped the back of Hiero's neck, Tim leaned in ever so slightly to whisper, "There is nothing about you I don't treasure." A flash of shock illuminated Hiero's brown-black eyes for an instant. "My methods, as you've noted, are rigid. Perhaps my lesson in all this is to bend a bit. Though I continue to fear that, in doing so, something within me will snap. The reason, I wager, I was so cross with you earlier."

"That and my utter lack of consideration in how I went about our little gambit." Hiero's shoulders sagged, as if the weight of Tim's arms forced repentance. "The trouble with an improvisational approach is that it flirts with carelessness."

"And fails, more often than not," Tim remarked. "As I have failed, and will again. The nature of the beast."

Shooting an inquisitive look Tim's way from under his thick eyelashes, Hiero cinched him in closer. "Awfully forgiving of you to see it that way."

"Difficult not to once reminded that everything you've done was out of concern for others." Tim met his gaze with one of steadfast affection. "Or perhaps I don't care to leave things as they are before sacrificing my queen."

Tim sought his mouth with surprising hunger, all the high emotion and deep disappointment of the day surging in him. If these were to be their last private moments together—and, in the back of his mind, he recalled Hiero's assertion that if Erskine was indeed alive, he and Han would head to the nearest port posthaste—Tim wouldn't deprive himself of a last embrace. A final press of Hiero's satiny lips, a final lick of his clever tongue, a final taste of the delirium that had entranced Tim for almost a year.

Not nearly long enough. Not when he'd been promised a lifetime.

Tim rested their brows together, caressing Hiero's cheek and ear, his neck, tugged loose his cravat to stroke a finger in the notch at the base of his collar.

"You'd best take care when among them. Think of yourself, as well as those you mean to save. Return to me."

Hiero held him close for several eternities before replying. "Then I shall indeed confront them alone?"

"And work your magic, yes." Tim pulled away to regard him with reluctance. "Callie and I will be near, of course, should you require us. In the Caledonian, perhaps."

"And if I fail?"

"Impossible." He forced a smile. "You are the incomparable Hieronymus Bash."

A sadness tinged the look they shared. Tim reached again to caress, but Hiero caught his hand, turned it over, and kissed Tim's palm before setting it back on his chest.

Then he snorted.

"You are, as predicted, an abysmal liar." Tim opened his mouth to protest, or perhaps to laugh, but Hiero shushed him. "We truly are a study in opposites. Fortunately, for you and your attempt at a performance, my dear Kip, your intentions are so transparent that I could easily decipher the moments of honesty and the moments of... well. To call them 'dissimulation' rather maligns the word."

Mouth agape, Tim didn't even bother to deny it.

"Though I do adore you, and admire the effort." Hiero sighed. "And, most crucially, have learned *my* lesson. 'Rogue and righteous, chaos and reason, Stoker and Bash,' I believe it was?"

Tim stammered.

"Quite," Hiero affirmed. "So onward together, hmm? Really, though, I wonder that you bothered, given how chastised I was after our last conversation. A bit of hectoring would have done the trick."

Tim recovered enough to comment, "History is against you there, I fear."

"Or you might have waited till I was in the bosom of the enemy, so to speak, to swing in and save the day."

"You're the dashing hero, not I. Besides, I wouldn't have been able to leave it so late."

"Because you fretted the lesson wouldn't take, and all would be lost?"

"No, you scapegrace." Tim let the full force of his ardor shine through. "Because I love you." Hiero's dark eyes widened. "I may only be a country squire with no flair or panache to speak of, but I will not let someone who is everything to me slay this dragon alone."

Tim hovered there awhile, near enough to kiss, far enough to give Hiero space to breathe. Hiero's lips quivered but emitted no sound. Tim permitted himself a small smile at having done the impossible: rendered Hieronymus Bash speechless.

When he could wait no more, Tim stole a second—delicate, simmering—kiss and led Hiero back to the round table.

"Now, most beloved and befuddling of minds." Tim chuckled to himself. "If you were a minion desperate to emulate his master, but also to defy him, how would you lure his archnemesis into your lair?"

This, finally, woke Hiero to the moment. "You do not believe Erskine is alive."

Tim allowed his small smile to grow to its full length.

"I do not," he acknowledged. "The trouble is, I wouldn't wager Han's life on a suspicion. Yet that is precisely what we must do."

Han almost missed the ruckus in the room below. Oppressive silence had followed Miss Marks's retreat from the room—to chase after Seraphine Vauquelin, result unknown—lulling him into a near-catatonic state. The prickles and tingles that heralded numbness in his arms and lower limbs had long since passed; his worries had fled with Miss Vauquelin. With no one else at risk, Han knew his life was forfeit, whether Hiero and their family flew to Portsmouth to board the latest steamer (unlikely) or Marius and Miss Marks used him as bait to lure Hiero into some final conflict (probable). As Han would not permit anyone in their family to suffer due to his colossal stupidity in trusting Miss Marks, he needed not waste valuable time and effort fretting over what was to come.

He knew his mind. Better to rest, to conserve his strength, to wait for the opportune moment.

At the first murmur of voices, Han thought his captors returned. Strained to hear if Miss Vauquelin had been recaptured after all. The unmistakable stomp of police footsteps jarred him out of his fugue. He'd participated in—and hidden from—enough searches in his time to recognize the sounds: bursts of conversation, door snaps, drawer squeals, the clatter of objects hitting the floor. No matter how discreetly the officers moved through the building, they could not disguise themselves from someone who'd spent years of his life listening for signs of a raid, even in his sleep.

Han slowed his breathing, stretched out his hearing as far as it would go. Silence from the room beyond. Marius and Miss Marks, trained by Erskine, would have planned for this and every eventuality. If they had returned. If they lurked near, listening as he listened, plotting as he plotted.

The police swept onto his floor, swift and merciless as a cyclone. A peculiar approach for Tim, who tended to know better than to authorize such a show of force. Han wondered what might have provoked him. Had Hiero been taken? Had Tim been dismissed from the case? Had Tumnus appealed to one of his friends in high places on Miss Vauquelin's behalf? Han dismissed the last as improbable and dreaded the rest.

A violent knock shook a nearby door. Officers in the main corridor conversed in curt, orderly exchanges. Not a rustle of movement or a whisper of discussion from the room beyond his own. No one entered Han's chamber to attempt to move or silence him. But would his captors pounce if he cried out? Or had they abandoned him, and this was Han's only chance of escape? Was this a test of his loyalty

Miss Marks had devised? Or another lethal game designed to make him the architect of his own demise?

Fortune, Han reminded himself, favored the bold. He gathered all the breath he could and bellowed, "Help! I'm trapped! Help, help!"

He shouted through the second and third round of knocks, through the slam of the door and the charge of footsteps so tantalizingly near. The scuffle and shuffle of the search of the rooms beyond, all too brief, before the officers ran off to search the next room, and the next, and the next. Han yelled until his voice croaked and his chest ached from straining his bonds, but to no avail.

Exhausted, he made peace with the severity of his predicament. Not only was he so well concealed the police never stood a chance of finding him, but his captors wanted him awake and aware, to be tempted by the possibility of escape and then denied. They wanted him weak and compliant and vulnerable. They wanted to crush every last speck of his hope to dust.

They couldn't know just what Han had overcome to become the man he was, and just who taught him to never surrender: his mother, his grandparents, his people. The People on the Water, always underestimated, who had thrived for centuries with nothing but their skill, their strong community, and a fleet of egg-shaped boats. For so long that their origins were as deep and fathomless as the waters they sailed.

Which did little to change the fact that he'd been expertly restrained. And he'd never been adept at emotional manipulation. The only way to lure in a small army of street-smart spies was, oddly enough, to treat them with respect and compassion. Then Han remembered Toby, the boy he'd sent after Erskine, and felt sick that his other rabbits might never know what became of him. But wallowing would not serve Toby or Randy Terriss or Silas Flint or Polly Nichols, or any of the Red Skull's victims.

Too many. But no more.

A barrage of thumps broke Han from his musings, the corridor beyond inhabited once more. He identified Miss Marks's smoky rumble and Marius's petulant whine. A third, muffled, distinctly feminine voice struck fear in him—had Miss Vauquelin been recaptured? If so, she put up quite a fight; from the yelps and smacks and thuds, they might have been wrestling down one of Pamplona's famed wild bulls.

The door crashed open. Miss Marks—hair disheveled, bodice ripped, blood dripping from a severed earlobe—strode in armed with a gun, which she aimed, point-blank, at Han.

At the click of the all-too-familiar MAS revolver's hammer, the fangs of a vengeful god sunk into his heart.

"We only require one of you," Miss Marks hissed at someone outside the room.

Beyond, the struggling ceased, though whether the bull had been tamed or slain, Han did not know until Miss Marks stepped aside and Marius shoved a bound and bitter Callie into the room. Turning the gun on her, Miss Marks threw her on the other bed. Callie's head collided with the headboard. With a snarl, she spat something at Miss Marks with such force that it just missed her eye, landing instead in the shreds of her torn dress.

The missing lobe of her ear.

Miss Marks plucked it off her bosom, walked over to a nearby candle, and held it in the open flame. The stench of burning flesh somehow made the reek of the roses less bearable. Han slowed his breathing so as not to void his stomach. Callie, still rabidly defiant, licked the blood from her lips.

Miss Marks lowered and uncocked the revolver, but not before shooting Callie and Han a warning glare.

"Not long now." Miss Marks smirked, then strolled out of the room.

At the clank of bolt, Han listened for a long while, but their captors did not resume their bickering. He wondered, not for the first time, how much of their behavior was genuine and how much another part of the show. Did Erskine have them so mesmerized that they could no longer distinguish between performance and honest interaction? If so, they were all the more dangerous for it.

"Can you move?" Callie asked him.

Han startled at the question. If he craned his neck, he could just meet her eyes. In their blue-diamond sheen, Han saw the last glimmers of her rage.

"Only my head."

A nod. "Miss Vauquelin?"

"Escaped." Han sighed. "I dearly hope." He noted she'd been bound much in the same manner as him, but not as high on the arms. Her Calvin guise had done her no favors—a bustle and corset would have been a greater challenge. "How..."

"The pair of them. Sprang atop me in the cloakroom at the Caledonian. Nearly suffocated by a mink stole. Still, I gave them no quarter. Or, rather, took more than a quarter of her ear." A look of deviant pleasure stole over her face.

"I meant how are you faring?"

She let out a low growl. "I'll play any part the case requires, save for damsel. So: exceedingly ill." She huffed a blustery breath, one tinged with frustration. "I won't be used against him, Han. We cannot allow it."

"No." When their gazes locked anew, Han did not shy away from the deep emotion reflected there. He would give her this and take something for himself in return. There was simply no other way forward, not with so much at stake. "Have you any room to maneuver?"

"How cunning of you to ask." He relished the archness of her grin. "I am, alas, properly trussed. But Miss Marks did not frisk me quite as thoroughly as she might have." A coy shrug. "Loss of blood, perhaps."

Han felt a flutter of an altogether different emotion when Callie rolled on her side to reveal the boot knife she'd been sitting on, clasped between her hands.

Chapter 22

"The stage has been set," Hiero declared to no one in particular from his seat in the lounge of the Caledonian Hotel. He nursed the third of his three allotted whiskeys whilst keeping a weather eye on the goings on in the main hall. There his Kip attempted to reassure the concierge and a caterwauling horde of disgruntled guests that only the subject of the current manhunt would be arrested by the constables searching the hotel.

This proved to be not the least bit persuasive. The initial cover story, concocted by Callie in their absence, was that all rooms needed to be searched under the pretense of checking the gas fixtures for leaks. Given the weeness of the hour and the worrisome nature of the request, the concierge had instead surrendered a list of empty rooms they might investigate. But the constables had raised such a clamor doing their diligence that the entire hotel was now on high alert, and Callie nowhere to be found.

Three taken in as many hours, and Hiero still as powerless as ever to prevent any more abductions. Oh, he'd thought himself so sly, faking his own death, torching any chance of resurrecting Horace Beastly on the most public of funeral pyres. But Erskine's minions had seen the flames of his plans from miles off and threw everything they had on the fire until it engulfed every aspect of Hiero's life. Little wonder he drowned his sorrows.

As for the overeager constables, they'd discovered a recently inhabited suite filled top to tail with bouquets of roses, for reasons unknown.

And a trail of blood staining the carpet.

Hiero drained the last of his liquid courage. But even the familiar sear in his throat couldn't soothe his stage fright—the worst bout he'd had in a decade. Tremors in his fingers, spiders up his spine, a guilty bladder… An ocean of dark liquor wouldn't salve his nerves with so much at stake. And then Kip had uttered those three impossible words. The ones he never thought he'd hear expressed sincerely, with so much passion and conviction, along with a promise of true partnership.

And Hiero had said nothing in return.

This, perhaps, was Erskine's true revenge, Hiero being given everything he could ever dream of whilst facing a threat to his very existence. More likely Erskine had planned for this night since the moment of Hiero's betrayal. He should have known the only way to kill someone was to sink the knife in yourself. And now there was everything to live for, and Hiero didn't know if he'd survive the night. Or worse, if his Kip or his Callie or his Han would.

And yet when Kip glanced his way and gave the signal, Hiero found the courage to stand, to walk, to venture into whatever trap Erskine's minions had set for them.

The cloakroom of the Caledonian Hotel had little to recommend it. Small, damp, a reeking mélange of the perfumes that lingered on the coats and cloaks housed there, Hiero wondered if the attendant kept a jar of smelling salts under the counter. Kip had already peeled back the strip of carpet that hid the square door leading down to the Dark Arches. He busied himself with dismantling the locks. An enterprising villain would inevitably find a way to bar the door, regardless—the minions doubtless kept several well-paid informants in the hotel—but any obstacle in their path might create the delay they needed to survive whatever gauntlet awaited below.

And a gauntlet it would be, testing not just physical endurance, but mental and emotional stress as well. Hiero attempted to clear his mind of all worries and regrets, not as herculean a task as he might have hoped, but they returned every time he glanced at Kip, thought of Callie and Han. It had been easier to trust his instincts when he had nothing but himself to lose. Less so when lives both near and dear hung in the balance.

"Tunnels," Hiero muttered to himself as the final panel shifted to the side, revealing the dank, seething nothingness beneath. "Why must it always be tunnels?"

"The Arches are quite cavernous," Kip reassured him. "And solidly built. Entire carriages pass through them. Nothing like the subterranean maze where the Daughters of Eden hid their sins."

"And what, pray tell, are these Arches renowned for?" Hiero asked. "Their darkness. Not metaphorical."

"Fortunately, we've prepared for most eventualities." Kip handed him a lantern. "First and foremost, illumination."

Hiero heard the echo of his words as they descended into the tunnel and the panel above shifted back into place. He reached for Kip's hand as they moved through the tight but far less suffocating passage, grateful for the dimness that permitted such an intimate gesture. Really, Hiero might have imagined himself under the stage at The Gaiety, were it not for the stench and the stalagmites of dust and the distant, squeaking chorus of vermin.

A chorus soon drowned out by the eerie tinkling of a music box, playing the same hypnotic tune as the night they'd searched The Gaiety, Daaé's *Nocturne*. Its familiarity did little to limp the hairs on the back of Hiero's neck. As they crossed into the Adelphi Arches proper, Hiero felt as if he stepped onto the grandest stage of them all. The only one that mattered, where he lived or died by the quality of his performance.

In the first alcove, Hiero confronted, rather unexpectedly, the specter of his own reflection. Kip, not quite so perceptive, bashed into the looking glass set before them. Distant torches flickered to life as they examined their surroundings. But no amount of light prepared them for the staggering effect of seeing themselves multiplied in every direction.

Their first trial of the night would be to navigate a Hall of Mirrors.

Kip whistled. "Spared no expense, did they?"

They shared a soft, nervous chuckle. Behind them, a panel slotted down from the blackness above, covering the passage to the hotel with another mirror.

"Heartening, in an odd way, the effort they put into confounding us." Hiero gravitated to the mirror with the best lighting, stole a moment to again admire his newly shorn hair and bare face. "Brings a tear to the eye."

"Perhaps they mean to delay us long enough to enact their escape." Kip's bemused expression hovered, expectant, over his left shoulder. "To the continent."

"And miss the final act?" Hiero scoffed. "Never." With reluctance, he drew back from the glass into the center of the octagonal room. He immediately realized his miscalculation—the move had lost him all sense of direction. Even if they found the trick panel that led them elsewhere, they would only find themselves in another similar room, with even less sense of which way to orient themselves.

Kip, who had of course leapt ahead of that rudimentary deduction, mused, "I do wonder if any of the routes lead to the next trial, or if following conventional logic will see us dumped in the street and forced to start anew."

"Perhaps the solution is more ephemeral," Hiero conjectured. "We're meant to reflect on our missteps until we reach genuine enlightenment."

"Meaning a path will be lit for us once we express contrition?" Kip sighed. "Dare I ask for what?"

"There's the rub." Hiero shut his eyes, unnerved by the infinite number of hims stretching out in all directions. Even his narcissism knew its limits. "The accusations of a deranged mind are hardly predictable. But!" He lit on an idea. "Erskine's methods are." Taking advantage of every chance to hold Kip's hand, even if briefly, he pulled him toward one of the mirrors. "Walk the perimeter in the opposite direction and knock on each one until we meet."

"To what end?" Kip inquired but obeyed. His third knock found only air, with one mirror placed a few steps back from the others. "Ah, I see." They slipped through the space into... another octagonal mirrored room, as Hiero had predicted. "You're aware, I imagine, of the quickest course to madness? Are we truly meant to find the trick panel in each octagon?"

"That is the brief, but not the game." Hiero looked to the heavens, but not for divine inspiration. "What would you say if I suggested you climb me like a wall?"

Kip chuckled. "Intriguing, but I hardly think it time for... Ah." Kip followed the line of his stare to the arched brick ceiling above. The one the mirrors didn't reach. "I'd tell you to cup your hands in front of you and gird your strength."

It took several attempts, a knee to the jaw, the scorch of lantern oil on Hiero's arm and, worse, his best skulking suit, and one very distracting groin to the face, but Kip eventually managed to hoist himself onto Hiero's shoulders. Charting a path to the exit from this higher vantage proved far less troublesome. Never had Hiero been so grateful for Kip's dogged and meticulous mind than when trailing behind him as he steered them through room after dizzying room. By the end, he almost—almost—grew sick of his reflection.

Kip shuttered the lanterns and glanced around the edge of the final trick panel, the color draining from his face.

"Another hurdle?" Hiero asked.

"No." Kip had never looked more sober, which terrified Hiero. "I'd say they are done playing."

Steeling himself, Hiero approached the final panel, then carefully moved into the empty space, angling himself just so. The scene before him shocked him such he nearly stumbled out prematurely.

In the middle of the road that traversed the Arches, an open stage had been erected. A long dining table stretched across it, Don Juan's fateful dinner with the devil painstakingly recreated. Mannequins dressed as all the players in their little drama—each of the suspects, the Red Skull, and the victims as well—filled the seats. Three enormous gold-fletched candelabra burned bright atop a blood-red brocaded tablecloth. No plates or platters of food marred its crimson silk, only an unfurled scroll bound in leather and a quill stood in ink, set before two empty chairs.

Hiero might have hurried to accept the implicit invitation and bring an end to this tortuous game, were those the only elements of this set piece. But three ropes bisected the table, a hairsbreadth above the three tongues of flame from the center candelabra, their bottom fibers just beginning to singe. The ropes stretched up to iron hooks on the high ceiling, then jutted sharply down to snarl around the bars of three suspended cages.

Cages in which Han and Callie, bound and blindfolded, lay slumped. One, in the middle, appeared empty. All three hung over a dead drop down to a secondary road. If the fall didn't kill Han and Callie, it would likely shatter every bone in their bodies. How long could ropes of that thickness withstand the licks of the flames?

Hiero recoiled. His head suffered a low-grade throb, war drums to a screaming migraine. But there was no escaping the game. Hiero had been mad to think something so trivial as death would keep Erskine from enacting his revenge, that he and Han could ever fly beyond his reach, let alone find safe harbor in the same city Erskine had preyed upon for decades.

That they'd preyed upon together. For Hiero had learned at the foot of the master.

A hand slid into his, splaying Hiero's fingers before latching tight around them. Palm to palm, grip to grip, with that heartful, forbidden clasp, Kip tugged him back into himself. Better, reminded Hiero of the stakes at play. Of the true nature of the life he'd worked toward in the years after Erskine. And of the steadfast and loving man who had not left his side since the moment they met.

"A point of clarification," he whispered, stealing a moment to admire the green-gold flashes of torchlight in Kip's eyes. "Am I the rogue or the righteous in your little *cri de guerre*?"

"You're the main event." Kip wrestled down a smile. "Isn't that enough?"

Hiero shrugged. "One would presume." He held fast to Kip's hand until the last possible second. But even after it slipped away, Hiero felt that solid presence beside him, around him, within him. No matter what transpired, those three impossible words would forever be etched in his heart.

Tim kept his senses on high alert as they approached the stage. The shadow play across the vaulting arches, the fetid atmosphere, the spine-tingling music, the dramatic setting... all so much artifice. But what did it mask? Where did the true danger lurk? Despite the certitude with which he'd urged Hiero forward, this was very much Hiero's domain. Tim's logician's brain struggled to make sense of this elaborate, murderous game with no rules and no reason, all in the name of vengeance.

There were simpler, more vicious ways of exacting revenge. That Erskine's minions had gone to such lengths suggested they had something to prove. But to whom? To their mentor? To the Yard? To others who sought to usurp their crown? Tim couldn't shake the sense that this was an audition. But who was being tested, and to what end, only time would tell.

He hoped they would survive long enough to learn the answer.

"Bonsoir, messieurs," an eloquent voice greeted, "et bienvenue."

Nothing could have prepared Tim for the sight of Marius, be-decked in the latest in villainous finery, blacks and crimsons and silvers, strutting onto the stage. Having molted the part of the woebegone costumier, his tone, his manner, and his bearing glinted like a new, scaly skin.

Before he knew what he was about, Tim found himself striding forward and jumping onto the stage so that he might confront Marius eye to eye, if across the vast dining table. And through a veil of candle smoke, the fecal fumes of the Arches air caused their flames to crackle and pop.

"You dare welcome us to such a place, one you have lured us to through acts so vile it wouldn't serve to hang you but once!" Tim barked. "And so we've come, at your beck, but I for one won't play your deadly game a moment longer. If you release your prisoners and surrender yourselves, I swear I will fight to spare you the noose."

Marius pressed a finger to his lips. Tim suspected it was to keep from laughing. He sensed Hiero fall in at his side, press a reassuring hand into the groove in his lower back.

But neither man, nor Tim himself, had estimated the depth of his fury.

"Do not condescend to me," Tim bellowed, "when you have so much blood on your hands your skin's gone scarlet." He shook his head, reined in his temper. "What's become of you, Marius? We tricked and trespassed as youths, but murder? Kidnapping? Torture? Whoever led you down such a path doesn't deserve your fealty."

"'Fealty'?" Marius cackled. "I have no sovereign. I take inspira-tion from my forebears, but believe me when I say my works are entirely of my own design."

"Then why set your sights on Hiero? Why involve me?" Tim demanded. "Every choice you make owes a debt to the past."

"Trust you to see only what's before your eyes," Marius retorted. "But that was always your way, the black and white of things. Be worthy, and fortune will favor you. Well, I will make my own fortune in this world, on the back of anyone who interferes with my plans!" Tim wanted to recoil from the hate that fired his eyes, but stood fast. "Before my work began, I read of your triumphs with Mr. Bash, and I thought to renew our acquaintance. To match wits with the brilliant Inspector Stoker. Finally, a true rival, a mind equal to my own. But I have strung the pair of you along by the nose for days, and all you can do is shout." Marius sighed. "Ça fait pitié."

Tim grabbed a chair and launched it at Marius. He dove to the side, tripped, and slammed down onto the hard boards of the stage.

"Release the prisoners!" Tim shouted. "Or suffer the consequences!"

"What fell specter, dare I ask, has possessed you?" Hiero inquired, sotto voce. "And might it sneak over my way when it's done?"

"The spirit of improvisation," Tim replied between heaving breaths. "As instructed."

Marius, his balance recovered, if not his mirth, stared daggers at them. More, he unsheathed one and began a slow stroll over to the ropes.

"Bold actions for one with so much to lose." He plucked at one rope, then another, shaking the cages above. Neither Han nor Callie stirred. "But then I should have expected nothing less from the redoubtable DI Stoker."

Marius pressed the middle rope into the full heat of the candle flame. With a sickening snap, the rope severed. The cage crashed to the ground. The sound painted as vivid a picture in Tim's mind as any amount of carnage might have.

"Your first and only warning," Marius said. "Do sit." He gestured Hiero toward his chair. "Not you, Timée. You must kneel."

"I will not," Tim growled. "Not before the likes of you. Not to anyone. Nor will we play audience to some tedious monologue detailing the hows and wheres of your crimes. There's no mystery, no riddle to be solved. You are the murderer. Case closed. Kill us if you must, but spare us the boredom."

"Kill you?" Marius chuckled. "What torment is there in that?" He moved back to the ropes, ran the flat of his dagger along their bristly lengths. "You've been conspicuously silent, Bash. Not terribly shocking, that you might watch as your friends plummet to their deaths, but I did expect a bon mot or two."

Hiero shrugged. "You're hardly worth the wit. Indeed, this whole..." He waved a lazy hand at the stage regalia. "...presentation is rather thin sauce after the buffet you served to get us here." He flopped his fingers toward the quill and open book. "Really, what did you mean to have me do, sign my name in blood to save my friends?" He folded his hands on his lap and sighed, his face a model of indifference.

"Not your name. A confession." Tim scanned the document. "To the ghost's crimes, to appearing as Horace Beastly, and... the blackmail of one Graves 'Dagger' Erskine."

Tim saw the effort required for Hiero to laugh. "And dare I ask what I gain in return?"

"The life of your ward, *or*..." Marius shifted the knife from one rope to the other. "...the life of your friend. Hardly the choice of Solomon, I grant."

Hiero clicked his tongue, then frowned as a teacher might to an uninspired student. "My dear boy, did Erskine never mention that the object of any and every game must be the chance of winning? If you remove a prize, what fool risks it all for victory?"

"The fool," Marius sneered, "standing before me." He angled his dagger like a razor and shaved at the side of one of the ropes. Callie's cage danced to his puppeteering, her limp body lurching to and fro. "Sign."

Tim glanced furtively around, searching for a clue or a hint as to what they must do to avoid disaster. His furious mind calculated and recalculated the odds, but the totality of the danger to their friends rendered his every sum a null. Hiero continued taunting Marius that he might reveal more information about Erskine, but he'd been well versed in excuses and aversions. When Han's cage began to jingle like a ringless bell, Tim knew their time was up.

"Sign!" Marius slid the dagger over the rope to Callie's cage, poised to slice. "And pray the devil be merciful!"

Hiero blew out a windy, exasperated sigh. "I suppose. If I must." He raised a brow in Tim's direction. "Kip?"

With a final, frantic count of all the pieces and the players, Tim whispered, "Let him cut the rope."

The only outward sign of Hiero's shock was the ever-so-slight parting of his lips. But within seconds, they firmed, and he smiled. "Quite mad, as strategies go. I approve." For Marius, Hiero struck a pose of haughty nonchalance and drawled, "No."

No amount of practice could mask Marius's disbelief. "You truly are a villain."

"Eye of the beholder," Hiero scoffed. "But, prior remarks to the contrary, I am no fool."

In one fluid sequence, Hiero kicked back his chair, rounded the edge of the table, and charged Marius. With a feral yell, Marius slashed through the ropes; both cages hurtled to the hard stone road. By the time the crash finished echoing through the Dark Arches, Hiero had Marius pinned to the table, dagger planted in the very hand that had wielded it.

After swallowing back a wave of nausea, Tim dared a look at the mangled remains of the cages. Torn limbs, twisted metal, a decapitation, tufts of straw... and not a drop of blood. The two mannequins had not survived, but somewhere, he hoped, Han and Callie had managed to overtake Miss Marks. He turned back to find Hiero twisting the dagger above a howling Marius and hurried to put a stop to it.

"My dear Mr. Bash, we won't learn much of use if you murder him." Tim clasped Hiero's wrist and pulled him back, all while keeping a knee planted in the center of Marius's chest.

"Erskine," Hiero snarled, his voice choked with emotion. "Tell us! Where is he?"

Marius let out a final deranged cackle and cried, "Now, you blackguards. Now!"

Tim yanked Hiero back from the table as the costumed figures, one by one, rose from their seats and turned toward them, knives out.

The denizens of the Dark Arches had come for their revenge.

Chapter 23

The bog stench of London revived Han's senses quicker than smelling salts. Worryingly, he did not remember falling asleep, but the cottonmouthed state of his head indicated chloroform, or some other method of sedation, had been involved. He dangled from a hook of some sort—not that his feet, if functional, could have carried him far—under a bridge. The stone pathway below would provide a solid landing should he fall, but the gull cries and the salt reek told him the Thames was near.

As was Callie, who Han looked for the instant his head cleared. She hung beside him, ash faced, sagging into her restraints, still unconscious. Or so he hoped. His only relief was the thought that Miss Marks would probably wait to kill her until he could bear witness.

The lady herself entered into his view, armed and dangerous, smiling a smile that, were she born several stations higher, would have sent her courtiers scurrying to obey. Han wished he felt unmoved by the sight of her, smug and imperious in this, the moment she had been scheming toward for months, if not years. Han spared a moment to regret that they hadn't met under different circumstances. That here, beyond the point of no return, all her elegance and daring and wiles would be lost to him, one way or the other. If only someone better than Erskine had recognized her potential before now. If only he hadn't been so attracted to her strength that he missed the hints of her villainy.

Han shook off the last of his sentimentality and concentrated on their surroundings. A chill in the air suggested they were out of doors, but the glow of the lanterns against the utter blackness of the night enclosed them in a chamber of soft light. Somewhere behind Miss Marks, what appeared to be an iron rail glinted weakly. A bank of fog kept Han from seeing beyond, though he heard the faint rush of the river. The Embankment path beneath Waterloo Bridge, if he had to guess, a stone's throw from the Thames and long rumored to hide a secret entrance to the Adelphi Arches. At present, the span directly beneath the bridge had been barricaded off by the Yard in order to prevent the criminal element from returning to their subterranean refuge.

In short, no one was coming for them.

"Your lesser half didn't care to accompany you on this particular killing spree?" Han attempted to channel Hiero's infamous banter in the face of certain peril.

Miss Marks smirked. "If he had, you'd already be sunk." She aimed Callie's MAS revolver at his chest as she strutted up to him, so close Han could feel the whisper of her breath. "And what a waste that would be."

Han met the challenge, and the temptation, in her eyes with one of his own. He recalled one of Erskine's cardinal rules: When in doubt, keep them talking. "Oh?"

"Steady." She pressed a hand, instead of the revolver's muzzle, into the center of his chest. "What the master always said of you. Steadfast, constant, dispassionate. Still waters. That he sought to get under your skin, but you never bared any."

"To him? No." Han confirmed. "Though he did try."

Miss Marks stilled. Her lips stayed curled, but her smirk seemed forced. "But the one you call Bash..."

"Astonishing," Han dryly remarked. "How you understand everything, and yet so little, of our time under Erskine."

Anger flashed in her eyes. "I understand more than you know. About loyalty. About betrayal."

"And yet you're about to ask me to turn my back on my truest friend in the world, and the family we made, and the life we've built together—"

"The life you stole!"

"I don't deny it." Han struggled to keep the emotion from his voice. "What choice do you have when you grow too big for your cage? What choice did we have, Hiero and I, when Erskine lured us off the streets? No choice at all. What choice, years later, to leave Erskine's company before he took such a risk that we'd all three of us hang? *No choice at all.*"

Han scrutinized her face for a sign his words stirred something in her other than blind fury. Enough to giver her pause. Enough to save one of them. The tension in her jaw and the faint creasing of her brow gave him cause to hope.

"Drown me," Han insisted. "Mark his revenge. Return to him with a pelt. But leave the rest of my family be."

At the lift of her chin, Han knew he'd lost.

"It's too late." Miss Marks smoothed a second hand onto his chest beside the first, the revolver, pointed at Han's head, snarled between her fingers. "For Bash and Stoker. Marius is relentless. A rabid dog."

"Who chased Randolph Terriss into the street, foiling your carefully staged murder scene in his flat?"

Miss Marks chuckled ruefully. "See what a pair we would have made?"

"And the faulty trapdoor. The dancer. Also his handiwork?"

"He tends toward the vicious. Wanted a grislier death. Instead she survived."

"Unlike Flint."

"Vive la révolution!" she proclaimed. "Every theater has a guillotine. One need only replace the blade."

Han nodded, though the thought sickened him. "But the archival newspapers. The coded reviews. The riddles. And then the headlines calling for Beastly's head. All by your hand, from your genial mind. I should have known then, Mademoiselle Arascain. Or should I say Miss Erskine?"

Her face erupted with delight. She gazed deep, deep into his eyes, caressed his cheek, ghosted a kiss over his lips. "Marketa Erskine," she whispered. "Enchantée de faire votre connaissance."

When she stepped back—to preen, of all things—Han saw what he'd been missing from the first. Or so he'd tell himself in the dead of night when he cursed himself ten ways a fool. The resemblance, once revealed, became an obsession to his sculptor's eye, tracing where her mother's features softened and shaded Marketa's looks just enough to conceal the truth of her origins.

Arascain. Erskine. Han wanted to put out his eyes.

Instead he rallied. "Your father hasn't returned to England. He sent you in his stead."

She laughed, a sharp, heady sound. "My father is dead. You and your gaoler saw to that. Oh, forgive me, your 'truest friend in the world.'" She pushed back against him, cupped his face in both her hands, the cool steel of the revolver biting into his temple. "I confess you were not at all what I expected. And if you had been more malleable, I might have wavered. I nearly did when Marius took the girl."

"Not part of the plan?"

Marketa scoffed. "The little imbecile should have nabbed Stoker. But Bash's theatrical coup distracted him, and here we are."

"She didn't escape. Miss Vauquelin. You let her go."

"I don't, as a rule, tend to endanger those of my own sex." She cut her eyes over to Callie, a warning. "But exceptions are made, when needs must."

Han was at a loss as to how to reply. If he begged for Callie's life, Marketa would end her without prejudice. If he renounced her, she would read the truth in his eyes. He'd given the game away before he even knew he was playing, and now she held all the cards.

"But you've been such a good boy," Marketa cooed. She brushed a thumb across his bottom lip, a faint look of longing coloring her face. "Notion after notion has bloomed and withered in those lovely brown eyes of yours, and you haven't let one take root. For that, and in honor of the adventures we'll never have, a gift. You may die first."

Han could only grunt as Marketa yanked him forward. Too late, he realized the hook that suspended him swung from a pulley system. He sailed over the rail and into the bank of fog, which parted to reveal the oil-black waters of the Thames far below. Even if he survived the plunge or the current, the ropes that secured him would surely spell his end. Han fought against his binds, wriggling enough to catch a final glimpse of Callie, to make one last, desperate plea for her life.

He turned in time to see her stab Marketa. The revolver clattered to the ground. Marketa howled a battle cry. Callie slashed at her neck but didn't cut deep enough. Marketa launched at her and slammed them both to the ground. She grabbed Callie's knife hand by the wrist, tried to bash it on the rail. Callie held fast. They wrestled, evenly matched. Marketa kicked at her legs, but the ropes that bound Callie shielded her. Callie screwed two fingers into one of Marketa's wounds. She cackled through the pain.

Han vigorously swung his legs, trying to help however he could, but he slipped farther from the shore. The snap of breaking twine warned him off his efforts; he could only watch, heart in his throat, as Callie fought for her life.

Marketa wrenched herself upward to jab her elbows into Callie's chest until she coughed for breath. Her arm gave out, and, with a sickening crack, Marketa dashed her fist against the cobblestone. Callie surged upward, tipped the knife over the rail.

Marketa seized her by the throat.

A gross miscalculation. One arm free, Callie punched her in the kidney. A second punch cracked the bones of her corset, pierced into her side. Marketa wailed. Han, remembering Marketa's strength from their own bout, was unsurprised when she held Callie's shoulders down with her arms and pressed her thumbs into her windpipe.

But he hadn't tracked the revolver's fall. Callie, who had, knocked it closer with her heel, hooked a finger in, and, with the last of her strength, clobbered Marketa in the head. She screamed, collapsed. Callie shoved her off and retrieved a second hidden knife. She lanced through the last of the ropes that bound her. Too weak to stand, she propped herself against the rail, revolver smartly aimed at Marketa as she stomped feeling back into her legs.

Her back to Han, it should be said, until she recovered.

He didn't begrudge her the privacy or her frustration. Or, perhaps, a deeper sense of loss. He'd been brought down from his pedestal due to everything involving Marketa. But Han couldn't bring himself to regret expecting the best of her, even if she'd upended his instincts.

In her corner, Marketa stirred. She moaned as she lifted her head, silenced at the click of the revolver. She stared down the barrel, at Callie, at Han for several heartbeats. Callie growled hoarsely, thrusting the revolver forward—a clear threat. Marketa leapt to her feet, staggered out of reach. Callie made to follow but could only crawl. She fired a warning shot, but Marketa had already climbed over the rail.

"No!" Han cried.

Marketa blew him a kiss, then jumped into the Thames.

"I'll have that back, if you please." Hiero pulled at the hilt of the dagger sunk into Marius's palm. And pulled. And pulled.

The dozen or so costumed mercenaries began to laugh, low and sinister, until their voices echoed through the Arches. They barricaded the table but did not attack, waiting for Hiero and Kip to make the first move in what would doubtlessly be their quick and brutal undoing. He looked to Kip for a gesture, a signal, anything that might give him some indication as to how they might extract themselves from this very well-laid trap they had willingly and, well, somewhat foolhardily walked into. Hiero watched as Kip's tactician's mind calculated the odds, the vectors, the alternatives, wishing he could trace the angle of his fox-red brows with a fingertip. He did not miss Kip's small frown at being observed.

"Hiero."

"Hmm?"

"Stall."

"Ah." He clamped a hand over Marius's mouth, clonked his head on the table. "Gentlemen. Or so I presume. Are there ladies among you? If so, you are welcome."

The laughter died out, replaced by a festering silence. Termite tingles crawled over his skin, but Hiero kept his face impassive. He stared into the black eye holes of each mask, appealing directly to the people hiding within and attempting to get a sense of who might be their leader. Other than muzzled Marius, whose increasingly gusty breaths soaked through Hiero's glove.

"I'll be brief. I presume my reputations precedes, but if not, here it is. I am Hieronymus Bash, consulting detective, patron of the arts, and very invested in continuing in both of those positions. Therefore… name your price."

Kip let slip a soft chuckle, but the others neglected to respond.

"Come now." Hiero clicked his tongue. "Don't play the shy violet. I am, I assure you, fully versed in the ways of the world, and my word is my bond. Also, I am in no way connected to the Metropolitan Police or the Yard. Consulting, as mentioned. And I dare say I have resources at my disposal that this"—he jutted his chin toward Marius—"unfortunate can only dream of. Because *I stole them from his master before I arranged for his murder.* Did he not mention?"

No one replied, but Hiero did not think he imagined a slight easing of the tension. Kip shifted his stance, sign enough that he readied for action. But an imperceptible nod urged Hiero to continue.

"Revenge is sweet, or so the saying goes. And I, for one, can attest to the truth of that. But sweeter still? *Profit.*" Hiero felt the thickness in the air that told a performer the audience was with him. "So you must ask yourselves what benefits you the most. Helping a penniless villain achieve his ends? Or lining your—"

Kip lunged across the table, grabbed a candelabra, and thrust it at the nearest aggressor, setting his costume aflame. He swiped at two more before they could retreat, their cries paralyzing the others. Hiero grabbed for the dagger and made a renewed attempt at freeing it, determined to be of use. Sounds of violence, and the hard thwack of Kip's truncheon, erupted behind him. Marius, no longer restrained or unconscious, pounced. Hiero rammed a fist over his shoulder but only managed to get himself flipped around and slammed back, knocking his wind out. He recovered in time to see Marius raise the dagger, blood gushing from the hand coiled around the hilt.

Hiero grabbed the tablecloth on both sides and tugged. Two candelabras toppled, setting the linen aflame. Only then did he remember he was the one lying down. Marius, a red menace firing his eyes, pressed the dagger to his throat. The hot rush of Marius's blood drenched Hiero's chest. Struggling against Marius's zealous strength, Hiero wondered if the fire would ignite him before or after Marius grew faint.

Kip denied him his answer as he clunked Marius on the head, nabbed the dagger, and hugged him into an equally perilous position, blade to throat. Their first hostage. Hiero might have beamed with pride, except...

"Hall of Mirrors," Kip whispered. "Run!"

Hiero dove into the shadows, not daring to glance back until at the mirrored maze. A dangerous distance back, Kip dragged a snarling, writhing Marius away from the stage, where mercenaries flailed in burning costumes. But a larger group, masks discarded, broke away from the pack to hunt them down. Hiero willed Kip to toss Marius over the edge—the fate to which he almost condemned Han and Callie—and be done with him, but Kip was determined to see him in irons. Better, Hiero thought, that they keep their lives.

He searched for something to delay or distract the hunters, but shattered mirrors would only endanger Kip. Instead he worked open the knot of his cravat, then rolled the silken fabric—too fine for the likes of Marius, but needs must—into a ball. Which he promptly stuffed into their captive's mouth once Kip shoved him over the threshold.

"You might have bound his wrists." Kip pushed him at Hiero. Once Hiero had him under the arms, Kip scooped up his legs. Marius, dizzied by blood and air loss, swatted the air like a drunken cat.

"I reserve such pleasures for a chosen few."

"Take many murderers to your bed, do you?" Kip chuckled as they wove their way back through the maze.

Hiero caught his gaze, winked. "Just the one." Once they'd navigated three turns, Kip set Marius's legs down and moved to a mirror beside the exit passage. He took hold of the frame, attempting to shift or turn it. Hiero forestalled his efforts. "Allow me."

He grabbed the mirror, lifted it just so, and slid it into the exit, creating a new configuration. He whirled around in triumph, only to meet Kip's glower.

"You might have done that from the first."

Hiero opened his mouth, shut it, smiled contritely.

"Hurry along, then." Kip waved a finger at the other mirrors, then carried Marius through so that they did not lose track of the return path. With no time to consider how to rearrange the mirrors,

Hiero created a series of impassable barriers.

They'd just slipped into the tunnel that led back to the cloak-room of the Caledonian Hotel when the shattering started.

Kip set Hiero at the head of their little caravan, bearing the dead weight of Marius's torso while he hooked his legs over an arm, truncheon at the ready. Though what a truncheon might do against all those knives, Hiero didn't care to contemplate.

Instead a needle-thin memory pierced through the tangled threads of his mind just as they reached the bottom of the ladder.

"My dear, a concern." He dropped Marius to the ground and climbed the first few rungs of the ladder. A quick push on the square panel confirmed his fears. "They've barricaded the door." Kip added his strength to Hiero's efforts. He'd have taken this as an insult, except he'd cultivated a reputation as a man of leisure. "We should have hidden behind the mirrors."

Their pursuers crashed through another barrier in the not-so-distance.

Kip shook his head. "They would have discovered us eventually. And reinforcements raced in from the street entrances behind them. Credit to him, Marius planned for every eventuality."

"Forgive my lack of charity as I await death by mob." Hiero straightened his waistcoat and brushed a hand through his hair, ready to face certain doom as every aesthete must: with peerless elegance. "And to think I once trafficked among them. How the tables have turned." He sighed, reached for Kip's hand. "I suppose there is no going back."

"To the Hall of Mirrors, or a life of crime?"

"Neither. Both. Whatever suits." Hiero shrugged but couldn't meet Kip's eyes. In addition to abject terror, he felt the weight of all that was still unsaid between them. Unsaid by him, specifically. He nodded toward the tunnel, which continued on past the Caledonian. "Perhaps we should abandon our prize and scuttle off into the unknown, disappearing into legend."

"And have another ghost haunt our every move? No. We will make our stand." Kip hopped onto a rung of the ladder, so that they stood eye to eye, and drew Hiero into his embrace. Mesmerized by the phosphorescent luster of his Kip's eyes, Hiero didn't even flinch when he heard angry boot steps hit the hard stone floor of the tunnel. "Unless your silver tongue has some other means of singing our pursuers to shipwreck?"

"Alas, I fear they are deaf to such sweet music."

Kip laughed. "We few, we happy few." He pulled Hiero into a fast, fervent kiss, then broke away. He leapt over the body and stood, weapon raised, staring into the black of the tunnel. "Slide Marius behind the ladder and sit on him. Throw your jacket over your head. I'll engage them for a while, then flee. With any luck, I'll lead them past you."

The leaden weight of the circumstances fell suddenly on Hiero's shoulders.

"Kip—"

"Hush now, love. They're near."

Hiero choked back his protest, or his guilt, or his despair, or he knew not what emotion—only that it burned like the fires of hell. Somehow he'd become Don Juan, too arrogant to see how his misbehavior endangered those around him until the devil himself demanded blood. But in this godless underworld, there would be no divine intervention, no—

Creaks and clamor from above. The scrape of large objects across the ceiling. A loud squeal, and then... a shaft of light! Perhaps the heavens did shine upon them.

Or simply Han, whose bruised, worried face peered down at them through the door to the Caledonian Hotel.

Hiero beamed up at him, eyes shining with relief. "Han! And here I thought you down for the count. Fancy a spot of mortal combat?"

"I *could* do with some exercise." He shouted something to one of the hotel staff, then leapt through the hole. To Hiero's astonishment, a passel of spring hares came bouncing down after him. Except these bunnyish lads had armed themselves with copper pipes, improvised maces, and spiked ball-chains, a veritable medieval rabble.

For the first time in his life, Hiero found himself raring for a fight.

A quick glance over his shoulder at the thugs racing one by one out of the tunnel muted that instinct. Kip swung at the leader as he charged, hammering blows to his face and neck until he fell to his knees. Kip crouched down to deliver a final blow; Han leapt over him into the fray, kicking the teeth out of two attackers. He baited three mercenaries into a corner and dispatched them with speed, the slice of his bare hands deadlier than any knife.

Kip's fists pounded jaws and kidneys and the occasional set of bollocks. The thugs fought just as dirty, spitting, biting, eye gouging, grabbing some of the rabbits by the scruff and tossing them against the wall. But they were no match for Han. He spun through them, a cyclone of destruction, every jab and crack seeming to exorcize another type of ache within.

But Hiero had no time to wonder why when Marius stirred beneath him. Before Hiero could react, Marius's nails snagged in the seam of his trousers and *tore off a strip of fabric.* Hiero shrieked, a cri de coeur than went unheard over the din. So he smashed his fist into Marius's smug face, indescribable pain mingling with minute satisfaction as Hiero swallowed a string of curses.

He looked for Kip, ready to crow of his triumph, but found him wheezing as he wrestled with a thug. Han fought his way out of a gang of foes as a steady stream poured out of the tunnel. Two rabbits flanking the entrance took turns hobbling them as they stumbled in, but it wasn't enough to ebb the rush. If the denizens of the Dark Arches could not have their revenge on the Metropolitan Police, then Hiero and the team would do.

Forcing down a surge of helplessness, Hiero lugged Marius to his feet, then up over his shoulder, grateful his mania had whittled him down to a wisp of a man. Hiero whistled at the boys defending the ladder, who pressed forward to form a barricade. Sneaking behind them, Hiero heaved up toward the door. Surely disappearing the mercenaries' captain would lead to some sort of mutiny? Or at the very least, conditional surrender?

Not to be. No sooner had Hiero dumped Marius onto the threadbare carpet of the Caledonian's cloakroom than he heard a rallying cry below. Han's rabbits roared in answer. The thugs stormed the barricade, chasing their master.

Hiero grabbed around for any type of weapon, caught the skirts of a maimed but flint-eyed Callie, who thrust out her revolver.

"Finish it," she rasped.

With a sly wink and shaking hands, Hiero descended anew. Hung a moment amidst the chaos, wondering where to aim. He looked to Kip, his north star, his better angel, for guidance. Framed like a Rembrandt in the sole shaft of light, surrounded by a tableau of toughs, Kip pointed at the archway over the tunnel entrance.

And Hiero, to his shock and elation, shot true.

The keystone split, cracking a passing mercenary's skull. Rock and dust rained down from the crumbling tunnel. Wary of collapse after years of living in the Arches, the thugs scrambled to escape, abandoning their injured on the field of battle.

The rabbits cheered in triumph. They'd won the day.

Hiero jumped down so that Han and his bunnies could hop up the ladder. He caught Kip by the arm before he could hare after any of their attackers, though, by the set of his jaw, it hurt his policeman's pride. On impulse Hiero tugged his bloodied, battle-worn Eurydice into a tight embrace, determined to guide him out of the underworld. Only Kip's halting breaths kept Hiero from squeezing the life out of him, or the love into him, or some such nonsense. Tears of relief stung the back of his eyes but went unshed.

Kip clutched him fiercely in return, massaging soothing circles into Hiero's tension-rigid back. His touch travelled lower, and lower, then lower still, tracing the frayed edge of Hiero's trousers and a patch of bare thigh. And, or so those curious fingers revealed, his partially exposed buttock.

"My dear, I expected to find you in a state, but not of deshabille." Kip, to Hiero's great annoyance, snickered into his lapel.

Until he started coughing. Hiero, ever the gallant in the face of mockery, offered his handkerchief. Kip wiped his mouth but couldn't hide his smile.

"Fortunately for us, Marius's only true revenge was sartorial." Hiero glanced around the dim space but saw only unconscious thugs sprawled on the sooty ground. "And perhaps an overdue scolding from my tailor."

"So long as the rest of you is quite intact, I claim it as a victory." With a final chuckle, Kip sank back against him for another stolen minute before they rejoined their friends.

In that moment, Hiero felt he held the entire world in his arms. That was consolation enough.

Chapter 24

A shock of lightning illuminated the lounge of the Caledonian Hotel, exposing the pale, drawn faces of the dawn
travelers and insomniacs who loitered there. No one startled. The
doom-gray sky had warned of a bleak morning. Rain battered the
windowpanes like an artillery barrage. Heavy-booted constables
pounded up and down the nearby staircase, chasing down every want
or witness the investigators above might require. The Yard had fully
invaded the hotel: every room searched, every guest and staff member
interviewed, no stone unturned.

In the aftermath of the night's tumult, Han had disappeared his
rabbits into a carriage before the hotel staff could take notice. Angus,
father of two and accustomed to shepherding unruly passengers
across town, drove them to Berkeley Square, where Minnie and Jie
would attend to their scrapes and bruises. With the boys settled, Han
shadowed Tim, first to help him track key players' whereabouts and
the events of his own abduction, then as an aid to further inquiries.
He'd questioned bedraggled guests, searched for hidden passages and
retraced important routes, bagged significant items, and listened to
the now testy concierge's list of complaints. He'd kept himself busy
until his vision blurred, until he swayed on his feet, until Tim
ordered him to eat something or he'd report him to Dr. Grieg.

Han stirred his tea, stared through the cascade of water at the
Thames beyond. He'd managed a few slices of buttered toast but

couldn't stomach the kippers or the sausage. He longed for Macau. For a simple bowl of fish and rice, for the lulling rock of the houseboat, the soft tinkle of wind chimes, the salt tang of the air as he gazed across the bay. Life there would have been just as complicated as the one he'd stumbled into, with just as much tragedy, he reminded himself. But some days he tired of the excess that surrounded him. Some days he wondered if he'd become a man his mother would be proud of.

"She made her choice." Han had not noticed Callie slip into the seat beside him but found himself grateful for her presence. "You must respect it."

He nodded, once, but didn't trust himself to speak. Or, rather, to speak with her about things he hadn't yet reconciled within himself. She hooked a fork into one of his kippers and eased it over to her plate, then attempted to slice it with the fork's edge. He remembered her hand, bones now set and bound tight against her chest, and cut the kipper into small pieces.

She frowned. Han set the cutlery down on his own plate and sighed.

"You mistake me." He cradled his teacup and took up his spoon again, the motion of stirring somehow soothing. "I mourn what might have been, had Hiero and I known of her existence before now." He raised the cup to his mouth, if only to give his thoughts some time to gather. "When we escaped Erskine... We wouldn't have left anyone behind."

"You believe he mistreated her?"

"She spoke of hardship, in her youth. I do not think it was part of the deception."

"Or she used the truth to sell the lie, as Hiero's always taught."

"As Erskine taught us."

Callie chewed on a piece of kipper, considering. "She has left a flood of questions in her wake. Did she even know Erskine in her youth? Was she ever apprenticed to him? Or is she acting in tribute to the father she never knew? But if that's the case, where did she learn his methods? What led her to follow in the path of one who abandoned her to hardship? Why did she feel she must take up his cause to the point of murdering innocents? Erskine, if I understand correctly, never committed such crimes."

"To my knowledge, no." Han took some solace in Callie's typical bloodless attack of the problem. He appreciated the distance, even if he could not match it in heart. "He was a thief and a cheat and a swindler, and certainly a master of deception, but we never saw him take a life by his own hand. Manipulate another into doing so, but never... Perhaps when he was younger.

"When Hiero first raised the idea of his resurrection, I believed it impossible because I thought these recent crimes out of character. Later, I thought Erskine's rage at our betrayal might have razed the last of his goodwill, whatever standards he had left to cinder. But he enjoyed a game too much, the look of someone when they realize they've been betrayed. Not..."

"And in that lack of understanding, her fatal mistake," Callie said. "She failed to enjoy the very game she devised to avenge her father as he would have."

Kipper demolished, Callie stabbed one of his sausages and ate it off her upraised fork. A reminder that she too had not always lived as largely as they did now. Han waited till she bit off another morsel to slide his plate over to her.

"The logical answer to all of my speculation, of course," Callie continued, rightly intuiting that Han needed the distraction, "is that she lied."

Han had been fighting very hard not to come to the same conclusion. "On which occasion?"

"Her claim that Erskine is dead."

Han blew out a long, slow breath but could find no counterargument. He retreated into practicalities to spare himself the anguish of believing that to be the case. "It seems my work is far from done, though the investigation may be concluded."

"I do wonder"—Callie's gaze lingered on Hiero, dozing on a bench by the door in a pair of ill-fitting trousers—"whether Marius will prove songbird or stone."

"Regardless, the Yard will squeeze. I don't envy Tim the task, if they request his assistance."

Callie harrumphed in her particular way. "I would happily take his place."

"And he'd be glad of it, I'm sure."

Only then did he find the courage to look in her direction. Despite her injury and the night of horrors they'd barely escaped, despite the sweat that mottled her clothes and the grime that mired her face, she glowed. Han felt his determination to do right by her weaken, as it always did in these moments, these quiet conversations that spoke of what they might be to each other. But then he saw the rain reflected in the ice-blue pools of her eyes, and the Thames beyond, and remembered himself. No matter what he felt for her, he would not wade into those waters and risk losing her friendship.

Callie, oblivious to his inner musings, smiled. "More toast?"

Han shook his head. "I've an errand that cannot wait."

"Rabbits to send hopping?"

"Something like." All of a sudden, the sadness struck him, hard and heavy on his chest. Poor, poor Toby—another victim of Marketa's wicked game. Another body they would never recover. Another soul who deserved so much better than his lot in life.

He felt the clutch of Callie's hand on his forearm, saw the question on her face. Han couldn't stop himself. "The boy I sent to inquire after Erskine, when I only suspected... They killed him."

"No!" Callie's outraged shout drew stares. She glared them off, gripped into his arm. "You sent your must trusted, I wager. Toby."

Han nodded. Of course someone with her attention to the minutiae of their work would remember his name.

"You mean to inform the others?"

"They await me at the house."

With a final, decisive pat to the back of his hand, she declared, "We'll go together. Bring them sweets, or ices, or... whatever they'd like best. Though I dare say Minnie has already done us proud in that regard."

She stood before he could protest, with a firm expression. But Han did not miss the forlorn glance at the plate. Han folded the last kipper into a napkin and stuffed it in his pocket. He threw back his lukewarm tea, hesitating only a second before joining her.

They caught Tim's eye while waiting for the bellhop to summon them a hansom. He waved them off with a half smile. Once in the safety of the cab, Han was surprised to find himself somewhat relieved. By her company. By her care.

They fell into a comfortable silence until—

"I have been thinking of late that I've got the wrong end of the stick, where the business of detective work is concerned."

Han raised a brow. "Oh?"

"When we first formed our partnership with Tim, I thought, 'At last, a chance to study under a real detective.'"

He chuckled. "I fail to recall much excitement on your part when Tim first came to us."

"Inwardly, I did," she corrected. "Not for Tim, per se, but what his methods might teach me. But now..." Callie bowed her head, fiddled with her mud-crusted sleeve. "Well. Not to dwell. But if we'd lost you..." She gnawed on her bottom lip, gnarled her fingers in the fabric. "What I mean is... I'd like to train as your apprentice."

"My... apprentice?"

She gave a vigorous nod. "I'll never be invited to join the Yard. I started down this path because it was the only one available to me. But I see now that yours is the better path. That what I should be learning are the ways around the rules, the methods of secrecy. Of stealth and subterfuge. Your methods." She dared a glance in his direction. For the first time in his adult life, Han couldn't control the look on his face. "Will you teach me?"

He gaped at her. Recognized that he understood her earnestness, her vulnerability as no one else would. And although every well-honed instinct he had warned him away, he found himself replying...

"I will."

Rain thundered on the roof of the hansom as it lurched through the traffic on the Strand, merrymakers and pleasure seekers undeterred by a spot of London weather. Word of the drama beneath the Adelphi Arches had winged its way through the leisure palaces; many of the pubs, clubs, and theaters hung a white sheet over their doorways to celebrate the unmasking of The Gaiety ghost—and in tribute to those fallen. Late of The Gaiety herself, where he'd related the events of the previous night and early morning to Mr. Tumnus, the Vicomte, Madame de Casterac, and the reunited Vauquelin sisters, Tim slouched across the carriage seat so that the space felt less empty. After two full days on his feet, every part of him ached.

And yet he couldn't help but smile as they passed door after door, rail after rail draped in white. He recognized this feeling for the rare treasure it was: the relief of knowing that the team had made the streets of London safer through their efforts. Assuring that the society secrets Lord Blackwood hoarded were kept by their bearers, or that the pregnant women trapped by the Daughters of Eden bore their babes in safety had been rewarding conclusions to those cases, but this...

Tim permitted himself a good measure of satisfaction at seeing Marius in irons. Pride, even, at having brought him down and cleared out the Dark Arches, not once, but twice. Superintendent Quayle, who eagerly and often cursed Tim's name to his face, had commended his work and privately asked what Tim thought should be done about Littlejohn. Quayle had even conceded that certain cases might be better suited to their mercurial methods than the brass tacks of the Yard. Tim would be back among their ranks for several days, tracking and organizing all the evidence—a victory if ever there was.

All of which added a slight spring to his step, despite the looming shadow of exhaustion, as he entered the Yard sometime later. Though deserted at this late hour given the all-hands-on-deck approach to capturing and processing their second batch of Dark Arches arrests, the front desk officers saluted him with vigor, and the gaol guards erupted in applause. And if they kept him from his final duty of the night for a quarter hour or two, recounting the previous night's events, to what harm? And if he indulged in giving them an extra warning as to the tricks and manipulations of their special prisoner, though they had doubtless been briefed by their actual superiors, why not? Tim had worked himself to the bone, paid his dues in blood and breath and grief, been beaten and poisoned and fed to lions!

A few compliments wouldn't spoil his supper.

Especially given that Marius had intended to serve him up to Hiero trussed like a Christmas goose. As one of the gaol guards escorted him to the windowless cell where Marius was being held— away from the other prisoners, for *their* safety—Tim struggled to understand what turn of fate or hidden aspect of his nature had brought Marius into league with Erskine. He recognized that any remnants of the boy he once knew were gone. And Tim would mourn him, in time. But before he took his rest that night, he would have some answers, even unsatisfactory. He would return to his Hiero armed with the knowledge that all his dragons had been slain.

Or, rather, awaited trial and execution.

To Tim's relief, Quayle had taken extra precautions. Not one, but two guards flanked the door to Marius's cell. The iron bars ensured the prisoner was visible at all times. Marius wore a straitjacket with additional chains crossing his chest. These linked to a ring embedded in the brick wall. They'd also been smart enough to gag him, but, as this would hardly serve Tim's purposes, he ordered the guards to remove the half bridle and await his whistle somewhere out of earshot.

After peering down the corridor to ensure they were indeed alone, Tim turned back to confront Marius's sneering face. Still, there remained a faint glimmer in his eye, a sharpness to his expression that warned of further mischief. Marius believed he still had an ace up his sleeve. Tim, in spite of, or perhaps because of everything Marius had put them through that night, didn't have the heart to bluff. He moved to the center of the room, just an inch or two from the maximum length of Marius's chains, if he judged correctly, and stared him down.

"Your card," he declared. "Your final card. Let's have it."

Marius's upper lip curled, a fangless snarl. "Not very sporting of you, Timée, to stride in here and make demands."

"Please disabuse yourself of the notion that I am here for any reason other than my duties as an officer of the law and the primary inspector on this case." He snapped his fingers, stretched out a hand, palm up. "Your trump card. Your ace in the hole. Details. Speak."

"I cannot speak of what I do not know." His lips twisted into a sinister smirk. Like most deranged killers, he could not help himself. "The whereabouts of my partner, for instance..."

"Miss Erskine? Jumped in the Thames." Tim struggled to maintain his poker face. When he thought of all the secrets lost with her... "Of which you've already been informed."

Marius scoffed. "And I'm to trust the word of a constable?"

"If I'm to believe anything that escapes your venomous mouth."

"Then why visit? Why not make me stew the night in my cell? You coppers are very fond of that technique, are you not?"

"Because I mean to be done with you. Until the day I watch you hang, that is."

Marius whooped in delight. "Quel sang-froid! Truly, I am humble enough to admit that I did underestimate your abilities as a policeman and as… this, this magnificent thing you have become. Heartless in the face of betrayal by your oldest friend."

"Murder has a tendency to chill the blood." Tim permitted himself a slight smirk of his own. "I reserve my sympathy for your victims. Amongst which I am told I should number Miss Erskine."

The trouble with feeding off hatred and rage for months, if not years on end, was that, despite any feints and protestations, one became very easy to provoke. Marius did not disappoint in this regard. His face flushed the color of an overripe beet.

"And just what accusations did she unleash, presumably before she dove into the Thames?"

Tim shrugged. "None you haven't claimed. That you masterminded the entire affair. That you hunted her down once you learned of her father's reputation and kept a stranglehold around her neck ever since."

Marius's chest heaved with the effort to rein himself in, his pupils blown. "Pity, then, that she took our last gambit to her grave. The final card, as you call it, was hers to play."

A lie. But Tim had expected no less. He suddenly had cause to question his intentions in coming here. Was it a futile search for some sort of insight into why his childhood friend had done so wrong by him? Was he avoiding Hiero and a possible contentious welcome home? Was he waiting for another shoe to drop, either out of instinct or intuition? Or was the most obvious answer the correct one: given her connection to Erskine, Marketa had been the one to provide the most damning evidence against Hiero and Han, which she hid from her partner when things took a murderous turn? Evidence now lost to the vagaries of fate.

Except…

"How convenient," Tim retorted, shelving his thoughts for later contemplation. "Their loss won't save you from the noose, but may spare us further trouble."

He tossed off that last sentiment like chum into the water, hoping his shark wouldn't resist a bite.

"You and your lover, you mean?" Marius's mouth stretched into a toothsome grin. "I hardly need dredge up the past to cause trouble, as you see."

"Ah, but two can play at that game." Tim stepped forward another inch, their faces in intimate proximity. "And a shared past cuts both ways. Make your claims. I will counter them. Only one of us has the means to dredge up the relevant evidence. Only one of us is prepared to fall on his sword."

"How disastrously noble." Marius coiled into himself, a scorpion ready to sting. "You might care to ask yourself who exactly you share your bed with before you sacrifice everything for him. And where that evidence might lead. And whether or not he might also deserve to be in chains."

Tim did not even give himself the satisfaction of a raised brow, though a million defenses and justifications leapt to his tongue. But to display even a hint of vulnerability would tempt Marius to make good on his threats and out them.

"Food for thought." Tim nodded, as if in approval. He did not miss Marius's mild surprise. "I'll leave you with one last morsel to chew over. Whom do you think the headlines would favor, were all this dark business—Erskine, Marketa, the complicated life of a certain consulting detective—revealed? Whom would they crow over? Write column after column dissecting his motives and affairs, his movements, his choices, his subterfuge, *his* relationship to all the victims, *his* connection to the murderer, *his* part in the great game that *he* instigated? Who would inspire books, plays, reenactments? Who would live on in infamy? Who would consume the public's memory long after the snap of your neck?

"Who, in the end, would truly get his revenge?"

He let his words hang in the air for a moment, then performed a short bow and left the stage, commanding the guards to replace

Marius's gag as he whisked past them. True to form, Tim replayed every beat and note of the conversation as he crossed over to the Yard's archives, Marius's threats prompting one final errand before he could take his rest.

Chapter 25

With a snort, Hiero threw his head back, blinking away the film that blurred his surroundings. He listed to the right, then forward, wrestling between sleep and equilibrium. He flapped a hand in hopes of slapping some wakefulness into himself, only grazed his cheek. Simple questions, like Where was he? How long had he been dozing? What day was it? eluded him. Then he caught the spiced aroma of his favorite Turkish tea and sighed.

Home at last.

With heavy hands, he poured himself a glass of the rich mahogany liquid, pleased to discover a plate of jewel box biscuits. It required several sips to regain a measure of clarity. Enough, at least, to consider his present circumstance: swathed in his favorite dressing gown, skin clammy from a recent bath, hair dripping down his neck, feet bare, top lip tacky but with no moustache, body a shambles. Some half-dozen boys noisily slurping noodles from fat bowls of soup encircled him.

Ah. The kitchen.

Another few sips of tea, and Hiero noticed Han bent over a steaming cauldron, which smelled not of his famous fish stew, but of laundry. With a meat fork, he pulled out a series of long white towels, then plopped them into a waiting bowl.

Hiero, sinuses aching and past decorum, asked, "What in blazes are you doing? The washing?"

Han chuckled. He spared Hiero a wry glance as he stretched out his back. "Go to bed."

"Not until you explain why you're boiling the linens and the kitchen's become a warren." He gasped in horror. "Is it fleas? Do we have fleas?"

"Says the bloke what went swimmin' in a sewer," one of the rabbits piped up.

"And wouldn'ta seen daylight if it weren't for us," another opined.

"Daylight? In London?" Hiero wiggled his eyebrows at them, and the rabbits snickered. He liked an easy crowd. "And very grateful I am to you, my young cavalry, even if we did emerge into a deluge." The hard patter of rain still rumbled the windowpanes hours... days... Hiero's fatigue had muted his sense of time. "And to you, Han, for corralling them after your own ordeal, of which I'll gladly hear more... if I've not already... Where's dear Calliope? Was her hand seen to? Has Kip returned to his duties?"

Shaking his head, Han poured him another cup of tea and shoved a few biscuits at him. "Drink up."

Hiero had just taken a nibble—decadent, delightful—when Aldridge raced down the stairs, grabbed the bowl of linens and a pot of hot water, and pounded back up again. Hiero raised an inquisitive brow; Han barked a laugh.

"Not long now. We'd best go up." He patted Hiero on the shoulder as he made for the stairs. "Boys, kip in the study. No pillow fighting, no nosying about."

Hiero toddled after him to a chorus of "Yes, sir!" He groaned up the stairs, his weary muscles pestering him all the while.

"Do I need to make myself more presentable?" he asked Han's retreating form. "Are we expecting company?"

"A new arrival is imminent, but I doubt they will stand on ceremony."

Hiero panted his way around the second landing. "Why do I

sense I am being mocked?"

That stopped Han long enough for Hiero to catch up. "Because it's the third time we've had this conversation." He set a hand on Hiero's shoulder. "I do wish you'd take some rest. Tim won't fail to rouse you upon his return."

It spoke much of Hiero's tiredness that he didn't comment on the amnesia or the double entendre. "But what of the new arrival?"

"I doubt they will even notice your absence."

A flash of insight finally dissipated Hiero's brain fog. "Shahida!"

"Indeed."

"It's no time for rest!" A reinvigorated Hiero tackled the next flight of stairs, matching the pace of a spirited tortoise.

Han hovered only a step or two behind him in anticipation of Hiero taking a tumble. "So you've said. Repeatedly."

"Then I have the good fortune of being right not once, but thrice."

"And we've climbed a few stories this time. Progress."

Hiero might have scowled back at him, but they'd reached the third floor. A good thing, too, as he'd begun to see stars. With a decided left turn down the corridor, away from his room, he felt more determined with every step.

A scream cut the air. Fatigue forgotten, Hiero rushed down the hall and up the back stairs to the attic, where he found Callie pacing in a strict military line by the windows, Aldridge listening by the bedchamber door in case they required his help, and Lillian knitting in her rocking chair, oblivious to all around her. A soft hum of encouragement punctuated by terrible howls sung out from the back room.

"Should I summon my physician?"

"Minnie and Jie have the matter well in hand," Han replied, to Callie as much as to Hiero. Han moved into her path, gestured for her to take a seat. She smiled but shook her head.

"When you find him that done this, stab him in the throat!"

Shahida screeched from behind the door.

"Fetch her mother, perhaps?" Hiero asked. "I'll have Angus—"

Callie paused long enough to answer. "She'd prefer not. Wants to present her grandchild as a fait accompli."

"Of course." Only then did Hiero permit the blanket of relief to cover him, such that he staggered over to a high-backed chair and sank into the cushions. Though the weight of the week's events pressed upon him, something like joy bubbled up within at the thought of another child in the house. Another plump pair of cheeks to pinch, another squeal to greet him when he returned home, another distinguished member of the Toy and Tot Tea Society, another bundle he could roam the halls with on late, lonely nights... Except that his nights, of late, were hardly lonely. But he adored every one of his tiny charges, and this babe would be the same.

He would do better by them, he swore, than those who had reared and mentored him. He held a brief moment of regret for Marketa Erskine, then banished such dark thoughts from his mind. Today he would rejoice in their victory and cherish his family.

Hiero reclined back in his seat and promptly fell asleep.

A familiar touch on his shoulder shook him back into consciousness. Kip sat on the arm of the chair, face wan and eyes dark rimmed, but also like the cat that ate the canary. He caressed a thumb across Hiero's cheek but did not bend to kiss him. The intensity of his gaze spoke volumes, ones Hiero could now read with the greatest of ease.

He made to smile but yawned instead. Lively chatter in the distance told Hiero he'd been dozing for quite some time. "I've missed the final act, I take it."

"As did I." Kip's smile was fond. "We must accustom ourselves to life after the stage."

"Oh, I daresay we'll have our fill of dramatics all the same."

"After some repose, I hope."

"Much repose," Hiero purred, attempting to tug Kip onto his

lap. "What's kept you?"

"Later," Kip whispered before claiming his kiss, a slow, sensuous brush of lips that promised much but stopped just at the edge of chaste. "Someone's quite eager to make your acquaintance."

"Not as eager as I."

Nestled in a cocoon of their loved ones, Shahida glowed. The entire household gathered around her on the bed: Lillian and Callie, Aldridge and Minnie, Angus and Jie, Ting and Feng, while Han poured out the champagne.

"And who is this treasure?" Hiero asked of the swaddled bundle in Shahida's arms, all burnished brown cheeks and pretty black lashes.

"The cause of a bloody uproar, inside and out," Shahida groused but beamed down at her daughter nonetheless. "And already tearing my heart out, besides." She cinched her arms around the babe, dropped a kiss to her brow. "This is Kashika, everyone. Kashika, this is..."

"Your family," Hiero concluded. Shahida met his eyes with a steady gaze full of understanding and affection.

"Our family," she whispered down to the wee one with a radiant smile.

Hiero, swollen with feeling and never one to let a celebration go un-toasted, raised his glass in the air. "To our dearest Shahida and sweet Kashi!"

"Long may she reign!" everyone cheered.

Some of the uncertainty of the past few days slid back under Tim's skin as his bathwater cooled. He'd left Hiero doting over Shahida and her daughter, retreating to the privacy of their bedchamber for a long remedial soak. But now that he'd scrubbed off two days' grime and inhaled enough steam to soothe his lungs, Tim felt his solitude most keenly. Along with the bone-deep need to be with his Hiero. In the aftermath of their adventure, they had barely shared a glance, let alone an embrace, let alone a private hour to pick through the detritus of what they'd experienced for nuggets of insight.

Not that Tim felt at odds with Hiero. If anything, his absence through Tim's day had been a distraction, a missing limb pulling his attention away from his duties. He believed neither of them would have survived Marius without the other. He only hoped Hiero felt the same on the matter of their partnership... and far more precious things.

And that the file he'd tucked away in the library would not be the straw that broke them.

Just as Tim began to contemplate the logistics of getting out—he was so eager to be clean that he hadn't brought so much as a slipper from the adjoining room—footsteps echoed in from the corridor beyond. He carded his fingers through his wet hair and reclined with his arms on the edges of the claw-foot tub, a pose Tim hoped affected a suitably relaxed air. Inviting, even.

Hiero eased open the door, only to still at the sight of him. Swathed in his most regal robe, mustard and marigold married together by turquoise swirls, along with his shorn hair and his stubbled cheeks, he resembled a dastardly prince come to charm a too-willing prospect out of her maidenhead. Given how his blood ran hot at the melding of their gazes, Tim planned to surrender anything and everything Hiero might desire.

"Home at last." He rose slowly, letting the clinging suds and gleaming waters work their magic on his muscles, his freckled skin, proud in his nakedness under Hiero's admiring gaze. "Fetch me a towel, won't you? I wouldn't care to drench the carpet."

Hiero padded in a few steps, mapping every inch of Tim with his lust-black eyes as if preparing to mold him in clay, and locked the door behind him. With his usual feline grace, he grabbed two towels from the linen basket and stalked toward him, depositing one on the carpet and folding the other over his arm without once breaking eye contact. A gentleman in all but origin, Hiero offered him his hand, then brought it to his lips once he helped Tim out of the tub. He caressed the knuckles as he turned over Tim's hand, planting an impassioned kiss in his palm, a little moan escaping as he pulled away.

Tim shuddered, need, relief, and soul-deep longing warring with his resolve, but he held fast. Though he yearned for every comfort Hiero could give, he knew how much better it would be if he played out his seduction. He reached for the towel, but Hiero drew back.

"Allow me." The husk in his voice hinted to Tim that he did not struggle alone.

Hiero flapped out the towel with flourish, then draped it across Tim's back. A twirl of his finger instructed Tim to turn around. Hiero set about his task with tenderness and delicacy. He massaged the aches out of Tim's shoulders and arms until he almost swooned. Hiero couldn't resist a long sniff after petting Tim's hair dry but dropped down to give his legs a vigorous rub, somehow ignoring his buttocks. Or perhaps not quite ignoring them, as Hiero gave one a quick nip before moving to the front.

He paused there awhile, on his knees, face inches from Tim's hardening prick, a saucy smile spreading across his lips, a question in his eyes.

"Enjoying the view?" Tim asked between pants, his body in every way betraying him.

"It's quite... arresting." Finally, he stood. Hiero stroked the towel up from his navel, over his chest, and pinched a nipple through the rough fabric. Tim gasped. "Anything else I can do for you this evening?"

Tim nodded, not trusting himself to speak. He stole the towel from Hiero and dropped it to the floor, then snared the sash of his dressing gown. Making quick work of the knot, he threw back the ends and parted the sheathes of silken cloth to expose Hiero, bronze and beautiful and hard as sin, in every way his for the taking.

"A fuck would be lovely." Tim grinned, feeling playful, feeling bold, nigh indestructible under Hiero's hot stare. "But do take your time getting there."

Hiero cupped his cheek, dragged a ready thumb across his bottom lip. "As you wish."

Their mouths met in a hungry kiss. Tim climbed into Hiero's arms, wanting to touch him, devour him, but also hold him, be held, be entwined and writhing...

Somehow he pushed up against a wall. Hiero crushed Tim into the satiny wallpaper, a delectable contrast with Hiero's slick, unyielding body. Tim moaned, and Hiero claimed his mouth anew, delving deep, drinking Tim down. Tim wove his arms around Hiero's waist and let himself feel: the size of him, the powerful weight, his sensual lips, the scorch of his roving hands, the jut of his cock against his navel. Everything he'd ever dreamed of, thrumming with need of him.

Tim eased Hiero's robe over his shoulders as gently as he could, too beautiful a garment to rip. Hiero, now blessedly naked, moved down to suck at his neck. Tim laughed at himself, at the things Hiero had taught him to dote over. Including himself. Tim suffered such a rush of love for him then that he cupped his head and kissed his crown. Hiero, eyes glinting with lust, dove back for another heart-stopping kiss before dropping to his knees.

Hiero rubbed his stubbled cheek along the length of Tim's straining cock, and he saw scarlet. Without warning, Hiero took him deep. No preamble, no gentilities, just heat and rough and the absolute bliss of fucking into his throat. The crudeness of it thrilled Tim. He twined his fingers in Hiero's velvety hair, gripped into the soft of skin on the nape of his exposed neck. How many nights had his buttocks scraped against a coarse brick wall whilst chasing a sensation nowhere near as intense as this? How many jittery, bumbling clods had he copped off with in alleys, against lampposts, desperate to feel something, anything akin to connection?

This was real connection. A lover who used him thoroughly and worshipped him utterly, who rode him raw whilst spoiling him rotten. Hiero worked his elegant fingers—slick with oil from Tim knew not where—past his bollocks to that sensate strip of skin behind, then farther, spearing him. Tim cried out, hoarse from a day of barking orders. Better to be commanded, he thought before a searing rush of pleasure melted his mind.

"Have me," he rasped, his legs collapsing under him. "Hiero, have me."

Hiero withdrew just as Tim began to sink down, nimble enough catch him on his lap and in a heady, tonguey kiss. He folded Tim's legs against his chest, adjusted the angles, penetrated. Their heaving breaths mingled as he thrust in; Tim moaned. They flicked and flirted with lips and tongues, never far from a kiss as Hiero took him, brutal, unyielding, his brazen stare breaking Tim apart.

Ecstasy howled through him, wild and heedless. Still he stretched, he opened, he gave, desperate for more. He pried one of Hiero's hands off the wall, twined their grips. Joined with Hiero at groin and chest and mouth and gaze as the sweet throb within him built and built and built, enflaming Tim, shattering him, and he spent with a strangled cry.

He hugged Hiero to him as he met his end with an eloquent shout, not relenting until they fell onto the bed in a tangled, sweaty mess long minutes later.

Exhaustion hit hard when his tipsy head found that perfect groove on Hiero's chest, the constant beat of his heart lulling Tim as little else did. But Tim fought against the heaviness that settled over him, thick as a quilt. Nothing needed saying, but Tim wanted to reassure himself that all trace of their disagreement had been burnt away.

"Rest," Hiero cajoled when he attempted to lift his head.

The touch he smoothed down Tim's back did not inspire wakefulness. He shifted so he could see Hiero's face, brushed a thumb through the darkening stubble on his cheek and neck. "Will you keep it? Grow a beard?"

"Gracious, no." Hiero curled his lip in distaste. Tim laughed. "I don't care to confront my father every time I..."

Hiero shut his eyes, likely against the memories. Tim propped himself on his elbows, now fully awake. He continued to caress the side of Hiero's face until the tension eased and his spark rekindled.

"Do you resemble him?" Tim asked gently.

"In my youth. Or so I was told. Though perhaps less now..."

"You carry him with you in other ways."

To Tim's relief, the thought made Hiero smile. "I do, at that. He was something of a raconteur. Owner of a coffee house, you know, keep the patrons chatting till they need another cup, or a biscuit, or some cake."

Tim chuckled fondly. "So you learned at the foot of the master."

"One of several, alas." His smile curdled. "Prior to this week, I'd never had cause to wonder if perhaps I should have been more willing to embrace my parents' way of life. If I've left too many bodies in my wake. No better, really, than our Monsieur Lamarque. Only less Machiavellian..."

Tim continued his caresses, letting Hiero feel supported by his closeness, his ministrations while he gave careful thought to how he might respond. How frail and brittle some parts of his Hiero were behind the pageantry.

"Hardship twists all its victims, sometimes beyond recognition," Tim observed. "Some are stuck in this final form, while others, by some miraculous strength of character, improve themselves. Marius did not suffer as you have, but still he could not break free. Instead he sought darker and darker ways to do others harm. You, my love, could have done the same. And perhaps did for a time when under the wrong kind of influence. But you escaped. And later chose to bring light and laughter to those in need, to forge a new path through loyalty and perseverance, and, when rewarded for it, you shared this new wealth with others. Erskine enshrouded many a minion in his darkness, but only you and Han lit a candle to ward off the gloom."

Hiero cleared his throat several times but seemed beyond the power of speech. Their gazes locked, lingered. Tim hoped he infused Hiero with some measure of contentment, of peace after their ordeal. But a part of Hiero still cowered, still condemned, still cursed himself for succumbing to Erskine's influence.

When he finally spoke, Hiero's tone turned delicate. "And you, dear Kip? Whose image do you sometimes see reflected when you look in the mirror?"

This startled Tim, but not for the expected reasons. "Have I never shown you?"

With considerable reluctance, he rolled off the bed and staggered into the adjoining room. Hiero sighed at his departure but indulged him. He'd settled under the covers, leaving a flap folded back to welcome Tim when he returned with his book of old photographs.

He flipped to the portrait of his parents and presented it to Hiero, who grabbed it away. His eyes glittered with curiosity as he compared the picture to Tim.

"Well?" Tim prompted.

"First, it must be said, they appear..." He worried the edge of the page, hesitant. "...enamored. Deeply. And quite devoted."

Tim swallowed a lump. "They were."

"As for the verdict..." He flipped his gaze up and down, from Tim to the portrait and back again. "You inherited your father's freckles and general appearance, but your mother's eyes." His own refocused on Tim, intense and admiring. "Were they of that same lush green?"

Tim cleared his throat, battling a blush. He marveled that no matter how intimate they became, Hiero's compliments could still reduce him to a schoolboy's shyness. "I believe they were."

The warmth of his smile drew Tim in close, as intended.

"Tell me of them," Hiero urged as he tucked them under the coverlet.

Tim shed a few layers of fatigue as he basked in the aura of Hiero's intense, undivided attention.

Chapter 26

*H*iero thought he had done quite well in waking before noon. Granted, the endless pummel of rain on the window had broken him out of his repeated attempts to doze for an hour or so, and the humidity this swelled up made burrowing under the sheets a clammy affair. The lack of a certain compact but muscular pillow to cling to also disturbed him. He'd hoped Kip might steal some extra... well, kip, before plunging back into police work, but the course of justice had swept him back up, constant and inevitable as the tide.

He sat propped against the headboard, unable to sleep but unwilling to rise as the clock chimed eleven. Cups of cooling tea and a congealed plate of half-eaten breakfast lay beside him in Kip's stead. With his part in the case concluded, no lover to entertain, and no theater to haunt, he felt as melancholy and lifeless as a ghost. Unmoored from anything and anyone who might give his life some tether. Which was ridiculous, since he and Han had grown their little family to give themselves and others the kind of sanctuary they'd not had under Erskine.

But Erskine's lessons shadowed him nonetheless. He drowned his memories in drink. He secluded himself from these people he sheltered. His vanity and neglect had almost brought the wolf to their door, almost blown down the very house where he worshipped:

The Gaiety Theater. And still, after a night of passion and communion, after almost sabotaging the truest connection he'd ever felt with another, he still could not bring himself to say those three impossible words to the man he loved.

Earlier that morn, Kip had nipped at his ear and whispered a soft message, as he always did before he left Hiero in bed after a night together. Except this time, he had added, "My love." Savored the words as he uttered them. Pressed a hand to Hiero's chest as he hugged him from behind. Hiero might have turned to him, cupped his face and vowed to him in return; instead he allowed Kip to depart un-caressed, unacknowledged, to spend another day cleaning up Hiero's mess.

And still some part of him resisted. Remembered Kip's horror after Hiero reappeared in the wake of Horace Beastly's "death". Remembered the fear he'd had to strangle in the crib just to go on when he thought Erskine still alive. Remembered how many had lost their lives—Randy, Flint, Toby—because a specter from his past sought revenge, sweet revenge. And even though Kip had proven to him the power of their togetherness, Hiero worried that asking too much of life, for someone hounded by loss and torment as he had been, would catch fate's notice. That some greater threat would be summoned into being if he succumbed to happiness.

As a pragmatic sort, these feelings vexed him. But they did not release him from their vise.

A soft knock at the door announced Aldridge, come to fetch his tray. With an unsparing look at Hiero, he untangled the sheets from his legs and stripped them back, threw a robe at him, and poured water into the washbasin. Despite the gloom outside, he parted the curtains, even opening the window a crack. A heavy breeze swept in, damp but refreshing, and the smells of the city with it, including whatever sweet delight Minnie baked in their kitchen.

Hiero's stomach rumbled. He snatched back the tray before Aldridge could claim it, then moved to his dressing table.

"Hot water, please," Hiero requested before daring a look at himself. Though his now-thick stubble did give him an especially roguish air, he'd meant what he said the night before. His father's richly bearded face flickered into his mind's eye the moment before he grabbed the razor.

Hiero was determined not to repeat the sins of the past, be they emotional or follicular.

Behind him, Aldridge grunted his approval. With his usual deft alchemy, he frothed up the shaving soap.

If still uncertain of himself, Hiero felt much improved as he snuck into the library some time later to discover Kip had not left for the Yard, but sequestered himself here to do… whatever he needed to do to conclude the case. Hiero made an unobtrusive—or so he hoped—amount of noise as he entered.

He found Kip frowning down at a fat, official-looking file open on the round table, with further documents and photographs fanned out around him. A page of his faithful notebook, written in a cipher—Hiero may have snuck a peek once upon a time—waited for his upraised pen. Research, Hiero knew, was Kip's favorite aspect of investigation. He lived to discover the hidden details, the unknown connections, the minutiae so many lesser detectives overlooked in their haste to resolve a case. This attentiveness extended to his every action, including the intimate. As Hiero approached, he smirked at the thought that Kip's brilliance as a detective also made him the ideal mate.

Kip caught the movement, glanced over, and smiled. The affection in his gaze warmed Hiero through. Kip reached out to him, and Hiero took his hand, curling around his shoulders from behind, enveloping him. Hiero kissed the soft of his neck, cinched his hold, feeling strange and vulnerable. He wished he could cart Kip off to the countryside, where they might cloister themselves for a fortnight and forget all this black business.

He did not fail to notice how Kip flipped the file shut.

"Sit with me awhile," Kip beckoned. He did not relinquish hold of Hiero's hand until he settled into a nearby chair, and then only to rise and move to the small bar Hiero'd had installed on one of the larger shelves. He watched Kip pour two fingers of whiskey, wondering all the while. He took up Hiero's hand again when he returned after setting the tumbler on the table before him.

One hand with the angels, the other with the devil, Hiero thought, recognizing a test when he saw it. He'd also thought they'd played their last game the night they trumped Marius.

"Hair of the dog?" Hiero pushed the tumbler to the side, twined their fingers. "Unnecessary, I assure you. Our interlude last night proved... quite medicinal."

"For me as well. I hope you will forgive me being the one to add to your aches."

Hiero chuckled. "Never apologize for such inspired agony. I live to be used by you."

"If only I referred to carnal matters." Kip nudged the file toward him. Hiero glared at it, suddenly so weary his bones might have withered to dust. And that was before he noticed the name on the file: Graves "Dagger" Erskine, aka Charles Arascain, aka Geraint Ernst Klein, aka Giacomo Aragona. "I thought it best we arm ourselves, should any other of Erskine's bastards decide to hunt you for sport."

Hiero nodded. "I applaud any and every effort to preserve my hide."

"And such a prize pelt it is." A decidedly predatory gleam lit Kip's eyes, though the only thing he pursued was his explanation. "I also don't care to take Miss Marks's word on matters of life and death. Especially when they concern your continued life and Erskine's possible death. But, fear not, I am at pains to preserve your anonymity. Nothing in my reports, if I gather enough evidence to share with Quayle, will connect you to Erskine."

Hiero laughed mirthlessly. "With the exception of everything."

"I cannot speak to your history—"

"But you must be curious."

"I am. Of course I am." Kip squeezed his hand so hard he cracked a knuckle. "I love you. Every suave and scintillating spark, every black, twisted impulse. I want everything in you. But most of all... I want to be worthy of your regard. Of the parts of yourself you still hide."

Hiero reeled at such a bald expression of ardor, compelled and overwhelmed in equal measure. And staggered by his own inadequacy. "If there's any question of worth, it is I—"

"I will listen to every tale you care to share," Kip reassured him, undaunted. "And I will make certain nothing in the Yard's records links you or Han directly to Erskine."

A tentative measure of relief eased the weight that had fallen on Hiero's chest at first sight of the file. Still, he'd lured many a mark into many a trap with the same shining look that lit Kip's open, earnest face. And perhaps if he'd ever harbored a moment's doubt where Kip's honor was concerned, he might have drawn back or tread more carefully. But Kip had scarified his ambitions, his reputation, and his security to be with Hiero, to say nothing of the risk to his life and the repeated declarations of love. Hiero could reward that devotion the only way he knew how: by sharing his story.

"Then I suppose I'd best begin." He cleared his throat. "After our escape from the asylum, Han and I lived rough in places much like the Dark Arches. In worse. In doss houses, if we begged or stole enough that day. If not, in the forgotten corners of abandoned buildings, in outhouses, on the streets themselves. But never for more than an hour or two, lest the constable happen by.

"After years of skilly and shackles, I was very frail. A day without left me too starved to stand. Han did his best, but his English was poor. I lived in fear of him being nabbed, forced into a workhouse. Without his help, I would have..."

Kip brushed a thumb across his knuckles. "You need not continue."

Hiero shook his head. "My dear Kip, as of this day, there will be nothing between us but care and devotion. Certainly not a black specter like Erskine. Who discovered us cheating punters out of their pennies at cards. A kindly friend had taught me a few tricks. I had a natural talent and improved on them. Erskine, a grifter by trade, lost almost a shilling trying to spot my deception. Then he offered me a pound—months of shelter, and full bellies besides—if I could fool him again, with a different trick."

"And so you did."

Hiero permitted himself a smile. "Do you doubt it?"

"No," Kip chuckled. "And he invited you to apprentice with him."

"Magic was his nominal trade. Three nights a week opening for Henri Robin at The Egyptian. On off nights, he trolled the music halls, searching for marks drunk enough to lose their wallets and watches, and not notice till the next morn."

"He performed a simple trick while you picked their pockets?"

"Precisely. In exchange, we learned his trade. Also performance. Erskine improved our vocabulary, our accents, our refinement. And kept us in what at the time seemed the height of luxury: clean quarters and full meals. For a time, Han and I thought ourselves the most fortunate lads in London. And for a time, we were. Until Erskine showed all his cards."

Hiero planted his gaze in the center of the table, still angry and incredulous fifteen years on. "Like many a fraud, Erskine's brilliance lay in his ability to mimic traits he saw in others. We attended less popular shows, where amateurs honed their craft, and if Erskine saw a trick he admired, he'd make us sneak backstage to see how it was done. He made a game of it, one we were both eager to play at first, especially since we earned rewards and special privileges. An extra helping here, a few pennies there.

"But it was a game that had very real consequences. Erskine had more than one acquaintance amongst the gangs that hunted the Strand. And as the rare criminal with erudition and savoir faire, he'd done them more than a few favors over the years. Enough to have them persuade these young magicians to abandon their careers. Enough to have them disappeared if they refused. More than once, the tables turned, and the inventor of a particular trick would recognize his work and come calling with his own dangerous friends. And Erskine would throw Han and me to the wolves.

"He began stealing from foreign magicians who performed in London for a month or two and then returned home to China or India or elsewhere. He forced us to serve as his assistants onstage. For authenticity, he said. When we refused, he set the peelers on us, and only my silver tongue kept us from being sent back to the asylum. As it was, we spent a fortnight in the workhouse. Sobered, we returned to him. What choice did we have? He held all our possessions, all our earnings. And he could summon my family or the police at any time. Have Han press-ganged again. And, as he often reminded us, he had given us so much.

"In truth, it wasn't always such a hardship. He had this… way about him. When he shined his light in your direction, you felt as if, with his help, you could conquer anything, fool anyone. When we were winning, he made the game *fun*. And when you failed him, Erskine somehow convinced you that you were to blame. That you'd chosen the misery that fell upon you."

"The very method of a master manipulator," Tim commented.

"With every societal advantage over us," Hiero concurred. "For a time, Han and I resolved to help him achieve his goals, in the hope success would preoccupy him and he would forget us. We begged him to let us invent an original act. He promised he would, if this latest gambit failed.

"But it was a sensation. Within two months, we were booked on the Strand, headlining our own theater. As our reputation grew, Erskine was invited to do private performances for visiting dignitaries, for royalty. He let a grand apartment, with a cook and a maid, and threw boozy bacchanals till the wee hours after the show. Han and I were granted a room of our own... if we agreed to provide 'entertainment' to one or two of his guests. Needless to say, Han always slept in the theater. I confess on occasion I did not."

Kip shook his head as if to dismiss Hiero's concerns. "You well know I can't claim to have behaved better in my youth. And with far less justification. And employers willing to turn a blind eye."

"And willing to employ you to begin with," Hiero said. "For us, it was the asylum or the workhouse or gaol. I began to think of myself as a prophecy fulfilled. I had become all that my parents feared I would be: a cheat, a thief, a deceiver of the highest order, a penniless dog serving a cruel master, willing to roll over at the merest instigation.

"Erskine grew bolder, prouder, more reckless. He encouraged us to steal from our hosts—baubles of little value to them but immeasurable to us. If we were caught, Erskine would act outraged, return the item with uxorious apologies, sometimes thrashing us before the injured party. The act was a ruse, but the blows were real. When we protested, Erskine called us ungrateful, that we only wanted to hinder his success, that we hadn't yet paid off our debt to him. And always the Sword of Damocles over our heads, the threat of returning us to the asylum, or calling the constable, or worse. His gangland acquaintances."

Kip looked fit to resurrect and re-hang Erskine, and draw and quarter him for good measure. Through gritted teeth, he said, "A tale as old as time."

"How well I know it." Hiero sighed. "We embarked on a tour of the great houses of Europe. We visited a few cities, but mostly small, remote villages. Erskine pushed us to steal ever more valuable items, or replace famous paintings with forgeries Han would paint, confident we'd be long gone if the theft was discovered. We, in turn, depended on him for everything, including our return to England.

But all that time away rejuvenated our spirits some. Travel opens you to the world and its possibilities. And while he could still cause us horrible trouble... he lacked the presence of certain authorities. All that resentment in which to stew helped us formulate a plot to rid ourselves of him once and for all."

"The Duke of Wellington." Kip knocked on the top of the file. "And the trove."

Hiero snickered, relishing the memory just a touch. "Our first engagement upon our return. The Duke's valet was a compulsive gambler. First we filched his half his wages, then we mined him for knowledge. We stole the family wedding ring, worn by every duchess for three centuries back, off the current duchess's finger. And arranged, with the valet's help and not a little subterfuge, for Erskine to be found by the duke, midthrust in his most beloved, very married sister, with a chest full of all the treasures pilfered on our tour, including the ring."

"Minus one or two trinkets to sustain you for a month or so?"

"No." Hiero felt a small pang of relief at being able to say so. "We broke clean. Debt paid in full. Nothing else to weigh on our hearts, only Erskine's blood on our hands."

Kip hummed. "A matter of perspective, that."

"Yours, or the Yard's?"

"Would that I could say both." He gripped Hiero's hand with renewed ardor. "I am no judge and refuse to play jury. I can only thank you for confiding in me."

A moment passed between them, solemn, devout. Hiero let out the breath he hadn't known he was holding. Still, the damned file lay between them, another, more treacherous bridge to be crossed.

"And what of the Yard? How intrepid were your fellows when investigating Erskine?"

He felt Kip tense as he shuffled through the pages. Only then did Hiero realize how anxious and uncertain his dear Kip felt about, of all things, prying into Hiero's past. About searching for the very answers he'd been owed all along, not from some police report, but from Hiero himself.

When he stepped back from the situation for a moment—not a meager task, given his tendency to eat rather than follow a trail of breadcrumbs—he was further struck by the realization that Kip must lie on his behalf in order to put the case to bed. No mention could be made of Marius and Miss Marks's true motives in targeting The Gaiety Theater. His brilliant, brave, steadfast, and unfailingly honest detective would break every oath of his office in order to shield him from suspicion. And redact any existing documents to preserve his secrets.

And Hiero choked on the effort to declare his love for such a man.

Until Kip pointed to a section of the file labeled *Known Associates*, and Hiero nearly shat out his stomach. For there, after a few names he recognized, a few he knew by reputation, and one of such inspired spelling Han had nothing to fear, was his father's name: Hakan Bachar.

The name he'd worn three lives ago, well before Erskine. The life he lived as a boy, a scion of a well-respected merchant, coddled in the womb of his family's insular community. He reached out and traced a finger over the clear cursive writing, not to erase the name, but to prove to himself it was real.

He looked to Kip, whose eyes shone with sympathy, with apprehension, with eagerness. His dearest beloved wanted confirmation that he had, at long last, uncovered the true Hiero. But Hiero felt no more kinship with that name than with any unexpected issue of one Graves "Dagger" Erskine.

And yet. If he had learned one thing from this ordeal, it was that no one else would suffer for his crimes. Including besotted detectives willing to forget the law in order to preserve Hiero's independence.

"Leave it," Hiero instructed before he could second-guess the impulse.

Kip raised his eyebrows. Not the response he'd expected. "But it is—"

"A name buried with my father's love." He inhaled a fortifying breath. "But not from those who might one day seek justice. I will not voluntarily admit my past wrongs to the Yard—permit me some sense of self-preservation—but if they discover it... I will pay the price for my mistakes."

Kip fell silent, giving the matter his usual thorough consideration. Hiero hadn't expected such a subdued reaction, but then Kip, for all his righteousness, had a greater appreciation for the shades of gray that colored a situation than most officers of the law.

In the end, he asked only, "You're certain?"

"I am."

And with a nod, the matter concluded. In Kip's mind. But Hiero, ever the flibbertigibbet, wasn't satisfied with quiet acceptance. It left too much room for doubt, and doubt led to misgivings, and misgivings led to distance, and distance led to...

"But what of Marius?" he demanded, startled by the tenor of his own voice. "Has he not sung of my involvement to every copper and gaoler who might listen?"

Kip chuckled. "And give another credit for *his* devious machinations? Marius's vanity wouldn't allow it. He is Erskine's creature to the end. He claims sole responsibility for every murder and injury, including the death of celebrated actor Horace Beastly."

Hiero gaped. When he recovered himself, he murmured, "You paid him a call."

"Perhaps." Kip indulged a private grin. "Regardless, I shall continue to plant the seeds of his madness in the minds of my superiors."

"But he will hang?"

"Oh yes. Killing Terriss sealed that particular fate. The Yard must play to their audience." Kip sighed. "As to whether he'll keep quiet once the noose is around his neck..."

"Hence your shadow investigation."

"I prefer 'protective measures.'" He gathered both of Hiero's hands in his. "And while I applaud your bravery in permitting your past to catch up with you, should another detective decide to give chase, I do hope, despite my better instincts, that no one ever does. Fagins like Erskine prey upon the poor and the desperate. Whatever crimes you committed on his leash, under threat of being whipped or deserted or imprisoned or worse, do not compare to the good you've done since cutting your own collar. I've heard a thousand tales like yours; I've seen such youths with my own eyes when I walk the streets of this city, pockets full of coins ready to be picked. That you escaped that life and his influence is more a testament than a condemnation of your character."

Hiero inched back, struggling to reconcile Kip's words with his inner sentiments, the danger that his choices had brought upon their comfortable life, the ever-present threat of further mischief. His need to express how giving and golden his sweet Kip's faith in him was, despite his concerns.

Then Hiero remembered he was a performer par excellence and could act his way out of any dire situation, even his own lack of confidence.

"That is, I fear, a rather rose-colored interpretation." He leaned forward, stretching to embrace Kip until he'd nearly drawn him onto his lap. "But since I prefer to paint with a gilded brush, I approve. And certainly I trust no other to discover that which still remains hidden from us." Before Kip could object, he amended, "With my help, of course. We, after all, make quite the pair. Dashing and dogged. Suave and sensible. Wicked and wise."

"Stoker and Bash?"

"Who other?"

Hiero drew his Kip to him then, all else forgotten in the heat and heart of their kiss.

Epilogue

*A*s the carriage drew up to the curb in front of The Gaiety Theater, Tim turned to Hiero for a final straightening of his cravat. After his cardsharp's fingers completed their minute, precision adjustments and took several liberties with his person, Tim received the Hieronymus Bash twinkle of approval. Though Hiero couldn't have failed to approve of what he had commissioned and styled, namely Tim's very fine, very formal evening wear in midnight blue with an emerald velvet waistcoat.

When Angus opened the carriage door, Tim rushed out. He parted the busy, crackling crowd with the sheer aura of his authority, a silent ringmaster making way for the greatest show in London. Hiero, of course, made them wait. How he timed his exit to the coincide with the flood of light from the open theater doors, Tim would never know, but that didn't in the least dim Hiero's magnificence. Swathed in a suit of deepest, richest violet velour harnessed by a gold and petal-red brocade waistcoat, to Tim he looked temptation incarnate.

Whispers susurrated through the crowd as they paraded into the grand re-reopening of The Gaiety, as special guests of the new manager, the Vicomte de Croÿ-Roeulx. Tumnus sold his stake and moved to the seaside in the wake of The Gaiety's woes after introducing the Vicomte to his fellow investors. Fresh off a sellout run as Don Juan, Genevre de Casterac, now Vicomtesse de Croÿ-Roeulx, would that night debut her Macbeth, with Seraphine Vauquelin as her Lady and Damiane as the stalwart Banquo. The events of the previous month had whetted a blood thirst in audiences all along the Strand, but none could compete with the site of actual murders (though The Adelphi Theater did try to lure punters away by staging Webster's *The Duchess of Malfi*). After the horrors The Gaiety's company had survived, the cursed reputation of the Scottish Play only enhanced their macabre allure.

The subject of what up-and-coming actors might fill out The Gaiety's troupe had preoccupied the residents of 23 Berkeley Square for many a gossipy family meal of late, though Tim harbored only a mild curiosity. Of far greater interest was how The Gaiety had been refurbished since its summer haunting season.

Navigating the path of fond friends and nosy acquaintances between the carriage and Box 5 took almost an hour. Fortunately, Hiero's newly fulsome mane and sneaky hands proved a suitable distraction from twenty versions of the same conversation: the whats, wheres, and hows of finding the phantom.

In the wake of solving the case, the headlines blazed, the Strand's demimondaines sung their praises nightly, and Hiero's popularity soared. Requests for their services flooded in. Invitations to balls, dinners, and soirées arrived so frequently that Aldridge hired one of Han's rabbits as an underbutler to sit by the front door and sort the envelopes. But, to Tim's relief, Hiero spent more time composing polite refusals than venturing out. A gutting sense of guilt still ruled him some days. On others he lounged in the library, content to read or reflect while Tim worked. A small part of Tim's heart broke each time his favorite tale-teller avoided retelling the tale of his greatest triumph to date. But he also understood that Hiero would not be able to distance himself from those ever-so-personal events for some time, if ever.

That he would forever mourn Beastly and regret how he took his final bow.

As they slipped into the royal foyer on their way to Box 5, Tim offered Hiero his arm. That tender grip proved a comfort as they segued into the refurbished box and tightened as Hiero beheld the tribute to Horace Beastly that adorned the walls. A small mural celebrating his greatest performances wrapped around the entire space. Copies of his best reviews had been framed and hung. On the back of the seat closest to the stage, a plaque paid homage to his most devoted patron, Admiral The Viscount Apollonius Pankhurst.

Hiero stared at the plaque for some time, and then, with a soft shake of his head, he turned to Tim. "Would it be in bad form to deface an honor on the very night you receive it?" he inquired, a mischievous glint in his eye. "I believe there's a name missing."

"I have it on good authority the box opposite has been redone as a tribute to Randolph Terriss," Tim replied.

"Ah, well done." Hiero's smile, and his mesmerizing gaze, were all for Tim. "But not the gentleman I had in mind."

He moved in for a kiss, but the curtains parted, and so did they. Hiero tugged Tim toward the shadowy nook they oft hid in. Then he heard the applause.

As they moved to the front row of the box, the entire audience turned in their direction, clapping furiously. The impromptu celebration was revealed to be, alas, not so impromptu when Tim spied the Vicomte center stage, leading the charge. Hiero basked a little too long, in Tim's opinion, but finally rewarded his audience with a deep and dramatic bow. Finally, the lights dimmed, the curtains parted, and they were alone.

Tim twined their hands beneath the drape of Hiero's cape. He found he took more pleasure in watching Hiero watch the perfor-mance than anything the actors portrayed. The peculiar noises he made, the growls of disapproval, the barks of delight, the scoffs of derision, were an entertainment unto themselves. His sigh of relief when the interval came almost inspired Tim to close their small curtain and remind Hiero of the many tangles they'd gotten up to in their favorite box. But, like The Gaiety itself, they had to feign respectability.

A knock on the door heralded the Vicomte, who escorted in a group of investors anxious to meet the famed consulting detective who had saved their theater. After that came an invitation to visit the Prince of Wales in Box 6, which they hastened to obey. (Tim thought him a mere silhouette of the man his late father had been.) Even Damiane Vauquelin dropped in for a smoke. Rakish and self-satisfied even in her spectral makeup—Banquo's ghost having just appeared to Macbeth—she thanked them quite earnestly for saving Seraphine and flirtatiously asked that they pass on her regards to both Mr. Han and Mr. Calvin.

At the final curtain, the Vicomtesse de Croÿ-Roeulx called out to them from the stage, insisting they join her for a late supper. In the same private room where Hiero and she had sparred, they were feted like kings, the Vicomtesse ceding the spotlight for the length of another spirited retelling of their encounter with Marius under the Dark Arches. Before a small audience of actors and patrons, Hiero orchestrated a masterful recreation, arms conducting each beat, voice rising and falling with operatic intensity, his eloquent face reliving every emotion. Tim observed the rapt gathering with no small pride, however eager he might have been for the evening to end.

To be alone with the man who owned his heart.

He took advantage of a short window of escape when the fleet of waiters descended to clear the main courses and prepare the table for dessert. With no terrace to retreat to, Tim wandered back into the auditory, standing at the rail of the balcony stalls so as to better appreciate the grandeur of The Gaiety stage. He too mourned old Horace, no matter how relieved he was that era of Hiero's life had ended. He vowed to return as a spectator, to support this new generation of actors and this theater they loved.

In the distance, someone sung a strange yet familiar tune. Excitement slithered up Tim's spine. He waited, smiling, as the voice approached, for the soft tap of footsteps descending behind him, for the cinch of Hiero's arms around his waist. Tim leaned back against his broad chest, hooked into his embrace.

"What refrain were you singing just now?" He sighed, basking in the stolen moment. "Not the one from the music box?"

"Good instinct," Hiero enigmatically replied, "wrong villain."

Tim considered this for longer than he would have liked, then conceded defeat. "I've not your artist's ear."

"A library," Hiero whispered, his hot breath licking Tim's ear. "A society gathering. A melting tooth."

"Ah!" Tim chuckled as that memorable evening at Lord Blackwood's flickered into his mind. "I didn't hear a note of the music that night. Not once you entered. I was too… enthralled." He turned in Hiero's arms, wove his own around his sinuous frame. A panther in all but name. "A year ago today, I believe. The night we met."

"So it was."

"Which you knew before I mentioned it."

"So I did."

"And you wish to commemorate here… and elsewhere?"

"Here, in our old home…" Hiero brushed a featherlight kiss across his lips. "…and later, in the one we make together. With the one I cannot live without. The one…" Hiero swallowed hard, stared at him. The dark wellspring of his eyes, fathoms upon fathoms deep, resounded with a vulnerability never glimpsed before. "The one I love. My dearest, most treasured Timothy."

Tim held there, silent, reverent before the man who was his everything, who held their future in the palm of his hand. His kiss, when Tim claimed it, began as tender, giving tribute, and then, as it deepened, roared with desire.

"Must we…" He gasped into Hiero's mouth. "Must we return?"

"Perish the thought." Tim followed, dizzy with lust and enchantment, as Hiero drew him up the steps. "This evening, dessert will be served in Box 5."

They stumbled into the corridor behind the boxes, giddy and groping, only to be confronted by the newly installed night watchman, cross armed and unamused. Hiero clamped a hand over his mouth but couldn't contain his laughter. Tim hid behind Hiero, conscious only of his burning cheeks and other, tumescent parts of his anatomy.

"Ah, messieurs!" a voice boomed. They swung around to find the Vicomte beckoning them from down the hall.

With a pointed nod to the night watchman, Tim whispered, "Let's hurry about our goodbyes and away."

"Quite," Hiero agreed in such a purr that Tim thought twice about defying them and dragging him off.

Sometime later, reclined against Hiero on the plush seat in the carriage, site of their first and most recent intimate bouts, Tim felt a deep contentment settle within. Though future dangers and strife no doubt awaited them—a detective's lot, after all—he would always have this moment, this man, this peace.

And yet. As voluble as if he spoke them aloud, Hiero's inner musings screamed into the silence. Tim and their evening's activities had conspired to exhaust him, but still something nagged at his soul. A voice Tim feared no amount of attention and care could quiet.

"My heart," Hiero exhaled sharply in the manner of one unburdening himself. "I find I am no longer content to continue as we have before. In investigatory matters, I mean. That is, of course we will serve where we are needed, dedicate ourselves to those cases that confound others. But we must, I feel, be more judicious in our selection. Accept only those most in need, or with proper references. Be wary of..."

"Ulterior motives?" Tim murmured.

He felt Hiero nod. "And I would that we undertake an inquiry that has fallen to the wayside during our other adventures. One that... that may be lost to time, but that we, as no others, may bring to light."

"My love." Tim turned around to face him, surprised and confounded. "What case is this?"

"The one that's haunted you, mon amour, for far too long," Hiero answered, a wealth of affection shining in his black-pearl eyes. "The murder of your parents."

The End

Stoker and Bash will return in... *The Song of the Siren*

Notes on the History Behind the Fiction

The magnificent Gaiety Theater did indeed exist on the Strand, in three different iterations, from 1863 to 1957. Originally known as the Strand Musick Hall, it was redesigned into the first Gaiety Theater in 1868, then updated in 1903. Those interested in its history can find extensive details on everything from its construction and interior design to blueprints, photos, playbills, and newspaper articles, thanks to the intrepid theater historians at arthurlloyd.co.uk. Every description of the theater in the book, with the exception of the workrooms under the stage, is based on the actual Gaiety as it existed in 1874.

Although they no doubt put on a burlesque of *Don Juan* at some point during their run, and very often French troupes were invited to perform on its stage, in the fall of 1874, the Gaiety bill consisted of comic operas, one based on Lecocq's *Cent Vierges* (The Hundred Virgins) called the *Island of Bachelors*, and another called *Oil and Vinegar*. John Hollingshead, manager of the Gaiety during the Victorian era, published a memoir rich with detail about the daily struggles of running a theater, performances, cast changes, controversies—an embarrassment of riches.

Only one archway of the original Adelphi Arches still exists, an exit from under the Royal Society of Art onto Lower Robert Street in London, and a few of the reconstructed tunnels can be found in the Society's basement. Originally built by the Adams brothers, famous eighteenth-century architect siblings, these Thames-side warehouses stored coal and other supplies offloaded from merchant vessels, all while supporting a row of luxury terraced houses. But with the advent of Joseph Bazelgette's Embankment sewage system, the arches that once bordered the shore were sealed off and no longer served their purpose. Though the palatial residence above drew prestigious artists like Charles Dickens and Théodore Géricault, the dark tunnels below became a hideout for gangs, pickpockets, thieves, and other unfortunates. Historians David Pike and David Allan have written vividly about the Adelphi's transformation, if you care to know more.

On the other side of the world, boat-living communities inhabit the ports and seaways of Southern China and Vietnam. These indigenous peoples have existed for so long that there is no clear record of their origins. They are often shunned and prejudiced against by their mainland counterparts. Their culture is as diverse as any, with different factions living in Hong Kong, various South China provinces, up the Yangtze river, and in Macau. Some of the Hong Kong faction sided with the British during colonial times and were renown for piracy, while the Macau faction, fishermen and ferriers, often intermarried with Portuguese sailors. These relationships have been portrayed in works by both Chinese and Portuguese writers, such as "A Chan, A Tancareira" by Henrique de Senna Fernandes.

A sharp-eyed reader may notice some changes to Han's backstory from book two. Thanks to two new sources I discovered while researching this book, a translation of an unnamed Portuguese sailor's diary from 1874 and a study of the boat people of Macau by Rui Brito Peixoto, I learned that "Tanka" was the name given to the boat people by mainland Chinese and not the name they themselves prefer, which the source translates to the "People on the Water." Many Western sources do not make this distinction. "Tanka" refers to the egg-shaped boats in which the People on the Water in Macau reside, not the junker I used in book two (although some other factions do use junkers). I am also indebted to the research of Wee Kek Koon and Nathan Kwan. I deeply regret these errors and will correct them in the next edition of *The Fruit of the Poisonous Tree*.

And finally, the popular stage actor William Terriss was indeed murdered in Bull Inn Court at the entrance to the Adelphi Theater (though in 1897, not 1874) by a fellow actor he had tried and failed to take under his wing, Richard Price. Price, an alcoholic, had become destitute as a result of his physical and mental diseases. Terriss, who had once worked with Price, often sent him money through the Actor's Benevolent Fund. But Price blamed Terriss for his troubles and, when the money dried up, stabbed him. The murder became a sensation in the London press. Price was found guilty but insane, and was sent to an asylum—causing a bigger scandal. To this day, a plaque by the Adelphi stage door commemorates Terriss, and his ghost has been said to haunt the theater most nights...

The list of incredible historians doing wonderful, detailed work on the Victorian era and other periods is too long to mention, but I was particularly helped by books/websites by Liza Picard, Dorothy L. Haller, Lee Jackson, Ruth Richardson, Judith Flanders, Moira Allen, Chris Payne, and Fern Riddell, and the plentiful resources at the V&A and the British Library. Any mistakes I made while transforming their sterling facts into fiction are entirely my own.

Acknowledgements

Writing this book carried me through one of the most challenging years of my professional and personal life (and that was pre-2020), so just the fact that it's out in the world is a small victory. I definitely couldn't have done it without the incredible, steadfast group of friends, critics, and collaborators who have shepherded all my books for many years now. Time is ever precious, but more so these days, and I will be forever grateful that they chose to devote their time and insight to this endeavor.

Nancy-Anne Davies, editor extraordinaire, reminded me to include moments of joy amidst the skulduggery. Anna "Tiferet" Sikorska, high sorceress of design, magicked another spectacular cover into being. My amazing betas, Liv Rancourt, Mel Ting, and Judie Troyansky, helped me prune and polish the story. Han's story and perspective were enriched by sensitivity reads by Vivian Lee and Day's Lee (not related), and Elena Meyer-Bothling consulted on Shahida—huge thanks to all of them for sharing some personal tales and traditions. Aljoscha Steiner gave this Quebecoise a French "from France" edit; merci mille fois! And Paul Salvette from BB eBooks is the formatting wizard who keeps the books looking as sharp on the inside as on the outside.

Elaine Lui and all the writers at *Lainey Gossip* have taught me how to show my work for over a decade now, the best kind of squad goals. Sarah Marrs—what a dream come true to be reviewed by your shrewd, empathetic eye.

Can't forget the debt I owe to Gaston Leroux and Sir Andrew Lloyd Webber, the first to put the goth in my love of romance. And Colm Wilkinson, the one true Phantom, for his sublime night music.

I wouldn't have gotten through this or any year without the love of my family and friends. I hope they feel as loved and supported by me as I do by them.

My eternal gratitude to Dr. Romain Javard and the team at the DMV for saving my dog's life, and Dr. Andrea Dolan for listening.

And to you, dear reader, for joining me on these adventures.

Share Your Experience

If you enjoyed this book, please consider leaving a review on the site where you purchased it, or on GoodReads.

Thank you for your support of independent authors!

Books by Selina Kray

Stoker & Bash Series
The Fangs of Scavo
The Fruit of the Poisonous Tree
The Death Under the Dark Arches
The Song of the Siren (coming soon)

Historical Romance
Like Stars

Contemporary Romance
In Wild Lemon Groves

About the Author

Selina Kray is the nom de plume of an author and English editor. Professionally she has covered all the artsy-fartsy bases, having worked in a bookstore, at a cinema, in children's television, and in television distribution, up to her latest incarnation as a subtitle editor and grammar nerd (though she may have always been a grammar nerd). A self-proclaimed geek and pop culture junkie who sometimes manages to pry herself away from the review sites and gossip blogs to write fiction of her own, she is a voracious consumer of art with both a capital and lowercase *a*.

Selina's aim is to write genre-spanning romances with intricate plots, complex characters, and lots of heart. Whether she has achieved this goal is for you, gentle readers, to decide. At present she is hard at work on future novels at home in Montreal, Quebec, with her wee corgi serving as both foot warmer and in-house critic.

If you're interested in receiving Selina's newsletter and being the first to know when new books are released, plus getting sneak peeks at upcoming novels, please sign up at her website: www.selinakray.net

Find Selina online:
Twitter: @selinakray
Facebook: Selina Kray / 23 Berkeley Square
(Stoker & Bash fan group)
GoodReads: Selina Kray
Email: selinakray@hotmail.ca
Website: www.selinakray.net